if the shoes fit

Buy them
in every
colour

Pauline
LAWLESS

POOLBEG

Published 2010
by Poolbeg Press Ltd.
123 Grange Hill, Baldoyle,
Dublin 13, Ireland
Email: poolbeg@poolbeg.com

1 3 5 7 9 10 8 6 4 2

A catalogue record for this book is available from the British Library.

ISBN 978-1-84223-388-7

Typeset by Patricia Hope in Sabon 10.5/14.5

Printed by
CPI Cox & Wyman, UK

www.poolbeg.com

NOTE ON THE AUTHOR

Pauline Lawless was born in Dublin but she has lived most of her life in the midlands. She was educated at Belgrove School, Clontarf and St Louis Convent, Balla, Co Mayo.

She started writing after she retired from business and her first novel, *Because We're Worth It*, was a bestseller in 2009. It came about as a result of her experiences running Superslim Slimming Clubs in the midlands for many years. Her second novel, *If the Shoes Fit*, was inspired by her years working as an area manager with an international cosmetics company, also in the midlands, except that the cosmetics have been replaced by shoes!

When Pauline is not writing she likes to escape to the golf course.

Visit her website at *www.paulinelawless.com*

Also by Pauline Lawless

Because We're Worth It

Acknowledgements

A big thank you to all at Poolbeg: Kieran, Lee, David, Lisa and Sarah. A special thank you to Paula Campbell whose fund of stories about her own Leo, Lucy and Grace, gave me much inspiration for Niamh's three lovely children.

To my editor, Gaye Shortland, the best in the business, a huge thank you. Your professionalism puts the sheen on my rough diamond.

I am eternally grateful to my family and friends whose support keeps me going.

To my daughter Ciara, with love. Thanks again for your input and proof-reading.

To my former colleagues at Avon Cosmetics, especially Mai, Maureen, Pat, Maura, Alice and Doreen, who were my inspiration for this book. I have such fond memories of the good times we shared. To my former reps Lorraine, Bernie and Deirdre – it was wonderful to see you at the launch of my first book, *Because We're Worth It*.

Thanks to Jackie Quigley of Easons in Newbridge for that fantastic launch. A day I'll never forget!

Finally, to you the readers, who made my first venture into writing such a success. I appreciate all your kind comments and hope you enjoy *If The Shoes Fit* even more.

To my mother,
with much love and gratitude.

Chapter 1

Amber was sitting on the balcony of her penthouse apartment in Malahide, watching the little boats bobbing about in the beautiful marina below. Her face, a golden tan and make-up free, was turned to catch the rays of the morning sun and her bare feet were curled up under her. She was wearing a comfy Juicy Couture velour leisure suit and her long blonde curls were caught up haphazardly in a ponytail. She sipped a vodka and orange as she reached for a glossy magazine and started leafing idly through it. It was then that she spotted the advertisement.

"I don't believe it!" she exclaimed as she read it. "I don't bloody believe it!" She smiled to herself as she realised that she sounded just like Victor Meldrew, that crazy character from the TV sit-com *One Foot in the Grave*. She read down through the ad again.

CALLING ALL SHOE ADDICTS!

Are shoes your passion? Are you enthusiastic and ambitious? Would you like to work for yourself?

*Not be tied to specific hours? Do you get on well
with people? If you answered "yes" to all of the
above, you may be the person we're looking for.*

IF THE SHOES FIT
(buy them in every colour!)

*We are launching in Ireland soon and we require
part-time area sales managers to introduce our
fabulous range of designer shoes to Irish women. No
age limit. No experience required. No initial cash
outlay.*

Applications with CV to:
If the Shoes Fit, 54, Lower Mount St., Dublin 2.

"*Buy them in every colour*" was Amber's motto. How often
had she bought the same shoe in two or three different
colours! "Am I a shoe addict? Are they my passion? Are they
what?" she exclaimed aloud. "Just come and see for yourself!"

She wasn't joking. Amber was the proud owner of the
most fantastic shoe-room in Dublin, if not Ireland. Not a
closet or a couple of racks, like most women, but a customised
room, especially for her shoes – and their matching bags, of
course. All her girl-friends were madly envious of her
collection of some two hundred pairs (give or take a few)
and she did sometimes feel a bit guilty about it. But what
the hell, she thought, Imelda Marcos had 1250 pairs!
Everyone had a passion and shoes just happened to be hers.
And she rarely paid full price for them. Most of them she'd
bought in sales in New York, Paris, Rome and Madrid for
a fraction of the original cost.

It had always been that way. She'd always been a sucker for shoes.

This love affair had begun when, as a three-year-old, she'd fallen in love with a tiny pair of red patent shoes. Her mother had chosen a pair of sensible brown leather Clarks but Amber wouldn't even try them on and had thrown herself on the shop floor, refusing to get up until she could have the red patent ones. Embarrassed by this tantrum and shocked at her little girl's determination, her mother had given in and had left the shop with her golden-haired, angelic-looking daughter clutching her shoes and smiling in triumph. Amber could still remember every detail of them. They had narrow ankle-straps with the cutest bows on the front and they were so shiny that she could see her own face reflected in them. How she'd loved them! She'd felt like a princess every time she'd worn them.

She read the ad a third time, hardly daring to believe it. It sounds too good to be true, she thought. She got scissors and cut the page out of the magazine, then poured herself another vodka and orange. This called for a celebration! Yes, she knew it was still not quite midday and she'd already had her mid-morning drink, but this job was just perfect for her and as the song said: *"It's five o'clock somewhere."* She'd always thought that was strange – saying five o'clock – as six o'clock was the boozing hour in Ireland. Mind you, we make up for that extra hour real quick, she admitted to herself with a wry smile.

She hadn't always been a drinker. When she'd first met Dermot, her ex-husband, she'd never touched the stuff but it used to infuriate him when she'd ask for a Diet Coke at the fancy corporate dinners and receptions they attended regularly.

"For God's sake, just try and drink a glass of wine. It won't kill you!" he'd say in exasperation.

3

So, to please him, she'd tried, although she'd hated the taste of it. Eventually of course, she'd grown to like it and now she couldn't get through the day without it. She knew she drank too much but she didn't know how she would have survived the past twelve months, since her divorce, otherwise. Twelve months of heartache – her *annus horribilis*, as she called it – during which her self-esteem and confidence had sunk to an all-time low.

Reading the ad, she had her first glimmer of hope. Be positive, she told herself. I adore shoes, I'm enthusiastic, good with people and I'm willing to work hard. I'll do anything to get back to the old me – to get back living again.

So, with a sense of purpose, she pushed away her vodka and went to the computer to print out her CV and application. She went straight to the post-box and sent it on its way, before she could change her mind.

Susie, her best friend, rang that afternoon. "I've something really interesting to show you," she said, excitement in her voice. "I'll pop in on my way home."

She arrived beaming and brandishing a copy of *It Magazine*.

"This is just perfect for you. Look!" She shoved the page with the ad for If the Shoes Fit at Amber. "You adore shoes, you're great with people and it's only part-time. It's made for you!"

"Oh, I don't know . . ." Amber shook her head.

"What do you mean you don't know?" Susie banged the table, exasperation showing in her face. Then she saw that Amber was smiling.

"Actually, I've applied for it already – this afternoon!" Amber replied smugly.

"You've what?" Susie couldn't believe her ears. For months now she'd been trying to get Amber interested in getting back to work, with no success. Susie had been very worried. She was aware that Amber was drinking too much and wasn't making any effort to move on with her life. Thank God, at last she'd found something to interest her.

"I'm so happy," said Susie, giving her dearest friend a hug. "The minute I read it I knew it was made for you. You're an expert on shoes, as we all know!"

"I have to agree with you there," Amber replied. "Have you time for a quick cafè latte?"

Susie looked at her watch. "Yes, if it's real quick. I have to collect Rachel and Joshua from the crèche in ten minutes."

They chatted enthusiastically about the ad as Susie gulped down the coffee – then she flew out the door, blowing a kiss at her friend as she did so.

Amber appreciated Susie's concern. She knew she was worried about her drinking and it touched her. There was nobody else who gave a damn. She owed it to her friend to make an effort. Feeling bad about her behaviour and grateful for Susie's loyalty, she decided then and there to put a stop to it. This new opportunity had given her something to aim for. She made a decision. That's it – no more drinking on my own any more! This is my chance to get my life together again and I won't blow it. With determination, she took the bottle of vodka and poured it down the sink. It felt good!

Niamh was waiting in the doctor's surgery in Clondalkin with her little son, Ian, when she spotted the advertisement. She couldn't call herself a shoe addict exactly, mainly because she couldn't afford to buy shoes for herself very often, but she did adore them and if she had the money she had no doubt but that she would indulge herself. As a teenager, while her other friends were spending their money on cigarettes and drink, piercings, tattoos and the Lord knows what else, Niamh had spent every penny of her precious pocket money on shoes. Now twenty-three years old with three children (four, counting her husband) and a mountain of debts, there was very little chance of her buying a pair of glamorous shoes anytime soon. Intrigued, but not thinking it could have anything to do with her, she read down through the ad. She did have a passion for shoes – those she saw on other women – and yes, she was ambitious and enthusiastic and did get on very well with people. She read on. Was it possible? No age limit, no experience needed and most importantly, no money outlay. That would have been a problem. She began to feel a tremor of excitement. Was God possibly taking pity on her and bringing this opportunity her way? She desperately needed to get a job to help pay off all her debts and now that the twins had started school . . .

It says part-time, she thought, and it looks like you can choose what hours you work – this would be perfect for me.

There was no way she could afford to pay a child-minder for three kids.

She felt buoyant with hope. She despised people who tore pages out of magazines that didn't belong to them – but she had no choice. She could never afford to buy the glossy magazine herself and she desperately needed this ad.

After the doctor had assured her that Ian was merely suffering from a cold, she rushed home to make out her application. Her hopes took a bit of a bashing when she realised that her CV was pitiful. She couldn't very well say: "Mother of three at nineteen and excellent at the job." She guessed that wasn't quite what they were looking for. However, she had achieved a very good Leaving Certificate and would have gone on to University to study law if fate hadn't intervened. Fate in the form of charming, sexy, handsome Gavin Byrne who had seduced a very naïve seventeen-year-old Niamh, which resulted in her getting pregnant. She didn't want to go there.

Wrapping Ian up well, she collected the twins, Lily and Rose, from school. They looked so cute and tiny in their uniforms and as they hugged her, her heart swelled with love for them. Yes, she had it tough, but not for anything would she give up one minute spent with her three precious babies.

She posted her application and then they took the five-minute bus ride to her mother's house. Normally they walked but today, what with Ian's cold and her exciting news, she decided to splash out and take the bus.

"Come in, my darlings, and give Nana a big hug!" Her mother, as always, was delighted to see her grandchildren and wrapped her ample arms about them.

"How is your cold, pet? And what did you do at school today, girls? I've baked some lovely fairy cakes for you and I'll make some of your favourite hot chocolate."

When the three kids had babbled their news and were seated at the kitchen table happily munching, her mother turned her attention to Niamh.

"You seem in high spirits today, love. What is it? Has Gavin got a job?"

"No such luck, Mam. But maybe I have," and with eyes glowing she handed her mother the advert.

Eileen raised her eyebrows as she read it. "No experience needed, no money outlay and you can work whatever hours you choose. This seems perfect, love. You should apply for it."

"I already have, Mam," Niamh replied.

"That's great, love. You know, you'll never get out of your mother-in-law's house if you don't do something about it yourself. You certainly can't rely on Gavin to help!"

"Ah Mam, give him a break," Niamh sighed. They'd been down this road many times before. "I don't want to breathe a word of it to him just yet, in case I don't get it."

It killed Eileen to see her bright, smart daughter tied to a waster like Gavin. She often thought that Niamh would have been better off as a single mother – as least she'd have had her own house by now and not be stuck living with that dragon of a mother-in-law. Eileen sighed. What a mistake we made! she thought. We should never have agreed to the marriage. Her dad never wanted it – I should have listened to him. Thank God he's not alive to see how hard it is for his little girl now. It would break his heart. She sighed again.

Niamh hated having to leave her mother's warm, homely kitchen and face back to the drab, cold house they shared with Gavin's mother, Bridget. The cottage was tiny – certainly not big enough to accommodate three adults and three children. Bridget had kept the biggest bedroom for herself and Niamh and Gavin had to make do with the box-room and a bed that wasn't quite a double one. The kids had no space to play with their toys and it was impossible to keep them from messing things up. On top of that, she had a job trying to keep them quiet while her mother-in-law watched the endless procession of daytime chat and game shows on television.

Her mother was right – she had to get out of there – and

it would be up to her to achieve it. Thank God for Mam, she thought. What would I do without her?

Niamh had left the advert with her mother just in case Bridget should find it. She knew all hell would break loose if she did. Bridget did not approve of working mothers and Gavin sided with her on this. In fact, he sided with his mother's views on practically everything.

Niamh's older sister, Val, dropped in to her mother's later that evening.

"Great news," Eileen announced, as she cooked up a big fry for her daughter. "Niamh applied for a job today. It sounds great."

"What kind of job?" Val asked, already munching on her mother's brown bread.

"It's a part-time job, selling designer shoes. She saw an ad in a magazine. It's there in the drawer." Eileen nodded towards the dresser.

"Let's have a look at it," Val said, full of curiosity.

Eileen dished up the bacon, egg and sausages and when she'd poured them both a cup of tea, she found the ad and handed it to her daughter.

"Mmm . . . interesting," Val remarked as she read it.

When she'd finished eating and her mother had left the room to answer the phone, Val slipped the magazine page into her pocket.

Chapter 2

Rosie woke sleepily, reaching over for Jack as she did every morning. The empty bed and the realisation that he was gone drove a dagger through her heart. It was ten months since he'd died but she still couldn't come to terms with it. They'd had thirty wonderful years together and now here she was, alone, facing her fifty-third birthday, not knowing how she would be able to go on without him. Her daughter, Gail, was constantly on at her to get back to her old hobbies, but how could she? She and Jack had been so close and had done everything together. She just couldn't face the bridge and golf clubs without him.

"It gets easier with time," everyone kept saying, but it wasn't getting any easier. If anything, it was getting harder and sometimes she panicked when she couldn't remember his face clearly and would have to look at his photo to recall it. She couldn't pray any more, except to Jack. She spoke to him constantly and felt he was listening to her. Every day she prayed to him to help her.

Gail, who lived nearby, arrived at lunch-time with her adorable baby girl, Holly, and was shocked to see her mother still in her dressing-gown. Seeing her daughter's look of disapproval, Rosie sighed.

"Don't be cross with me, Gail. I took a sleeping pill last night and overslept. Anyway, I'm not going out today so why bother getting dressed?" She shrugged her shoulders.

Gail felt the tears prick her eyes and the anger bubble up inside her. She couldn't keep it in any longer, so she let her mother have it.

"Mum, you know how much I adored dad. Don't you think it's hard enough on me that I've lost him, without losing my mother too? You're not here any more. I know how much you miss him but I miss him too and I need you now." Gail was pacing up and down the kitchen floor. "Dad had so much zest for life. He must be going crazy up there watching you wasting yours. He would be very unhappy to see you like this." Seeing the tears in her mother's eyes, she spoke more gently. "Mum, you owe it to him, and to me and Holly, to start living again."

Rosie was crying now. She knew what Gail said was true and that Jack would be furious with her, seeing her like this, but somehow she couldn't get back into the real world. She couldn't let go of him.

"Mum, whether you like it or not, I'm going to make an appointment for you with the bereavement counsellor. She even offered to come and visit you here in the house, if you preferred."

Sighing, Rosie reluctantly agreed. She knew Gail was right. Life had to go on, but how?

Gail reached for the box of tissues and handed them to her mother. "By the way, Mum, I saw a job advertised in this magazine, which would suit you down to the ground," she remarked casually. "Please take a look at it. It might be just what you need."

"Job? How on earth could I cope with a job, the state I'm in?" Rosie asked, ignoring the magazine Gail held out to her.

Gail left it on the coffee table, open at the If the Shoes Fit ad, in the hope that it might rouse her mother out of this limbo that she was in.

When her daughter had left, Rosie glanced idly at it. Sounds interesting and fun, she thought, as she read down through it, but I could never do it. But she understood why Gail thought that it would suit her.

She had to admit that her big passion was shoes. When she had accumulated all the jewellery that she would ever need, Jack, knowing how much she adored them, had started buying her beautiful shoes, for birthdays and anniversaries, or whenever he was abroad on business. It had never ceased to amaze her, or her friends, that he knew exactly what to choose and that they always fitted perfectly. He never got it wrong and she had quite a collection now. Since he'd died, she hadn't been able to bring herself to wear any of them.

Gail was as good as her word and later that week, Sheila, the bereavement counsellor, came to visit. Rosie was surprised to find her so understanding and non-judgemental. She spent the whole hour talking about Jack and, somehow, it was easier to talk about their life together with a total stranger than with any of her old friends.

"Jack took early retirement so that we could travel the world together and do all the things that we'd missed out on because of his work commitments," she explained to

Sheila. "Then the day after his retirement party, just one week short of his sixtieth birthday, he had a massive stroke and that was the beginning of the end."

"Oh, that must have been awful for him, and you," Sheila said, her voice full of sympathy.

"It was," Rosie said. "We had to cancel the round-the-world trip, of course, and Jack, being the kind of man he was, was more concerned about me missing that than he was about himself." She wiped a tear from her eye. "He went downhill fast and it was horrible watching helplessly as he lay immobile, unable to do anything for himself."

"That's the worst thing, that feeling of helplessness as you watch your loved one suffer," Sheila said softly.

"Yes, it was. He so wanted to communicate with us, but was unable to, and I couldn't bear to see the tears in his eyes as he tried to make the effort." Rosie had a faraway look in her eyes as she relived it. "He'd always been such a virile man, full of energy and fun and now he lay wasted, waiting to die. The end, when it came, was a merciful release for him and I was happy that he was in a better place," her voice sank to a whisper, "but the bottom fell out of my world."

"I do understand, my dear," Sheila said kindly, patting her hand. "It seems so unfair. Life is very cruel sometimes."

Rosie found it easy to talk to this gentle woman who seemed to understand. She'd kept it all bottled up inside her for so long that now she found it a great relief to let it out. Tears rolled down her cheeks as she shared her memories.

"I think you're very lucky that you had such a wonderful husband who obviously loved you very much," Sheila said, handing her a tissue from the box on the table. "Let's dwell on that for the moment and be grateful for the years you had together." She smiled at Rosie, taking her hands. "Not every woman is so lucky, you know."

Gail arrived later that evening to see how things had gone and was delighted to see her mother smiling and in better form.

"She's a lovely lady and understands completely," Rosie told her.

"Well, that's what she's there for," Gail replied. "So you found it a help to talk to her?"

Rosie smiled. "Absolutely. I feel much better after our chat."

Gail hugged her mother, delighted with what Sheila had achieved in just one visit.

"By the way, did you do anything about that ad?" she asked, looking around for the magazine.

"The shoe one? God, no! I'd be much too old," Rosie grimaced.

"It says no age limit," Gail persisted.

"I know but I'm sure they don't mean over fifty!"

"No age limit means *no* age limit," insisted Gail. "Anyway, you're only fifty-two and they say fifty is the new thirty. Please think about it, Mum."

"Okay, I'll think about it," said Rosie resignedly. When Gail got the bit between her teeth, she just wouldn't let go.

The counselling session with Sheila, early the following week, went even better.

As they sipped their tea, Rosie told her about the job Gail was on about.

"You know how you told me that you talk to Jack all the time and feel he is watching over you?" Sheila remarked, looking thoughtful. "Well, why not ask him about this?"

When Sheila had left, Rosie did just that. She took out the ad and, reading it again, said a quiet prayer to him asking what she should do. She felt a sense of peace come over her and could just imagine him laughing heartily. She could almost hear his voice.

"Selling shoes? My God girl, you're the expert there. Only thing is, you'll probably buy more than you sell – and sure why not? You deserve it!"

When Gail dropped in later, she found her mother smiling gently to herself. She hugged her tightly.

"Mum, you're looking great! It's good to see you wearing make-up again. But why are you smiling to yourself like that?"

"Well, I was just thinking what your father would say if he heard I was thinking of applying for a job selling shoes," Rosie chuckled, as she lifted Holly out of the buggy and gave her a big kiss.

"He'd say you'd be your own best customer!" Gail laughed.

"Exactly what he did say!"

Rosie laughed and Gail's heart lifted to see her mother's old smile light up her face again.

"Mum, will you seriously consider this? It would suit you down to the ground!" Gail pleaded with her.

"Well, I suppose you won't let up till I do, so I may as well give it a go. But I don't have much of a CV." Rosie bit her lip.

"It's only selling shoes, Mum – not lecturing in university. Here, let me help you with it, now." Gail was nothing if not determined.

15

"You know, you're as relentless as your father when you want something," Rosie smiled, shaking her head. Putting Holly down on the rug, she went to put the kettle on, while Gail got out a pen and paper.

"I can't say I'm fifty-two," Rosie said. "They'd never even consider me." She frowned as she set out the cups and saucers for the tea.

"We're not going to say you're fifty-two. We'll say you're forty-four. You could easily pass for that. Everyone says so."

"Oh God! What if they find out?" Rosie looked at her daughter nervously.

"How can they?" said Gail, brooking no argument. "And anyway, according to you they won't even call you for an interview – so you've nothing to worry about."

"I suppose," Rosie replied, unconvinced.

It took some time to do out her CV because they had to change all the dates, due to the fact that she was now saying she was eight years younger. Rosie took Holly on her knee and, dipping a biscuit in her tea, gave it to the baby who rewarded her with a big smile. All the while, she marvelled at her daughter's determination.

Rosie heaved a sigh of relief as they finally finished the CV. "Thank God that's done," she said, as she handed Holly back to Gail.

"I'll take it with me and do it up on the computer," Gail said, "and then I'll post it off tomorrow." She was afraid Rosie would chicken out. This way, she couldn't.

"God, but you have your dad's drive and determination," Rosie laughed as she handed it over. She didn't hold out much hope of getting a reply.

Chapter 3

Tessa heard the door close behind George and heaved a sigh of relief. She waited as he drove down the drive and out the gate before fetching Napoleon, her golden Labrador, into the kitchen. There, he snuggled down in front of the Aga, showing his appreciation by practically licking her hand away. George wouldn't allow him in the house, which Tessa thought was ridiculous. She then put on her favourite Juliet Turner album and, flinging off her shoes, danced around the kitchen, singing loudly along with it. Her delight when George had to go to Dublin for the day made her feel a little guilty but never for very long.

She loved these days to herself when she could walk around barefoot, play her own music, read a book, soak in a bath for hours, eat lunch in front of the telly or gossip with her friends. George didn't approve of any of these things – he considered them trivial and frivolous. Napoleon's pleasure at being allowed into the house added to hers and increased her sense of freedom. This was the only time that she could really be herself. The more she enjoyed these days, the more she realised just how restricted her life with George had become. It hadn't always been like this. When they'd met, six years before, her free spirit had enchanted him and he'd fallen in love with her, faults and all.

When Tessa was only sixteen, she was spotted in Grafton Street by an agent from Storm Models, who whisked her off to London where she'd become a highly successful model. She was a canny businesswoman, and at the age of thirty, tired of posing for the camera and knowing that it wouldn't last forever, she had started up her own modelling agency. In the meantime, she'd managed to get herself married and then divorced from Isaac, a highly successful New York fashion photographer. She'd been crazy about him, but too late she'd discovered that he was a serial shagger and his philandering had finally caught up with him when his photo was splashed all over the tabloids, cavorting with a famous young actress. They say the wife is always the last to know, and Tessa still cringed at the fact that half of London had known about it before she did. A leopard doesn't change his spots and her ex-husband had subsequently cheated on the actress. He was now on his fourth wife and still up to his old tricks. Tessa wondered if the girl knew about it. Probably not!

Her self-confidence had taken a nosedive after this and she'd found it very hard to trust men after Isaac. It was George who'd finally won her round. They'd met at a dinner party in London, shortly after she'd started the business, and she'd found him a breath of fresh air after all the luvvies of the fashion world. They became close friends and for five years they regularly spent weekends and holidays together, commuting between Dublin and London. George had restored her self-confidence and was a welcome respite from the manic world she lived in.

He was fifty-one to her thirty when they'd met, but the age difference hadn't bothered her. He'd made her feel safe which was a nice change from her boyish, immature husband. After the roller-coaster ride that had been her life with Isaac, the stability George offered had seemed very attractive. George had never been married and lived in a small town in Ireland. He was a property dealer and his home was a magnificent Georgian house, less than an hour's drive from Dublin.

She was quite happy with their arrangement when, out of the blue, Tessa's whole world, and she herself – quite literally – collapsed. Right in the midst of London Fashion Week, she'd suffered a heart attack and was very lucky to have come out alive, with the words of her surgeon ringing in her ears: "Unless you change your lifestyle, Tessa, you're quite likely to have another one and next time you might not be so lucky." That had been her wake-up call. She'd taken stock of her life and realised it would have to change. The stress and pace of life in London, the madness that was the modelling world, the partying and drugs, had all been too much and she'd had enough. She wanted out. She had no choice but to sell the agency.

George – nice dependable George – had flown over and stayed by her bedside throughout her ordeal. When he heard what the doctor had said, he'd taken her hands in his.

"Marry me, Tessa. Come and live with me in Ballyfern," he'd said softly. "It's so quiet and peaceful there. It's just what you need." His eyes had pleaded with her.

She'd been tempted. He'd asked her many times before but she'd always said no – citing her business as an excuse

– but the real reason was that although she was very, very fond of him, she didn't love him the way she felt she should. She wasn't *in* love with him. Mind you, she'd been madly in love with Isaac and what a disaster that had turned out to be!

"Oh George, that's sweet of you but I'm not sure I want to be married again," she'd told him, trying to let him down gently.

"I know your first marriage has left a bad taste in your mouth," George had said, "but I love you, Tessa, and would never be unfaithful to you."

"I know that, but it's just that we're both pretty set in our ways, and let's face it we're not exactly young things," she'd replied, smiling.

"I'm not anyway, whatever about you," he'd replied. "People laugh about long Irish courtships and look at us! It's been five years since we started going out together. Don't you think it's time?" He was being very persuasive. "We're not getting any younger and it will be nice to grow old together," he'd added. "That can be a very lonely place if you're on your own."

She had to agree with him there. He was now fifty-six and she thirty-five and she'd been working for almost twenty years in the crazy world of fashion. She was tired of it all and, still frightened by the doctor's words, she compromised and agreed to come and live with him, but to hold off on marriage for a while.

That, she realised now, was the most sensible decision she'd ever made because things were not working out between them. She wondered why she hadn't seen it before now.

She and George were total opposites. Tessa had always been full of life. Flighty, the nuns used to call it – she preferred to think of it as *joie de vivre*! George, on the other hand, could best be described as serious and conservative. This glaring difference in their personalities hadn't been so obvious when she'd been living in London but had become much more apparent since she'd come to live with him in Ireland. She remembered her father's old adage: *"If you want to know me, come and live with me."* How right he was! She'd often wondered if he'd been referring to her stepmother, Claudia.

Tessa's father, Edward, was a very wealthy landowner in County Galway, whose photo was constantly in the newspapers and social columns. He owned a large stud farm and a string of racehorses. He'd met her mother at the Dublin Horse Show when he'd been a member of the Irish international show-jumping team and she'd been a member of the Italian team. They'd fallen madly in love and, three months later, were married. Tessa was their only child. Her mother was the daughter of an Italian count, hence the name they'd given her, Contessa. Both her parents had been high achievers and, as a child, Tessa had always had the feeling that she somehow hadn't come up to scratch, although both her parents adored her.

She was ten years old when her world fell apart. Her mother was killed in a fall from a horse. Three years later, her father had remarried. It was hate at first sight for Tessa and her stepmother. Claudia was insanely jealous of Edward's affection for his daughter and a year later persuaded him to send Tessa to boarding school. She'd hated every moment of it, missing her "Daddikins" as she called Edward, and also her beloved ponies. Small wonder then, that she'd grabbed the opportunity to go to London modelling, when it had presented itself.

Now trying constantly to reach George's very exacting standards and failing miserably had catapulted her back to her teen years when her stepmother Claudia had exerted the same pressure on her and she had come up sadly short then too. Her stepmother had been a control freak and, little by little, she was beginning to realise that George was the same.

She had the strangest feeling that in the year since she had come to live with George she had lost herself – lost her enthusiasm for life. He had somehow managed to dampen her spirit. She knew he meant well but it was getting her down. What she had perceived as mature and steady, now seemed to her stuffy and controlling. Maybe she'd been right. They were too set in their ways to start again.

She'd thought that coming back to live in a country house in Ireland would mean a big warm kitchen with the dogs lying by the Aga cooker, just like the big house in Galway where she'd grown up. She'd imagined friends joining them for supper around the big wooden kitchen table. How naïve she'd been! When she'd shared this vision with George he'd been horrified.

"Dogs in the house? You can't be serious, Tessa, and entertaining friends in the kitchen when we have a perfectly good dining-room?" he'd spluttered, shuddering at the thought. "Why do you think we have a beautiful mahogany table and Chippendale chairs, not to mention the silver and Waterford crystal?" He was so irate that she quaked under his gaze. "Eating in the kitchen – and dogs there too! Unthinkable!" He shook his head, still disbelieving.

She never mentioned it again.

Now that George was gone for the day she could relax and enjoy herself. She had invited her friend, Kate, for lunch and as Kate plonked down at the kitchen table, Tessa took a bottle of Sancerre from the fridge and poured them each a glass. In between sips, she bustled around the kitchen, putting the finishing touches to the Greek salad she'd prepared earlier.

She'd first met Kate in the golf club and they'd clicked straight away and were now good friends. Tessa knew she'd never be any great shakes as a golfer, she'd left it too late for that, but it was nice to make new friends and she enjoyed the game. Kate was really sweet and the only person Tessa would ever dream of confiding in, knowing that she could trust her.

"This salad looks delicious, Tessa, and the dressing . . . mmmm . . . it smells great," Kate sighed, inhaling the lovely aromas wafting up to her.

"My secret recipe," Tessa grinned, sitting down opposite her.

"I love these trendy square white bowls. Very Japanese-looking," Kate continued, reaching for a slice of crusty bread. "Presentation is everything, isn't it? It enhances the food so much."

"I agree. I got these bowls in Dunne's Stores, would you believe? Mind you, George would have a fit if he knew. It gives me a perverse pleasure to be eating off them – and in the kitchen – with Napoleon basking by the Aga!" She grinned triumphantly, like a child who'd been naughty and got away with it.

Kate silently agreed with her. There were very few people Kate didn't like but George was one of them. She found him stuffy and pretentious. She would never understand how Tessa had ended up with him. They were like chalk and cheese. Of course, she would never let Tessa know how she felt.

"He's driving me crazy at the moment, Kate," Tessa confided, popping a forkful of salad into her mouth. "He's so meticulous and fussy. Yesterday, he complained about the way I was loading the dishwasher. The day before, it was that I was eating my lunch without a napkin. He's such a bloody stickler for etiquette, it's making my life hell."

"That does sound a bit over the top, I have to say. I suppose it's just his way," Kate reflected.

"I broke a cup last week and honestly he behaved as if I'd smashed the whole china dinner service on the floor," Tessa continued, her voice rising with indignation. "It was just one cup and it was an accident, for God's sake. You've no idea, Kate!"

"Does George never have an accident like that?" Kate asked her, dabbing her chin with her napkin where some of the dressing had escaped.

"No, never! He's so bloody careful. He says I don't watch what I'm doing." Tessa rolled her eyes. "I suppose he has a point. I am a bit of a day-dreamer," she admitted, her pretty mouth turning up at the corners.

Kate thought how beautiful she was and such a lovely person too. George should appreciate her and not be so niggly over – let's face it – unimportant things. She felt that he was damned lucky to have met Tessa, but she didn't voice these thoughts, not wanting to fire her friend up even further.

"He's set in his ways, I suppose," she said lamely.

"You can say that again!" Tessa was on a roll. "I was cooking dinner last night and he comes in and starts telling me how to make lasagne. I ask you! I'm half Italian, for God's sake!" She spilt some of her wine as she banged her glass down on the table.

Napoleon jumped and, sensing her distress, ambled over to sit at her feet. Absentmindedly, she stroked his soft coat.

"I suppose the fact that he's lived on his own for so long makes it difficult for him now," Kate said, playing devil's advocate.

"Well, he'll be living on his own again soon, if he doesn't cop on," Tessa continued, wiping up the wine she'd spilt with some napkins. "Dear Lord, he's like an old woman sometimes. You know he hits the roof if I don't fold the towels in a certain way. God, who the hell cares if the towels are folded facing the wrong way or not? Life's too short for such nonsense."

"George apparently doesn't think so."

"I've tried doing everything his way, for the sake of peace, but it's difficult. I feel like I'm losing my identity. I'm a thirty-six-year-old woman for God's sake! Surely I can fold the towels any damn way I want!" She speared an olive with so much gusto that it flipped across the table.

"I understand but you should calm down," Kate said, retrieving the olive. "You're stressing now and that's not good for your heart."

"Sorry, you're right," Tessa replied sheepishly. "You know, I'm really concerned that George might be suffering from that disorder . . . you know the one . . . what do they call it?" She frowned, trying to remember. "You remember, Jack Nicholson suffered from it in the movie *As Good As It Gets*?" She looked to Kate for help.

"Obsessive-compulsive disorder – God, I loved that movie!" Kate was laughing as she said it. "Do you remember the scene with the dog? It was so funny!"

Tessa was laughing with her. "It was a howl. I remember I laughed so hard I wet my pants."

"Ooohhh . . . Jack Nicholson was brilliant!"

"Yes, he was. Obsessive-compulsive disorder . . . that's it . . . well, I honestly think George is suffering from it." She paused, suddenly serious. "I don't know what to do."

"I think your problem, Tessa, is that . . ." Kate hesitated, trying to find the right words. "Well, because George works from home, you're together all the time. What you need is a job to get you out of the house." She looked at Tessa questioningly as she drained her glass, wondering what she'd think of the brilliant idea she was about to propose.

"I'd love to work again, Kate, but it was work stress that caused my heart attack. I wouldn't want to go down that road again." Tessa grimaced as she poured more wine.

"It doesn't have to be anything stressful," Kate insisted. "Actually, I think I have just the thing for you." She got up from the table and went to her bag. Taking out a magazine, she handed it to Tessa. "There's an ad on page sixty for a job that would suit you down to the ground. I thought of you when I read it. It's part-time and it would suit you to a tee."

Tessa took a sip of wine as she read the ad, intrigued. "Gosh, this sounds interesting but I don't know if I'm what they're looking for."

"Why not?" Kate demanded. "I'm always admiring your shoes and you certainly have a passion for them. You have such great taste, you look gorgeous and you'd be a great saleswoman. And," she continued, leaning across the table to Tessa, "it would give you some breathing space from George."

"I suppose so, but let's face it, I'm no spring chicken. They're probably looking for young women. I'm thirty-six."

"For God's sake, Tessa, that's not old and anyway it says *no* age limit." Kate had all the angles covered.

"Yeah, but do they really mean that?" Tessa looked doubtful.

"You'll never know until you try it."

"I suppose," she said, reading the ad again.

"Go on, Tessa! Apply for it. You can always change your mind." Kate clapped her hands and Napoleon jumped up out of his cosy sleep again.

"George won't like it," Tessa said, frowning.

"To hell with George!"

Kate raised her glass and Tessa clinked hers against it.

"To hell with George!"

They drank off their wine, laughing so hard they almost cried, and the big Labrador stood up and anxiously ran from one to the other of them, licking them furiously.

"Oh, Nap! You silly boy!" Tessa said hugging him. "I'm fine, really I am."

Kate wondered if this was true.

Chapter 4

Niamh knew that she'd no chance of even being called to interview for the job. It was two weeks now and she'd heard zilch. Who in their right mind would give her a job, with her CV? They'd probably thrown it in the bin straight away. She'd heard that most companies didn't even reply to applications these days unless they wanted to interview you. How rude, she thought. I'll just have to see if I can get a morning job in one of the local shops. She knew she was clutching at straws. Every young mum wanted a job like that.

Every day her mother asked if she'd heard anything and every day it was the same negative reply.

"Forget it, Mam. They're not interested."

"I don't know. I've got a good feeling about this. I even started a novena for you." Eileen desperately wanted her to get it.

"You and your novenas!" Niamh smiled at her. Her mam – ever the optimist and a great believer in the power of prayer!

She was sorting the washing out on Thursday morning when she heard the post dropping through the letter-box.

"Post for you," Bridget cried out in her pseudo-posh accent that fooled nobody.

"Coming," Niamh replied, thinking – not another bill!

Taking the letter from Bridget, she saw that it was hand-written on very expensive stationery. Hardly a bill! Bridget had noticed that too and stood waiting to see what was in the envelope.

"Thank you, Bridget," she replied, putting it in her pocket, enjoying her mother-in-law's crestfallen face. She was so damned curious!

Niamh couldn't wait to read it but finished loading the washing machine and then went into the bedroom to read it in private. Her heart was hammering violently. It couldn't be the job, could it? She was afraid to open it, in case it was a rejection, but eventually she plucked up the courage. She thought she was seeing things but no – there it was, in black and white. She read it again and again in disbelief, "*We would like you to attend for interview, on Wednesday next, at noon, in The Davenport Hotel.*"

Hardly able to contain her excitement she rushed over to her mother's.

"Mam, they want me to come for an interview!" she said breathlessly, bursting in the door.

"I knew it. I told you. My novena to St Jude worked!" Eileen was overjoyed and pressed her hands together.

"Mam, he's the Patron Saint of Hopeless Cases!" Niamh cried.

"Well, it worked, didn't it?" her mother said, sheepishly.

She was so happy to see her young daughter's face aglow with hope. Better start another novena to be sure she gets it, she thought, although how anyone could not see Niamh's potential, she didn't know. She said a quiet prayer of thanks to St Jude. "But you've some more work to do," she told him.

Niamh was in a tizzy as to what she would wear to the interview. She'd bought a lovely green print, crossover dress in Oxfam last year and she'd seen a pair of gorgeous shoes, that exact same colour, on sale in Dunne's last week. Could she possibly spend some of Tuesday's Children's Allowance on them? Yes, she decided. This was a shoe company and she really must wear smart shoes to the interview. She had nothing remotely smart enough in her wardrobe and, as she was only a size three, she couldn't borrow from her sisters or friends.

To her relief, the shoes were still there the following Tuesday and reduced yet again, to €15. What luck! Maybe this was an omen. They were divine and their platform soles made her look much taller than her five-foot-one. She loved them.

The next morning, she had to sneak out with the dress and shoes, in case Bridget would get wind of where she was going. She still hadn't said a word to Gavin, who was still asleep in bed.

She went to her mother's to get ready. She was a bundle of nerves and Eileen wasn't much better.

Val was hovering around.

"Do you think that dress is suitable?" she asked, wrinkling up her nose.

"What's wrong with it?" asked Niamh, anxiously.

"Oh, nothing," Val shrugged, leaving Niamh full of doubts as to whether it was okay or not.

"Don't mind her! You look lovely, pet," Eileen reassured

her, glowering at her older daughter. "Those shoes are perfect with the dress. Thank God it's a lovely day and not raining."

Niamh had been terrified of that very thing, as she had no suitable coat to wear, but someone up there was looking out for her – St Jude, maybe? She smiled to herself. She was getting as bad as her mother!

"Are you sure you don't want me to come with you?" Eileen asked, anxiously.

"No, Mam, thanks all the same. I'll feel much happier knowing that you'll collect the kids from school, if I'm delayed. Just say a prayer that it all goes well," Niamh said nervously.

"I won't stop praying till you're back," her mother said, giving her a big hug.

"Thanks, Mam."

"Good luck, love," Eileen cried after her, tears in her eyes for her brave young daughter.

Rosie had known that she'd hear nothing back. She was too old for the job. They would want young glamorous women, not old fogies like her. When she mentioned this to Gail, ten days later, her daughter exploded.

"Mum, for God's sake, you're talking like you're eighty years old! You're still young and vibrant. Anyway, as I keep saying, it said *no* age limit in the advert."

"Oh, they have to say that. Otherwise it's considered ageist," Rosie said with authority. "Like they can't specify sex or race or the next thing they know they're up in court for discrimination."

Gail gave up. But she was cock-a-hoop two days later when Rosie rang to say she'd been called for interview.

"I'm not going to say 'I told you so' – but I did," Gail said delightedly.

Rosie was a nervous wreck for the next five days, wondering what to wear and what to say. Gail was afraid she might chicken out at the last moment, so she insisted on driving her mother to the interview.

Calling to collect her that morning, Gail let out a low whistle.

"Mum, you look terrific. Wow! You could pass for forty. We should have lopped another four years off your age."

Rosie was flattered, though she knew she was looking her best. She'd bought a new Paul Costello suit, in her favourite shade of coral. She'd had her hair cut and coloured – it was now a lovely silver blonde – and for the first time in her life, she'd had acrylic nails applied. She'd always had a problem with her nails. They kept splitting and she envied all those women who had long, beautiful talons. Now, she was one of them and she kept waving her hands in front of her, admiring the elegant coral manicure.

"Mum, your nails!" Gail shrieked, catching sight of them. She couldn't believe her eyes. Thank God, her mother was back in the land of the living again. Please Lord, she prayed, let her get this job. It will be the making of her.

Rosie was very apprehensive. But at least I'm feeling again, she thought. She gabbled nervously, non-stop, till they reached the hotel.

"I got a good-luck card from Sheila this morning," she told Gail. "Wasn't that very nice of her? She thinks this is just what I need."

So do I, thought Gail, but she didn't say it aloud.

Rosie said a little prayer: *Wish me luck, Jack.* And she

felt him there with her, holding her hand. A strange calmness came over her and she smiled at Gail.

"I'm ready for them, love."

Tessa hadn't given much thought to the job application until she received the letter asking her to come for an interview. She debated whether to mention it to George and then decided not. Better to wait and see what came of it. They might not offer the job to her and, even if they did, it might not suit her. No, she'd wait until it was a definite proposition. She felt a flutter of excitement and hoped that this would be, as Kate had said, the solution to her problem.

Trying to figure out a way to go to Dublin without George wanting to accompany her, she hit on the bright idea of asking Kate to come with her.

"Why not?" Kate replied. "I feel I have a vested interest in this job as I persuaded you to go for it. I'll ask Lauren to baby-sit Caoimhe for the day. Caoimhe was Kate's cute, fourteen-month-old, baby daughter. "I need to buy her some winter clothes as she's growing so fast. We can go shopping and have a nice lunch. Great! I look forward to it."

Tessa was quite excited and looking forward to the day too.

George lifted his eyebrows when he saw her dressed in her Gucci print silk dress, mustard Jimmy Choo heels and matching bag.

"My oh my! You look like you're going to a fancy lunch – not shopping with a friend," he remarked, raising his eyebrows. "And pray tell me, my dear, how do you expect to walk down Grafton Street in those outrageous heels?"

Trust George – ever critical! Somehow it really irritated her and she answered him sharply.

"I do not intend to look like a country bumpkin come to town. This is how I always dressed in London. Dublin's no different."

"Well, don't say I didn't warn you if you fall and break a leg," he frowned.

God, let me out of here quick, she thought, and she left without giving him the customary kiss, her long silky black hair swinging behind her.

Amber had been as good as her word and hadn't had so much as a single drink, while on her own, since the day she'd sent off her application. She'd started walking every day and also going to the gym three times a week. She was feeling so much fitter and surprisingly she hadn't missed the vodka. She had, of course, had a few glasses of wine when out to dinner but that was it. No more drinking alone! It was worth it, to see the relief on Susie's face when she told her. She'd also contacted some of her other old friends who were delighted to see that she was back in circulation.

"Was I crazy," she asked Susie, "to let Dermot ruin my life like I did?"

"Yes," Susie replied, "you were, but none of us could tell you that. Well, thank God you woke up to it in time. I was so worried about you, but now I'm so proud of you." She gave Amber a hug.

"I'm sorry, Suze. I was stupid." Amber hugged her back.

When she had received no reply from If the Shoes Fit after two weeks and had just about given up hope of hearing from them, a letter arrived summoning her to an interview in the Davenport Hotel. She was as nervous as a four-year-old on their first day at school. The last time she'd been for an interview had been fifteen years ago, for her airline job, but she'd been young and confident then, with no fears. Today, she was terrified. Having finally found the motivation to try for something she was surprised at how desperately she wanted to get it.

She, who was normally so confident, was now a bundle of indecision as she tried on everything in her wardrobe. The room was like a disaster area with clothes strewn all over the place, discarded because they were either too fattening, or revealing, or short, or frumpy. In the end she settled for her coffee and cream, silk-jersey, Richard Lewis suit. She felt very good in it and loved its beautiful waterfall collar. It had taken her months to find the perfect matching pair of shoes to go with it. She'd finally located them – gorgeous Manolo Blahniks in the exact coffee and cream colour as her suit – at DSW in Union Square, New York, reduced from $650 to $200. What a steal! She couldn't believe her luck. Although they had four-inch-high heels they were butter soft and extremely comfortable and made her look taller than her five-foot-seven. The antique pearls that had been a wedding gift from Dermot and a coffee Fendi clutch bag completed the ensemble.

Surveying herself in the mirror she had to admit that she did look good. Thank God for the tan she'd acquired in Marbella last month. It meant no tights and gave her an added glow. She spent ages trying to decide how to wear her newly highlighted, layered, wavy blonde hair. She normally wore it cascading around her shoulders but with the waterfall collar it looked a bit much so she twisted it up in a knot. Yes, much better. Neater for an interview, she decided, although she couldn't stop the tendrils from escaping the clip. Damn! I should have used the straightener. Too late now! She set off with trepidation.

Chapter 5

Amber entered the interview waiting-room to find an incredibly attractive young girl sitting there. She looked to be about fifteen. Good God, Amber thought with dismay, I hope they're not only looking for young things. But no, the ad had definitely said no age limit. She smiled at the girl who, she noticed, was inexpensively but very stylishly dressed and who smiled nervously back.

"Are you here for the shoe interview too?" Amber asked her.

"Yes, but I was here much too early," the girl said shyly. "My appointment isn't till noon."

"I'm early, too. Better to be safe than sorry," Amber smiled. Extending her hand, she introduced herself. "I'm Amber Gileece."

"Niamh Byrne," the girl replied, shaking her hand.

Amber sat down on the sofa beside her. She could see that the young girl was very nervous. "Are you okay?" she asked gently.

"Not really. I'm desperately nervous," Niamh replied, biting her lower lip. "I've never been for an interview before, you see."

All the years of dealing with nervous airline passengers came into play as Amber reassured her. "Don't worry, you'll be fine. It sounds fun and it will be interesting to hear what it's all about. You like shoes, do you?" She was admiring the green patent platforms the girl was wearing.

"I adore them," Niamh answered with a shy smile.

She was, Amber thought, attractive in a natural unpolished way. She had short feathery auburn hair that framed her very pretty face. Her eyes were a startling emerald green and had a gentleness and vulnerability about them that was most appealing. Amber guessed that men would find Niamh very attractive and feel the need to protect her.

"Unfortunately," Niamh continued, "I don't get to buy them very often. I've got three kids at school and I'm afraid their shoe needs come before mine." She smiled, shrugging her shoulders.

Amber gasped in shock. "My God, you can't be serious!" She looked at Niamh, open-mouthed. "You look young enough to be at school yourself. You must have started very young."

"Seventeen," Niamh said shyly. "Ian is five and I have twin girls of four. I'm twenty-three."

"Criminal! You don't look old enough to have even one child, let alone three – and at school!" Amber could scarcely believe it.

Niamh laughed at her reaction.

She had visibly relaxed and was looking much more confident by the time she was called in for her interview.

"Good luck!" Amber whispered.

"Thanks," Niamh said, giving her a little wave.

Twenty minutes later Niamh emerged, smiling.

"Phew, thank God it's over. I think I did okay. They're really nice. They'll let me know by Friday. I really hope I get it. It sounds terrific!"

"That's great! Hope I find them as nice," Amber replied with a grimace.

"I'm sure you will. Best of luck!" Niamh said, waving goodbye as she left the room.

"Well, Carlo, what do you think?" Grace asked her fellow interviewer after Niamh had left the room.

"She's very sweet. I really liked her," he replied in his deep sultry voice.

Grace frowned. "Yes, me too, but I'm concerned that she's never actually worked before."

"Well, she's very young still and I suppose having three children meant she couldn't, before now." Carlo had found it hard to believe that the lovely young girl already had three children. She was no more than a child herself and seemed so vulnerable.

"Incredible," Grace said. "She must have had a tough time."

"Exactly! I think she's a strong, determined girl and I feel she'll make a great success of anything she takes on."

"Okay, we'll shortlist her," Grace said, trusting Carlo's judgement. "You'll like the next candidate," she grinned at him as she went to call Amber in.

When the door opened, Amber was amazed to see Grace Taylor, who she knew from her airline days, standing there. They'd worked together often and had always hit it off really well. She recalled that Grace had taken winter leave and gone to Italy where she'd met a dashing Italian, married him and settled down there.

"Grace! What a surprise," Amber said, as they hugged.

"Amber, it's wonderful to see you again. You're looking terrific, as always. How are you?" She ushered her into the interview room. "Let me introduce you to Carlo."

Amber's heart skipped a beat as the very tall, impossibly handsome man took her hand and drew it to his lips. His shiny jet-black hair was curly and a tad on the long side and his deep velvet-brown eyes looked up at her from under long black lashes. She felt the soft touch of his lips on her fingers and it sent a thrill through her body that shocked her. Sensing this, he smiled sexily at her, his eyes half closed. God, he's gorgeous, she thought, and smiled back at him. His olive skin was deeply tanned which made his perfectly even teeth look absurdly white. Her heart was racing as she took her hand away.

"Grace didn't tell me that she had such a beautiful friend," he said in a deep languid voice, with an obviously Italian accent.

Amber found herself blushing. "I'm not surprised you decided to stay in Italy," she grinned at Grace, embarrassed by the effect he was having on her.

"Oh, Carlo's not my husband," Grace replied, laughing. "He's my brother-in-law, and a director in the company."

"Oh!" Amber said, her mouth open in surprise. She wondered if he was married and was then angry with herself for thinking like that. It doesn't matter one way or the other, she reminded herself. I've sworn off men forever – remember? His eyes were regarding her with admiration. She felt like a teenager under his scrutiny. She tried to regain her composure but was hugely aware of his presence. No doubt he has this effect on all women, she thought, annoyed to think that she might be a victim of his charm too.

"My husband, Massimo, is the managing director of the family shoe business which is located just outside Rome," Grace continued. "We are the largest shoe manufacturer in Italy and make shoes for all the top designers. If the Shoes Fit was my idea and I'm really excited about it." She moved over to sit on a sofa and patted the seat for Amber to join her. Carlo took a chair opposite them.

"It's a very exciting concept based on direct selling and I thought Ireland would be as good a place as any to launch it. You'll be perfect for it," Grace continued. "I remember you dragging me into every shoe shop in New York, and Athens, and Madrid. Need I go on?" She laughed, as did Carlo.

His laugh was deep and husky and Amber liked the way his eyes twinkled as he laughed.

"I see you are wearing beautiful shoes," he remarked, his eyes half-closed as he looked at her feet, a smile playing around his mouth. The languid way he said it made her feel as though she were wearing nothing else.

Grace looked at them. "Actually, they came from our factory. Manolo Blahnik, aren't they?"

Amber was impressed. Their company was obviously top-notch.

"Direct selling is hugely successful here in Ireland," Grace continued. "Witness the success of companies like Avon who have diversified from cosmetics and are selling lingerie, clothes, jewellery and even handbags and household goods. Add to that the fact that Irish women have got used to wearing designer shoes and I think we're on to a winner." She looked at Amber, to gauge her reaction.

"Absolutely! I think so too," Amber replied, her voice excited. "I'm an Avon customer and I buy from the Next catalogue too. It's a great idea. Women today are too busy to spend their free time trawling around shopping malls."

"Exactly," Grace said. "The time is right and there's no one specialising in designer shoes."

"How will it work?" Amber was very interested now. It seemed like a great business idea.

"Initially, we're starting in Dublin with seven area managers," Grace explained. "Hopefully, if all goes well here, we'll take it nationwide, then the UK and then, who knows?"

"Gosh, how exciting!" Amber's eyes were glowing.

Grace smiled at her obvious enthusiasm. "You'll each be given an area within which you'll work. You'll have to recruit representatives to sell for you within that area and you can also hold parties yourself in other areas, as you'll possibly have friends and family who would be happy to host a night for you."

"That sounds fair enough," Amber agreed.

"We'll have a week's training, starting next Tuesday. I know it's short notice. Would that be a problem for you?"

"No problem." Amber was beaming.

"Great!" Grace said happily. "Carlo – will you explain the financial aspect to Amber?"

"With pleasure," he said, smiling at Amber.

God, he's handsome, she thought as his sexy Italian voice washed over her and his deep brown eyes regarded her solemnly. She could barely concentrate on what he was saying. She sat twirling a curl around her index finger, which was a habit of hers when she felt nervous.

"We'll be offering you a six-months contract, during which time you'll be paid a retainer of €100 per week,"

Carlo explained. "You'll also earn a commission of 15% on your sales, plus you'll get expenses."

"That seems very generous," Amber remarked.

"As it's a new venture, things may change, depending on how it goes," Grace took over again. "But we'll work things out as we go along. We'll go into more detail during the training week. It goes without saying that the job is yours, if you want it, and I hope you do. I've a feeling Carlo will be disappointed if you turn us down. Am I right, Carlo?" She grinned across at him.

"Most definitely," he replied, his smile lighting up his face again as he looked at Amber.

"I heard you took early redundancy, to travel with your husband," Grace said, turning back to Amber. "How is it?"

"Ex-husband." Amber grimaced. "We divorced a year ago."

"Oh, I'm so sorry." Grace reached for her hand.

Amber was conscious of Carlo's eyes on her. She glanced at him and got caught in his gaze, like a deer in the glare of headlights. She had a feeling that he could read her thoughts. She was blushing again, much to her annoyance. Men didn't usually affect her like this. She never blushed, yet here she was as bad as any teenager!

Trying to ignore him, she asked, "Have you had many replies to this ad?"

"Unbelievably, hundreds!" Grace told her. "We weeded out a lot, of course, but we've been interviewing all week. I never realised there were so many shoe addicts in Ireland!"

"It sounds fascinating. I'll definitely come on board. I really need something right now." Her voice wobbled as she said this.

Grace caught the tremor in Amber's voice, as did Carlo. "Are things okay with you?" Grace asked.

"It's a long story. I'll tell you about it sometime." Amber smiled, embarrassed.

"I'm flying back to Rome tonight but I'll be back in Ireland next Monday," said Grace. "I'd love if you could meet me for dinner Monday night and we could catch up."

"I'd love that," Amber smiled. "I want to hear all about your life in Italy."

"How's Susie?" Grace asked. "Still flying the skies?"

"Yes, she's still working the European route," Amber told her. "She's very happy and has two adorable children now."

"Me too. Lord, where does the time go? Maybe she could join us on Monday night. I'd love to hear all the gossip."

"I'm sure she'd love to. I'll ask her."

They arranged to meet in the Shelbourne on Monday night and exchanged phone numbers.

"I'm really delighted you're going to join the company, Amber. I hope you'll be as excited about the potential of this business as we are," Grace said, taking her hands.

"I am already," Amber told her. "By the way, the girl who was in just before me – Niamh – do you think you'll be taking her on?"

"Well, we have shortlisted her. I liked her a lot although I'm worried that she's had no work experience whatsoever. Carlo was very impressed with her. Did you talk to her – what did you think? I remember how you used to size up the passengers – and you were always right."

They both laughed at the memory.

"I think she'd be great," Amber replied. "I had a long

chat with her and I have a good feeling about her. She's very bright and motivated."

"That's settled then. We'll make her a definite, Carlo," Grace said smiling.

Carlo gave Amber the thumbs-up.

"God, there's a pair of you in it," Grace chuckled. "Carlo can read people like a book" – Amber hoped not – "and you're never wrong about people."

They stood up and hugged goodbye. Carlo raised Amber's hand to his lips once more, and held it there for an indecently long time. She felt a lurch in her stomach and was furious with herself for blushing again. She'd always found Latin men attractive but they were trouble – big trouble – as many of the cabin crew on the Italian routes had found to their sorrow. Still, he'd undoubtedly stirred feelings inside her that she'd feared were dead forever. That had to count for something.

On her way home she thought about Niamh and was pleased she'd been able to help her. Such a sweet girl! Amber had laughed when she'd heard about her mother's novena to St Jude. Now she thought that maybe it had worked. She smiled, looking heavenwards.

"Go knock them dead!" Kate told Tessa, as she dropped her off at the hotel for her interview. "You look sensational." Kate wasn't kidding. Tessa did look stunningly beautiful.

Both Grace and Carlo were taken aback at the glamorous creature striding into the room. She threw them a dazzling smile, one that Grace thought could have been used by Colgate for their "ring of confidence" ads. Grace stood up, feeling like a minnow beside her. Some women have all the luck, she couldn't help thinking.

"Hello, Contessa. I'm Grace, the managing director of If the Shoes Fit. Thank you for coming." She extended her hand and Tessa shook it.

"Please call me Tessa, everyone does. I had to put my full name on my CV but nobody uses it at all."

"Let me introduce you to Carlo, one of our directors," Grace said.

Tessa turned to shake hands with the most drop-dead gorgeous man she'd ever seen. He was at least six inches taller than her, which in itself was highly unusual, as she was five-feet-eleven, but it was his dark Latin looks that really rocked her. This man was d-i-v-i-n-e! She loved his large serious brown eyes and long curly dark hair. Italian, no doubt about it. No other men in the world could wear clothes with such elegant chic. He took her hand in a firm handshake – another plus – and then spoke in a deliciously deep, sexy Italian voice. She had to restrain herself from sighing.

"*Incantata, Contessa,*" he smiled a devastating smile. "What a beautiful Italian name."

"Yes, my mother was Italian," she explained, smiling back at him. "She always called me that – she died when I was a child – but here in Ireland people take the mickey, so I prefer Tessa."

For a moment he frowned, puzzled, but then realised what she meant and threw his head back laughing. She loved the way he laughed and how his dark eyes sparkled as he did so. He was *soooo* sexy.

"Very well, when we are in Italy I shall call you Contessa," he replied, still laughing.

Oh boy! Tessa thought. You can call me anything you like.

Because of her stunning looks, Grace and Carlo had half-expected her to be arrogant and full of herself. The fact that she was so sweet, so nice and down-to-earth came as a surprise. They found her story interesting and it didn't take them long to realise that she would be perfect for the position.

"You would be working in Dublin initially. Would that be a problem?" Grace asked.

"Not at all. Ballyfern is only a forty-minute drive from the city centre."

"We could, in fact, assign Dublin West to you so it would be even less," Grace said, studying a map in front of her.

Tessa supposed that them saying this was a very positive sign and she was impressed with the company and with what they were offering. It sounded just the thing for her. She felt the interview had gone very well and she left with a spring in her step, throwing a dazzling smile at Carlo. I would have no problem working with him, she thought. No problem whatsoever! Now she really wanted the job. Coming out of the interview, she smiled at Rosie and Gail who were in the waiting room.

"Wow!" Carlo exclaimed when Tessa had left the room.

"She *is* stunning," Grace said, sighing. "She makes me feel plain and dowdy but she is a lovely girl."

"She'd make Heidi Klum feel plain," Carlo said kindly, "and she seems totally unaware of how beautiful she is."

"Yeah, I thought that too. If anything she seems a bit shy. Strange!"

"I think that she's a very suitable candidate, don't you?" Carlo asked.

"Absolutely! She's a definite," Grace replied, marking a large tick on Tessa's file and placing it on top of Amber's and Niamh's. "Three definite and three possibles – we're doing well, so far."

Tessa had adjourned to the bar after her interview, as she had twenty-five minutes to spare before she left to join Kate for lunch. She ordered a cappuccino and was about to sit down when Gail walked in.

"Are you not waiting for your interview?" Tessa asked her.

"Oh, I'm not going for it. It's my mum who's in there now. I hope she does okay."

Tessa introduced herself. "Would you like to join me while you're waiting?"

"Thanks. That would be great. I'm Gail and my mum is Rosie."

Gail ordered a coffee while Tessa chose a table and sat down.

"I really want Mum to get this job," Gail confided in Tessa when she joined her and then somehow found herself telling her all about Jack's death and how it had affected Rosie.

"How sad! I do hope she gets it," Tessa said. "They're looking for seven people, so fingers crossed."

Fifteen minutes later Rosie joined them, smiling.

"Well, that wasn't too bad. Much better than I expected!"

"Mum, this is Tessa," said Gail. "Tessa, my mum Rosie."

The two women smiled and said hello.

"The job sounds good, doesn't it?" Tessa remarked to Rosie.

"Yes. I wasn't too interested in the beginning, thinking I was much too old, but now I'd quite like to get it."

"Me too," laughed Tessa. "I thought they'd be looking for much younger people!"

Rosie couldn't understand how Tessa could have felt too old. She was young and beautiful to Rosie's eyes.

"Isn't Carlo the most divine man you've ever seen?" Tessa sighed.

"Gorgeous," Rosie agreed. "Very sexy."

"Mum!" Gail cried, in a shocked voice.

"I'm not dead, Gail," Rosie replied, pretending to look affronted, and they all laughed at this.

"They asked if I would be available to start training next Tuesday," Tessa said when they'd stopped laughing, "so I hope that's a good sign."

"They asked me that too and I thought the same," said Rosie. "Maybe we'll both get it – or maybe they just ask everybody."

"I don't think so. Fingers crossed then and hope to see you next Tuesday." Tessa bade them goodbye as it was time to meet Kate for lunch.

"How did it go?" Kate asked, as she joined her in the Unicorn.

"Good, I think – I hope! It sounds good. I really hope I get it and there was this divine man interviewing me. He's Italian," Tessa enthused.

"Uh-oh! Watch out there! He could spell trouble," Kate warned.

In fact, Tessa had been more than a little disturbed by Carlo. It wasn't just that he was so good looking but that he exuded a sex appeal that was irresistible.

During her modelling days, she had developed a marking system for men that rarely failed her. She awarded marks for kind eyes, a nice smile, a firm handshake – amongst other things – and it looked like Carlo had ticked all her boxes. Most importantly, a man had to be taller than her, so that she could look up at him, even in four-inch heels. Not too many men were and Carlo had certainly earned points there! She didn't care how fantastic Tom Cruise was, she could never fathom how Nicole Kidman and Katie Holmes – both tall women – could have fallen for him. She wouldn't have given him the time of day! But Carlo – he was pretty much perfect!

Grace and Carlo had found their fourth definite. Rosie had impressed them very much and they agreed that she would be perfect for the Dublin South area that they had decided to allot to her. Matching the right person to the right area was crucial, as Grace had found out when doing her market research.

"We're doing well here," Grace remarked. "I think we have the basis of a great team."

"We sure do, and a good-looking team at that. I can't wait to work with them," Carlo grinned wickedly.

"I bet you can't!" And Grace smacked his hand playfully.

"What a lovely girl Tessa is," Rosie remarked to Gail as they drove home.

"Yes," said Gail, "she told me she'd been a model in London and even had her own modelling agency there before she came to live in Ireland."

"She's so glamorous. She certainly looks like a model –

or even a film star. She reminds me of that Hollywood actress . . . you know . . . the one with the young husband. She was married to that guy from the *Die Hard* movies . . ." Rosie waved her coral-tipped hands about, trying to remember the name.

"Demi Moore? Yeah, she has that same dark, exotic look. I saw the resemblance also, but Tessa is a lot taller and probably a lot nicer too."

"I'm sure she is."

"It will be great if you both get it. When will they let you know?"

"They said they'll ring on Friday," Rosie said anxiously.

Gail was delighted that Rosie wanted the job and hoped desperately that she would get it. All they could do now was wait and pray.

Chapter 6

That Friday, Rosie, Tessa and Niamh received the longed-for phone call from Rome.

Rosie danced around the kitchen and invited Gail and Sheila out that evening to celebrate with her.

"Looks like you won't need my counselling any more," Sheila said, over a delicious meal.

"If it wasn't for you, I'd never have had the will to go for it," Rosie told her. "And if it wasn't for my wonderful daughter here . . ." Full of emotion, she couldn't continue. And if it wasn't for Jack taking care of me – she thought secretly – well, I don't know where I'd be.

Niamh rushed around to her mother's as soon as she got the news. Eileen was overjoyed. She brought out the sherry and insisted that Niamh have a glass. "Has Val been in?" Niamh asked as they sat at the kitchen table, sipping the sweet sherry. "I thought we might all go out for a few drinks tonight, to celebrate."

"No. Strangely, I haven't seen her since you were going for your interview on Wednesday." Eileen sounded perplexed. "She didn't even ring to see how you'd got on. I'll call her this afternoon and give her your news and ask her to come out tonight."

"Now I have to think how I can break the news to Gavin," Niamh told her mother, a worried look on her face.

"Hrrmph!" Eileen snorted. "He should be delighted that someone in the family is willing to work. He certainly isn't."

"Oh, Mam, give over!" Niamh said in exasperation. "He does try to find work but it's not easy."

Eileen could never understand why Niamh always defended the lazy son-of-a-bitch. It seemed that she still loved her waster of a husband. Eileen would have thrown him out years ago.

They finished their sherry and as Niamh walked home, she wondered why it was that she always felt the need to defend Gavin. She knew that he was immature and irresponsible but she blamed that on his mother. Bridget still treated him like a teenager and did everything for him. Niamh knew they had to get out of there if they wanted their marriage to survive. He would never grow up while under Bridget's roof.

Niamh was the youngest of a large happy family – an afterthought, her mother always said – but her father had called her the twinkle in his eye. Her older brothers and sisters had all left school early but she had loved studying and had been the brightest student in her class. Her parents had had great hopes for her. She'd had great hopes for herself.

Unfortunately, none of them foresaw that she would fall in love with Gavin Byrne and get pregnant, all in her final year at school. From the moment she set eyes on him, at the Soccer Club disco, she'd been hooked. At twenty-two, he'd been six years older than her. He was tall and muscular with blond film-star looks, not unlike a young David Beckham. He was the star of the soccer team and girls for miles around flocked to the matches every Sunday, hoping to catch his eye. Even her older sister Val had been crazy about him. He had a charisma that drew people to him, male and female, young and old. Niamh was no exception and she still couldn't understand what he'd ever seen in her. She'd been a late starter when it came to boys, preferring to curl up with a book than go out clubbing with her friends, so she'd been quite unprepared for the feelings that had overwhelmed her when she'd fallen in love with him. Crazily, wildly, madly in love with him!

It was a piece of cake for him to seduce her and when she discovered she was pregnant, she was distraught. She almost died of happiness at his reaction to the news.

"Well, now you'll have to marry me," he'd said, with his lopsided smile.

"You don't have to," she'd replied, although spending the rest of her life with him was what she'd wanted more than anything.

"I want to. I love you and we're going to get married someday, so why wait? Why not now?" he'd asked.

This was like music to her ears. The way he'd said it had made sense.

Her parents had been very disappointed with her and she'd felt very bad about that. They'd secretly harboured hopes that she'd go to university but those dreams had now flown out the window. At least Gavin was standing by her, which was something. Her father was totally against the marriage, believing Niamh deserved better, but in the end he gave in. Gavin's mother was furious with him and treated Niamh like a pariah, come to prey on her darling son.

They were married quietly, the week after she finished her Leaving Cert., with just the two families present. She was two months short of her seventeenth birthday and six months pregnant. Not quite the wedding she'd always dreamed of, but she was madly in love with her gorgeous husband and blissfully happy. Her baby boy, Ian, was born three months later and she adored him from the moment she set eyes on him. He was so tiny that Niamh was almost afraid to hold him. Gavin wouldn't hold him at all, in case he hurt him or Lord forbid, drop him, but he was very much the proud father.

"He's going to play for Man. United one day," he'd say later when Ian had become more sturdy. He spent hours throwing a ball to him and playing with him but he would get irritated when Ian cried. As for things like nappy-changing – forget it – he would have none of it!

Living with Bridget – a widow, who worshipped her son and spoilt him rotten – was not the ideal start to their marriage. She was jealous of Niamh, convinced that she had trapped her beloved son into marriage. Bridget had scowled throughout their wedding day, as could be seen in all the wedding photographs. Niamh tried to keep out of her way as much as possible but it was difficult in the small cottage. They had put their name down for a council house but Niamh knew that the waiting list was so long, it would be years before they would get one.

Gavin was perfectly happy living as he'd always done – his mother taking care of him, washing and cooking for her darling son. Niamh sometimes felt that Gavin still thought of himself as a single man. All he wanted was an easy life. Marriage and fatherhood had changed nothing for him, whereas *her* whole world had been turned upside down.

She knew he loved her and she still loved him madly. He

had a voracious sexual appetite and in the beginning they'd made love every night and every morning and sometimes he'd want her during the day as well. Niamh wasn't complaining. She adored sex with her handsome husband. However, she was always conscious of the paper-thin walls and the fact that Bridget could hear them, put her off somewhat.

To her horror, when Ian was only six months old, she discovered that she was pregnant again. This time Gavin suggested that she have an abortion but she wouldn't hear of it. Not only was she pregnant but she was expecting twins. Lily and Rose arrived two months early, kicking and punching their little fists in the air and perfectly healthy, although they were very, very tiny. They were hungry babies and Niamh, who was breastfeeding them, was exhausted all the time. Her sexual marathons with Gavin became a thing of the past – sleep became more important – and eventually they were down to once-a-week sessions. Gavin showed little interest in the babies and she knew he felt trapped.

Although it was tough going, she was happy with her little family and longed for the day when they would have their own place. She was still very much in love with her charming husband, despite his faults.

Gavin was working as a carpenter, but he didn't earn very much and they were always short of cash. Bridget didn't do them any favours and expected them to pay rent and help with the household bills. Niamh paid for all the groceries, Bridget's included. On top of that, she couldn't believe how much the babies cost. Gavin still didn't get it. He still spent as many evenings in the pub, with his mates, as ever and no match went unattended by him. No matter how much she scrimped and saved, there was never any money left over to put aside towards a deposit on their own house.

Then the unthinkable happened. Gavin lost his job. That was when their troubles began in earnest. He didn't seem interested in looking for another job. They started arguing a lot and, when she tried to tackle him about it, he would walk out, slamming the door after him. His mother was no help and always sided with her son. Niamh found it a struggle but she couldn't trust anyone to look after the babies as well as she did herself, so taking a job and leaving them was out of the question for the moment.

The twins had thrived over the years and now that they'd started school Niamh decided she absolutely had to get a job. She had accepted the fact that if it was left to Gavin they would be living with Bridget forever. She knew it would be up to her to make a life for her family. She didn't know where to start as she'd had no training or experience. When she spotted the If the Shoes Fit ad in the magazine, she'd felt it might be fate. Now it looked as if it was.

Tessa was delighted when Grace rang with the good news. Luckily, George was out playing golf, otherwise she would have had to tell him about the job and she hadn't quite decided how to break the news to him. She drove over to Kate's.

"I got it, I got it, I got it!" she cried, whirling Kate around the kitchen.

Kevin, Kate's husband, came in to see what all the shrieking was about.

"Tessa got the shoe job I told you about," Kate said, thrilled with the news.

"Congratulations!" he said, swinging her off her feet, which was quite a feat, given her height.

"This calls for some champagne!" Kate cried.

Kevin duly brought out the bottle and some glasses.

Caoimhe, their baby daughter, was laughing and clapping her hands, having no idea what the grown-ups were so happy about but determined not to be left out. Tessa took her out of her high chair and twirled her around the room. She squealed with excitement, chuckling happily and wriggling her chubby arms and legs in the air.

When things had settled down, Kate asked, "Have you told George yet?"

"Hmmm . . . no, not yet. I was thinking of taking him out for a meal tonight and breaking the news to him then."

"Yeah, well, it's time you did," Kate advised her.

"I'm sure he'll be pleased for you," Kevin said.

"You don't know George," Tessa replied, apprehension in her voice.

As they sat in the Ballyfern Inn, later that evening, George remarked, his voice very serious, "You've been jittery all afternoon, Tessa. Is something bothering you?"

"No . . . well, yes." She didn't quite know how to begin, so she just blurted it out. "Actually, I've got a job." She looked at him, dreading his reaction.

"A job?" he said, wrinkling his nose with distaste.

"Yes, with a designer shoe company. It's only part-time and I'll be a sales manager, managing a team of women who'll sell direct to the customer."

"And do you mind telling me how you got this job – behind my back?" he asked, his voice icy.

"It wasn't behind your back. I just didn't want to say anything until I was sure I'd got it."

"You still hid it from me. I don't like secrets," he replied, his face grim.

She looked at him helplessly.

"I don't want you to work. I earn more than enough to keep us both in comfort. Why do you want to do this?" His eyes were hard and his lips compressed in annoyance.

"I really need something, George, other than golf and riding. I feel I'm stagnating." Tessa prayed that he'd understand.

"Remember what the doctor said: 'No stress'. I presume this job is in Dublin?" he asked archly.

"Yes, but there won't be stress and anyway I can't stay wrapped up in cotton wool for the rest of my life." She looked at him hopefully, willing him to understand.

"You know my feelings on the subject," he replied tersely, pressing his fingertips together. "What will everyone think? Selling shoes indeed! Now I don't want to discuss it further." Straightening his tie, he opened the menu, signalling that the conversation was over.

After that, their conversation was stilted and general and when they got home, George went straight up the stairs to bed. When she went up, thirty minutes later, his light was off and he was lying rigid, way over on his side of the bed. She knew that he was still awake. He was angry with her but she didn't care. She wanted to take on this job and he had no right to stop her.

Niamh had decided to break the news to Gavin and his mother over tea.

"I have some good news. I got a job." There really was no other way to say it.

"What kind of job?" he asked suspiciously – thinking babyminder, lollipop lady, cleaner.

"It's with an Italian shoe company. They sell designer shoes and I'll be an area manager."

"You can't be serious!" he exclaimed, his mouth dropping open. "What about the children? Who'll look after them?"

Niamh could see he was worried that it might be him. "I can work when they're at school," she told him. She was so anxious for him to agree that she couldn't touch the macaroni cheese on her plate.

"I hope you don't expect Gavin or me to mind them while you're off gadding about?" Bridget had to put in her tuppence-worth, as usual. "You young ones! All these fancy notions about working! You should be home looking after your children. It's not your husband's job to do that," she sniffed.

Niamh wanted to throttle her. No, it's my husband's job to bring in some money, she wanted to scream at her, and why shouldn't Gavin look after his own children occasionally? She knew better than to voice this aloud. She knew Gavin would side with his mother and she couldn't hope to win against the pair of them.

"Ma's right, I don't think it's a good idea," he said petulantly, stuffing a forkful of macaroni in his mouth.

Nothing affects *his* appetite! Niamh thought bitterly.

She dropped the subject, determined to bring it up later when Bridget wasn't around to stick her nose in.

"Can you baby-sit tonight, Gav? I'd like to go down to Daly's with Mam and Val for a drink."

"Sorry, no way, I'm meeting the lads. Maybe Ma will." He looked at his mother hopefully.

"Well, I suppose," Bridget said grudgingly, "as they'll be in bed. But mind," she threw the words at Niamh, "if they wake up, I'll be ringing your mobile and you'll have to come home."

Niamh felt the tears prick her eyes. It was so unfair. She couldn't remember the last time she'd gone out on her own.

Please God I won't have to stand this much longer, she thought. If this job works out we'll be able to move into our own place. This thought put her in better form as she met up with her mother in Daly's.

"Where's Val?" she asked her mother, taking her coat off and slipping in beside her.

"I've no idea, love. I've left messages on her mobile but she didn't ring back."

"That's strange. I hope she's okay," Niamh said worriedly.

"You know her, love. She probably met some guy and is shacked up with him," Eileen spoke resignedly, as if she was well used to this. "Anyway, you and I will celebrate your new job together. I'm so proud of you and your dad would be too, if he was alive."

Niamh felt a lump in her throat. "Mam, I don't know what I'd do without you," she said, giving her mother a hug. She meant it from the bottom of her heart.

She ordered two Bacardis and Coke and they settled down to enjoy the evening. There was no sign of Val all night and, luckily, no phone call from Bridget either.

When she got home she checked on the kids and, pulling the covers up on them, kissed them gently. They looked so sweet and vulnerable that her heart welled up with love for them. When they were sleeping, they reminded her of the cherubs in Raphael's paintings – her little angels. She tiptoed into bed and lay awake, waiting for Gavin to come home. When he climbed into bed beside her, she broached the subject of the job again.

"Gav, I'd really like to try this," she said, her fingers crossed under the covers. "I know I can work while the kids are at school. You won't even notice I'm doing it."

He'd had more than a few pints and just wanted to go to sleep. "I suppose," he mumbled, and then he started to snore gently.

She hugged herself tight, thinking that this was going to change her life. Gavin would get used to it. As long as she made sure it wouldn't inconvenience him or interfere with his life, he wasn't bothered. She'd be sure to keep it like that.

Chapter 7

On Sunday afternoon, Amber was sitting in Susie's garden enjoying the last of the summer sunshine. After a delicious lunch, Susie's husband, Tony, had taken the two kids off to visit his mother, leaving the girls chatting over a glass of wine.

"I'm so delighted you got the job. It will be a new start for you." Susie beamed at her friend. "And to think that Grace Taylor is running it! I always liked her. You'll enjoy working with her. I'm really looking forward to seeing her on Monday night."

"I'm glad you're able to make it. In fact, I'm dreading it now because I'll have to tell her my whole sorry story," Amber said with a grimace, twirling a curl around her finger, "and you know, Grace, she'll want to know all the gory details."

"Amber," Susie said gently, placing a hand on her friend's arm, "I think it's time. You haven't spoken about it in a year, not since your divorce came through. It's time to let it go. Move on. Maybe talking about it will release it and then you can start this new phase in your life and put the past behind you."

Amber knew Susie was right and she thought about it later that night as she lay soaking in her bath. She had tried to block all memories of her marriage out of her mind. It was too painful to even think about. The drink had helped but now that she'd cut that out, the memories were more raw than ever. She knew Susie was right. It was time to let go and move on. If she didn't do it now she'd never do it. Lying in the delicious warmth of the bubble bath, candles flickering all around, she let her mind drift back.

She'd first met Dermot on a flight to New York and although she'd never believed in all that "eyes across the room" lark, it was actually how it had happened. He was older than her but very attractive, in a mature way, and he'd made it obvious that he fancied her from the off.

Just before landing he'd invited her to dinner that evening. Seeing her hesitation, he had reassured her by saying, "It's quite okay. I promise you, I'm not a married man. I'm divorced, actually."

Whew! Thank God for that! Amber's last relationship had ended disastrously when she'd discovered that the man she had been seeing – and sleeping with – for over a year, had neglected to mention that he also had a wife and four children. She had sworn off men after that but now she couldn't resist Dermot's invitation. He took her to Tavern on The Green, in Central Park, a restaurant she'd often admired. She was utterly enchanted to find it a blaze of fairy lights and lanterns. Amber thought that it was surely the most romantic place on earth and over the course of the evening, it cast its spell and they'd fallen deeply in love. Six months later they were back there, celebrating their wedding dinner. It was like a fairy tale; she was the princess, he the handsome prince and they would live happily ever after. Or so she'd thought.

Initially, she'd been blissfully happy. Dermot was a high-powered financier and he opened up a whole new world to her that she'd never known existed. He was passionate about opera and took her to The Metropolitan in New York, La Scala in Milan and to the Verdi Festival in Verona. He also had a yacht in the South of France, where they spent many glorious weekends. For holidays they sailed the Mediterranean. No matter where they travelled, he'd been there before and he introduced her to beautiful quiet places, off the beaten track. She'd travelled a lot in her job but all she'd ever really seen were hotel rooms and shops. She now realised just what she'd missed.

After their marriage, she'd sold her apartment in Clontarf and moved into his big spacious house in Foxrock. He had a large coterie of friends who shared his interests: sailing, golf and opera. Like Dermot, they were all quite a bit older than Amber, but they welcomed her with open arms and were very pleasant, with one exception. Maeve was the wife of his best friend Jeff and she was a bitch. The first time they'd met she'd informed Amber, "We were all terribly upset when Dermot divorced Camilla. They were perfect together. However, young things have always attracted him and you are obviously cleverer than those who went before you."

Amber was so gobsmacked by her remark that she couldn't think of a reply. She was very upset after this encounter but Dermot brushed it aside. "Don't mind her. She and Camilla were best friends and she was upset at our divorce. Don't give her another thought."

Easier said than done, Amber thought. She tried to

ignore Maeve's remarks, hoping they might become friends but Maeve tried to undermine her at every possible opportunity and in the end Amber gave up on her.

Her marriage was everything Amber had ever dreamed of and she and Dermot were very much in love. She was still working and would be away for three days at a time, flying transatlantic. She enjoyed the camaraderie between the cabin crew, not to mention the fantastic shopping in New York and Los Angeles, but she was always happy to get back home. She missed Dermot dreadfully when she was away.

Life was perfect and then, out of the blue, Dermot was headhunted by one of the biggest European Financial Institutions and things changed. In his new position he had to regularly entertain foreign financiers and their wives. He wanted Amber by his side. She didn't want to give up her job but just then the airline offered early redundancy. She loved flying and the *craic* she had on overnights in foreign cities, not to mention the shoe shops in New York! She also treasured her independence but Dermot was adamant. He expected her to comply with his wishes. She held out for as long as she could but she didn't stand a chance in the face of his determination. She loved him too much. In the end, she gave in and resigned.

She didn't miss work as much as she'd expected she would and the first five years had been great. It had been very exciting: dinners, receptions, fascinating people, foreign travel, invites to all the best parties. But then Dermot had been promoted and sent to Brussels. He didn't need her there. She went over occasionally but mostly he left on Monday morning and returned on Friday evening. She felt bereft and didn't know what to do with herself. She rambled around the big house, alone, all week long.

The crazy thing was that all of her married friends thought she had the perfect life: husband gone on Monday, back on Friday. "Oh, how I wish my husband would get a job like that – you lucky thing!" she heard over and over. Amber didn't see it like that. She adored Dermot and hated being away from him. She felt that they were drifting apart and she was scared. She started learning Italian and joined the local tennis club but there were still a lot of empty hours to fill. She was lonely and felt her life was aimless. She thought that maybe now was a good time to start a family – after all she was thirty-two – it was time! When she broached the subject to Dermot, she recoiled at his vehemence.

"Forget it, Amber. I don't want children. I never have. Anyway I'm too old to start all that. This was the main reason Camilla and I got divorced. She used to go on and on about it. So just forget it. I'm just not father material."

She was shocked. They'd never actually discussed it but she had always assumed that they would have kids some day. Lots of men had children in their fifties. Why, some celebrities like Al Pacino and Anthony Quinn had kids in their sixties and seventies! She couldn't believe Dermot's attitude or the fact that he wouldn't consider her wishes at all. After all, she was still a young woman and it was only natural that she would want children.

This was when Amber started drinking. Whether from boredom, loneliness, or disappointment, she couldn't have said, but the alcohol helped. In the beginning, she only drank after six o'clock. Maybe a gin and tonic or two and then she'd open a bottle of wine with dinner. She never intended to finish it but it was very easy to keep pouring as she sat alone watching television, night after night. Then one Friday evening, Dermot didn't arrive home. She was beside herself with worry, imagining an accident or some other awful tragedy. That was until the phone call that exploded her life into tiny fragments.

It was Dermot on the other end. He pulled no punches. "I'm truly sorry, Amber," he said. "I don't know how to say this and I really hate having to hurt you, but I've met someone else. I want a divorce."

She sat looking at the phone, like an idiot, thinking that he was joking. She even thought for a moment that maybe it was April Fool's Day. It wasn't, and it wasn't a joke either. She couldn't understand it. She felt as though she'd been punched in the stomach and her mouth went dry. She groped for the nearest chair and sat down.

"Amber, are you still there?" Dermot's voice was full of concern. "Did you hear what I said?"

When she finally found her voice she replied. "Dermot, please tell me this is not true."

"I'm really, really sorry, Amber. I don't want to hurt you but our marriage is over." His voice sounded final.

"You can't mean that, Dermot. Please, darling! You're just feeling lonely over there. We have to talk." She could hear the panic in her own voice. "I realise that being apart all week is a strain," she rushed on, "but we'll get over this. I love you. I could come to live in Brussels with you. We'll work it out." She was pleading with him now, her voice tearful.

"There is nothing to work out, Amber. I'm sorry. Please don't make this more difficult than it already is. You'll be looked after financially – have no fears there – but I want a divorce, and as quickly as possible."

He sounded so cold. "Who is this other woman?" she cried. "Do I know her?"

"No."

"How did you meet her?" She had to know what she was up against.

"Amber, that is not important," he assured her.

"It's bloody important to me!" she yelled. "I want to know who is stealing my husband and wrecking my marriage."

"It's someone I met here. She's the daughter of a colleague," he said, sighing. "I knew you'd make a scene," he continued. "That's why I didn't want to tell you in person. Goodbye, Amber. My solicitor will be in touch with you."

Before Amber could say more, he'd hung up.

She couldn't understand it. She sat staring at the phone. Had this really happened or was it just a bad dream? They had a happy marriage. They loved each other. Of course they argued from time to time, like all married couples, but her marriage was as solid as they come. Or so she'd thought. She'd even given up on her wish to have children because that was what he wanted. How could this be happening? The daughter of a colleague, he'd said. That meant that she was probably a young thing. He was trading her in for a newer model! She started to laugh hysterically. She'd been the newer model once and now she was being thrown on the trash heap.

She couldn't come to terms with it. She'd often heard of women who'd thought they were happily married and who were shocked when their husbands upped and left them. As if, Amber used to think, sceptically. She didn't believe a word of it! How could they not have known that their husbands didn't love them? Frankly, she thought they were fools and now it looked like she had joined their ranks.

And how cruel of him not to tell her face to face! That's

Dermot all over, she thought bitterly. Couldn't stand a scene!

In tears, she rang Susie, who rushed over straight away. She hugged Amber and made her repeat what Dermot had said, word for word.

"I can't believe it, Amber!" Susie was shocked. "He adores you. All the girls say so. God, if your marriage is in trouble then there's no hope for the rest of us!" There was anguish in her voice. "You'll have to talk this out together. He can't just end it like that, with a phone call. He was probably lonely and some girl took advantage of it. It's probably just a silly affair – male menopause and all that!" She put her arm around Amber's shoulders and felt her shaking. "Dermot loves you. I'm sure of that. You'll have to sit down with him and talk about it."

"How can I? He's in Brussels," Amber replied, tears welling up in her eyes.

"Well, go over there and talk with him. You can't just give up without a fight," Susie said firmly.

"I don't know, Susie. He sounded so cold on the phone," she said, the tears rolling down her cheeks. "What can I do? I can't live without him. I love him so much!"

Susie got her a box of tissues and then poured them both a drink. "Here, take this," she said, handing Amber the glass.

In between sniffs, Amber took a long swig.

"Go to Brussels and talk to him. Pretty lousy way to break the news to you, I have to say." Susie was furious with Dermot.

Amber wasn't so sure that going to Brussels was a good idea, but it was worth a try. Anything was worth it, if she could salvage her marriage. Susie helped her pack an overnight bag and set out her clothes for the following morning. "You're doing the right thing, Amber," Susie assured her as she folded clothes in the bag. "He can't just end it with a phone call." She would have stayed the night but she was working early the following day, so seeing her friend safely tucked up in bed she hugged her and wished her luck.

Amber caught the midday flight the following day, feeling as though she was in a dream – a nightmare, to be exact! She hoped to God she was doing the right thing but she had nothing to lose, did she? She planned to arrive at Dermot's hotel at four thirty and wait for him there.

Having time to spare, she ambled down the Boulevard de Waterloo. Normally, she would have been in her element, window-shopping in all the fabulously expensive designer boutiques. They were all here: Armani, Prada, Dior, Chanel, Escada, but today she felt like a zombie and barely glanced at them – until she spotted the red shoes in Versace. "Oh my God!" she cried aloud. "What divine shoes!" They were red patent stilettos, cut very low in front, with the daintiest straps she'd ever seen across the instep. They were to die for! They reminded her of her first pair of tiny red patent shoes. She checked out the price, €350. Not too bad, considering they were Versace, and *sooo* gorgeous. However, having more serious business to attend to at the moment, she turned her back on them.

She arrived at Dermot's hotel, the Hilton, just after four thirty and, as he wasn't in his room, decided to wait for him in the lobby. Surprise was everything, Susie had warned her. If she'd let him know she was coming, he would have either put her off or been well prepared for her. She ordered a bottle of Perrier water. She was sick with nerves, rehearsing what she would say to him. After an agonising half-hour her heart lurched as she saw him come in. With a shock she saw that he was holding the hand of a stunning young girl who couldn't have been more than twenty years old. She was exquisite, small and slim with long silky black hair, smooth olive skin and almond-shaped eyes. Thai or Malaysian, Amber guessed.

As Amber approached him, Dermot's eyes opened wide in surprise but he kept his composure. Turning to the beautiful girl, he spoke to her in French.

"*Camille, excuse-moi. Tu peut monter chez nous et j'arrive tout de suite.*"

"*D'accord, chérie,*" she replied, kissing Dermot on the lips and giving Amber a questioning look as she left.

Amber knew enough French to understand that he'd told her to go up to their place and that he'd join her as soon as possible.

She felt like laughing hysterically on hearing that his lover's name was Camille – French for Camilla, the name of his first wife – but somehow she kept her hysteria under control.

"Amber, what are you doing here?" Dermot asked, steering her to a chair in a quiet corner of the lobby.

"We have to talk, Dermot. We can work things out." She reached for his hand but he pulled it away.

"I'm so sorry, Amber, but it truly is over. There's nothing to talk about."

Her heart was pounding. She couldn't believe he could be so cold and callous. Where was the man she loved and who had promised to love her "till death do us part"?

"Is that the girl you're leaving me for?" She tried to keep her voice under control.

71

"I'm sorry, I truly am, but yes she is. I love her and . . ." he hesitated.

She saw the red colour suffuse his face and realised he was embarrassed.

"But she's young enough to be your daughter, your granddaughter even. Just how old is she?" Amber's voice was rising, her eyes wild.

"Mmm . . . twenty," he replied, looking abashed, "but don't forget, you were quite a bit younger than me too."

"Dermot, I implore you, please think about this carefully. This is just infatuation. She's only a kid." She couldn't stop herself reaching for his hand again and felt her hopes rise when he let her take it. "This girl wasn't even born when John Lennon was killed," she continued, "let alone Elvis Presley or JFK. How can you possibly consider marrying someone so young? You have nothing in common. You're two generations apart." Her eyes pleaded with him. She knew she sounded pitiful but she had to make him see sense. She started crying. "I love you," she said.

People around were beginning to look at them and Dermot shifted uncomfortably in his seat. He hated scenes. Amber knew this. He pulled his hand away from her.

"I'm sorry, my dear, I know it's a shock for you but my mind's made up . . ." he hesitated again, looking away, not able to meet her eyes. "Actually, Camille is pregnant so you understand why I want a divorce, as soon as possible."

Shock! That was the understatement of the year. She felt like she'd been hit with a sledgehammer in the gut. She doubled over in pain. She couldn't believe what she was hearing.

"You'll be very well taken care of financially, of course," he continued, ignoring her anguish. "You'll have nothing to worry about on that score. Now I must go," he said, standing, embarrassed at this public display of grief.

"Please, Dermot, please!" she cried, sobbing.

"Goodbye, Amber," he said and, turning on his heel, he left her.

Amber couldn't take it in. She was too shocked to feel any other emotion as she stared after him. She felt the bile rising in her throat and just made it to the Ladies' in time to throw up. She couldn't believe it. Her marriage was caput. Was he serious? He was almost sixty, for God's sake! This relationship could never last. And the cruellest blow of all – he was going to be a father! How often had Amber pleaded with him for a baby but he had adamantly refused. Now this slip-of-a-thing, whom he barely knew, had managed to get from him that which he had denied his wife. The only way she could survive this was to go on automatic so, pulling herself together, she repaired her make-up and left the hotel with as much dignity as she could muster.

She realised that she'd better find somewhere to stay the night as it certainly would not be in her husband's bed. But first she needed a drink. She went into the nearest café and ordered a large brandy. This calmed her down and, leaving the café, she walked back down Boulevard de Waterloo trying to come to terms with what had just happened. She passed the Versace shop again. The red shoes were still there. To hell with it, she thought, pushing open the door of the elegant shop. A very chic woman was just about to close up.

"I'm sorry I'm so late but could I please try on the red shoes in the window?" Amber managed to ask, in her halting French.

"But of course, my dear," the woman replied in perfect English. "They are so beautiful, no? Every woman should have a pair."

They were gorgeous on and Amber agreed with her, handing over the credit card. Retail therapy – nothing to beat it! She saw the incongruity of it. Here am I, my world and my marriage crashing around me and the first thing I do? I buy a pair of shoes! She felt quite light-headed and giddy. She realised that she had eaten nothing all day so went into the Taverne de Copenhagen where she ordered a salade niçoise and a glass of white wine. She rang Susie from there.

"Oh, Amber, I've been so worried about you. How did it go? Did you talk to Dermot?"

"No dice, Susie. He says there's nothing to talk about. He's in love with a twenty-year-old who also happens to be pregnant and he wants to marry her," she said bitterly.

Susie was flabbergasted. "Amber, you can't be serious! Twenty – and pregnant? He's lost his marbles! You poor thing! I can't believe this."

Amber could hear the utter disbelief in her friend's voice.

"Look," Susie continued, "I'm just in from Madrid and still at the airport. If I dash, I can try and get a standby to Brussels. I'll get back to you," and with that she was gone.

"*A friend in need, is a friend indeed*," Amber remembered her mother droning on when she was a child. She was right, she thought ruefully, as always. God only knows what her mother would make of this mess she was in. Her mother had never liked Dermot.

"He's too old for you and he's inscrutable," her mother had said. She made him sound like a villain in a James Bond movie.

"What do you mean 'inscrutable'?" Amber had asked.

"I don't trust him. You never know what he's thinking.

His face is like a mask. He says one thing but underneath he's thinking another."

Amber had pooh poohed her mother's fancies. Now she had to admit that her mother had got it right.

Susie rang back five minutes later.

"I'm on my way. I'm boarding in five minutes. Have you booked a hotel?"

"No, not yet."

"Okay, I'll give the Charlemagne a ring and book us a room. You know it. It's beside Kitty's. The crews stay there when they overnight on the Brussels route."

"Susie, I don't know how I could get through this without you." She felt close to breaking point but Susie shushed her.

"I'll meet you in Kitty's at, say, ten o'clock? You go and check in now. I'll see you soon."

"Susie, thanks."

Amber was waiting in Kitty's and felt the tears welling up inside her when she saw Susie rushing in the door, her face full of concern.

"You poor thing," said Susie, giving her a hug. "What a bastard he is. Frankly, I think you're better off without him but I know it doesn't feel like that at the moment. How are you? Are you okay?" She looked at Amber, her face creased with worry.

"Numb really. I just can't believe that I didn't see it coming. But honestly, I hadn't a clue." Amber shook her head.

"Dermot always played his cards very close to his chest. I never knew what he was thinking."

"Well, I thought I did, but obviously I was wrong," Amber said, her mouth turning down at the corners.

"I need a stiff drink and you certainly do too," said Susie, ordering two large brandies.

Many brandies and a few tears later, they made their way to the Charlemagne where they talked long into the night.

That was just fifteen months ago. Fifteen months of heartache which had almost led her to self-destruct, drinking vodka and orange at eleven in the morning, hoping to dull the pain and get her through the day. She'd changed from gin and tonic. It was a giveaway; everyone could smell it! She had done very well out of the divorce, or so everyone said. Dermot had offered her two million euro and a very generous monthly allowance. Guilt money, she called it! He was so anxious for a quick divorce that he'd have agreed to any demands she would have made. It had meant that she was able to buy this gorgeous apartment in the Marina in Malahide but her life had become empty and meaningless. She was glad to be back on the north side of Dublin where she'd grown up and where Susie and all of her old friends lived. She felt more comfortable there. She would have hated bumping into Dermot's friends every day. She did meet Maeve once, shortly before she moved out of Foxrock, and she could see that the other woman was delighted at her misfortune.

Maeve couldn't keep from gloating. "I must say, I'm not surprised and neither is Camilla."

Amber couldn't let this go. She hadn't wanted to stoop to Maeve's level but couldn't resist it. "Well, I don't think his new wife will make her any happier. She's young enough to be Camilla's granddaughter."

It was worth the bitchy remark to see the shock on Maeve's face. Amber smiled again at the memory.

Chapter 8

Tessa hardly saw George on the Sunday. He was obviously still annoyed with her about the job and trying to avoid her. He had risen at seven and, by the time she'd come downstairs, he had left for golf. It was such a lovely day that she saddled up her horse, Kilkenny, and went for a long exhilarating ride.

When she got back, in the early afternoon, she found a note from George to say that he'd gone to visit his mother and wouldn't be home till late. That in itself was unusual. He rarely went to visit Doreen. Twice a year at most – her birthday and early December – that was it! He'd almost had a seizure last year when she'd suggested having his mother for Christmas.

After a quick snack she took Napoleon for a walk. The lovely weather and the thought of starting work again put a spring in her step that even George's behaviour couldn't dampen. After their walk a delighted Napoleon curled up beside her on the sofa as she watched the *Sex and the City* movie. The film reminded her of her years in London. Sometimes, she felt homesick for the life she'd left behind and wished she was back there. If it wasn't for Kilkenny and Napoleon, she reckoned she'd have jumped ship long ago. Now she had this job to look forward to. George would just have to get used to it!

When he arrived back that evening she was watching her favourite soap *Fair City*.

"How can you watch this rubbish?" was his greeting to her. "You're an intelligent woman, Tessa. I just don't understand it."

"I like it," she'd replied. "Most of my friends watch *Coronation Street* and *Desperate Housewives* and other soaps."

"Desperate housewives is right," he'd replied, opening his book with a bang.

So, she'd turned off the television and gone up for a bath, crying, wondering what the hell she could do while at the same time wondering what was happening on *Fair City*. The following morning she rang Kate to find out about the soap.

"Why don't you drop over and I'll tell you?" Kate had said.

Relieved to be getting out of the house for a while she put the leash on Napoleon and walked over to Kate's beautiful home. Kate ran a catering business and the delicious smell of baking wafted out as she opened the door. Kate had the coffee ready and had cut Tessa a generous wedge of a marvellous chocolate cake.

"Why didn't you watch *Fair City*?" she asked Tessa.

"George again! He hates me watching television. Especially dumb programmes, as he calls them." She took a huge bite of the chocolate cake. "Mmmm, this cake is delicious, Kate," she said, her mouth so stuffed she could hardly get the words out. "Aren't you having any? It's terrific."

"Don't tempt me. I can't risk it. Too many calories! Lucky you, able to eat everything you want," Kate sighed.

"Well, I'll have your slice then," Tessa grinned, licking the chocolate from her lips.

Kate grinned as she cut another big wedge. "Okay – there it is when you're ready for it."

"It's the same with magazines," Tessa continued. "It's no problem if I come home with *Vanity Fair* or *Vogue*, but Lord forbid I buy *Hello* or *OK!* George would go mental. Crap, he calls them!"

"Oh, for God's sake, all women love them," Kate said in exasperation. "Tell him everything doesn't have to be high-falutin' all the time."

It was great to be able to talk freely to Kate. She understood her problems. She was that kind of person. Everyone confided in her and she was full of good common sense.

"I'm really looking forward to the training tomorrow," Tessa told her. "I'm so grateful to you for suggesting this job. If only George could accept it I think it could really help us." She continued dejectedly, running her fingers through her long silky hair, "Things can't go on like this. Something's got to give."

"I'm sure things will improve," Kate told her, although more in hope than with conviction.

Chapter 9

Amber took ages getting dressed for her dinner with Grace on Monday night. She wondered if Carlo would be there. Probably not, but still she took much more trouble than usual over her appearance, just in case he was. Walking into her shoe-room, she looked around, feeling that thrill she always got when surrounded by her beautiful shoes.

"Well, new beginning – past behind me – moving on. There's only one pair of shoes for this occasion!" She took down the red Versace shoes that she'd bought on what she still considered to be the worst day of her life. She'd never worn them. They'd sat there forlornly, unloved. That was about to change. God, they were beautiful. To hell with Dermot! He wasn't worth it, she thought, admiring the shoes in the mirror.

She was ready and waiting when Susie called for her. Tony had very kindly offered to drop them off at the Shelbourne as he had a meeting in his club, which was just a few doors down from the hotel on Stephen's Green. They would meet up with him there later which meant they could enjoy a drink without the worry of driving home.

"Oh my God! You're wearing *those* red shoes!" Susie squealed as she spotted them. "They're gorgeous!" She hadn't seen them since that fateful night in Brussels. She knew what this meant. Her friend was indeed moving on.

Amber was walking on air as they entered the Shelbourne to meet Grace. She flashed a dazzling smile at the doorman. She felt great – light-hearted in fact. She was excited about this new opportunity offered to her.

Grace hugged them both. "It's wonderful to see you again, Susie. I'm dying to hear all your news. And yours too, Amber," she said, turning to her with a smile. "I didn't want to pry too much at the interview, what with Carlo there."

"Just as well you didn't," Amber laughed. "He'd have thought I was a nut-case."

Grace had a bottle of champagne on ice and when the waiter had poured it for them they settled down for a good natter, all of them talking at once.

"It's great to have a night off like this. I'm actually working harder than I ever did," Grace told them, sipping her champagne. "Especially with this new venture, but it's worth it to have nights like this." She raised her glass to them.

"To If the Shoes Fit!" Amber said, and they all clinked glasses.

"Well, girls, tell me what you've been doing with yourselves," Grace said, looking at each of them.

"You first," Amber said to Susie.

"Not much to tell really," Susie said. "I got married to Tony seven years ago and we have two little terrors," she rolled her eyes to heaven, "Rachel and Joshua, four and five."

"Don't mind her! They're adorable," Amber said, giving Susie a poke in the arm.

"Well yes, they are, actually," Susie smiled. "They're my life." She held out her glass to the waiter who was offering more champagne.

"Mmmm, delicious," Amber said, noticing that it was Krug they were drinking. Grace had always had great taste.

"I'm still working away," Susie continued, "but I don't fly transatlantic any more. I couldn't bear to be away from the kids for so long."

"Is there still a lot of the same old crew working?" Grace asked her.

"Indeed there is," said Susie, shaking her head in disgust. "Some of them should be collecting their pensions! They practically need a wheelchair to meet them off every flight!"

All three roared laughing at the vision she'd conjured up.

The waiter came with menus and they sipped the delicious champagne as they decided what to order.

When he'd taken their order, Grace turned to Amber, raising her eyebrows, and said, "Tell me, what was all that about you being divorced?"

Amber found herself actually laughing and making jokes as she told Grace all that had happened to her in the intervening years. Susie couldn't believe her ears. Amber had never, ever, joked about Dermot before, yet here she was, talking about it as though it wasn't that important.

"You poor pet!" Grace sympathised with her. "What happened since? Did the twenty-year-old have his baby?"

"No idea," Amber replied, her eyes blank. "I'm not interested. He's not my business any more." This wasn't strictly true. Privately, she often wondered how he was doing and whether he'd had the child. Somehow, she'd always expected that he would come back to her, begging her forgiveness and admitting he'd made a terrible mistake.

Susie squeezed her hand. "That's my girl," she murmured. She felt that Amber was finally moving on. She certainly hoped so. "It's left her royally pissed off with men," she told Grace.

"I'm not surprised," Grace said, kindly. "Poor Carlo is in for a disappointment then." She turned to Susie. "Did Amber tell you about her conquest of my brother-in-law?"

"What conquest? She never mentioned anyone." Susie looked at Amber reproachfully.

"Carlo's quite fallen for her. He couldn't talk about anything else, all the way to Rome. It got boring, believe me!" Grace rolled her eyes as she spoke. "He's flying in tomorrow morning. He was hoping to be here tonight but he had a previous dinner engagement in Rome."

"I'll bet. Probably with some supermodel," Amber replied sarcastically.

"Really, Amber, you've got him all wrong," Grace tried to assure her. "He's not a womaniser, not at all."

"I'm sure." Amber didn't believe it for a moment.

Susie wondered what was going on. She'd heard nothing about this Carlo fellow from Amber. Knowing her friend well, she was surprised that she hadn't mentioned him. She must like him. Well, time would tell!

Grace told them all about her kids and her life in Rome, which sounded idyllic. Her children, Silvio and Lucia were the same age as Susie's.

"You'll both have to come over and visit for a weekend," she told them, "and bring the children, Susie. Mine would love to meet them and Carlo will be delighted, that's for sure," she said, glancing slyly at Amber.

Susie was amazed to see Amber blushing. Uh oh, something's going on here definitely, she guessed.

Chapter 10

The following morning, Amber arrived at the Red Cow Hotel for the training course and was directed to the Leinster Suite where she found Niamh sitting in an ante-room, talking to two women. Amber was relieved to see that one was about her age and the other a bit older. Thank God she wouldn't feel like an old fogey amongst a crowd of young ones.

"Hi, Amber!" Niamh called out.

"Hello, Niamh. Great to see you!"

"I'm delighted you're here. I knew that you would be!" Niamh was beaming. "We met at the interview," she explained to the two women, introducing Amber.

"We met at the interview too," the older woman said. "I'm Rosie and this is Tessa. I was delighted to see her here today too," she smiled. They shook hands and Amber sat down beside them.

Rosie was in her late forties, Amber guessed, very elegant and beautifully dressed. She was a big woman with short sleek ash-blonde hair and a good figure. Amber took in the expensive jewellery, bag and shoes. "A real lady," her mother would have said.

Tessa was drop-dead gorgeous. Not pretty-pretty but exotic and striking. She was very tall and slim with smooth olive skin and high sculpted cheekbones. Her hair was the colour of dark chocolate and fell like a silk curtain, almost to her waist. It was so shiny and glossy that she could have done the commercials for the L'Oréal TV ads. As if all that wasn't gorgeous enough for one woman, she also had perfect white teeth and wide-set amber eyes, like a tiger's. Amber thought she looked familiar.

"Have we met before?" she asked Tessa, a slight frown wrinkling her brow as she tried to recall where it might have been.

"I don't think so. I'm sure I would have remembered you," Tessa replied smiling, a twinkle in her eye.

Amber liked her at once and guessed she would be good fun.

Amber was a dab hand at these quick once-overs. Her cabin-crew colleagues used to tease her about how quickly she could size someone up. Standing at the door of the aircraft as the passengers boarded, she would size them up in a split second and signal any potential problems to the other crew members. Nervous; drunk; diva; demanding; troublesome kid; Casanova. Sometimes she'd alert them to "eligible bachelor" or "shoes-to-die-for"! She had a private code for them all. The amazing thing was, as her colleagues soon found out, she was always right. They learned to heed her advice and give a wide berth to those whom she saw as trouble. She couldn't stop the habit and she was doing it again now, as she sized up the other women.

I wonder how they see me, she asked herself. Do they see "sad divorcée, verging on the alcoholic"? I hope not but that's how I'd see myself, she thought with a grimace. She stuck her chin out. Well, all that was about to change!

In fact, the others were all very impressed by Amber. Although not beautiful in the true sense of the word, her sheer force of personality made her seem so. She had a golden glow about her – like an aura, Rosie thought – and she charmed them all. She appeared confident and self-assured. None of them could have guessed what she had been through – how empty her life was and how low her self-esteem. Tessa was sure that if there had been only one vacancy, Amber would have got it. Amber would have been surprised, and delighted, if she'd known what the other women were thinking.

Niamh was thinking that everything about Amber was perfect. She was so glamorous – how Niamh wished she could be like her! Noticing Amber's beautifully manicured nails, she was embarrassed by her own, and tried to hide them. Having them constantly in hot water, she could never get them to grow.

Tessa envied Amber's bubbly personality. Although Tessa was stunningly beautiful, she was lacking in confidence and she wished she had Amber's self-assurance. She'd sort George out jig-time, Tessa thought. How I wish I could!

Rosie thought how Jack would have admired Amber. He'd always had an eye for an attractive woman, though always adding, in his debonair way, "But she's not a patch on my Rosie!" She'd loved him for that. Yes, he'd have appreciated Amber.

As they sat chatting, taking stock of one another, the door opened and another girl joined them. She was small and slim with purple hair, a nose stud, and larger-than-life breasts. Silicone – I'll bet my life on it, Amber thought. What was this girl doing here? She was a slapper! Amber shuddered and threw a glance at Tessa, who raised her eyes to heaven.

"Val!" Niamh jumped to her feet when she caught sight of the newcomer. "What is it? Is something wrong at home?" Niamh had visibly paled.

"No, nothing," the girl replied, shrugging her shoulders.

"Then what are you doing here?" Niamh asked, perplexed.

Amber could see that Niamh was distressed and wondered what she could possibly have to do with this dreadful person.

"I'm here for the training," the purple-haired one replied, lounging up against the wall.

Niamh looked confused. "You're here for the training? I don't understand."

"What's not to understand?" said Val. "I've got as much right to be here as you do."

The others were shocked at Val's aggressive attitude.

"But why didn't you say something?" Niamh asked her, a look of bewilderment on her face.

The girl called Val shrugged and said nothing. It was obvious to the other three girls that Niamh was very upset.

"Do you know each other?" Amber asked.

"She's my sister," Niamh replied.

Amber gasped in surprise. She found it hard to believe. They couldn't have been more different. Val was as nasty as Niamh was sweet. What's going on here, she wondered? She took in Val's tight black pants and vertiginous black studded heels. Amber loved her stilettos but these were ridiculous. How could she even walk in them? She looked like a dominatrix. All she was missing was a whip! Amber could see that the others were equally shocked.

She was about to quiz Niamh some more but just then Grace came out of the meeting room to greet them.

"Hello, girls, and welcome," she said, smiling. "If you'd like to help yourself to coffee and biscuits" – she directed them to a table at the back of the room – "we'll be starting in approximately ten minutes. If you'll excuse me, I just have some final things to prepare." She smiled as she left them and went back into the room.

They headed for the coffee table while Val went outside for a smoke.

"I get the feeling she's trying to avoid you," Amber whispered to Niamh.

"So well she might," Niamh replied, with a grimace. "She never even mentioned that she'd applied for this job, or that she'd got it. She never said a word, not to me nor my mother." Her lips trembled as she spoke and Amber felt very sorry for her.

As they sipped their coffee, Carlo came and said hello and poured himself a coffee. At that moment, another girl arrived. She was about thirty, Amber guessed, with a mane of jet-black curls framing a pretty, delicate face. She had startling blue eyes that were cold as they looked over the four women. She had a fantastic figure and was dressed in a tight pink brocade suit with high sparkly pink satin shoes. She nodded to them but didn't say hello. She went straight up to Carlo and Amber noticed that her face lit up as she greeted him. He poured her a coffee and stood chatting to her.

The four women looked at each other, each thinking the same thing – tacky!

"Where does she think she's going?" Tessa whispered. "A wedding? All she needs is a big pink hat," she giggled.

"Most inappropriate," Rosie murmured.

"She's very sexy though, isn't she?" Niamh sighed.

Amber had to agree that the newcomer was oozing sex appeal and she noticed with dismay that the fact wasn't lost on Carlo.

"God, we're a motley bunch," Tessa remarked, laughing.

"You said it," Amber agreed. "I reckon we'll be having some fireworks before the week is out."

"Variety is the spice of life," Rosie smiled.

Niamh said nothing. She was still feeling upset at Val's behaviour.

As they finished their coffee, Grace reappeared. Although the last girl still hadn't put in an appearance, Grace had decided to start the meeting. She ushered them into the room.

"Well, girls, we can't wait any longer for Phoebe. Please be seated and we'll go ahead without her as we have a lot to get through."

She waved them to the chairs which were arranged in a semi-circle around a table. She and Carlo sat together at the top of the table.

"Welcome, ladies, to If the Shoes Fit," Grace began. "Carlo and I are delighted that you are joining us in this very exciting new business. We'd like to start by asking you to introduce yourselves, so that we can all get to know one another. Amber, would you like to start?" She smiled at her friend. "You can go next, Niamh."

Amber did as she was asked and, as she was speaking, Niamh started to panic. What could she possibly say about herself?

Amber finished and Grace signalled to Niamh to take her turn.

Shaking with nerves, Niamh was about to speak when the door opened.

"Helloooo!" trilled a voice. "Frightfully sorry to be late but the traffic – it was horrendous. And trying to get parking – impossible!"

This was obviously Phoebe – making a grand entrance. The others gaped at the technicoloured vision before them. Tiny and plump, she looked like she'd strayed off the set of *South Pacific* – in full stage make-up. She had a mane of blonde hair, flicked back in that old Farah Fawcett style. It was much too long for someone just barely the right side of fifty. She had enormous pendulous breasts which knocked Val's siliconed ones into the small category. Her blouse was orange, her long skirt was acid green and she wore green and yellow shoes. A myriad of glass beads, green, yellow and orange, jangled on her heaving bosoms. She had two bags slung over her shoulder: one capacious green one, one smaller yellow one.

The others couldn't believe their eyes. Mutton dressed as lamb, Amber thought. Had the woman not looked in the mirror before she came out?

"Just take a seat, Phoebe. The girls have been introducing themselves," said Grace.

"Oooh dear, have I missed that? Frightfully sorry." She spoke in a pseudo-posh Dublin 4 accent, which the girls later discovered became a flat working-class one when she was excited.

She doesn't look a bit sorry, Amber thought. Not my type, most definitely not!

"Well, in that case let me tell you about myself," said

Phoebe, still standing. She dumped her bags on the table and opened her mouth to address the group.

"No, it's Niamh's turn now," said Grace coolly. "Please sit down."

Phoebe looked as though she were about to protest, then she ungraciously relinquished the floor.

She seemed quite oblivious to the effect she was having on the group. Rosie looked stunned and when Amber caught Tessa's eye she could see that she was trying to stifle a laugh.

Niamh's introduction went down well, as did Rosie's who was next. Then it was Tessa's turn. The others were very impressed by having a successful London model in their midst. They were not surprised as she was exquisitely graceful and striking. And clever too by the sound of it, even running her own modelling business. Amber, Rosie and Niamh smiled at her as she sat down. The dark sexy girl was next. She now had a name – Lesley. In a very strong Dublin accent, she told them that she was married with no children and had worked as a representative with a direct-selling cosmetic company for three years but she now wanted something more challenging, hence her move to If the Shoes Fit. She oozed ambition as she spoke.

"I felt my talents were not properly recognised and there was no chance of promotion to senior management, which is where I feel I belong. I'm hoping this company will give me that opportunity," she finished up, flashing a dazzling smile at Carlo.

"Let no one stand in her way!" Rosie whispered to Tessa, who dissolved in giggles.

Dream on, girl, Amber said silently. You have me to reckon with.

She couldn't believe the arrogance of the girl though it looked like she had impressed Carlo. She wondered if Grace had swallowed it.

Val went next and hadn't much to say. It took her no more than thirty seconds to introduce herself.

"Well, Phoebe," said Grace, "maybe you'd like to tell us now about yourself?"

"With pleasure." Phoebe rose as regally as her four-feet-eleven would allow.

According to herself, she was Superwoman incarnated. She mentioned about six companies she'd worked for, where, she claimed, she'd risen to the top. The others didn't believe a word of it. If she'd been so successful, what was she doing here?

After about ten minutes of this self-praise, Grace interrupted her. "Thank you, Phoebe. That will be sufficient. I think we get the picture. We need to move on now."

Phoebe looked offended as she reluctantly sat down. The girls enjoyed her discomfiture, glancing at each other and grinning.

Grace passed round the schedule for the training and they could see that there was a lot of ground to cover. She then outlined the goals of the company and how it would work.

"As I explained at your interview, your job is to recruit salespeople in the area we allot to you to sell our designer shoes, either by direct selling or on a party-plan basis." She looked around at their eager faces and then went on to elaborate on how they could achieve this. "I also informed you that we would offer you a three-month contract initially – renewable, depending on your performance. Obviously, if you're not delivering, we would have to

93

review your position. Carlo will give you a copy of the contract now and you can peruse it in your own time or show it to your legal advisors but we would like it back, signed, by Friday."

She smiled around at them as Carlo handed out the contracts.

"Does anyone have any questions?" she asked.

Phoebe, of course, had, despite the fact that she had already interrupted Grace on at least three occasions to ask totally irrelevant questions. Grace was patient with her, but firm.

Tessa glanced over at Amber when Carlo had passed them and mouthed "Phew", fanning herself with the paper. Amber grinned back at her.

Grace continued. "Now for the most important thing – money!" They smiled at her. "How much you earn will depend on you. The more reps you have and the more they sell, the more you'll earn. Simple!"

To the girls it sounded great. The wonderful thing was that they could do it in their own time – no nine-to-five – and as Grace explained, they would get out of it what they put in. The atmosphere in the room was upbeat and positive.

Grace was pleased. "You all understand that this is a new concept in Ireland so we'll be pretty much winging it, but we have done a lot of market research and feel it is very viable. We hope eventually to cover the thirty-two counties and maybe go even further afield. So you," she held her two arms out to them, "are the pioneers, as it were, and will have the possibility of rising to senior management level with us."

The girls looked at each other, smiling.

Amber noticed Lesley staring transfixed at Grace, a

determined tilt to her chin. She nudged Tessa and surreptitiously rolled her eyes in Lesley's direction. "She sees herself as managing director already," she whispered, behind her hand.

Tessa giggled. "Not with you to contend with," she whispered back.

"Bloody right!" Amber muttered. "Let the battle begin!"

Grace was gathering up her notes. "I think you've had enough for one morning, so if you'd care to make your way to the dining-room, lunch is waiting for you. Just tell the waitress to charge it to If the Shoes Fit. Enjoy your lunch, ladies, and we'll meet back here at two."

Niamh's head was spinning trying to take it all in. She felt like pinching herself just in case she was dreaming. She looked across at Val, still hurt by her behaviour.

What if there had only been six places and she'd got in and I'd missed out? she wondered. I would never have forgiven her. She was finding it difficult enough to forgive her now. Val was obviously avoiding her and went outside with Phoebe and Lesley for a smoke as the others headed to the restaurant.

"I think it's going to be a case of 'them' and 'us'," Tessa remarked as she sat down beside Amber, having picked up a salad from the buffet. The four girls had grabbed a table together and Val, Phoebe and Lesley sat at another.

"I could do without their company, to be honest," Amber replied, checking that Niamh was still at the buffet counter and couldn't hear her.

After Niamh and Rosie had taken their seats Amber leaned in and said in a low voice, taking care not to be overheard. "Isn't that Phoebe something else?"

Rosie rolled her eyes to heaven and Niamh giggled.

"I've come across this type of woman often in the modelling business," Tessa confided, keeping her voice quiet too. "Supremely self-confident and very loquacious, but an empty vessel behind it all."

"She is rather boastful," Rosie agreed.

"Pain-in-the-arse, if you ask me," Amber muttered, to the amusement of the other three. "But let's forget her for the moment." She turned to Tessa. "I know now why you looked familiar to me. I've seen you on the cover of *Vogue*. You said you had retired as a model when you introduced yourself but don't you still do some modelling? I'm sure I've seen your photo lately, in a magazine."

"That's possible, but I'm well past my sell-by date. However, I do still have a contract with a cosmetics company so that's probably where you saw it. It's just four shoots a year but it pays well and of course my face is completely airbrushed!" Tessa laughed.

"You still look fantastic," Amber said admiringly.

"I wasn't surprised that you'd been a model," Niamh said sweetly. "You look stunning."

"It must have been very exciting running a model agency," Rosie said. "What made you give it up?"

Tessa told them about her heart attack, moving to Ireland, and how she needed something to keep busy.

"It must have been a shock to your system – leaving London – and work," Niamh said sympathetically.

"Imagine coming from the hectic London fashion world, to retirement in a small Irish village! However did you cope?" Amber asked her.

"I didn't. That's why I went for this job. I'm not cut out for retirement."

"You're much too young to be retired," Rosie said kindly.

"How about you, Niamh? What made you go for this?" Tessa asked.

"Well, my husband is unemployed and we live with his mother, who is a dragon." She rolled her eyes to heaven as the others laughed at her woebegone face. "I want to get the money together for a deposit for our own house and since the twins started school in September, I decided to look for work. This job seems like the answer to my prayers."

"I couldn't believe it when you said you had three kids," Tessa said. "God, you're only a kid yourself!"

"Not quite," Niamh said blushing. "And what about you, Rosie? Why are you here?"

"My husband died a year ago," she told them, the sadness evident in her voice, "and I really couldn't come to terms with it. My daughter, Gail, bullied me into applying and I'm so glad she did." She looked around at the others, tears not far from her eyes. "Besides the fact that I'm very excited about the business, I've a feeling I've made three lovely new friends."

Tessa squeezed her hand and Niamh put an arm around her shoulders.

"I'll drink to that!" Amber raised her glass of water and they clinked glasses.

"What about you, Amber?" Rosie asked. "What made you apply for this job?"

"Besides my addiction to shoes?" Amber replied, making the others laugh.

She then told them about her divorce and how she desperately needed a new start.

"It's a new start for all of us then," Tessa smiled.

They finished up their lunch and made their way back to the meeting, all of them sensing that they'd become good friends.

Chapter 11

Back at the meeting, the six shoe styles that would comprise the first collection were on display. They were exquisite and the girls descended on them like a flock of locusts on a cornfield. They positively drooled over them. Niamh had never seen such beautiful shoes in her life.

"I can't believe it," Amber shrieked, pointing to a pair of silver shoes. "These are identical to the Manolo Blahniks that were stolen from Carrie on *Sex and the City*!"

The others crowded round the said silver shoes, remembering the scene and agreeing with her. They were peep-toe, with one side cut out and a rosette on the front.

"Not identical," Grace smiled at them, "but very, very similar." She winked at Amber. She was delighted with their reaction to the shoes. She knew that if they loved them, they would have no trouble selling them. "You will each get a set of these shoes and we would like you to wear them as much as possible, because by doing so you demonstrate them."

There was a gasp from the girls.

"Wow!" Niamh exclaimed.

"Fantastic!" said Amber, and she and Tessa high-fived each other.

Even Lesley came down from her high-horse and looked excited.

Grace and Carlo laughed at their enthusiasm.

"We'll take your sizes today and have them for you before you leave on Friday," Grace told them. "We would also like to invite you for dinner on Friday night – a sort of graduation, if you like. Can everybody make it?"

Phoebe of course had a problem. "I do have other plans for Friday night but I'll see if I can rearrange them," she said condescendingly.

"Yeah, probably shopping in Tesco," Amber whispered to Tessa who dissolved in giggles, earning a dirty look from Phoebe.

Grace continued. "If, after six months, we feel you've got what it takes, we'll take you to Rome for five days, for further training – all at our expense, of course. Will any of you have a problem getting away?"

They looked at each other, disbelievingly. This *was* too good to be true.

Niamh would have to have the kids taken care of but she was sure that her mam would take the kids again, as she had this week, to give her this chance. Wow! Rome! She'd never even been out of Ireland. She was so excited!

Tessa knew that she would have a problem. How will I tell George? He'll have a fit. He doesn't even like me going to London to visit my old friends. Well, fit or no fit, I'm going to Rome. He'll just have to get over it.

Rosie said a little prayer. *Thank you, Jack.*

Have a problem getting away? Amber thought. Are you kidding? This is a lifesaver for me. I'm going to give it one hundred per cent and I'll make a success of it if it kills me. And I'll make senior management, Lesley be damned! I was born for this company.

She had caught Carlo looking at her several times but had avoided his eyes. Then she thought she must be imagining it. How could he be interested in her when Tessa was so gorgeous and Lesley so sexy? When the meeting was over she thought she saw him heading her way but he was intercepted by Phoebe and Lesley. He's a womaniser, no doubt about that, she thought. Look how charming he is, even with those two. No, thank you! I need another Casanova like I need a hole in the head. She sighed. There was no denying that he was absolutely gorgeous, though.

The four girls decided to go into the bar for coffee.

"To hell with coffee, girls – we're having champagne. My treat," Amber said. "This is a special day." She ordered a bottle of Moët.

"Isn't this a fantastic opportunity?" Rosie exclaimed. "I can hardly believe it."

"It's great, though I wish my partner felt the same way. He's not too pleased about me taking it on," Tessa admitted.

"My husband isn't too happy about it either," Niamh told them.

Amber heard the tremor in her voice. Poor kid, she thought – a sister from hell and now a problem husband too!

"What is it with your sister? Why didn't she tell you she was applying too?" Amber was very curious about Val. She couldn't understand how Grace had chosen her. She never would have.

101

"No idea. She was there in Mam's last Wednesday when I was leaving for the interview, and she never said a word. Mam certainly didn't know she was going for it, or that she got it." She looked really perplexed. "I don't understand it. I'm sure she must have had a reason to keep it quiet." Niamh, for the life of her, couldn't imagine what it could be. "Maybe she resents me a bit. She was the baby in the family for six years and then I arrived. I suppose she wasn't happy about that . . ." She trailed off, conscious that she was trying to make excuses for her sister's actions.

The other girls didn't buy it.

Val went out for another cigarette and came back into the room, hoping that Niamh would have left. Relieved, she saw that she had gone so she joined Phoebe and Lesley, who were talking to Carlo. The last thing in the world that she wanted was to bump into Niamh. She knew she would get a rollicking from her mother when Eileen heard that she'd gone for the job. Well, too bad! Val fancied Carlo like mad but she'd seen the way he'd looked at Amber. So, he's interested in that posh bitch, she'd thought furiously.

As she was leaving the hotel she spotted Niamh and Amber chatting cosily in the bar with the older woman and the stuck-up model. Trust Niamh! She twists everyone around her little finger, her sister thought bitterly.

Val had hated Niamh from the very beginning. She'd been six years old and she still remembered the shock she'd felt when her mother had arrived home from the hospital with the tiny bundle. She'd asked her parents to send Niamh back and when they wouldn't, she'd proceeded to offer her to anyone who came to visit. Up till then, Val had been the pet in the house and no way did she want this upstart around. She was jealous whenever anyone paid the slightest bit of attention to the new baby. She was especially angry that her father seemed enchanted with his new baby daughter. It hadn't helped that Niamh had been so pretty and placid. She had big green eyes and golden hair and when she smiled, which was pretty much all the time, two little dimples appeared in her cheeks. The only time she'd ever cried was when Val had pinched her, which was often, and once when Val had bitten her.

Eileen had been very concerned about that.

"Maybe we should get counselling for her," she'd suggested to her husband, Dan. "None of the others ever behaved like that. She's so jealous of Niamh. I'm very worried."

"She'll grow out of it," he consoled her. "Don't worry."

But Val hadn't grown out of it. Twenty-three-years on, she still considered Niamh a usurper.

The crunch had come when Val had fallen in love with Gavin Byrne. She'd been crazy about him and had even offered to let him go the full way with her, but he'd turned her down. When she discovered that he was in love with Niamh she'd been distraught and had even considered suicide. But then she decided that it would be better to bide her time and find a way to get even.

She found it incredible that Niamh had no idea just how much she hated her. It amused her to see the perplexed look on her sister's face when she said, or did, something nasty to her. Niamh couldn't quite get it and always made excuses for her.

Mam was another story. Her mother had guessed her true feelings and warned her off Gavin. Eileen would sure as hell be furious with her about this job. Well, it was worth it, she thought, with glee. I damn well took the wind out of Niamh's sails today. Her face when I walked in – it was priceless! She laughed mirthlessly to herself at the memory.

After the meeting, Niamh went straight to her mother's to collect the kids. After she had hugged them and kissed Lily's knee, which she'd hurt at school, she sat down with Eileen in the kitchen.

"Mam, you won't believe it! Do you know who was there? Val!"

"Val? What was she doing there?"

"She went for the interview last week and got the job too. I couldn't believe it when she walked in. I thought something had happened to you or one of the kids. Why didn't she say something?" Niamh couldn't keep the hurt out of her voice.

"The bitch!" Eileen cried. "I'll kill her when I get my hands on her . . . Oh, sorry," she apologised to the children, seeing their shocked faces.

"Naughty Nana," Rose shook her finger at her.

"Bad word," Lily got in on the act.

"Yes, that was a very bad word. I'm sorry."

"Are you angry at Mammy?" Ian asked her, a worried frown on his little face.

"No, of course not, pet," she said, giving him a hug. "Why don't I put on the *Disney Channel* for you and we'll see if there's something good on?"

She ushered them into the living-room and settled them down there so that she could talk freely with Niamh.

She returned to find Niamh putting on the kettle.

"Bad as Val is, I didn't think she was capable of doing that," Eileen said bitterly. "The sly thing! That's why she didn't return my calls, I swear I'll kill her, Niamh. This really is the last straw." She was incensed with anger.

"I can't understand why she didn't tell us," Niamh said, shaking her head.

"Oh, I can. She's so jealous of you that she'd do anything to get at you," Eileen was vehement. "You'll have to be very careful with this job. Don't let her spoil it for you, pet. She will if she can."

"But why?" Niamh asked, a bewildered look on her face.

"Because she's so jealous of you that she'll do anything to bring you down." Eileen's face was thunderous.

"I just don't understand it, Mam."

"Well, never you mind. I'll sort her out tonight," Eileen said, in a very determined voice. "I'm going round there right now, when you're gone." Niamh had never seen her mother so angry. As she went in to check on the children while Eileen made the tea, she found herself hoping her mother would calm down before confronting Val. She decided she wouldn't refer to her sister again that day.

"Oh Mam, I'm so excited!" she said as they sipped their tea. "If we make a success of it, after six months they'll take us to Rome for further training. Can you believe it? Of course, I'd need you to take the kids while I'm there." She looked at her mother anxiously.

"You know I will, love. Rome. Imagine! I've always wanted to go there. Do you think you'll get to see the Pope?"

"I hope so, Mam. That would be brilliant. I'll get your rosary beads blessed by him, if we do see him."

Her eyes were shining and Eileen was very happy for her

youngest daughter. She deserved it all. Now to sort out the other one!

She mused over it as she made her way over to Val's. Despite everything she and Dan had tried to do, that awful jealousy had continued to gnaw at Val and obviously it was still there. Thank God that Dan or Niamh had never found out that Val was in love with Gavin. Eileen had warned her to keep away from him and that she'd never talk to her again if she did anything to damage Niamh's marriage. Val was afraid enough of her to obey, but now this! Eileen knew her daughter well and, although she loved her, she didn't like the woman she'd become. She'd never admit this to anyone, of course, and she often worried that somehow she'd failed Val.

She pressed Val's doorbell. No reply. She knew her daughter was in. She kept her finger on the bell and, when Val still didn't answer, she used the key Val had given her, to let herself in.

Val came sheepishly down the stairs.

"I know, I know, I should have told you . . ." she started, scared of the murderous look on her mother's face.

"You are a bitch – a mean jealous bitch! My God, what would have happened if you'd got the job and Niamh hadn't?" Eileen clenched her fists by her side.

"That would have been something!" Val couldn't resist the jibe.

"Val, I actually want to slap your face," her mother spat out. "Thank heaven your father isn't alive to see what a nasty person you've become."

Somewhat chastened by this remark, Val replied. "Of course Niamh was going to get it. Everybody loves her. Even though she's never worked a day in her life, she got the job, didn't she?" She couldn't keep the jealousy from her voice.

"That's because they could see she's a nice person, unlike you. And she works bloody hard looking after those kids and that useless husband."

"Don't call Gavin useless!" Val's face became suffused with colour.

"Oh, so you're still carrying a torch for your brother-in-law! I'll tell you one thing, missy," Eileen came up close to her, her face practically touching Val's, "if you do anything to hurt Niamh in this job, you'll never darken my door again."

Val was quaking. She'd never seen her mother so angry.

"Now, I'm going. I can't stand to look at you any more." Eileen turned on her heel and left.

"Ah, Mam, I'm sorry, I didn't . . ."

But her mother had marched out, leaving Val very shaken.

Rosie was in great form. She was in Gail's for dinner and her daughter was all agog to hear how the first day had gone.

"It was terrific," Rosie was glowing. "The shoes are beautiful and I've made three new friends."

She told her all about them and the champagne they shared afterwards.

"What about the others?" Gail wanted to know.

Gail pealed with laughter as her mother described Phoebe and Val.

"Somehow, I don't think we'll be friends," said Rosie. "They're quite dreadful. Twin Peaks, Amber calls them, because they both have enormous boobs, not entirely due to nature. Amber has a wicked wit and she's great fun. I'm so glad you forced me into this. Thank you, darling." She gave Gail a kiss on the cheek.

"I'm so glad to have you back, Mum," Gail said, wrapping her arms around Rosie.

Rosie uttered a silent prayer. *Thank you, Jack darling.* She knew it was his doing.

George was listening to Wagner when Tessa got home.

"What's for dinner?" he asked, looking up from his newspaper.

"Hello to you too! I'm fine, thank you." She marched to the fridge and took out the lasagne she'd made the day before and stuck it under his nose. "Dinner will be on the table in twenty minutes."

"Sorry," he mumbled, going back to his newspaper.

Over dinner Tessa made an effort to act as normal, as did George, so some semblance of civility returned. Still he never mentioned the training and neither did she.

Lying awake beside him that night, she wondered what had happened to them. She wasn't happy and George didn't seem to be too happy either. She thought back to when they'd first met and remembered a lot more laughter and fun in their relationship. It seemed that George didn't do laughter or fun any more. When had he started to change? When had he started to take life so damned seriously? She didn't want to spend the rest of her life like this. If her brush with death had done nothing else, it had taught her that life was precious and that she should treasure every moment and live every day to the full.

She'd give this job a chance and if things didn't improve between them then she'd have to seriously consider her options. She thanked her lucky stars that she'd held out against marriage. She still had her lovely house in London and she could always go back there but it was rented out now and, anyway, she didn't want to go back. She was very excited about this new job and didn't want to give it up. If she decided to leave George then it would make more sense for her to rent a place in Dublin. God, I can't believe I'm thinking like this, she said to herself. But her heart attack had changed her attitude to life. Life was not a dress rehearsal – it was the real thing – and she intended living every moment of it, to the best of her ability.

She was thrilled to be starting this job. It was exciting and she loved the other girls – well, Amber, Niamh and Rosie anyway – Phoebe, Val and Lesley were another story. It was good to be back interacting with women once more. She hadn't realised how much she'd missed it. This was her last thought as she drifted off to sleep.

Amber was thinking exactly the same thing. They'd had such fun over their champagne. Tessa was a scream and Rosie and Niamh were two smart cookies. She had a feeling they would all become great friends. She hadn't realised how much she'd missed the company of women. There was nothing to beat the *craic* when a group of like-minded women got together. God, it felt good! They were all so different but that's what made it interesting and fun.

Chapter 12

The rest of the week flew by. Niamh couldn't believe how much there was to learn. It felt good to be using her brain again. Being around small children for the past five years hadn't exactly taxed it too much. There was so much to get through: accounting, tax, sales techniques, recruiting, interviewing, business management, staff training, time management, computers and lots more. It was exhilarating. She couldn't wait to get started.

She was still upset with Val and ignored her as much as possible. She could sense that Amber, Tessa and Rosie had no time for her at all. Amber couldn't understand how Niamh was even civil to her.

"If my sister did that to me, I swear I'd never talk to her again," she'd said.

"Yeah, well, Mam gave her an earful," Niamh assured her.

Despite the difference in their ages, Niamh and Rosie had bonded really well. There was something about Niamh that brought out Rosie's maternal instinct. I could be her mother, Rosie thought. She's even younger than Gail and David, for God's sake, yet we're fast becoming friends. Niamh found herself confiding in Rosie, telling her all about Bridget and how impossible it was living under her roof.

"That's really why this job is so important to me," she said. "If I make a success of it then we can move into a place of our own. That's my ambition and I'm going to work as hard as I possibly can to make it happen."

Rosie admired her courage and determination.

On Wednesday it was time for the allotment of areas and Niamh was delighted to find that Grace had given her Clondalkin, the area where she lived and the surrounding areas. She knew lots of people there and it would mean much less travelling.

"Thanks, Grace, that's great." She smiled gratefully at her.

Amber was given Malahide, where she lived, and the neighbouring areas. She knew these well and was already mentally making lists of all her ex-colleagues who lived there, hoping to line them up for parties. She knew they'd love the shoes.

Grace had been true to her word and given Tessa the closest area to Kildare.

Rosie would have worked any area at all, she was just so pleased to be doing it, but she also got the place where she lived, Dun Laoghaire, and the surrounding areas. She was more than happy.

Phoebe made a face when told that she would be working the inner city area. She was not a happy bunny.

Val was given a much rougher area on the north side of the city.

"I'd prefer to have the area Niamh has," she grumbled.

Amber threw her dagger's looks as Grace, with a voice as cold as ice, informed her, "I'm afraid you have to work the area I've decided to give you, Val. You don't have a choice. And in no circumstances can you recruit or have reps selling in Niamh's area, or anyone else's, for that matter."

That shut Val up.

Lesley was also given a very rough area and, although it was obvious from the way she pressed her lips tight together that she wasn't happy, she didn't complain.

She's a clever lady, Amber realised. She knows better than to go against Grace's decision.

When they broke for lunch Phoebe, Lesley and Val hightailed it outside, to feed their nicotine addiction and to grumble and complain. What a trio! They deserved each other. Amber noticed Grace watching them. She was no fool. Amber supposed she knew what she was doing.

Just then Grace came over to Amber and whispered. "Could you meet me for coffee after we finish this afternoon?"

"Of course," Amber replied. "I've nothing on this evening."

"Let's go to City West, where I'm staying. I wouldn't want any of the others to see us and think it's favouritism." Grace waved her hand in the direction of the others.

"Well, I know Niamh, Tessa and Rosie wouldn't think that. They know we worked together before. As for the others – well, God knows!" Amber made a face.

"Exactly!"

As Amber returned to her seat, Carlo took her aside.

"I was wondering, Amber, if you'd like to meet me for a drink this evening, after we finish?"

"I'm sorry, Carlo, but I have a previous appointment," she said, smiling sweetly. She was relieved that she could honestly say that. He was very sexy but there was no way she wanted to be alone with him. It was a long time since she'd felt this attracted to a man – not since Dermot, in fact. Her husband's betrayal had crushed her. So much so that she'd lost all sense of her sexuality. In the fifteen months since her divorce, she hadn't looked at another man. Not that they hadn't tried, of course, but she just wasn't interested. She was dead inside. She'd more or less resigned herself to a life of celibacy and now here was Carlo, upsetting that plan. Yes, she was very attracted to him, but there was no way she would give in to an Italian womaniser. No, siree!

When they met up later Grace asked Amber how she felt it was going.

"Fantastic. We're all really excited and can't wait to get started. Well, I speak for my friends anyway."

Grace sighed. "Yes, the other three are something else."

"What I can't understand is why you took them on?" Amber looked at her questioningly.

"Well, I thought about it carefully. I need a certain type of person for certain areas. I couldn't have put you or Tessa into their areas, for example. I hear from other direct-selling companies that some of their agents actually need bodyguards going into certain areas in Dublin. Can you believe that? I think Val, Phoebe and Lesley are tough enough to handle that kind of environment. I had to match the manager to the clientele." She shrugged. "We'll see how it goes."

"Phoebe would drop dead if she heard what you're saying. She considers herself oh-so-posh!" Amber laughed. "But are you sure the women in those tougher places have the money for designer shoes?" She looked doubtful.

"You must be joking! They certainly have and they don't mind spending it on shoes."

Amber was amazed.

"Mind you, if I'd known that Val and Niamh were sisters I wouldn't have taken them both on," Grace continued.

Amber, realising that this meant Niamh might not have made it, disliked Val all the more.

Thursday morning was scheduled for the accounting side of the business and the girls arrived to find a very attractive man seated beside Grace and Carlo.

"Let me introduce Pete Clancy, our accountant," she said as he smiled at them and gave them a little wave. "He is going to take you through the financial side of things which is a very important part of your business.

Pete was the total opposite of Carlo, Tessa noted. He had bright blue, twinkling eyes which, coupled with his dimpled smile, gave him a very disarming air of innocence. He had a Brad Pitt-style, unshaven look about him and Tessa wondered if his blond hair had been helped along by a good colourist. She reckoned he was probably in his mid thirties. Although he was wearing a very expensive suit, and a shirt and tie, he somehow made it look casual. He's a right charmer, Tessa thought, as he flashed his boyish smile. It was obvious that all the girls felt the force of his attraction as they had suddenly perked up, giving him their full attention. Even Amber, Tessa noted, was hanging on his every word.

He made the boring business of finance seem fascinating and by lunchtime he had them all eating out of his hand. He was vibrant and funny and moved about with a restless energy as he spoke. He was obviously highly intelligent and he made each of them feel like they were the only person in the room.

"He's a pet, isn't he?" Amber remarked as they sat down to lunch.

"A sweetheart," Niamh agreed.

"He's lethal," Tessa exclaimed. "He should have a sign on his forehead – 'Danger to Women'!"

"Surely not," Rosie said. "He looks like an innocent little boy."

"Exactly!" Tessa replied, her mouth full of pasta. "The most dangerous kind of man! Mark my words, Carlo is a pussycat in comparison." She looked pointedly at Amber.

Amber giggled and almost choked as a result. When she'd stopped coughing and Niamh had poured her a glass of water, she turned to Tessa. "He's sweet and harmless, you'll see."

Niamh and Rosie agreed.

"Ladies, I'm the expert, believe me," Tessa continued, her face solemn. "I know a Casanova when I see one and I met one today."

The other three pealed with laughter at the notion.

Val rang her mother on Thursday but got no joy.

"I really have nothing to say to you, Val," Eileen said, hanging up on her.

Eileen had never done that before. She'd always come round. She was obviously still really angry with her. Val decided that the only way she could get her mother to talk to her again would be with Niamh's help. With this in mind she suggested she and Niamh share a taxi to the dinner on Friday night.

Niamh rebuffed her. "No, thanks. Grace says she'll send one for each of us."

Niamh was still hurt but Val knew she would come round. She always did.

Chapter 13

There was a great atmosphere at the final day of training. Carlo gave a superb talk on marketing and advertising and then Grace asked them to prepare a plan to get their business up and running successfully. They had thirty minutes to do this and they even surprised themselves with what they managed to come up with.

"I can't believe it! All these wonderful ideas!" Grace enthused.

"*Fantastico!*" Carlo replied, lounging in his chair and smiling delightedly at them.

"I think we have ourselves a group of entrepreneurs here, boys," said Grace.

"A very pretty group of entrepreneurs, if I may say so," Pete replied, his boyish smile sweeping over each and every one of them.

They all automatically smiled back at him.

He was such a charmer. He really had it down to a fine art. Tessa wondered if there was any animosity between

Carlo and himself. There didn't seem to be, but Italian men were very macho and she was sure there must be some rivalry between the two men, especially when there was a gaggle of women to compete for. It should be interesting to watch. She brought her thoughts back to the meeting and Grace, who was speaking.

"We have a bottle of champagne for what we consider the best thought-out business plan . . . and the winner is . . . Niamh!"

The girls clapped and cheered – Val and Lesley with some reluctance.

Niamh was blushing as she shyly went up to accept the champagne and receive kisses from Grace, Carlo and Pete. Tessa thought that Pete took rather longer than was necessary and held Niamh a little too close. She was blushing furiously as she took her seat again.

Phoebe couldn't believe it. She thought her plans were terrific – driving through Dublin with a loudspeaker, hailing people and letting off a thousand balloons with shoes printed on them – were two of her least outrageous ideas. She couldn't understand why she hadn't won. To her ears, Niamh had merely said that recruiting representatives was the way forward.

In fact, Niamh had put forward a very detailed plan of how she would target future representatives so that she would have every street in her area covered. Her friends thought her plan for recruiting was great and Carlo and Grace obviously thought it was a blueprint for success too.

When they came back after lunch they found beautiful pink boxes, tied up with silver ribbons, lined up on a table.

"Your shoes are here with your name on top," Grace

told them. "Please try them on to make sure they fit and let me know if there's any problem."

She laughed as they all made a beeline for the shoes, oohing and aahing over the boxes.

"Then, when you've tried them all on, please keep on the shoes you prefer most," Grace continued, laughing at their enthusiasm. This was a little game she was playing. From her experience, Grace knew that a woman's choice of shoe could tell you a lot about her personality.

They had great fun for the next half hour trying them all on and Niamh felt a lump come into her throat as she realised just how much her life was changing. The shoes were out of this world – all different, all beautiful, all with incredibly high heels.

"Oh, my God!" Amber made a beeline for the red kid sandals which were divine. They were exactly like the Emilio Pucci ones that she'd admired on Net-a-Porter. They had five-inch slender heels and narrow straps which wrapped around her foot and extended way above her ankle. She particularly loved the zip at the back of the shoe. She tried them on and as she twirled around admiring them in the mirror Grace had provided, Tessa laughed at her.

"You're like Dorothy on her way to Oz!"

"I feel like The Good Witch of The East has waved her wand over me," Amber exclaimed. She was in seventh heaven.

Niamh, meanwhile, was falling in love with the purple suede shoes. She caressed the buttersoft suede and marvelled at the wide cuff around the ankle.

"These are seriously sexy. A girl could get into trouble wearing these," she giggled.

"Not you, goody-two-shoes!" Val bitchily replied. Niamh blushed and pretended not to hear her.

"Purple is *sooo* in this year," Phoebe announced. She was having trouble deciding between the red, purple and silver.

Rosie had gone for the grey patent pump which started out a pale grey at the toe, graduating in ever deeper shades to dark grey at the heel. "Gosh, everyone will think these are Christian Louboutin, with this red sole," she said, lifting her foot to show the others. "And for less than a €100! Nobody will believe me."

Grace noticed that Tessa had preferred the classy, sophisticated pale gold sandals. They had a strap across the toe and two narrow straps which criss-crossed the instep and went into an ankle strap. The heels were four inches high and they looked wonderful with her tanned slim legs

Val had gone for the black gladiator-style platform shoes with studded straps which were currently popular with young women. Grace wasn't surprised. Val was a bit of a Goth, always dressed in black and slightly dark and menacing.

Lesley had chosen the silver *Sex and the City* shoes. The flashier the better for Lesley, Grace thought. If we had one covered in crystals or diamante she'd have gone for that. Grace shuddered at the idea.

Amber, ever the extrovert, had, as she'd expected, fancied the red strappy kid shoes.

"These should be a doodle to sell," Amber remarked, convinced that no woman could possibly resist them once they laid eyes on them.

The biggest surprise of all was that Niamh had gone for the sexy purple suede. Hmmm . . . Grace thought, I never would have expected that.

And Phoebe . . . well, Phoebe was Phoebe and still couldn't make up her mind!

There was an atmosphere of excitement in the room all afternoon and Grace finished up early, to allow them time to get home and prepare for the dinner that evening. Tessa had arranged to stay with Amber, as it would have been too far to travel down to Kildare and back and too expensive for a taxi.

Chapter 14

When Niamh arrived home that evening, she was surprised to see Gavin and the kids having their tea. She wondered what had got into him. Gavin didn't do cooking – he left that to his mother and Niamh – unless you counted toast, which he generally burnt to a cinder. This usually meant that the windows had to be left open for hours afterwards, to get rid of the smoke and the horrible smell. This evening he'd got it right and he'd also opened a tin of beans, which was his other culinary talent.

He gave her his lopsided smile and pushed back his long blond hair.

"Surprise! I thought I'd give you a chance to get ready for tonight, so I collected the kids from your mam's and made their tea." He looked absurdly pleased with himself, like a small boy waiting for a pat on the back.

Her heart melted. "Oh, Gav, pet, thank you so much. That was so thoughtful."

He could be wonderful sometimes. She really did love

him. She sat down with them and heard the day's news from her children, smiling at Gavin fondly as they prattled on.

"And Daddy is going to wead us *Willy Wonka* tonight," Rose told her.

If only it could be like this all the time! Bridget had gone to visit her sister so they were just like any normal happy family.

"What have you got there, babe?" Gavin asked when he saw the boxes in the hall.

"These are the shoes I'll be selling. I had some job getting on the packed Luas with them," she laughed.

She showed him the shoes and he was silent for a moment.

"Don't you like them?" she asked, with a worried look.

"They're beautiful," he said with awe, lifting the purple suede shoes out of the silver satin-lined box. "And seriously sexy," he added.

"That's exactly what I said when I saw them," she laughed. "And that's not all," she told him, her eyes glowing. "I won this bottle of champagne for having the best business plan of anyone. Can you believe it? And they're all much older and more experienced then me."

God, she's so hot when she's excited like this, Gavin thought, pulling her to him. "Good on you, babe! Maybe this job will work out after all, even though Ma thinks it's crazy."

"Well, it's not. We'll show her when we move out to our own place," Niamh answered with more vehemence than she'd intended.

"Yeah, I met Andy today and told him what you're doing and he thinks it sounds great."

Now she understood Gav's change of heart. Andy was

his idol. He'd played soccer for Ireland and now owned a chain of pubs in Dublin city. Where Gav was concerned, Andy's word was law, so if Andy approved of her job, then it was okay. He was such a kid sometimes but she wouldn't look this gift horse in the mouth. Thanks, Andy!

She got the children ready for bed before getting showered and dressed for the evening. She was wearing yet another Oxfam dress. This time it was a Chinese style dress in a purple and gold print. With her petite figure, she looked a dream. Luckily she had her new purple shoes to go with it. They were beautiful and made her feel quite sexy. They were so high, yet soft and comfortable.

"You look pretty, Mammy," Ian said showering her with kisses when she went to say goodnight to him.

"Bootiful Mammy," Rose lisped.

Lily couldn't be outdone. "Mammy weally pwetty."

"Thank you, my munchkins," she said, kissing them goodnight.

Gavin whistled as she came down the stairs. "Wow! I hope there won't be any guys there tonight. If there is, they'll all fancy you like mad."

"Don't be silly," she said, putting her arms around his neck.

"I'll be waiting for you tonight, babe," he said huskily, kissing her deeply.

Luckily, Bridget wasn't there to see them.

Oh, God. We have to get out of this house. Everything will be perfect then, Niamh thought as she waved him goodbye and got into the taxi.

Tessa gave a low whistle as she arrived at Amber's apartment.

"Wow! What a divine place, Amber. And what a wonderful view!" She looked out over the marina. "It's like a picture postcard with all those pretty yachts."

"Yes, I love it here. I bought it with my divorce settlement," Amber replied, pouring them both a glass of Pinot Gris.

"You live here alone?" Tessa asked, taking in the very feminine décor. "No man around?"

"You must be joking!" Amber replied, taking a sip of her wine. "I've given up on men."

"Have you not been dating since your divorce?" Tessa was curious.

"No way! I'm finished with men – forever." Amber made a cutting motion with her hands.

"Oh, don't be daft," Tessa replied, not believing her. "Forever is a long time. You're young and beautiful and Carlo really likes you, you know." She glanced at Amber to gauge her reaction. "I've seen him looking at you. I can tell he's interested."

"No way would I go there. Not in a million years," Amber said adamantly. "The last thing in the world I need is an Italian Casanova."

"Mmmm, this wine is delicious," Tessa said, sipping blissfully. "Seriously, I don't think Carlo's like that. I think he's sweet and genuine and *ohhh soooo* sexy. *I* wouldn't charge him a penny," Tessa drooled. "If I wasn't with George . . ."

"He's all yours," Amber replied. "Be my guest."

Tessa was surprised at the bitterness in her friend's voice, although she'd known some girls who'd gone off the deep end after a divorce. Still, Amber had got this divine pad out of it. That was something!

They finished their wine and went to the bedroom to

prepare for the evening. Tessa was gobsmacked when she saw her friend's shoe-room.

"My God, Amber, you've more shoes here than the whole flipping shoe department of Brown Thomas!" She gazed around, not able to believe her eyes. She flitted from shoe to shoe admiring, exclaiming, and occasionally taking one down.

"I've never seen so many red shoes in one place," she gasped. "Dorothy, eat your heart out!"

Then she spotted the boots. "Oh my God, I've died and gone to heaven. These boots are divine. And your bags . . ." Amber had opened up the cupboard where all her bags hung on hooks, colour-graded, as were her shoes.

"I thought I had a good collection but I'm only in the tuppence-ha'penny place compared to this!" Tessa exclaimed.

Amber had to drag her away to get showered and dressed or they wouldn't be ready when the taxi arrived.

Amber was wearing a mid-calf, gold silk sheath dress with slits up to mid-thigh. It shimmered as it clung to her curvaceous body and flashed a glimpse of tanned, toned legs when she moved. She wore matching Manolo Blahnik gold sandals and no jewellery except for gold drop earrings. Her hair fell softly in curls to her shoulders. She was pure golden glamour.

"Poor Carlo. You'll break his heart tonight," Tessa remarked.

Amber gave her a mock slap. "You don't look too bad yourself."

Tessa was wearing a white, off-the-shoulder gypsy blouse over an incredibly soft, short beige suede skirt. She had matching knee-length, beige suede stiletto boots which emphasised her long, bare, tanned legs. She had worn her hair up for most of the week but tonight it hung straight and shiny and she wore big gold hoops in her ears. She was a master with the make-up brush and Amber marvelled at the way she wielded it. The way she had done her eyes made her look more exotic than ever.

They were just ready when the taxi arrived and they set off in high spirits for La Stampa, which was the restaurant Grace had chosen for the evening. Every head in the room swivelled to look at the two beautiful women as they made their entrance. All the women envied them and all the men fancied them. They greeted the others and accepted a glass of champagne from Carlo. He did the hand-kissing thing again, but this time Amber snatched her hand away.

"You look beautiful tonight," he whispered. She pretended not to hear and, leaving Tessa with him, moved away to join Grace.

"You both look sensational," Grace said, hugging her. "In fact, everyone looks extremely glamorous. It's amazing what we women can pull out of the hat when we want to," she laughed.

There was a very attractive man talking to Niamh and Rosie. Grace brought her over and introduced him as her husband, Massimo, who had flown in from Rome, especially for the evening. He was charming and very chic and Amber found herself warming to him. He didn't make her feel uncomfortable, as Carlo did.

Val arrived just then and made a beeline for Carlo. She was very heavily made up and the purple hair was spiked on top of her head. She was wearing a ridiculously low-cut, tight black dress. Amber was afraid that her huge boobs would pop out at any moment. She felt a bit piqued as she saw Carlo leaning towards Val, smiling.

"Don't tell me that he's interested in that tart," she whispered to Tessa, who was beside her.

"Well, you don't want him, so can you blame him?" Tessa replied. "She's certainly making it obvious that she fancies him."

Somehow, this bothered Amber.

Pete was hugely looking forward to the night. In fact, he couldn't believe his luck. He'd been doubtful about taking on this job but Grace, whose brother Tim was his best friend, had persuaded him to do it and boy was he glad that he had. So many gorgeous women! Tim was convinced that his friend was a sex-addict, like David Duchovny and Michael Douglas (before he met Catherine Zeta Jones, of course), but Pete knew it wasn't about the sex.

Pete loved women – all women – whatever their age, shape or size. He loved the way they thought. He loved their idiosyncrasies, the very things that often drove other men mad. Growing up with five sisters and a mother, who had all doted on him, had given him a deep understanding of what made women tick. And women of all ages recognised this and responded warmly to him.

As he looked around the room he saw that he was spoilt for choice.

Tessa was exotic and a stunner – and boy what legs! But he had a strange feeling that she could read him like a book. She understood men. She'd been around the block and some. No doubt about it!

Amber was glowing tonight. What a body! He liked a woman who looked after herself. And what a personality! She would be good company but he could tell that she was wary of men. Well, he was confident that he would be able to soothe those fears.

Niamh was a cutie. The way she looked at him with those big emerald eyes! She was so young and vulnerable, appealing to his protective instincts. But underneath it all, he knew she was a little sex kitten. He had a great instinct for this and he was never wrong. Yes, he certainly fancied her!

Rosie was a lovely lady and very maternal towards him. Although some of the best sex he'd ever experienced had been with older women, he'd heard she'd been recently widowed – and well, he wasn't a complete cad!

Val was another kettle of fish. Hard as nails, but fond of sex too. He'd been very surprised to learn that she was Niamh's sister. They were very different but they obviously both shared a healthy sex drive. Val would be easy. Niamh would be a challenge and he was never one to resist a challenge. My God, Val was certainly letting it all hang out tonight, he thought, as he caught sight of her rigout.

There was no sign of Phoebe or Lesley yet.

Phoebe was a nut case – completely off-the-wall. One of the very few women who didn't hold some kind of attraction for him.

As for Lesley – she scared the daylights out of him. Nothing soft or feminine about her! He'd watched her at the training and had seen how focused and ambitious she was and he knew that she would let nothing get in her way. She would chew him up and spit him out, without a thought. She had an obsessive personality – the type that could easily become a bunny boiler. He knew that she was married but she'd never let *that* get in her way. She was dangerous which made her all the more exciting. And she was damn sexy. Whew! He got a hard-on just thinking about her body.

Pete joined Amber and Tessa, filling up their glasses and letting his eyes move slowly up and down their bodies.

"Wow, you two make a stunning pair. Are there two lucky men waiting at home for you? If so, I'm madly jealous of them." He smiled that boyish smile of his, as Amber giggled.

"No one waiting for me, I'm afraid," she said.

Tessa didn't bother replying. She suspected that it wouldn't matter a damn to him whether there was or not. If he wanted someone, he would go all out to get them. She saw that he was flirting with Amber now, who seemed to be responding. I have to get her away from him, she thought. She needn't have worried. He was one of those people she detested, who look over your shoulder constantly to see if there is anyone more interesting around. It seems there was! She saw his eyes widen as he excused himself and left them, mid-sentence.

Tessa turned to see what had distracted him to find that it was Lesley, who had just arrived.

"He's cute, isn't he?" Amber giggled. The champagne was having its effect already.

Lesley was wearing a pale blue, satin trouser suit which clung like a second skin to her every curve. The blue matched her eyes exactly and under the jacket she wore a black strapless corset which showed off her ample endowments. Her hair hung in loose curls on her shoulders which emphasised her pale, pretty face and of course she had on the ubiquitous sparkly shoes – blue with the diamante she loved so much. Damn it, but she was sexy!

Tessa could see that the men's eyes were all drawn to

her. Pete was already pouring her a glass of champagne as Carlo and even Massimo went over to greet her.

"What does she have that we don't?" Amber asked, ruefully.

"She oozes sex, that's what. Stupid men can never see beyond that," Tessa replied as Niamh and Rosie joined them.

All four grudgingly admitted that Lesley did look good, although none of them would ever have worn anything so tacky.

They were on their third glass of champagne when they were called to their table. Amber wangled it so that she was sitting as far away from Carlo as possible. He was so damned attractive and she was afraid of the feelings he aroused in her. She was afraid of what might happen after a few more drinks and she didn't trust herself. Val was directly across from him and Lesley was beside him. I'm sure he's happy – Amber couldn't help thinking – surrounded by all that cleavage!

Phoebe, as usual, was late.

"Wants to make a grand entrance, I suppose," Tessa laughed.

She wasn't far wrong. They were looking at the menu when they heard her.

"Helloo, everybody! Sorry I'm a little late! Hope I haven't missed anything."

She was wearing a red off-the-shoulder dress with a huge frill at the neckline which exposed quite a lot of her enormous bosom. The full skirt was frilled and flounced, which made her look even more plump than usual. Her hair was tied up with a red rose and she had big hoop earrings. Roaring red lipstick and nail polish completed the look.

131

"Where does she get them from?" Amber asked.

"She'll get up on the table and do some flamenco for us at any moment," Tessa whispered and indeed she'd hit the nail on the head. That's exactly what Phoebe looked like.

The others giggled as the champagne was now taking effect. Even Grace found it hard to keep a straight face as she introduced Phoebe to her husband.

What on earth does he think of us? Amber wondered.

They had a truly great night. The food was fantastic and Carlo had ordered wonderful wine to go with it – Italian, of course. Amber was amazed to hear Tessa speaking to him in Italian.

"How are you so fluent?" she asked her.

"My mother was Italian," Tessa explained. "She spoke it to me all the time but sadly she died when I was ten." The girls heard the catch in her voice.

"That's where you get your dark good looks from," Rosie smiled at her.

Rosie was looking ten years younger than her fifty-two years. She couldn't believe she was having such a good time. She knew Jack was looking down at her, happy to see her enjoying herself.

Pete was sitting between Niamh and Amber and he enjoyed himself flirting with each of them in turn. Amber was really taken with him. He didn't arouse the scary feelings inside her that Carlo did. He was much safer so she flirted right back. He whispered in her ear and asked if she would meet him for a drink some night. She agreed. He was a little sweetheart.

Unknown to her, he was also getting very audacious with Niamh on his other side. In the beginning she laughed and flirted – just a little – with him, but as he got into sexual territory she pulled back and when he asked her out she told him she couldn't possibly meet him. She was a married woman!

Tessa caught his eye once or twice and he winked at her. She laughed back at him. He was truly outrageous! She was having a wonderful time. Carlo was the most interesting man she'd ever met. He'd travelled extensively and had so many interests that she could have spoken to him for hours. She saw how Lesley and Val were doing their best to attract him, getting ever more blatant with each glass of wine. He very adroitly evaded their advances and Tessa felt sorry for him as he tried to be polite, in the face of their increasing vulgarity. He was a true gentleman and she thought Amber was crazy not to be receptive to him. Tessa fancied him more than ever.

"Are you flying back to Rome on the midday flight tomorrow?" Amber asked Grace, as they finished the delicious desserts.

"Actually, no. Massimo came over on the family jet, so we're going back on that in the morning."

Family jet! My God, that was something else. All the girls were very impressed with this piece of information. After the meal was finished, Grace said a few words.

"I'd like to thank you all for your hard work this week. I know there was a lot to take in but you're now very well equipped to go out and build a successful business. Carlo will be running the Irish operation for us," she said, smiling and gesturing to him. "He'll be coming over to Ireland every second week, initially, to meet up with you individually and give you any support you might need. We'll have a general meeting together every six weeks or so. Of course, Carlo is always available, by phone or e-mail, should you need him, as are Pete and I. I do hope you'll all succeed and that we'll be welcoming you all to Rome, in six months, for a further training session." She smiled, looking around the table at them all. "And Carlo has a little surprise for you." She held her hand out to him, asking him to take the floor.

Carlo stood up, smiling broadly around the table as they all went silent.

"To help motivate you, we have a further exciting incentive for you." He paused, enjoying the eager looks on their faces. "The girl with the highest sales, in the first six months, will have the use of a car for a year, which will be presented to her when she returns from Rome."

Some of the girls gasped and then they all clapped and smiled at him.

"*Grazie, Signore e Signorine,*" he said, sitting down.

Niamh had never been so excited. A car of her own! It was too good to be true. She was determined to be the one to win it.

"I can't wait to get home to tell Gavin about this," she beamed around the table. Her friends smiled at her excitement.

Amber noticed the disdainful look Lesley gave Niamh. She obviously had no intention of letting Niamh win it. She noticed that Lesley was more than a little drunk and was flirting with all the men, even Grace's husband.

As they said their goodbyes and prepared to leave, Amber heard Val and Lesley trying to persuade Carlo to go on to a nightclub with them.

"No way! Do I look like a nightclub person?" he asked, throwing back his head and laughing.

"You certainly do," Lesley purred, stroking his arm.

He turned to Tessa and asked, "Are you and Amber going?"

Before Tessa had a chance to reply, Amber answered for her.

"No, we're not," she said sharply.

He shrugged and bowing, said, "*Buona sera, signorine*." Then he turned on his heel and left.

"You're crazy," Tessa said, frustrated with Amber's attitude towards Carlo. *She* would love to have gone to a nightclub with him.

"He's not my type," Amber answered.

Tessa didn't believe her.

As they were waiting for their taxi, Pete pressed a note in to Tessa's hand.

On it he had written his private mobile number and a simple message: "*Call me.*" She looked at him and laughed. Was he for real? Did he intend to bed each one of them? She wouldn't have been surprised to discover this was his goal. Well, he can count this girl out, she thought, still laughing at his audacity.

"I've a feeling that Val will be playing gooseberry for the night," Tessa said, as Val and Lesley headed off with Pete. "Lesley appears to be in a distinctly amorous mood and Pete seems more than happy to accommodate her."

Amber was shocked. "Oh, I don't think so," she replied. "Lesley is married."

"I don't think that will worry either of them too much," Tessa said, cynically.

Amber looked at her in disbelief.

She's such an innocent, Tessa thought, as they climbed into their taxi.

On the way home, Tessa tried to talk to her. "Carlo's really sweet, you know, not at all like you think, or like Pete," she said gently. "You should give him a chance. I think he's simply divine."

"I'm not interested in him," Amber insisted, looking out the taxi window, winding a curl round and round her finger.

"Well, I think you're crazy. I think he's really genuine *and* he's *verrry* sexy. How can you resist that Latin charm?" She couldn't figure Amber out. "I'm telling you, if it wasn't for George, I'd go after him myself," she sighed.

Niamh was exhilarated as she travelled home in the taxi.

The taxi driver caught her mood. "You look like you enjoyed yourself tonight."

"Oh, I did. But it's not just tonight. Everything is just going great at the moment." She smiled at him.

"Well, I hope the guy you're going home to appreciates you."

"Oh, he does," she replied, nodding her head.

"Some guys have all the luck!" He grinned back at her. She laughed.

Coming quietly into the cottage, she took off her shoes and tiptoed up the stairs. She looked in on the children, covering them up as she kissed each of them softly. The last thing she wanted to do was wake Bridget. She'd never hear the end of it, if that happened. She crept into her own bedroom where Gavin was still awake, waiting for her.

"Come here, sexy babe."

"Oh, Gav, I have some news to tell you . . ."

"Sshh," he said, pulling her down on the bed and kissing her hungrily. He started to undress her slowly while

136

nuzzling and kissing her face and neck. It felt wonderful and she forgot all the news she had for him as she gave herself up to the delicious sensations that were flooding her body. He'd always been a superb lover and took a long time to pleasure her before he sought his own. As he made his way down her body she felt the longing and desire consume her. She lost count of the orgasms she experienced before they finally collapsed, exhausted, wrapped around each other.

Chapter 15

The following morning, Niamh woke to feel Gavin caressing her again and within seconds she was climbing on top of him. It was as if the years had melted away and they were young lovers again. She thought she'd die with happiness. The kids came in shortly afterwards, surprised to see Daddy awake and smiling and Mammy cuddled in his arms. They jumped on the bed and squealed with delight as Gavin tickled them all, in turn.

Bang! Bang! Bang! There was a loud knocking on the wall.

"Oh, God, your mother!" Niamh cried, realising she'd forgotten all about Bridget in the room next door. Jumping out of bed, she got the kids up and dressed and was in the kitchen, giving them breakfast when Bridget came in, scowling like a banshee.

"What hour of the night did you come in at, Miss?" she demanded. "This is not proper behaviour for a wife and mother!"

Niamh, realising that she'd probably heard them making love, blushed to the roots of her hair.

"Oh, Ma, get a life," Gavin said, coming into the kitchen in his boxers, his hair all tousled, his feet bare. "Niamh hardly ever goes out and anyway it wasn't that late. I was awake."

He looked so sexy! She couldn't believe it. Gavin had never, ever, sided with her against his mother. This was a first. Niamh wanted to throw her arms around him and hug him.

"I'm well aware that you were awake," Bridget snorted. "You kept me awake half the night with your shenanigans."

With a shock Niamh realised that her mother-in-law was jealous. Living here is the cause of most of our problems, she thought. I've got to make a success of this business and get us out of here.

Gavin was thrilled to hear that, if it went well, she had a chance of a company car in six months. He wanted a car, more than anything, even more than he wanted a house.

"Oh, that'd be fantastic, babe! You need to work really hard, to make sure you win it." His eyes were alight at the idea of their own car. He's just a kid at heart, she thought, ruffling his hair. She reckoned she'd have his support now.

To her surprise he offered to take the kids to the park so that she could go and have a chat with her mother. Gosh, what had come over him? It was years since he'd done anything like this. Things were really on the up! She went to call on her mother.

Eileen was heartened to see the happiness in Niamh's eyes. "I'm dying to know how last night went," she said, hugging her daughter.

"Has Val not been in touch to tell you?"

139

"I don't want to hear from her. I told her so," Eileen replied stiffly.

"Ah, Mam, that's silly," Niamh said as she put the kettle on. "You'll have to talk to her sooner or later. I've forgotten about it, so you should too. Life is too short to let something like that fester."

"I suppose. Well, you look happy," she said, bending to take an apple tart out of the oven. "I take it you had a great time?"

"It was brilliant. The girls are so nice and great fun. It was a very posh place and the food was out of this world." Niamh's eyes were aglitter as she continued, "And now for the best thing of all – the person with the best sales in the first six months will win a car, for a year. Can you believe it? I know I can be the one."

Eileen clapped her hands. "Oh, love, that would be fantastic! Just think where we'd be able to go: shopping to Liffey Valley and Blanchardstown and we could take the kids to the beach in summer! We could even go to visit all your cousins in Athlone and Birr."

Niamh grinned as her mother made plans for them all. "I have to win it first," she laughed as she set out the tea things, "but I know if I work like mad, I could. Thank God Dad taught me to drive."

"How I wish he was here to see this!" Eileen said. She took a bowl of whipped cream from the fridge then paused as a thought struck her. "What about Val? She can't drive."

Niamh was too charitable to say that she really didn't think Val had a hope in hell of winning the car.

"I suppose if she won, she'd have to learn," she replied, making the tea. "I'm really happy because Gavin is thrilled about the possibility of us getting a car. That means he'll help me and won't be against me doing this job." She looked at her mother hopefully.

I bet he won't, not if he has a chance of having a car to swan around in, Eileen couldn't help thinking as she handed Niamh a slice of hot apple tart and cream.

Niamh dug into the tart immediately. "Mmmmm, Mam, you're the best cook in the world!" she said, her mouth full.

Meanwhile, Tessa and Amber were feeling the worse for wear. After numerous cups of coffee, Amber suggested that they go for a walk in Portmarnock. It was a cold but sunny morning, so they wrapped up well and set out.

As they walked briskly along, Tessa took the bull by the horns. "Okay, are you going to tell me why you're so antagonistic towards Carlo?"

"First, he's a man – and second, he's an Italian man. Need I say more?"

Tessa could hear the bitterness in her voice. "God, Amber, you can't tar all men with the same brush. I know your husband hurt you badly. Do you want to tell me about it?"

They walked briskly, linking arms, and Amber told her the story of her marriage and divorce, leaving nothing out. She also told her about her previous disastrous relationship and she even told her about the drinking and the feeling of self-worthlessness she'd felt.

"So, now you see why this job has saved my life and why I'm so wary of men. I'll never trust a man again," she said, her voice full of pain.

Tessa had tears in her eyes as she heard the hurt in Amber's voice and realised how she'd almost hit rock-bottom.

"I see where you're coming from but, you know, not all men are bastards like Dermot. I had a similar experience with Isaac, except that he was a dreadful womaniser – a serial shagger, I prefer to call him. I discovered after I left him that he'd been screwing everything in a skirt, all through our marriage. I was desperately hurt and embarrassed but I haven't let that stop me looking for love again."

"You're braver than I am, then," Amber replied. "I'll never let a man hurt me like that again. It almost destroyed me."

"Well, I felt a bit like that after Isaac but then, after my heart attack, I learnt to grab each day and live it fully. Life is so unpredictable and love can be the most wonderful thing. Mind you, I think I've made a huge mistake with George, but that's another story."

Amber looked at her sharply. "Why do you say that?"

"It might sound strange but I feel I'm not *me* when I'm with him." She hesitated, looking at Amber. "I feel like I'm trying to be what he wants me to be, all the time. Do you understand? This job is pretty much a life-saver for me too. I rather hoped that it might repair my relationship with George. Now, I'm not even sure I want it to. Life is too short to settle for second best."

"I envy you your optimism and willingness to try again," Amber said sadly. "I wish I could but I'm just not brave enough, I'm afraid."

Tessa wished she could do something to help her new friend.

Rosie spent €40 speaking to her son, David, in Australia, regaling him with all the changes in her life during the past two weeks. He was delighted to hear his mother back to her old self. He'd been extremely worried about her in the aftermath of his dad's death. He had actually considered leaving Melbourne and going back to Ireland to live, thinking his mother needed him. He and his wife and two boys were very happy and had settled well in Australia, but as he said to Gail in one of their numerous emails, family is family, and if his mum needed him, he'd come home. Thank God he'd listened to Gail and stayed put, as it looked as if his mother had come through it okay. He was relieved and genuinely happy for Rosie.

She was like a new woman and couldn't wait to get started selling the beautiful If the Shoes Fit shoes.

Tessa hated leaving Amber and heading back to Ballyfern, but she couldn't put it off any longer. She was pleased to see that George was out when she arrived home. He'd left her a note to say he was playing golf and would be home around six.

She was relieved and went up to have a nice long, relaxing bath. She was finished by four and decided to take Napoleon over to Kate's for a walk.

Kate was delighted to hear all the news of the course and pleased that Tessa had enjoyed the week so much and had made some new friends.

"Amber sounds lovely. I'll have to meet her. And Carlo sounds divine. If I wasn't so happily married, I'd ask for an introduction! I insist on being the first one to hold a party for you. I have some friends who are crazy about shoes – although I don't think any of them have a shoe-room like your friend Amber." She checked her diary. "How does next Friday suit? I'll get all the girls at the golf club to come and I'll ring my friend in Dublin and invite her down."

Tessa was delighted. "Way to go!" she said, giving Kate a high-five.

George was home when she got back.

"Where have you been?" he asked, his voice surly.

"I decided to take Napoleon out for a walk, so we went over to Kate's."

"Huh," he replied, burying his head in his newspaper.

He didn't ask her how the dinner had gone the night before and she didn't volunteer any information. George wasn't big on female bonding. He couldn't understand how women could reveal their innermost feelings and thoughts to each other. He'd have had a fit if he knew that Tessa had discussed their relationship with both Kate and Amber. What he doesn't know won't hurt him, she thought – not for the first time.

Later he spotted the six pairs of shoes in the den.

"What's this?" he asked, frowning.

"These are the shoes I'll be selling. Aren't they beautiful?" She opened the boxes to show him.

"You're not serious! They're much too trendy, very inappropriate." He looked appalled. "I do hope you're not thinking of wearing them?"

She bit her lip and said nothing.

"If you must indulge yourself with this little job, at least do it with taste," he said disdainfully.

That's what this business was to him – her indulgence. Well, she'd bloody well show him. She vowed she'd make him eat his words.

Chapter 16

On Monday morning all the paperwork was delivered to the women. Niamh opened the boxes with excitement. There were the brochures that she would give out to her reps, featuring the six pairs of shoes, photographed in glorious colour from every angle. She had to admit that they looked very seductive and hoped that any woman looking at them would feel she just had to have them, whatever the cost. There were also posters, equally seductive, which she would hang up in shops and anywhere else she could, to attract representatives. And lastly, leaflets to drop into individual homes.

She was determined to recruit as many representatives as she could, as quickly as possible, and she wanted to go for quality women. She'd received this advice from a very successful Avon manager that she knew. She preferred this to the party-plan way of selling. If she was having parties, she would have to work at night. This way, she could work while the children were at school. She didn't want to give

Bridget anything to complain about. She had considered using the landline phone for the business but her mother-in-law would certainly have made that difficult for her, not to mention sticking her nose in and knowing too much of what was going on. The company was paying her phone bills anyway so she bought a new mobile, specifically for the business, and put it down as an expense.

She decided to start in her own area and work out in a circle from there. She wore her most comfortable shoes and set off on her bike. She returned to the house three times for more posters before it was time to collect the kids from school. Each time she had to put up with Bridget's disapproving scowls. By this stage she was starving as she hadn't eaten since breakfast so on the spur of the moment she took them to McDonald's on the way home. This unexpected treat had the kids in an exuberant mood. When they had done their homework she allowed them to watch a DVD as she wanted to complete stamping the leaflets that she would use the following day. The kids thought it was their birthday. Bridget thought otherwise.

"Is this how things are going to be from now on? McDonald's after school and watching DVDs during the school week?" she whined, sniffing, as she always did when she was annoyed.

"Today is special. Our lives are going to change and I want to get this up and running as soon as possible."

Just then, Rose came running in, making things even worse.

"Can we watch a other DBD?," she lisped.

She never could pronounce her Vs, Niamh thought, scooping her little daughter up into her arms.

"Indeed you cannot," her grandmother snorted. "You're a right little diva!"

"I'm not a diba!" Rose's lower lip trembled as she started to cry although she had absolutely no idea what a diva was. However, even at four, she knew from her grandmother's tone that it wasn't good.

Lily, hearing her twin cry, came running into the kitchen in support and naturally joined in the tears.

"Now look what you've started!" Bridget spat the words out. "I really can't take all of this."

Flabbergasted, Niamh took her two little daughters on her knee and tried to calm them, thinking: you won't have to take it for too long more, you old bag!

That night she finished stamping the leaflets and was delighted to receive six phone calls from women who had seen her posters already. She arranged to meet three of them the following morning and the others on Wednesday. They all seemed very interested, except for one who seemed only to be looking for free shoes. She fell into bed exhausted but with a gut feeling that this was going to be a huge success. Gavin was, as usual, out with his mates.

Amber decided that dragging around door-to-door was not for her, so she decided that parties would be how she would start her business. God knows, she had enough friends and ex-colleagues who were shoe fanatics and besides she liked the idea of actually being the front woman herself. She'd often been told that she could sell snow to the Eskimos, or sand to the Arabs. Now was her chance to prove them right. Could she sell shoes to Irishwomen? That should be a piece of cake!

She spent Monday working her way through her

address book and contacting every woman in it. She scanned the shoe brochure and emailed it to everyone. She knew that they wouldn't be able to resist them. Many of her friends emailed straight back, wanting to hold a party for her, as soon as possible. Susie was having a party for her on Wednesday. She bought a big diary for the wall, so that she could co-ordinate things at a glance. She was on a winner here. She just knew it.

Rosie discussed her ideas with Gail. They decided that approaching ladies' clubs would be a good strategy. That way she could target a lot of women in the one night and also get leads from them for representatives and parties. She would also try golf clubs, tennis clubs, bridge clubs and gyms. She knew a lot of women from all around south Dublin, through all her activities in these areas. So many of them had turned up to Jack's funeral and offered to help her in any way they could. Now was their chance. She felt truly alive again.

Gail was having a party for her on Thursday night and had invited all her friends and neighbours. Rosie was nervous but excited and was glad her first outing would be at Gail's.

As Tessa didn't know all that many women in her area, she couldn't rely on parties alone, although Kate assured her that some of the women she'd invited for Friday night would also throw a party for her. She sure hoped so.

She was going to have to put out posters in her area. Like Amber, she didn't fancy going door-to-door, but if push came to shove she'd do it. She hoped it wouldn't be necessary. She had better ideas than that. She had contacted a friend in Dublin who designed websites and he was currently working on one for her. She had scanned the brochure to him and was busy putting the website address on her posters. She had squared this with Grace, who said it was okay, as long as she forwarded any replies from prospective representatives in other areas to the appropriate manager. She hoped she wouldn't get any replies for Phoebe, Lesley or Val's areas. She'd be delighted to help out the others.

She had also contacted the local newspapers in her Dublin area and had placed adverts in them. Her good business sense and experience would see her through. She felt very confident.

While the four friends were busy getting things underway, Phoebe was in the beauty salon, having her weekly manicure and pedicure. She was loudly telling one and all about the fabulous new shoes that she would be selling.

"Well, I'm not selling, of course, I'm the sales director," she preened, "but I'll be running a team of representatives to sell them. Anyone interested?"

The staff of the salon, who dreaded her Monday morning visits, pretended not to hear.

"Who wants to start the week, after a hectic weekend of partying, listening to that one?" the manicurist muttered to the junior. "I swear she makes me feel like staying in on Sunday nights. Imagine facing her with a hangover? Total nightmare!"

Phoebe, secure in her self-confidence, was totally unaware of how they felt about her. She figured she must be their most popular customer. After all, she always tipped well. She couldn't understand why none of them were interested in selling her shoes.

"If it was anyone else, I'd be mad keen to do it, but I wouldn't risk having to deal with her on a day-to-day basis," the beautician confided to the others after Phoebe had left.

"Imagine it!" the manicurist shuddered.

One of the other clients, who didn't know Phoebe very well, had said she'd like to learn more about it.

"Fantastic! Can you come around to my house now and I'll fill you in?"

The poor woman did as she was asked and, completely railroaded by Phoebe, found herself, twenty minutes later, a representative for If the Shoes Fit. She didn't know quite know how it had happened.

Phoebe, delighted with her first conquest, rang Val to share her good news. There was no reply. She must be busy working, Phoebe thought, leaving a message.

Val wasn't working. She was still in bed, although it was almost noon. While all the others were busy getting their businesses under way, Val had other things on her mind.

She'd had a dreadful row with her boyfriend, Keith, on Sunday evening. He'd stormed out of the house and hadn't returned home that night. She guessed that he was hanging out with one of the groupies who followed his rock band. These girls were always there, willing to drop their knickers for any one of the guys in the band, or indeed all of them, if necessary. The guys regularly took them up on it. (Val conveniently forgot that that was how she had met Keith herself.) Not that it bothered her if he was with someone else. It wasn't as if she was in love with him but still, he *was* her boyfriend and they'd been living together for over a year. He owed her.

In the beginning it had been exciting. Sex, drugs and rock-and-roll – what a potent mix! She'd loved going to his gigs and the crazy parties afterwards, where cocaine was as plentiful as booze and everyone got as high as kites. It still happened, of course, but she'd tired of it. Well, that wasn't strictly true – the fact was that Keith didn't want her there any more. She knew he was screwing around and that was another problem. He refused to use condoms and she was terrified of catching something. God only knew what slapper he'd been with. They fought about it a lot and now their sex life was non-existent. Fine for him, he was getting it elsewhere. What about her needs?

She'd had really had high hopes of getting Pete into bed the previous Friday night. She'd seen the way he'd been looking down her cleavage all night and had thought that things would heat up in the nightclub. They'd heated up all right – but for Lesley – not for Val! Not that she blamed him. Lesley was fabulous. She was so hot. Val really admired her. The way they were groping each other on the dance floor – it was almost pornographic! She sighed. She really wouldn't have minded a threesome but she wasn't invited to join in.

Bringing her thoughts back to Keith, she knew it was the beginning of the end, which was why she'd gone for this job. It was all very well for Mam to say she shouldn't have. Where would she go, if Keith threw her out – which she knew he would, any day now. Her mother, who'd always been her rock, wasn't talking to her, so she couldn't go back there. She didn't get on with her older sisters and Niamh's was out of the question. They were cramped enough in Bridget's little house as it was. Niamh was forever going on about getting a place of her own. If she did, Val knew she'd be welcome there. But could she bear to live in the same house as Gavin, knowing he wasn't hers? Seeing him every day with Niamh would be too much for her. She couldn't bear it.

If only he'd fallen in love with her and not Niamh, everything would have been perfect. Lying beside him every night, feeling his gorgeous body next to hers – what bliss it would be! She started to get aroused, as she did every time she thought of him and touching herself, imagining it was Gavin, she brought herself to orgasm.

Afterwards, crying softly to herself, she thought how unfair life was. The only two men she'd ever loved, Dad and Gavin, had both preferred Niamh. Was it any wonder Mam called her a jealous bitch? Anyone would be, in the circumstances. Her very handsome father used to take her on his knee and call her his little princess. Then Niamh arrived and spoilt it all. He called Niamh his "little twinkle". Somehow it had sounded more important than princess.

Val was twenty when she fell in love with Gavin Byrne. She fell hard. She wanted to make love to him more than anything else in the world. She did everything she could think of to catch his attention but although he was friendly and sweet to her, he never even asked her out. When he fell for her kid sister, he broke her heart.

Their wedding day was the worst day of her life. She still didn't know how she'd got through it. It was all so unfair. She could barely look at Niamh who had been glowing with happiness and pregnancy. Val had wanted to die and the only thing that stopped her was the hope that one day Gavin might change his mind and realise that he'd married the wrong sister. Six years down the road, she still loved him and still hoped it would happen.

The Angelus bell, ringing from the nearby church, roused her from her thoughts and she crawled out of bed, knowing that she should get down to work but somehow she couldn't face it today. She had too much on her mind.

Chapter 17

Amber's party at Susie's was a great success. She sold twenty pairs of shoes, arranged a party for the following Friday, and came home with promises of other future parties. She'd also found three women who were interested in becoming reps.

She realised that this was the way to go – networking. It was all word of mouth and women were the specialists at that. No doubt about it, it was going to be a huge success. She loved it.

Tessa was busy all week and was delighted to get calls from women who'd spotted her posters. She interviewed four of them on Thursday and signed them up. She had hoped that George would come around to accepting what she was doing but if anything, he was even more hostile.

On Thursday night she had to sit through a boring dinner with three of his boring friends and their boring wives. She looked around the dinner table wondering what on earth she was doing there. She had absolutely nothing in common with any of these people. She was barely aware of the conversation drifting about her, as she planned her business for the next week. At one point she did start to tell the other women about If the Shoes Fit, but George's scowl stopped her in her tracks. Obviously, he was embarrassed by it and didn't want his friends to know what she was up to. She gave up and withdrew into herself.

She was wearing a cashmere twinset and pearls with low-heeled ballet pumps. Her hair was up in a chignon. She felt like a fraud. This wasn't her – it was someone else! She felt like a sixty-year-old matron and she reckoned she looked it too. She would love to have worn a pair of her new shoes but after George's remarks she thought it was safer to leave them where they were. She wondered what his reaction would have been if she'd worn her beige suede suit and boots. God, he'd have had a seizure!

She was beginning to understand that George didn't want *her* – he wanted what he thought she represented. He'd been attracted to her because of her background, not for herself.

The first time she had taken George home to meet her father and stepmother, she'd been surprised at his behaviour. He'd been so impressed by them and had spent the weekend fawning over them. Her father had hated this and she suspected that he hadn't liked George very much either.

She'd wondered why George had behaved so obsequiously towards her father and Claudia. She finally understood why when, months later, she met his mother, Doreen, a dear little woman who lived on a suburban estate in Dublin.

"Oh, my dear, you're very posh for our George," she'd

whispered to Tessa, as she'd flustered about the little kitchen, preparing tea for them.

Tessa had laughed and hugged her. "I'm not at all posh," she'd assured her. "I'm really very ordinary."

"Well, you're a very nice girl anyway. George always wanted to be posh, you know." Doreen gave a little sigh. "He thinks he is now, but people can always tell," she said sadly.

Tessa had become very fond of Doreen and visited her regularly. George never accompanied her. It was obvious that he was ashamed of his mother and where he'd come from. He was an out and out snob.

Tessa rang Kate the following day and told her about the awful evening she'd had with George's friends and how she felt her relationship with him was deteriorating faster by the day.

"I'm so sorry to hear that," said Kate. "I really thought it would improve things for you if you had an interest of your own."

"Sadly not," Tessa replied, her voice dejected. "If anything things are getting worse."

"How about bringing George over for supper tomorrow night?" Kate suggested brightly. "The Smithsons are coming and I know George thinks very highly of Jonathan."

"That's because Jonathan is a successful barrister and what George considers upper-class," Tessa retorted. "But thanks, Kate. You're right. It might help. I'll tell him. Gosh, I'm quite nervous about this party tonight," she added, sucking in her breath.

"Don't be daft. It'll be great," Kate reassured her. "All the girls who are coming are friends of mine and believe me, they're big into shoes."

Kate could not understand Tessa's lack of self-confidence. She was bright and funny and beautiful into the bargain. It's all bloody George's fault, she thought angrily as she put the phone down. He saps her self-confidence.

Tessa's nerves melted away quickly after meeting Kate's friends that evening. They were a terrific group of women. Kate had pulled out all the stops and the house was looking beautiful. There were candles everywhere, sixties music playing in the background and a Cosmopolitan cocktail handed to each woman as she came in. They'd come from everywhere: Kildare, Meath and as far away as Dublin. The atmosphere was electric and they were all drooling over the shoes.

"They are divine," Marcia, a friend of Kate's from Dublin, remarked. "I pay six times the price for similar shoes in Dublin and London." She laughed. "This means I can afford to buy all six pairs for the price of one!"

She wasn't joking. She ordered all six pairs. Tessa was exhilarated. There were eighteen women there and some of the others also ordered more than one pair.

"They're all so gorgeous I can't make up my mind. I'll have to take both pairs," she heard, over and over again.

This was fantastic. What a start to her business! Not only that, but Marcia wanted to host a party for her in Killiney. This was too good to be true. In all, she sold thirty-two pairs of shoes – in one night – wow!

Kate had prepared a lovely selection of hors d'oeuvres and, after the Cosmopolitans, numerous bottles of Chablis were consumed. It was a brilliant night. At the end of it, Kate's best friends, Lauren, Tara and Jenny, remained for one last drink. They were such fun and Tessa felt at home with them straight away.

"It's wonderful to feel the bond between you all," she told them, a little enviously.

"Well, we've been through a lot together," Kate said.

"We'll tell you sometime," Lauren smiled at her.

"If you have about a month to spare," Jenny added, and they all laughed.

"To us girls!" Tara raised her glass.

"Because we're worth it!" they all chorused, howling with laughter now.

Seeing Tessa's bewildered look, Lauren added, "We'll explain all to you next time we meet. It looks like you'll be a new member to our little group."

The others nodded their agreement. She hadn't had such a good girls' night out since she'd left London. The three women offered to have a party for her and she said she'd ring them over the weekend to discuss it.

She didn't know how to thank Kate. Well, she did actually. She was going to give her a pair of the grey patent shoes that she liked so much.

Niamh had set off on Tuesday, wearing the red strappy shoes which she hoped would wow the prospective representatives. She was nervous as hell about inter-viewing the women but it went wonderfully well and they all signed up. The fact that they adored the shoes, helped to convince them. The following day she signed up two more women, this time wearing the purple suede shoes. It amazed her that these ordinary women were so crazy about shoes. Who'd have thought it in the Ireland of the noughties!

She found that she had a good instinct for people. The girl she had thought would be a waster, when speaking to her on the phone, turned out to be exactly that. Niamh didn't waste too much time on her.

Her hard work putting out posters and leaflets had paid off and by Friday she had signed up ten representatives who, as she told Gavin, were all out there working and making money for her. She'd had phone calls from another twelve and she was planning to sign them up the following week. It was exhilarating.

Rosie rang her on Friday evening to find out how she'd got on and when she heard, congratulated her on her success. Although Rosie hadn't done as well as Niamh, she was very happy with the ten pairs she'd sold at Gail's party. She was pleased with the response she'd got and had some meetings planned for the following week.

Val rang Phoebe on Saturday to see how things were going for her.

"Fantastic, absolutely fantastic, darling! I've employed six women to put around posters and leaflets for me. It's looking good."

Val was taken aback. She couldn't afford to pay women to do this for her.

"Have you signed up many reps?" she asked Phoebe.

"Just one, but it's still early days. This will take time. I feel very confident."

Val wished she could share Phoebe's confidence. The fact was that she hadn't done a tap all week except mope around the house, wondering where Keith was. He had finally showed up on Thursday, behaving as though everything was normal and as if he hadn't been missing for four days. She played along with it. She had no choice.

She'd finally managed to get her mother to talk to her

again. Val was green with envy when Eileen told her that Niamh had already signed up ten women and had twelve more to interview the following week. Val just had to find out how she'd done it. She went around to her mother's that afternoon.

"Well, Miss. I hope you're sorry for what you did. If it wasn't for Niamh asking me to make up with you, I never would."

"Ah, Mam, you don't mean that!" Val's voice was wheedling.

Eileen knew in her heart that she didn't, but she was damned if she'd let Val know it.

"How is Niamh recruiting so many reps?" Val asked, her eyes all innocence.

"You'll have to ask her that," Eileen replied, making the tea. "I do know that she's been in touch with Amber and Tessa and they've had a great week too."

Val felt that old jealousy rise up inside her. Typical Niamh – the two posh ones ringing her. She'd have to find out more. That meant swallowing her pride and ringing Niamh. Well, one does what one has to do.

Niamh was surprised to hear Val, all sweetness and light, on the other end of the phone. She was glad that they were talking again. She hated any kind of conflict. She'd had enough of that to last her a lifetime with Bridget.

"How's it going for you?" Val asked, all innocence, as if she hadn't heard.

Niamh couldn't keep the excitement out of her voice as she told Val all that had happened.

"What about the others?" Val asked sweetly.

Niamh naïvely told her how well Amber, Tessa and Rosie had done.

"Oh, Niamh! You've all done so much better than me. I feel such a failure," she said, her voice trembling. Her performance was worthy of an Oscar. "Could you help me and show me how you went about it?" she asked plaintively.

Niamh, ever the softie, couldn't refuse. "Of course," she replied. "Can you come around tomorrow? About three."

"Gee, thanks." Val couldn't believe her luck. Her stupid sister would not only tell her how she'd managed it but she'd get to spend time with Gavin too. Yipee!

Tessa and George were having an aperitif at Kate's. He was fawning over Jonathan, as he always did, and ignoring Kevin, Kate's lovely husband.

"We've decided to eat in the kitchen as it's such a miserably cold night," Kate informed them. "The kitchen is nice and cosy and, as it's just the six of us, we thought it would be more informal."

Tessa saw the way George pursed his lips together with disapproval.

"Lovely, I prefer that," Jonathan said in his lovely, deep, rumbling voice.

George, the hypocrite, concurred.

Tessa really liked Lauren, Jonathan's wife, who was also Kate's best friend. She'd been a top model in Dublin, so they had a lot in common. Tessa was pleased to be sitting across from her, between Kevin and Jonathan. Kate served up a superb meal and everyone was at ease and relaxed. Everyone, that is, except George. For starters, he'd come dressed in a suit and tie although she'd told him it was casual. Kevin and Jonathan were both dressed in sweaters and polo shirts. Well, she'd warned him – it was his own fault. He looked most uncomfortable but she daren't suggest that he take off his jacket and tie. Lord forbid!

It was a great evening although Tessa didn't say very much. Every time she started to voice an opinion, George either put her down or cut her short. Kate and Lauren couldn't bear to watch it. Even Jonathan thought it was too much.

"I believe you relieved my wife of a pretty penny last night, Tessa," he turned to her smiling, hoping to ease the tension. "She tells me that she just couldn't resist your shoes. Seems to me you've got a very successful business on your hands. Congratulations!"

"Yes. It was great –"

George stopped her in her tracks. "Oh, it's just a little nonsense. You know women," he said to Jonathan. "They need their playthings and we must indulge them. Ha-ha-ha!"

Nobody else laughed, least of all the women. Kate and Lauren were both seething. Tessa was afraid she would disgrace herself by bursting into tears.

Shortly afterwards, George said they had to be going and they said their goodbyes.

"How could you embarrass me like that?" Tessa asked, as soon as they had reached the privacy of the car.

"Don't be silly, you're overreacting," he snapped back. "Let's face it, we both know this shoe thing won't last. You'll get bored with it. In the meantime I've decided to indulge you."

He looked so smug that she didn't know how she restrained herself from hitting him, but she did. Pompous asshole, she thought. I'll show you!

Back at Kate's house, Lauren was saying those exact same words.

"What a pompous asshole! What on earth does she see in him? He's dreadful!"

"He was very patronising. She seems like a very bright woman," Jonathan remarked.

"She is. She's fantastic," Kate joined in. "She's very intelligent and funny and normally great company. But did you see the way he kept putting her down?" Kate spoke furiously. "It's dreadful! In the end she just stays mum and she's usually so lively and such fun."

"Why does she stay with him?" Lauren asked.

"God knows. I wouldn't," Kate replied with some vehemence. "I do know she's not happy and now he doesn't want her doing this job."

"Oh, for God's sake – this is the twenty-first century," Kevin joined in. "Women are not chained to the kitchen sink any more."

"Well said, my darling," Kate patted him on the arm.

"Agreed," Jonathan backed him up, hoping for a similar show of affection from Lauren. She pushed him playfully – not quite what he had in mind!

Chapter 18

On Sunday afternoon, Bridget opened the door to Val, glowering at her skimpy outfit.

"Did someone rob your clothes on the way over?" she asked her, with a snort.

"This is called fashion, Bridget," Val replied cheekily, as she brushed past her, nose in the air, "not that you'd know it if it jumped up and bit you!"

"Common as muck!" Bridget shot after her.

Niamh had heard this exchange and tried to get Val out of Bridget's way as quickly as possible.

She had to admit that Bridget had a point though. Val's skirt was little more than a pelmet and her top was so low that it left nothing to the imagination. Niamh just couldn't understand why Val dressed like this. It was no wonder men got the wrong idea.

"Come on up to the bedroom. We'll have privacy there," she said.

"Where's Gav?" her sister asked, looking around.

"Where do you think?" Niamh laughed. "He's watching the football, in the sitting-room."

"Can we not go in there?" Val asked, heading in that direction.

"God no!" Niamh replied, pulling her away and directing her up the stairs. "He'd hate it if we disturbed his game. Anyway, I keep all my stuff in our bedroom so the kids can't mess it up." She followed Val up the stairs.

"Where are they?" Val asked. "The place seems awfully quiet."

"They're at a birthday party till five, so we can work in peace."

Val made a face. She'd gone to so much trouble to look good for Gav, and for what? She mightn't even meet him!

Niamh sat at the little table she had installed in the bedroom while Val lounged on the bed.

"Which side of the bed do you sleep on?" Val asked her sister.

Niamh couldn't figure out why she wanted to know. "The right, why?" she replied, raising her eyebrows.

"Just wondering," Val said nonchalantly.

She took the pillows from Gavin's side and put them behind her head, inhaling his scent as she did so. God he had such a sexy smell!

Niamh spent the next hour explaining how she'd operated during the week.

"That seems like so much work," Val complained.

"Well, it is work. That's what we're supposed to be doing. You get nothing for nothing, Val." Niamh was perplexed. Did Val not understand that it was a job and, as Grace said, you got out of it what you put into it? Seemingly not!

"It's all right for you," Val whined. "You've got a great area."

"Women everywhere will love these shoes, Val. You just have to make sure they get to see them." Niamh picked up a pen. "Here, let's make a plan for you."

Val wasn't convinced but she knew she had to do something. She listened to Niamh's ideas. They'd obviously worked for her and she had to admit they made sense.

"Okay, I'll start with posters on Monday but can you come out with me?" she asked, turning big puppy-dog eyes on her sister.

"Oh, Val, putting out posters is child's play. Anyone can do it. I honestly need every minute I have, to work my own area," Niamh explained patiently.

"Well then, will you come out with me when I go out to interview?" Val asked, in a wheedling voice.

What could Niamh say? She agreed, as Val knew she would.

"Okay, let's go have a cup of tea in the kitchen," Niamh said when they'd finished.

"Will that dragon, Bridget, be around?' Val asked. "If she is, I'll go. Honestly, I don't know how you stick her!" She stuck out her tongue.

"No, she isn't – she goes out every Sunday afternoon," Niamh assured her, laughing.

"Okay so, but I'd much prefer a glass of wine. Do you have any?"

Niamh looked at her sister in exasperation. "Val, how the hell do you think we can afford wine? We're bloody lucky to have tea."

"What about all the money you're making?" her sister demanded.

"I haven't seen any of it yet," Niamh informed her, "and trust me, when I do, I won't be spending it on wine. I'll be saving it for a deposit on a house." She stuck her chin out in the defiant way Val recognised. Niamh didn't often put her foot down but when she did, she was immovable. Poor Gav, Val thought, as they came down the stairs. What a miserable time he must have between his mother and his wife.

"I'll just pop in and say hello to Gav," she said, sticking her tongue out at Niamh, whose back was turned to her as she headed for the kitchen. She was gone before Niamh could say anything.

Val pushed open the sitting-room door. "Hi, Gav," she greeted him, in her sexiest voice.

"Oh, hi, Val," he said, not taking his eyes off the television screen.

"That's a nice way to greet your favourite sister-in-law," she replied, coming between him and the TV.

She bent over and gave him a kiss, full on the lips, aware that her top had sagged, giving him an eyeful of her boobs. She was gratified to see that he had forgotten about his football and was taking them in. He was turned on, she could tell. God, she was glad that she'd spent the money on that boob job. Men just couldn't resist them. Well, *she* hadn't actually spent the money on them. Keith had paid for them but she reckoned he'd got his money's worth. He hadn't stopped groping them for six months. It was different now, she thought, he's feeling up some other tits. But you know what they say, plenty of other fish in the sea and Gavin was the one she would not let get away. Pleased with his reaction, she left him and went into the kitchen, a smug smile on her face.

"That was a great night in La Stampa, wasn't it?" Niamh remarked as she poured the tea.

"Yeah. You should have come on to the nightclub. It was great *craic*," Val told her, refusing milk and sugar. "I'm on Atkins," she explained.

Niamh threw her eyes to heaven. Val was so slim, yet she was always on a diet.

"Lesley is fantastic, isn't she?" Val continued. "Pete was glued to her all night. They were practically at it on the dance floor." She grinned, remembering how the bouncers had told them to cool it. "She's been out with him since and they seem to be really into each other. The sex is fantastic, according to Lesley. Lucky her!"

"But she's married!" Niamh exclaimed, her green eyes open wide in shock.

"What difference does that make?" Val asked, looking at Niamh to see if she was serious.

"A lot, I would think," Niamh replied, munching on a biscuit.

"Oh, for God's sake, Niamh, grow up!" Val said scornfully. "Everyone's at it nowadays."

"Gav and I aren't," Niamh replied primly.

"Maybe you're not," Val sneered, "but how can you be sure Gav's not?"

Niamh went pale. "You're not saying . . . ?" She stopped, the lump in her throat preventing her from saying more.

"I'm not saying bloody anything but honestly, Niamh, you're so naïve. Hey, that's a good one, Naïve Niamh!" she laughed. "Cop on. Most men stray. It's the nature of the beast."

She saw with satisfaction that she had rocked her smug sister's boat.

"I'd better be off," she said, a few minutes later. "I'll just pop in and say cheerio to Gav."

As she left, she looked over her shoulder at Niamh and was pleased to see her sister was clearly upset.

It was half-time in the match.

"I'm off, Gav," Val said as she bent over him once more to kiss him goodbye.

Her top sagged even lower this time and he couldn't take his eyes off her fabulous breasts. She had no bra on and he could see her nipples, large and erect. For one crazy moment, he was tempted to take them in his hand and caress them but luckily he stopped himself, just in time. Val didn't move. He knew that she knew what he'd been thinking.

"Very nice," he said, nodding at her breasts. "More than a handful there, eh Val?" he grinned.

"They're all yours. Anytime you want, babe. Just say the word," she whispered, jiggling from side to side.

Holy Christ! He drew back like a scalded cat, realising she was serious. He pushed her away. So, she still had a thing for him then. He'd thought she'd got over that, years ago. She was a little witch. He watched her sashay out of the room, wiggling her bum in that ridiculously short skirt. He knew she was trying to turn him on. And she'd succeeded. God, you'd want to be a saint not to be turned on when it's shoved in your face like that, he thought, adjusting his trousers so that Niamh wouldn't notice the bulge in them.

Val saw him do it and grinned cheekily at him over her shoulder as she let herself out.

Phew! That was close! He was sweating. Can you imagine if he had touched her or Niamh had walked in on them? God, it didn't bear thinking about. Funny thing that, he thought. If this had happened six months ago when he and Niamh were fighting all the time over money, then he might have gone there. But not now – not since Niamh got this job. She'd changed. She was excited and confident and damned hot too. Things were going great between them and he was damned if he was going to let Val ruin that.

The match had resumed so he quickly forgot all about her.

Shortly afterwards, Niamh brought him in a mug of tea and biscuits.

"Thanks, babe," he said, pulling her down for a kiss. "Hey, did you get a look at Val's bazoukas in that top? They're really something. Maybe you could have a boob job like that, if you make money with this crowd!"

"You wouldn't really like me to have breasts that huge, would you?" Niamh asked him, shocked and not a little hurt.

"Why not? I think they're great. Mind you, they don't seem to be enough to keep Keith from straying. Word is that he is hanging around with an eighteen-year-old bimbo." He turned his attention back to his television programme.

"Oh, God! Poor Val. What will she do?" Niamh exclaimed, forgetting her own fears for the moment.

Gavin was engrossed in his football again and didn't hear her. Was it true what Gav had said? Had Keith really met somebody else? Poor Val! Where would she end up?

Niamh went back up to the bedroom and, despite her concern for Val, she lifted her top and perused her breasts. They were small but nice and firm, despite the three kids. She was quite proud of them but were they not enough for

Gav? Did he really want her to have massive boobs? Is that what he fancied in a woman? She would hate to change hers, as Val had. She hoped that he didn't mean what he'd said. And she hoped it wasn't true what Val had said about all men straying. Gav would never do that to her, would he?

She pulled her top down and put her jacket on to go and collect the kids, worrying these things over in her head. Things were just beginning to go right for them. Six of her representatives had already got an order for her. She figured out that she'd earned about €400, in commission alone, this week. It was so exciting. She didn't dare mention this to Gav. He'd be out spending it if he knew about it. No, she had great plans for this money.

Firstly, she was going to clear off their debts. Once this was done, every penny would go into a savings account which she thought of as their "House Account". She was meeting with the bank manager on Tuesday to set this up and would outline her plans to him then. She hoped he would see how determined she was to make a success of the business and realise her dream of owning their own home.

New boobs indeed! Was Gav serious? Not a penny of this money would go on something as ridiculous as massive mammaries!

Chapter 19

Grace arrived at her office shortly before eight on Monday morning, feeling exhausted. Weekends were meant to be for resting but there was no rest where Massimo's family were concerned. She loved them, each and every one, but there were just so many of them – uncles, aunts, cousins, nephews, nieces, grandparents, not to mention his father, brothers, sisters and their families. They all descended on her, every weekend, and she found it utterly exhausting. The kids loved it, of course, and were spoiled rotten by everyone. Massimo was the eldest son and his father, Roberto, had moved in with them after his wife's death so it was the natural gathering place for the family.

The house was perfect for entertaining and they spent every weekend there. It was a beautiful villa, overlooking the sea, about twenty miles from Rome. They had a yacht moored in the harbour and Massimo loved to take all the men and children out in it after Mass on Sunday mornings. Then they would come back, ravenous for lunch, which was always a boisterous, happy, typically Italian family meal. Grace had a cook and a maid but she liked to do a lot of the preparation herself. By the time they all left on Sunday night she was ready to collapse into bed but instead had to lock up and face the drive back into the city, where they had a luxurious apartment.

Up till now she had been able to take Mondays off but because of If the Shoes Fit, Monday looked set to become the busiest day of the week.

She probably could have stayed home today as it was highly unlikely that any of the girls in Ireland would have an order after just one week in operation. However, this was her baby and she really wanted to prove to them all that it could be a success. Roberto had been very sceptical about it and it was only after Carlo had interceded for her and offered to run the Irish side of things, that he had given the go-ahead. Massimo didn't really think it could be viable either but he was supportive of her, as always. She checked her emails anyway and to her delight, saw that Amber, Niamh, Rosie, Tessa and Lesley had all placed an order. And my God, they were good!

She could hardly believe that Niamh had already signed up ten representatives and had twelve more lined up for the following week. What a star! I was right to put my faith in her. Nothing, of course, from Phoebe or Val but in fairness it was early days yet. However, if the others could manage it . . . !

She wanted to ring them immediately and congratulate them but, realising that it was only 7 a.m. in Ireland, had to hold out for another two hours.

When at last she rang, she could hear the pride in their voices as they told her how they had done it. She could feel their excitement and knew they were enjoying it. She was delighted with their enthusiasm and with what they had already planned for the coming week.

She had Carlo with her and he spoke to each of the girls too.

Grace couldn't wait to tell Massimo and Roberto how well the first week had gone. They were both surprised but happy for her.

"I thought I understood women," Roberto said, shrugging his shoulders, "but I obviously underestimated you Irishwomen!" He smiled at her. He was as big a charmer as his two sons and must have broken lots of hearts in his youth. He still had an eye for the ladies and could flirt with the best of them even though he was in his late sixties.

Amber was happier than she'd been for a long time. To her surprise, Pete had called and asked her out to dinner on Friday night.

"I'd love to, but unfortunately I have a party that evening and I won't be finished till nine thirty," she'd explained.

"Oh, that's a pity," he said, disappointment in his voice.

Amber felt sorry for him. He was a sweetie. She'd been thinking about starting to date again, after Tessa's little sermon. So why not with Pete? He was such a pet.

"I could meet you for a quick drink then, if that's okay with you," she said.

"Great," Pete replied, his voice showing his delight. "Where's your party?"

"Here in Malahide. Is it too far for you to travel?"

"Not at all," he told her. "I'll pick you up at nine forty-five, if you'll give me your address."

She did so, thinking that a drink was better than going for dinner on a first date. If things didn't go well, they wouldn't have to spend hours together. She would see how things went over a couple of drinks first and she could always leave if they weren't hitting it off.

She was glad she'd agreed to meet him. Tessa was right. It was time to move on.

She was busy arranging parties and had three lined up for this week and four for the next. It was unbelievably easy. Word of mouth was spreading and women she'd never met were ringing her, asking if they could have a party too. Luckily, she wasn't restricted to her own area for parties. She was having them all over Dublin and had even had a call from a woman in Navan and one in Dundalk, for God's sake! Ireland was her oyster.

She realised that she was lucky she had the freedom to work every night if she chose. Her airline years had acclimatised her to unsociable hours, so it didn't bother her. She felt sorry for poor Tessa who was getting a lot of grief from George. He was not happy with her working at night and was making her life miserable. As for Niamh, she had her own problems, with three small children and no one to support her, except her mother.

She rang Niamh to congratulate her, after hearing from Grace that Niamh had recruited ten reps in the first week.

"Good girl, I knew you would do it," Amber told her.

She could hear the happiness in Niamh's voice. "Amber, this is the best thing that's ever happened to me – well, after the kids and Gav, of course. You know what I mean . . ."

"Of course I do. I feel the same way," Amber assured her. "I'm sticking with parties. I don't know if recruiting reps is for me."

"Oh, it is, Amber," Niamh exclaimed, excitedly. "My reps are holding their own parties this week. It's all business. Delegate – that's my new word," she laughed.

"I never thought of it that way," Amber mused, her interest piqued. "Maybe I'll stick a few posters out. How is Val doing?"

"Not great. Well, she had a bit of trouble with her boyfriend last week which held her up."

Amber could tell that Val had done nothing and Niamh was making excuses for her.

"She came round to me yesterday and I drew up a plan for her," Niamh continued. "I'm also going to go out with her when she starts interviewing."

"You're too soft. Let her bloody well get off her arse and work, like you and I have had to!" Amber couldn't help the outburst. Niamh was far too generous.

"She will, I'm sure," Niamh replied. "I really appreciate your call, Amber. It's great to have friends to share things with."

"Speaking of sharing with friends," Amber continued, "I was hoping the four of us could get together next Saturday evening. I'd like to have you all to supper. Can you make it? Tessa could pick you up on her way and you could get the DART home with Rosie. It should be fun."

"Gosh, Amber, I'd love to," Niamh replied, delighted with the invitation. "Gav goes out every Saturday night so I'll have to check and see if Mam can take the kids, but I'm sure it won't be a problem."

"I do hope she can," Amber replied. "Let me know."

Poor kid, Amber thought. Her husband seems to do nothing to help her. You'd think her mother-in-law would be happy to baby-sit, seeing as how her selfish son won't even give up one night to look after his own kids. Men!

Niamh realised that Amber hadn't mentioned Val or the others so she guessed it would be just their gang, as she thought of them. Ah, well, I'm not my sister's keeper. I must warn Mam not to tell Val where I'm going. She'd be furious.

Tessa was at her wits' end. She was keen to follow up all the leads she'd received but George did not want her going out to work at night. She was feeling very frustrated because, when she did stay in, he barely said five words to her. She couldn't see the point in suffering this fate every night when she could have been out building up her business.

She'd done a big cook-in on Sunday, to make sure she had lots of home-cooked meals in the freezer, but still he wasn't happy. She knew he would not be happy until she packed in this job. She decided that she'd rather pack in George and the way things were going that day wasn't too far off.

On Monday night she decided to make one last effort. Nervously, she sat down opposite him in the study.

"George, I think we should sit down together and discuss our problems," she said, her voice shaking.

He looked up at her from above his glasses, as he lowered his newspaper. "There's only one problem, as far as I'm concerned," he said gruffly, "and that is you spending so much time on this silly job. Once you pack that in, I think our problem will be solved." He went back to his newspaper and continued reading.

She felt like grabbing the paper from his hands.

"This attitude of yours shows me just how bad our problems are and I'm beginning to think they're insurmountable," Tessa retorted sharply. "I'm not willing to give up this 'silly job' as you call it. Why should I? You have your job and I don't complain. I really think that we have to work this out."

"Well, you know my feelings," he replied, closing his newspaper and standing up stiffly. "Now, I'll say goodnight." Turning on his heel, he left her.

She looked sadly after him. She'd hoped, once, that they would be together forever but now she had her doubts. She could, of course, do just what he wanted and pack it in but she could never live with herself if she gave in to his bullying – for that was what it was – plain and simple bullying.

She went up to bed much later, to find that he'd moved all his stuff into the guest room. Okay, George, so be it! She felt sad.

Niamh was over the moon. Her meeting with the bank manager had gone even better than she'd expected. She'd seen the look of respect in his eyes when she told him what she was doing and her plans for the future. She'd presented him with her business plan and it had obviously impressed him. She rushed to her mother's to tell her the good news.

"Mam, I can't believe it. He said that if I can prove to him, in the next six months, that I can earn enough to pay a mortgage, he'll give me one," she spoke rapidly, her eyes glowing. "All I have to do now is save every penny for the deposit. Imagine! Our own house!" She twirled her mother around the kitchen. "It's like a dream. I feel like pinching myself," she laughed excitedly.

"You deserve every bit of it, love." Eileen hugged her, delighted for her daughter and proud of her determination. God knows, she'd need lots of it with that waster, Gavin, contributing nothing. She knew things had got even more difficult for Niamh with that witch Bridget, since she'd started this job. Please God, she'd be able to get out of there soon.

Chapter 20

Pete was late for his meeting with his old friend Tim, who happened to be Grace's brother. Tim sat waiting for him in McDaid's, an old haunt of theirs since their student days in Trinity College. They'd been best friends since the age of seven when Tim's family had moved in next door to Pete's. Although they didn't meet as often since Tim had married Lucy, they still kept in touch. Tim wished Pete would get married and settle down but he knew there were two chances of that: slim and none.

Lucy refused to invite Pete to their dinner parties any more since the time he'd seduced a married friend of hers who, convinced she was in love, had left her husband for him. It hadn't lasted, of course, and now the poor girl was alone and very bitter. As a result, Pete was barred whenever there would be women present although they often invited him on his own or to guys-only nights.

From his teenage years, Tim had been envious of the way Pete could manipulate women and have them eating out of his hand. Pete's mother and five sisters, Tim's own mother and his sister Grace, the teachers at school, and just about every girl who'd crossed his path since, had fallen for his charm. When Tim had met Lucy he'd been terrified of introducing her to his friend, scared that she'd succumb to his charm too but, thank God, Lucy was one of the few women who resisted Pete and had remained immune to him.

Tim had just taken a slug of his Guinness, licking the froth off his upper lip, when he saw Pete coming into the bar.

"Hey, buddy, how are you?" Pete grinned, giving him a high-five.

"Great altogether. And you? How has my sister been treating you?" Tim asked, signalling to the barman to bring the other Guinness.

"Hell, Tim. If you'd told me that Grace had so many gorgeous women working for her, I'd never have hesitated for a second to take the job. I owe you, buddy."

"Oh no," Tim groaned. "You're not hitting on her girls already?"

"You should see them! Even you would be tempted."

"No way, man! I'm happy with my lady," Tim grinned, paying the barman for the pint he put in front of Pete.

"They are simply gorgeous," Pete told him, taking a long slug of the cool Guinness with a sigh of pleasure. "I've been out with one of them – Lesley – but each one is more fabulous than the next. I'm spoilt for choice!" Pete smiled his charming boyish smile, full of enthusiasm.

Tim couldn't fathom it. Pete was in his mid thirties now and he still had women of all ages eating out of his hand. Now it looked like Grace's women were joining the throng.

Grace herself had had a major crush on Pete as a teenager. Thank God she'd got over it fairly quickly and was now happily married in Italy. Tim wondered whether he'd done the right thing, suggesting Pete to Grace when she had asked about a good accountant.

"So who's this girl and what's she like?" Tim was curious.

"Lesley is amazing," said Pete, grinning at his friend. "She has the face of an angel and the body of a sex goddess. What more could a man ask for?"

"But what's she like – as a person?" Tim wanted to know.

"Strange, actually," Pete replied, his brow puckering up as he considered her. "She looks like butter wouldn't melt in her mouth but behind it she's as cold as steel. She knows what she wants and she goes out and takes it. A bit scary, actually, but fascinating too."

"Uh, oh," Tim warned. "Remember *Fatal Attraction*? Be careful, Pete!"

Pete blanched a little at the memory of the film that Tim had insisted he watch.

"Is she married?" Tim asked, aware that Pete had the morals of a rabbit.

"Well, yes, but not happily," Pete replied, his blue eyes sincere.

"God, Pete, you're priceless," Tim laughed. "Are you never going to grow up and settle down?"

"Why?" Pete asked, innocently. "I've plenty of time."

"You're thirty-six-bloody-years-old, that's why! It's more than time, though God help the poor girl that gets you."

"Well, Lesley is most definitely not wife material – more

the sexy mistress type," he laughed. "But I do have a date with another girl, Amber, for this Friday night and she is much more wife material. You'd like her."

Tim raised his eyes to heaven. "You're impossible."

"I know," Pete agreed with him sheepishly and Tim laughed, not able to be serious with him for very long.

Amber had come up with a brilliant idea. She'd decided that, as it was coming up to Christmas, she would contact all her male ex-colleagues and suggest that they might surprise their wives with a beautiful pair of shoes for Christmas. All those guys who'd constantly asked her advice on buying presents for their wives. Hell, she'd often gone herself and bought the gifts for them. She could just imagine their wives' delight on Christmas morning, to find a beautiful pair of designer shoes under the tree instead of the usual red or black frilly underwear, which was what men, everywhere, thought women wanted. Yes, what a good idea. Why, she might even target all the men of Ireland!

She rang her old friend, Luke O'Brien, a pilot that she'd often worked with and a real sweetie. He was delighted to hear from her and she told him what she was doing.

"So, I was thinking that maybe you'd be interested in buying shoes for Emma this Christmas. I remember how you never knew what to get for her," she laughed.

Luke was silent for a moment. "Haven't you heard, Amber? Emma and I divorced earlier this year."

"Oh my God, Luke, I'm so sorry, I hadn't heard," she said, her voice shocked. "How are you coping?"

"Fine – considering," he said.

He didn't sound it.

"I understand, believe me. I've been in the same boat,"

Amber told him, her voice gentle. "You know Dermot and I divorced last year?"

"Yes, I heard and I'm sorry, Amber," he said guiltily. "I should have contacted you but with the problems in my own marriage at the time . . . Well, you know how it is."

"I sure do! We must meet up some time and compare notes. I take it you won't be in the market for designer shoes then?"

"Actually, I might. I need to buy a present for my co-pilot, Fiona. I've been racking my brains trying to think what to get her this Christmas. Designer shoes might be just the thing for her." He sounded relieved.

"Great! Would you like me to call around and show you what I have?" Amber asked. "I'm free Thursday night."

"Yeah. Look, why don't I try and get some of my buddies round for a beer. Who knows, maybe they'll be interested in buying for their other halves too. You know how hopeless we men are in that department," he laughed. "I'll give you a call tomorrow."

Amber was delighted. What a pet he is, she thought. That Emma was a damn fool to let him go. She must ask Susie to fill her in on the details.

Luke rang back that evening. "Thursday night it is," he told her. "The guys all think it's a great idea." He hesitated. "Would you like to come around for a bite to eat first?"

"That would be lovely. It will give us a chance to catch up. What time?"

"Six okay?" Luke asked.

"Great. See you then!" Amber said, looking forward to meeting him again.

Lesley came off the phone smiling broadly.

"Yeeesssss!" she cried, punching the air with her hand.

She'd been talking to her sister, Yvonne, giving her a blow-by-blow account of her date last night with Pete. And what a night it was! Yvonne had been green with envy when she'd heard about Pete. *She'd* never scored with an accountant and Lesley could hear the jealousy in her sister's voice. There was fierce rivalry between the two sisters. In fact, there was fierce rivalry between Lesley and whoever else she came up against. She was ambitious and greedy and always had to be top-dog. Scoring with Pete had been a huge feather in her cap.

She'd seen him chatting up Niamh the night of the dinner but to her relief Niamh had turned him down primly. Why were men so stupid? They all fell for that little-girl-big-vulnerable-eyes look that Niamh had. They felt that she needed protection. Bah! She was stronger than any of them. Then she saw him chatting up Amber and realised that he fancied her too – the stuck-up cow. Ha! She'll realise soon enough that she has me to reckon with, Lesley thought. Thank God, Amber hadn't come to La Cave after the dinner that night. She hadn't and now Pete was all hers.

They'd been so hot for each other in the nightclub that the bouncers had asked them to cool it on the dance floor. She smiled, remembering, and then they'd had sex in the back of his car afterwards. It had been so exciting. She shivered at the memory. They'd met for a drink last week and had sex again – in the back of his car – again. Okay, it *was* a gorgeous BMW but she was beginning to want more. She would like him to take her out somewhere nice and have sex somewhere other than the back of his Beamer. When he'd rung on Monday to ask her to meet him last night, she'd decided to put her foot down. He had to show her some respect.

"I'd really like to go out somewhere nice and make love in a bed for a change," she'd informed him.

"Sweetheart, we have to be discreet," he'd replied. "After all, you're a married woman. We have to be careful."

"It doesn't bother me," she'd said sulkily.

Pete felt a little alarmed at this but his need to have her again overcame his fears.

"Okay, tell you what. I'll book us in somewhere nice if you can organise to stay the night. Can you manage that, sweetie?" he asked.

She was thrilled. "No problem," she'd replied, excited at the prospect.

It was even better than she'd hoped. She'd had a fabulous night. He certainly knew how to please a woman and she'd hardly been able to walk this morning, after all the sex. She'd delighted in telling Yvonne all the intimate details and hearing the envy in her sister's voice. She'd been on a high all day and had expected him to call, but he hadn't and she was getting anxious. She tried calling him but got his voicemail. She could barely concentrate on her work because of him and she absolutely had to, if she was to top the sales league and win that car. She was determined to win though she knew that Amber and that namby-pamby Niamh and even that long-legged gazelle, Tessa, were out to challenge her. She wasn't worried about them though. She felt very confident of winning.

Chapter 21

Luke enveloped Amber in a big bear hug when she arrived at his house in Sutton on Thursday night.

"God, you're a sight for sore eyes. You look marvellous," he said, taking her coat and the bottle of wine she proffered. "Single life is obviously agreeing with you!"

"You should have seen me two months ago," she replied, grimacing. "I was a mess."

He poured them both a glass of wine and led her into the kitchen where he was putting the finishing touches to a delicious-smelling Thai curry.

"Let me serve this up and you can tell me all while we eat," he said.

"Gosh, I never knew you could cook like this," Amber exclaimed, sniffing at the pot.

"Necessity, I'm afraid," he said ruefully. "I have about five signature dishes and that's it."

Over dinner, they exchanged the stories of their marriage break-ups. She told him of her drinking, holding back nothing. She described her downward spiral until this job which, she said, had saved her. It was amazing how easily they slipped back into their old close friendship. It was as if they'd seen each other only last week, not ten years ago. She told him about Grace, this new venture of hers and of her great life in Italy.

"She's as elegant as ever," Amber told him. He'd always been very fond of Grace but had lost touch with her also. "Mmmm – this curry is divine – best I've ever tasted."

"Thank you." Luke glowed with pleasure at the compliment. "I'm sorry we lost contact, Amber, but I don't know if you knew that Emma was always very jealous of you. That's why I drifted away. It just wasn't worth the hassle from her," he said, shaking his head. "I remember how pleased she was when you resigned."

"Silly," she replied, as she held her plate out for another portion of the delicious curry.

"Yes, indeed," he agreed. "How did you stop drinking? Did you go to AA?"

"No. I just stopped. I wasn't quite an alcoholic, though I was certainly headed that way." She grimaced. "Funny, I'm so involved in this business now that it never crosses my mind to pour myself a drink. I love a glass of wine if I'm out for a meal or if I'm out with friends, of course, but I don't drink on my own any more."

"Good girl! I could have gone down that road too but with my job that would have been suicide.

"Now, let's see these shoes of yours," he said, after they'd finished coffee and rose from the table.

Luke would not have been a connoisseur of women's shoes but as Amber opened the boxes he could see how beautifully made they were.

"I'm not surprised," he smiled. "Grace always did have exquisite taste."

He chose the pale gold sandals for Fiona and then decided to buy two more pairs, for his sisters. He had found out Fiona's size from one of her friends and he now rang his mother to find out his sisters' sizes.

"Size 38. Same as me," she told him.

He wondered if that was a hint.

"I'd really love to get the grey patent ones for my mother," he told Amber later, stroking the soft leather. "She adores shoes. But do you think they're a bit high for a sixty-two-year-old?"

"You're never too old for a pair of glamorous heels and these are quite a classic style. Even though they're high, they're extremely comfortable," Amber assured him. "If she doesn't like them, I'll take then back," she added.

"Okay, that settles it. I'll take them too." He rubbed his hands together. "Great, that's most of my Christmas shopping done, then." He smiled at her, pleased.

"You're a gem. This is so exciting," Amber said happily.

"Well, I've no doubt you'll have many, many more sales," he said. "You could sell snow to the Eskimos. I know you'll be a great success."

She helped him clear away and set out the shoes so that his friends could see them. She should have known that Luke never did things by half. One hour later, there were twelve of his friends in the living-room, drinking beer and inspecting the shoes they were hoping to buy for their wives or girlfriends. Amber wondered if some of them were buying for both, as they bought two identical pairs, in two different sizes. Well, that's none of my business, she decided. A sale is a sale!

There was great merriment and joking and she had to model all the different styles for them. A few of them hit on her and she suspected that they asked for her number, not to phone in their girlfriend's shoe size, as they claimed, but so that they could contact her.

It was a huge success and she sold twenty pairs of shoes in total. She couldn't believe it. Some of the guys told her that they had friends who they were sure would be interested and they took brochures with them and promised to contact her. When they had left, she hugged Luke and thanked him. "Your mother's shoes are on me," she told him.

"Don't be daft," he replied. "I'm delighted to be able to help. And it was a great night, wasn't it?" he smiled. "I'm delighted we're back in touch."

"Me too," she told him, kissing him goodbye.

Pete picked Amber up at her apartment on Friday night. He let out a low whistle . . . "Very nice pad," he said, handing her a bouquet of freesia.

"Oh how lovely," she said, burying her nose in their wonderful scent. "I love freesia!"

"I had a feeling you were a freesia kind of girl," he said, beaming his irresistible, boyish smile. He looked like a small boy who had done something wonderful and expected a pat on the head.

Gosh, he's charming, Amber thought. Tessa definitely has him all wrong.

She'd decided not to say anything to any of the girls about her date with Pete, just in case it all went horribly wrong.

They walked up to Gibney's, her local pub, which was

jam-packed as usual. They luckily found a seat and Pete ordered two glasses of Chardonnay.

"I would have thought that you were a pint man," she said laughingly.

"Oh, I am," he replied, "but when I'm out with a beautiful woman I like her to think that I'm sophisticated." He gave her that quirky, boyish smile again and Amber laughed at his honesty.

She relaxed then and started to enjoy herself. Pete was funny, and entertaining and charming, but she felt no sexual attraction towards him. The chemistry she felt with Carlo was missing. Pete had none of Carlo's smouldering sexuality. He was rather more like an enthusiastic little boy.

She enjoyed his company and she sensed that he was somehow lonely.

"Have you never been married?" she asked him curiously.

"No. I came close a couple of times but they had a lucky escape," he grinned. "I suppose I've never met the right woman."

She thought she heard a wistful note in his voice.

With a shock Pete realised, as he said this, that it was probably true. Looking at Amber, her blonde waves falling on her shoulders, blue eyes sparkling and her face alive and glowing – he wondered if she was the one. She was intelligent and bright and he loved her vivacious personality. She was certainly very different to the girls he usually dated.

"How about you? Is there anyone special in your life?" he asked.

"There was," she replied, "but we divorced just over a year ago."

"Do you want to talk about it?" he asked her. As soon as he said it he saw the closed expression that came onto her face and knew she didn't want to go there.

"No," she replied.

The waiter brought two more glasses of wine and they chatted comfortably. He told her about his sisters and had her laughing at their antics. He obviously loved them very much. She told him about her years in Aer Lingus and her travels. They were having such a good time that they decided to have one more glass.

"I really should have a coffee as I'm driving but I don't suppose there's a hope in hell of getting one here," he remarked, seeing how busy the bar staff were. "I haven't had much to eat today."

"Me neither," Amber told him. "Let's have one more glass of wine and we can get fish and chips on the way home and I'll ply you with coffee," she giggled, feeling the effect of the wine.

They left the pub in high spirits and bought ray and chips, in what Amber told him was the best chipper in Dublin.

"Oh, you're a real Dub," he told her, grinning. "Do you know they don't sell ray and chips anywhere else in Ireland? Only we Dubs are lucky enough to enjoy it."

"Lucky us," she said, not able to resist picking at the fish as they walked home.

"You'll have to come up and see my shoes," she said as she opened the door.

"Oh, not your etchings?" he asked, laughing.

"Definitely not," she giggled. Then it dawned on her that maybe he expected her to give him more than a cup of coffee. Surely not, she thought with alarm. He must know I'm not that type of girl.

They ate their fish and chips, both pouring vinegar on the chips. He was amazed at how alike their tastes were.

As she was turning on the espresso machine he came up behind her and put his arms around her waist. She froze. Turning towards him, she said in a cool voice, "Pete, please. When I asked you up for coffee, I meant coffee. Nothing more!"

Pete felt as though she'd doused him with icy water. He wasn't used to this. They'd had a wonderful evening so why was she behaving like this? He'd half hoped that she'd ask him to stay the night. Looks like that's not going to happen, he thought, feeling rejected. Did she not fancy him? He sure fancied the pants off her. She was perfect in every way. Maybe she was playing hard to get. That's it, he thought. These classy birds didn't like to let on that they had sexual feelings. She'd come round. She probably wanted to be wooed.

They drank their coffee and got back to their previous easy conversation as if the moment hadn't happened but Pete couldn't help feeling a little rejected.

Driving home he wondered whether Tim was right. Was he getting too old for this lark? Was he losing his touch? He broke into a sweat just thinking about it.

Chapter 22

On Saturday night Gavin answered the door to the most stunning woman he'd ever seen. He couldn't have been more surprised if it had been Angelina Jolie herself.

"Oh, I think you've got the wrong house," he mumbled, overwhelmed by the gorgeous woman standing on his doorstep.

"Tessa!" Niamh cried out, coming to the door and hugging this beautiful creature.

Gavin was dumbfounded. Even Bridget was speechless for once. This woman could have been one of the stars walking down the Red Carpet on any of the awards shows that she watched on TV. She was beautiful. And calling for Niamh – well, I never, Bridget thought. Wonders will never cease!

Gavin was even more impressed when he saw the car Tessa was driving. My God, a Porsche! I wouldn't mind driving off with that babe, in that car, he thought enviously.

"Nice car," Niamh laughed, as she strapped herself into the passenger seat. "Gav is probably green with envy."

"Your husband is quite a looker," Tessa remarked.

"Oh, thanks!" said Niamh, blushing, but she looked a little troubled at the compliment.

Tessa knew enough about men to recognise Gavin's undeniable sex appeal. She wondered if Niamh had a problem keeping him for herself. She hoped not.

As they crossed the M50 they chatted about how they'd done over the past two weeks and they both agreed that sales were much better than anything they'd expected.

"I love it," Niamh told her. "I can't wait to get out of bed every morning to get going at it again."

"Me too!" Tessa agreed. "The response is even better than I'd hoped. I'm having a problem with my partner, however." She sighed, her mouth turning down at the corners. "He really doesn't want me doing it."

"Can't you talk him round?" Niamh asked her. "I did with Gav."

"Unfortunately not. He's a bit more set in his ways, I'm afraid. But I've no notion of giving it up," Tessa said, her chin set defiantly.

"I'm glad."

They arrived at Amber's apartment just moments after Rosie and there was a great flurry of kisses and giggles as they all greeted each other. Tessa insisted that they see Amber's shoe-room before they even sat down. They were as bowled over by it as every other woman who'd ever seen it.

"My God, I've never seen the like," Rosie exclaimed.

"What size are you, Amber?" Niamh asked her and pretended to be crestfallen when Amber informed her that they were not the same size.

Amber popped open a bottle of champagne and when she had handed them all a glass they toasted each other.

"Okay, let's hear all the news," Amber said, looking at them expectantly.

"Well, Niamh has done fantastically well," Rosie told them. "How many reps do you have now, Niamh?"

"Twenty-five, last count," she told them, blushing a little. "I can hardly believe it. I never imagined it would go so well. Just think," she looked around at the others, smiling, "they're all out there now making money for me while I sit here quaffing champagne."

"I'll drink to that," Amber laughed, refilling their flutes.

They had a wonderful night, regaling each other with stories of the people they'd met. After listening to Niamh they all began to think that maybe her modus operandi was the way to go. Imagine having people earning money for you while you sipped champagne – that sounded good! Tessa wondered if recruiting representatives to do the selling for her would be better for her relationship with George than having to go out selling herself, at parties. She mentioned this to the girls.

"Has George still not accepted it?" Amber asked her.

"'Fraid not. I don't know why he's so against it. The nights I'm in, we do nothing anyway. I watch TV and he goes into his study and listens to music or works. It's as if he's jealous of the job." She shook her head slowly. "I really don't know what to do about it. The atmosphere at home is terrible. I can't wait to get out of the house."

"That's ridiculous," Amber said. "He's obviously very out of touch with today's world."

"I think he's just insecure. He's afraid of losing you," Rosie remarked, with her usual wisdom. "He wants you at

196

home, dependant on him. He probably feels that this business is making you independent again."

"You're maybe right," Tessa agreed. "I know he feels insecure because I don't want to get married but, to be honest, I'm glad now we didn't. I just wish he'd accept that I really want to do this."

"Gav felt a bit like that in the beginning," Niamh butt in, "but he's accepting it a bit more now. He's beginning to realise that I'll be bringing in money so he'll have an easier life."

"Is he helping you at all, by baby-sitting?" Amber asked.

"Not really, but I can manage. Mam is great."

She then told them about her visit to the bank manager, her eyes shining as she recounted what he'd said. "I'm so excited. It's made me even more motivated to do well."

"Oh Niamh, I'm so happy for you and I know you'll do it," said Rosie, giving her a hug. The others followed suit. She was such an inspiration to them.

Once Tessa put George out of her mind, she started to relax and feel like her old self. It was great to be having a girls' night again. She hadn't laughed so much in ages. Niamh had them all in stitches recounting her experiences.

"I had a reply from a woman who sounded awfully strange so I asked her to meet me in a hotel, instead of going to her home. Luckily I did! I nearly died when I arrived and found this guy, dressed in drag; full make-up, earrings, the works and wearing heels." She stopped for a moment, enjoying the looks of amazement on the faces of the other girls. "He was really interested in the shoes and asked if we could make them in size ten. I couldn't wait to get out of there!" she laughed. "I needn't tell you, I didn't sign him up."

"Why not?" Amber asked. "He probably has a whole crowd of fellow-transvestites who could be customers. Think of the business you're losing!"

"Okay, I'll give you his number. You can sign him up," Niamh replied, calling her bluff.

"No, he's not in my area. I can't have him, he's all yours," Amber shot right back while Tessa and Rosie almost collapsed with laughter.

"Actually, he's probably just a cross-dresser, as they prefer to be known nowadays. The word transvestite has more of a sexual connotation," Tessa informed them.

"How do you know all this?" Amber asked her.

"Experience," Tessa replied, nonplussed. "Believe me, in the modelling world you come across every possible sexual computation."

"Can you imagine Carlo's reaction if I started sending him orders for sizes ten and eleven?" Niamh asked them.

"Speaking of Carlo – are you all meeting up with him this week?" Rosie asked.

They all nodded their assent.

"He's coming out with me on Thursday morning," Niamh informed them. "He wants to see how I recruit and sign up girls. I'm so nervous about it."

"Don't be daft," Amber reassured her. "You've been so successful he probably wants to see how you do it!"

"He's coming out with me on Wednesday evening and Amber on Thursday," said Tessa. "He's here to help us and see how we operate," she added, hoping to reassure Niamh some more.

"He's meeting me to help me with my paperwork on Wednesday afternoon," Rosie told them. "Isn't he just the dishiest?"

The girls looked at Rosie, surprised at her remark.

"I'm not blind you know, just because I'm a widow," she laughed at them.

"Dishy isn't the word," Niamh agreed.

"I think he fancies you, Amber," Rosie remarked.

"He more than fancies her but she's not interested," Tessa added, disapproval in her voice.

"Definitely not interested," Amber informed them.

"Why not? He could be your knight in shining armour," Niamh sighed.

"They went out with the Round Table," Amber snorted.

"*The lady doth protest too much, methinks*," Rosie murmured.

Amber was fed up of them constantly throwing her at Carlo. Time to stop it once and for all!

"Actually," she said sweetly, "I met Pete for a drink last night."

Having dropped this bombshell, she turned on her heel and went to serve up the supper.

The others looked at each other in stunned silence.

Tessa couldn't believe what she'd just heard. "Did she just say she's been out with Pete?" she asked the other two.

"I'm afraid so," Rosie said, equally perturbed and thinking that Amber was no match for that silver-tongued-devil, charming though he was. She was bound to get hurt.

Niamh had paled visibly. Besides the fact that Pete had tried to chat her up at the dinner, she knew that he'd been seeing Lesley. Was Amber aware of this? She doubted it. She didn't know what to do. Should she say something? Not much point now, she supposed. Oh God! If what Val said was true he was two-timing both of them. What a mess! She put it out of her mind. No point in spoiling the evening. Nobody mentioned Pete again.

They had a wonderful night together as their friendship blossomed. They all agreed that they would have to get together like this on a regular basis.

Amber and Tessa sat chatting after Rosie and Niamh had left.

"I'm really sorry that George is not coming around," Amber commiserated with her. "What are you going to do about it?"

"I don't know. Things are really bad at the moment," Tessa stared sombrely into her glass of Sancerre. "Things are so tense at home that I feel stressed all the time. That's not doing my heart any good," she grimaced.

"Would you consider leaving him?" Amber asked. "It might shake him up a bit."

"I've thought about it, Amber, but I hate giving up on us. I'd really hoped it would work." She looked so dejected that Amber's heart went out to her. "I've already got one divorce behind me," Tessa continued, "and I feel such a failure because I don't seem able to sustain a permanent relationship."

"I know how you feel," Amber replied, in a heartfelt voice. "That's why I don't want to get involved again. I'm afraid it wouldn't work out."

"What about Pete?" Tessa asked her. "I can't believe you went out with him and yet you won't go out with Carlo."

"Pete is a sweetheart and we had a great night," Amber smiled, "but I wouldn't be serious about him. Carlo's another story. I'd be much more afraid of getting involved with him."

So she does fancy him, Tessa thought glumly.

"If you leave George where would you go?" Amber wanted to know. "Would you go back to London?"

"No, I don't want to go back there, that's for sure," Tessa replied. "Now that I've started this job, I really want to stay here and make a success of it."

"Well, you can always come and stay with me for a while," Amber suggested. "Maybe a trial separation would make George see sense."

"Perhaps you're right but I doubt it," Tessa said gloomily. "I'll think about it and thanks for the offer. I just may take you up on it."

Gavin was having a few pints with the lads in Murphy's. Some of them had been drinking since late afternoon and were more than a little drunk when Val entered the pub. She was wearing tight skinny jeans and a low-cut vest top which left nothing to the imagination.

"*Whoar!* There goes one hot babe," Billy, one of the guys, remarked, letting out a low whistle.

Gavin turned to check out the babe in question. "Hey, that's my sister-in-law you're talking about!"

"Lucky sod! Call her over and let's get a better look at that smashing bod," Ryan, a serious lecher, said.

"Hey, Val!" Gavin called out to her. "Come on over and say hello."

She sashayed over, swinging her butt, thinking what great luck it was to meet him here, sans Niamh.

Gavin grinned at her, knowing that she was putting on a show for the guys.

"Why aren't you at the dinner with the girls tonight?" he asked her.

"What dinner? What girls?" Val didn't know what he was talking about.

"Your shoe crowd. A fabulous-looking bird called for Niamh tonight. She was one hot babe," he whistled. "The spit of Demi Moore – Tessa, I think her name was."

Val was furious. Imagine! Tessa called for Niamh to go to a dinner! Why wasn't I invited? Why hadn't Niamh mentioned it? She was more annoyed still that Gavin seemed to fancy Tessa.

"Didn't know you liked flat chests," she snapped back at him, leaning towards him so that he could see that hers was anything but flat.

"*Miaow!*" he said laughing. "Don't worry, babe, yours are definitely way more to my taste."

She sat down on his lap, putting her arm around his neck and leaning into him.

His pals started teasing him.

"Hey, Gav, don't be greedy, share her around!" Ryan said.

"Why do all the birds always go for him?" Billy grumbled.

It was obvious to one and all that Val wasn't interested in any of them. She wanted *him*. She was flaunting herself at him now, wriggling about on his lap, and she knew that she had turned him on.

Gavin was angry with himself and realised that this was going too far. He wished she'd leave him alone.

"Better go join your friends," he said, pushing her up.

She took the hint and walked away, but the lads teased him unmercifully all night.

Chapter 23

Niamh had a problem. Her first delivery of shoes arrived on Monday morning and as the deliveryman carried box after box into the tiny living-room, Bridget stood, arms akimbo, her scowl deepening with every new box that appeared. This was Niamh's first order and already the tiny living-room was full. Where was she going to put next week's order which was twice as big? She'd have to think of something, and quick, if they weren't to be evicted by Bridget who was threatening that right now.

"You're not turning my home into a warehouse, Miss!" she shrieked. "Look at it, for God's sake! I can't even sit down to watch telly!"

"Calm down, Bridget, I'll find a solution, somehow," Niamh said. She had no idea how but obviously this wouldn't work out.

Admittedly, the boxes wouldn't be there for long as she planned to deliver them straight away but the following week's deliveries would be much bigger and would pose more of a problem.

She had been lucky enough to find an old school friend, Sharon, to help her deliver the shoes. Sharon drove a massive, luxurious Range Rover. Her husband, Dean, was in business but what business exactly nobody could say. One thing was for sure, he was loaded. Niamh had often wondered where he got his money. She'd heard he was a car dealer but surely they didn't make that much. She'd said as much to Gavin

"I wouldn't ask, if I were you," Gavin had told her. "He's dealing more than cars, that's for sure."

Niamh didn't want to believe that but, still, they did seem to be awfully well off. There were rumours of massage parlours and brothels and, Lord forbid, even drugs and she hoped, for Sharon's sake, that it was just that – rumours. She was sure that her friend knew nothing of her husband's dealings though she seemed happy enough to be spending his money.

Niamh had been wearing the red shoes at the school gate one morning when Sharon, whose daughter Willow was in the same class as the twins, had spotted them and practically had an orgasm on the spot.

"Oh my God, they're divine! You have to tell me where you got them," she'd cried.

When Niamh explained that she was selling them, Sharon was over the moon and insisted on going home with her to see the rest of the collection.

"Oh my God, they're fabulous," she'd cried, when she saw the other shoes. "I want them all. How did you get this job? I'd love something like that. I simply adore shoes."

"Why don't you become a rep for me?" Niamh had

said, grabbing the opportunity. "You can hold parties or sell to your friends."

"Gosh, I'd love that. That'd be fantastic," Sharon had exclaimed excitedly. "I'm so bored now that Willow has started school."

Niamh signed her up on the spot and when she mentioned that she was going to have to hire a taxi to deliver her orders, Sharon exclaimed, "Don't be so silly! Don't even think of hiring a taxi!" She was adamant. "I'd be delighted to drive you around to do your deliveries. I'm free all day while Willow is at school. Please say yes!"

Niamh began to understand that despite all her money Sharon was lonely, and from her own point of view, it was a terrific bonus that she wouldn't have to pay for a taxi. Besides, she'd enjoy Sharon's company as she did her rounds.

She sorted out the deliveries and invoices, Bridget glowering in the background all the while. She was just about finished when Sharon arrived, rearing to go. They had good fun and her reps were delighted to get their first delivery of shoes. By lunchtime they were done and when Sharon refused to take petrol money from her, Niamh insisted on taking her for lunch to Joel's.

"I've haven't had so much fun in ages," Sharon exclaimed, her eyes shining. "I'm really glad you let me help, Niamh. I'm so bored at home all day. I just love anything to do with shoes and it's great to have an interest like this. Thanks so much. I really appreciate you letting me help."

Niamh felt that she was the one who should be saying thanks and felt sorry for Sharon, who appeared so humble and grateful. Seemingly, Dean was never home and Sharon was obviously very lonely. Niamh appreciated her help and was happy to have her on board. Next, she had to sort out the storage problem. She confided the problem to Sharon.

"Leave it with me," Sharon said confidently. "I'll think of something."

Niamh couldn't imagine what.

Another problem Niamh was discovering was that although she was on the road recruiting every minute that the kids were at school, there was still a lot of paperwork to be done at home and she knew it would get increasingly difficult as the business grew. Gavin was no help – he didn't even want to baby-sit occasionally and Bridget was more of a hindrance than anything else, constantly interrupting and complaining about the children. With Bridget on her case she couldn't very well put them in front of the telly or let them watch DVDs all day, although they'd have been quite happy to do just that. She was mulling over this problem when she had a brainwave.

She wrapped the kids up well and walked them over to her mother's house. Eileen was delighted to see them and welcomed them with open arms. The kids felt so free there. They could run around and make as much noise as they liked. Her mother never minded, not like that battle-axe Bridget. They were so happy here.

As always, the first thing Eileen did was put on the kettle for a cup of tea.

"Mam, I have an idea. Could I have my old bedroom back?" Niamh looked at her mother hopefully. "I can't work in Bridget's. The kids have no freedom there and I thought that if I could come here every day after school, until tea-time, I could work on the computer in my bedroom and pay you to baby-sit." She crossed her fingers behind her back, anxiously waiting for her mother's reply.

"Don't be ridiculous," Eileen replied. "I couldn't take money to baby-sit my own grandchildren!" She laughed at the notion as she set out the mugs and the scones she'd baked earlier.

"Of course you can. It would mean so much to me. I'm earning it now and you can use the extra few bob, for holidays or whatever. Please say yes!"

"Of course you can do that, sweetheart! I'd love it. It would be great to have you here every day – it's lonely here with all of you gone. I'll clear out the room tonight. But I'm not taking any money!"

Niamh decided to let the money issue lie for the moment – but she would make sure her mother accepted payment. "Great, Mam! And, you know, I won't be working all the time so when I'm not we can take the kids to the park or for outings."

"It'll be wonderful!" Eileen's eyes were shining.

Niamh was delighted that she'd thought of it.

As she sat munching a warm scone, Niamh told her mother about Sharon and how well the deliveries had gone.

"I'm really glad," Eileen said kindly. "I always liked Sharon and felt very sorry for her and now that she's married to that crook, she could do with a good friend."

"Is he so bad?" Niamh asked, frowning.

"Worse," her mother said with a snort. "He's a sleazebag."

Niamh reached for another scone. "Mam, you'll have to stop all this baking when I'm here – otherwise I'll be as big as a house."

Just then the kids rushed in, all excited because there was a spider in the bath. The girls were squealing but Ian wanted to catch him in a jar.

"Some things never change," Eileen laughed, going to get rid of the offender.

Lesley was in a state. It was Monday afternoon and she hadn't heard from Pete since the previous Wednesday. She hoped he was okay and that he hadn't been in an accident or anything. You never knew these days! She couldn't think of any other reason why he wouldn't have contacted her. She tried his mobile again – for the umpteenth time. She got his voicemail once again. Damn! Then finally, the long awaited call. She was overjoyed. Pete wanted to meet her that night.

"Where have you been?" she demanded. "I've been worried sick."

"Long story, sweetheart," he replied. "I'll tell you when we meet." God, I'd better come up with something, he thought irritably. Why can't women just be glad when we do ring? He was still smarting from Amber's rejection.

Later that evening, as Niamh was sitting watching *Coronation Street* with Bridget, Sharon rang. Gavin was, of course, out with the lads.

"Is this going to go on every night?" her mother-in-law demanded, as Niamh left to take the call. The tension in the house was becoming unbearable.

Sharon sounded really excited. "Niamh, great news! Dean says you can use our garage to store your deliveries. What do you think?"

What do I think? I think I have to get out of here as soon as possible, Niamh quipped to herself.

"Are you sure, Sharon?" she asked. "Is Dean really okay with it?"

"Absolutely!" Sharon sounded very positive. "We have a huge double garage but we never put the cars in it. Oh please say yes, Niamh."

Niamh smiled at her friend's enthusiasm. Obviously, Sharon was really keen for her to accept and it would certainly solve her problem – for the moment anyway.

"Well, if you're absolutely sure then I'd be delighted," she replied.

Sharon was thrilled. Niamh realised that she was even lonelier than she'd suspected so maybe they would both benefit. In fact, if business continued to grow she would need to enlist help and who better than Sharon? She'd give it some thought.

Returning to the living-room, she ignored Bridget's scowl and smiled sweetly at her. Thank God, she'll see less of us from now on, Niamh thought, and by this time next year we should be in our own place.

Lesley took extra care getting dressed, hoping that tonight Pete would take her back to his place. She'd told Paul, her husband, that she was going out with Val and would probably spend the night with her. He accepted this information with his usual calm and went back to his golf programme. He'd given up on Lesley years ago. She did exactly as she pleased – and he didn't have the balls to stop her. His escape was the sports channel on the TV.

Lesley threw her eyes to heaven as she left the house. Honestly, you'd think he'd show some interest in what she did. But no! All he cared about were the bloody sports, on the bloody television. He'd never played a single sport in his whole life but there he sat, night after night, glued to the damn thing. It didn't matter which sport: football, rugby, golf, hurling, motor racing, tennis, darts, horse racing – he watched them all, regardless. He even watched the cricket for God's sake! I mean, who the hell understands cricket? It's the most boring game in the world – when you're in, you're out and when you're out, you're in – I mean, I ask you! What kind of idiots play such a stupid game? And what kind of idiots sit watching it on TV? With a toss of her head she turned her thoughts to more pleasant things – Pete Clancy and the fantastic time they would have together.

She'd always been the cool one when it came to men but Pete was different. He was getting under her skin and besides what a catch! An accountant! She'd had lots of affairs before but none of them had been as exciting as Pete. She had a gut-feeling that he would be *the* one to help her escape from her hum-drum marriage.

He'd asked her to meet him in a small pub in Kilmainham. She would love to have gone to one of the big plush hotels in the city but Pete said they had to be careful – because of her husband. Well, she had no intention of spending the rest of her life with Paul so it didn't worry her too much, one way or the other. She was wearing a low-cut, flimsy top and skin-tight leather jeans and she enjoyed the stir she caused amongst the men who, distracted from their pints, watched her undulate across the room to kiss Pete. She could tell that he was hot for her as she bent down to him. She was pretty turned on herself!

After two drinks, he suggested they leave and she smiled smugly, thinking he couldn't wait to have her and was probably taking her to his pad. She was dying to see it. To her surprise, he drove into the Phoenix Park and, parking in a quiet secluded spot, pulled her to him.

"Hey, what's all this?" she asked, coquettishly. "Can't you wait till we get into bed?"

"I'm sorry, sweetheart," he said, opening his big blue eyes wide. "I probably should have said something before now, but I'm afraid I have to leave early tonight. I should be at a business dinner right now but I told them I'd be late." He cupped her face in his hands and slowly ran his tongue over her upper lip.

Ooooohhhh, she loved the way he did this and she found herself getting aroused. "I thought we'd be spending the night together," she pouted. "It was so fantastic last Wednesday. Don't you want another night like that?" She looked at him sexily from under her long black lashes.

"Of course I do, sweetheart," he replied silkily, "but I thought having this little time was better than no time at all. Don't you agree?" He started on her lower lip now.

"Mmmmm," she murmured. "I don't know . . ."

"I did give up the dinner for you," he said in a hurt voice. "Come on, baby, I'll make it up to you," he said, slipping her top from her shoulders.

Once again, they had sex in the back of his Beamer.

Chapter 24

Carlo arrived in Ireland on Wednesday morning and met up with all seven women over the next two days. He quickly saw who was working and who was not and was pleased to be able to help those who needed his advice. He soon realised that Phoebe was a disaster and wouldn't last the pace. Val had got off to a very slow start but she seemed to be trying harder now. Lesley was very determined and was doing extremely well – but there was something about her that disturbed him. He saw the way she bullied her reps and treated them with utter disdain. They seemed to take it from her and he had to concede that her sales were terrific. Still, it wasn't how he liked to do business and he knew Grace would not approve either.

Lesley had mentioned to him, casually, that she was dating Pete. Was Pete out of his mind? Carlo would have to have a word with him and see if it was true. She was a married woman, for goodness sake. Carlo had no time for infidelity.

He was delighted to see that business was going great for the other girls. Tessa and Amber had more demand for parties than they could handle and he advised them to delegate these. It would be impossible for them to keep doing it solo, as the demand for these would certainly increase in the run-up to Christmas. Having seen how successful Niamh was at recruiting, he encouraged them to follow her example.

Niamh was the biggest surprise of them all. She was so young and yet she had a wonderful way of dealing with her reps, who all worked harder than they would have normally, in an effort to please Niamh. This showed in her sales which were way higher than any of the other managers. She was a little champion and justified his faith in her. He remembered that Amber had recognised her potential also.

Rosie seemed quite happy to have three meetings a week – she didn't like calling them parties – and she had also recruited ten representatives. Helping her with the paperwork, he advised her that it would save her time and help her business enormously, if she could become computer literate. She agreed with him and enrolled in a computer course that very day. She'd missed the first week but they assured her that she'd have no trouble catching up. She hoped they were right. *Am I mad, Jack?* she asked him that night. But she knew that he'd want her to go for it.

Carlo enjoyed being out on the road with the girls. They were all so different. The more he saw of Tessa, the more he liked her. They had a lot in common and she was great fun but, from little things she said, he suspected that she was having marital problems. He didn't like to pry, of course, and she didn't volunteer any information.

Amber was wonderful. He went to one of her parties

with her and was very impressed with the way she handled her customers. She was a natural saleswoman and her personality made the evening fun for everyone. She was obviously enjoying the job enormously. She'd been on a high after her party and they'd had a drink together afterwards. She'd been relaxed and happy and he asked her if she'd come out to dinner with him the next time that he was in Dublin. To his surprise, she agreed.

Rosie was very nervous as she set off for the computer course but she relaxed when she saw that there were a couple of other older students there. Why, some were even in their late fifties and sixties. There was even one old dear who must have been eighty-five if she was a day. Rosie had been afraid that they'd all be kids. She surprised herself by how quickly she picked it up. It wasn't as difficult as she'd expected. At the coffee break, she sat beside a very nice man who told her he'd been very nervous on his first night too.

"I know all the kids take to this technology with ease," he confided to her in a low voice, "but I'm hopeless. I can't even text."

"Me neither," Rosie confessed. "My late husband, Jack, used a computer all the time for business so I just left everything to him."

"Same here. My wife, Marian, who died nine months ago, was a wizard on the computer too so I never bothered," he said sadly. "My daughter, Ursula, enrolled me on this course, to give me an interest. My kids are worried about me as I'm finding it very difficult to move on since Marian's death."

Rosie heard the pain in his voice and her heart went out to him. She knew exactly how he was feeling.

"I understand completely," she told him gently. "Jack died last year and, honestly, I was like a zombie for twelve months. I couldn't face going back to golf or bridge. I might as well have been dead too." She gulped, tears not far away. She took a deep breath. "Then my daughter insisted that I apply for this job that I've just started and somehow I'm slowly getting my life back together."

"Well, that gives me hope. Ursula really had to force me onto this course. I didn't want to do it and like you, I can't face going back to bridge either. Marian was my bridge partner and it would feel strange without her."

"I know exactly how it is," Rosie said with feeling.

"I know this sounds crazy, but I still feel as if she's there," he said quietly. "I talk to her every night and I really feel that she can hear me." He looked a little embarrassed to be admitting this.

"It's not crazy. I talk to Jack all the time too," she smiled gently at him.

Just then they were called back to the computers.

"It was nice talking to you," he said, extending his hand to her. "I'm Hugo, by the way."

"Rosie. Nice to meet you too," she replied, smiling.

What a sad man, Jack, she told him, as she lay in bed that night.

I met a really nice woman tonight, Marian, Hugo told his wife, as he had his nightly, one-sided chat with her.

Chapter 25

Tessa was determined to make one last effort with George. After her meeting with Carlo, she decided she wouldn't do any more parties herself but put all her energies into recruiting and getting the reps to hold parties for her. This was the way to go. Since then, she had signed up twelve representatives and four of them were selling really well; six more were doing okay; and the last two were a bit of a disaster. This was exactly as Grace and Carlo had told them it would be.

As a result of her decision, she stayed in every night with George but they seemed to have practically nothing to say to each other. You could have cut the atmosphere with a knife. She could feel the underlying fury in him and he was still sleeping in the guest room. Eventually, she braved herself to have it out with him.

"George, I've given up working at night to be here with you, but you don't seem to appreciate that."

"Oh, I should be grateful that you deign to stay home with me?" he replied icily.

"George, I'm making an effort here but you have to meet me halfway," she pleaded with him. "We both have to compromise."

"If you love me, you'd give up this job," he said, staring at her stonily.

"And if you loved me, you wouldn't ask me to do that!" she threw back at him.

"I'll ask you one more time, Tessa. Will you marry me and give up this nonsense?"

Tessa couldn't believe her ears. Things were so strained between them and he thought marriage was the answer. Did he think that, as her husband, he could forbid her to work? She conceded defeat. In that instant, she knew that it was over between them. It shocked her to realise that what she felt most was relief.

"You can't control me, George, which is what you seem to want. That's no basis for a happy marriage and I realise now that we have no future together. I'm sorry. I'll go and stay with Kate tonight and tomorrow I'll arrange to move my things out."

George looked at her in shock and without another word left the room.

Tessa threw a few things into a bag and drove over to Kate's.

"Tessa, what are you . . . ?" Kate stopped mid-sentence as she saw the look on her friend's face.

"I've left him, Kate," she said dully. "It's over."

Kate poured two large gin and tonics and sat her down to hear what had happened. She didn't make any effort to persuade her to try again with George, which is what she'd

217

normally have done in this circumstance. She knew that this wasn't just a lover's tiff and secretly she thought that Tessa was doing the right thing.

"You can stay here as long as you like," Kate told her.

"Thanks, Kate, but it's too close to George. Tomorrow I'll go and stay with Amber till I sort out a place of my own."

"That's a good idea," Kate agreed. "It'll give you some breathing space."

"You know, it's crazy, but what I'm more concerned about is missing Kilkenny and Napoleon, not George!" She laughed a little hysterically. "Can you believe it? My horse and dog are actually more important to me than the man I thought I'd spend my life with – the man I thought I loved!"

Her laughter turned to tears. Kate put her arms around her friend.

"You're still in shock," she said, as she calmed Tessa down. "And don't worry about them. I'll take care of them until you get settled and can have them back with you."

Tessa smiled through her tears. "Oh Kate, would you? That would be fantastic. I was worried about where I could leave them. That way, I could come down and visit them at weekends."

"That's settled then." Kate beamed at her. "We can collect them tomorrow when we go for your things."

Later, Tessa rang Amber to tell her that she'd left George and was warmed by her friend's concern and insistence that she come and stay with her.

She and Kate talked long into the night about men, love, marriage and all those things that women talk about together. It helped Tessa that both Kate and Amber felt she was doing the right thing.

Amber wasn't surprised to hear that Tessa had left George. She'd known for a while that he was not the right man for her. She understood Tessa's feeling of failure, but far better to leave than stay with the wrong person. Amber was sure that had she still been married to Dermot, he would have felt exactly the same as George about her job. Men!

She was looking forward to having Tessa stay with her although they'd have to organise a warehouse somewhere to store the deliveries. Her own garage was too small. She'd been thinking about it anyway, as business was booming and Christmas promised to be huge. Now with Tessa here, it was essential and urgent. She was amazed at how little Tessa actually brought with her. She'd left the bulk of her stuff in the house in Ballyfern until she could find an apartment of her own.

"Thank God you didn't bring all your shoes. I can fit what you've brought with you on one shelf, so I won't need to retire any of mine which I'd hate to have to do," she told Tessa sheepishly. "I'm delighted you're here and I honestly think you've made the right decision."

"I think so too. Probably should have done it ages ago but you know how it is. I feel relieved, which is sad, but I can't wait to get back to the old me."

Amber rang Luke to tell him that his shoes had arrived and arranged to deliver them the following night. He suggested that they go out for a bite to eat afterwards and she readily agreed. She was delighted that they'd picked up their friendship again. He was easy and relaxing and she could just be herself with him.

"A date?" Susie had asked, her eyebrows raised and an impish grin on her face, when Amber told her what a nice evening they'd had.

"Definitely not a date, it was just pizza with an old friend," Amber insisted.

"Well, how about asking your old friend to lunch, on Sunday week," Susie suggested. "We're a bit top-heavy with women, what with you and Tessa fancy-free and my sister's husband away too. Poor Tony will be overwhelmed by all these females," she laughed. "Will you invite Luke? I've always liked him."

"Yeah, sure," Amber agreed. "He was asking about you, actually, and I'm sure he'd love to come, if he's free."

Luke was delighted to accept. He found weekends difficult since Emma had left him and Amber and Susie were great fun. He was looking forward to meeting this Tessa that Amber was so fond of. Yes, he was looking forward to the lunch very much.

Chapter 26

Tessa had heard nothing from George since she'd left a week ago and she wondered how he was coping.

"Not your problem any more," Kate told her when she rang to see how Napoleon and Kilkenny were settling in, "but he seems to be okay."

They decided that she would move the rest of her stuff to Kate's spare bedroom as it would be some months before she would have her own place. This meant that she had to ring George to arrange to pick it up. She was dreading talking to him as she was afraid that he might ask her to go back, but he did no such thing.

"Hello, George, Tessa here. How are you?" Silence! "I'd like to come and collect my things on Saturday, if that's okay with you." She was trying to keep her voice from breaking.

"That's fine." Click . . . he'd hung up on her. What the hell?

She was in such a state on Saturday morning that Amber

insisted on driving down with her. She dreaded coming face to face with George. She needn't have worried. The house was empty. He was nowhere to be seen. She sighed with relief but felt sad that it had come to this. They piled her stuff into Amber's car and just about got it all in. She took one last look around the lovely old house and then left the key on the hallstand.

"Another chapter in my life closed," she said sadly.

Val was getting on Niamh's nerves.

As promised, she had arranged to go out with her for a day, to help her interview potential representatives. Val had arrived at Bridget's on the morning in question wearing a low-cut sweater and a mini-skirt.

"For God's sake, Val, you're going out to interview women," Niamh had said, exasperated. "That is no way to dress. You'll only alienate them. Have you no cop-on? Here, take this and cover up!" She'd thrown a sweater at her and Val meekly had done as she was told.

It had been a successful outing and Niamh had signed up six reps for her. Two days later, Val wanted her to go out again.

"Val, I showed you how to do it. You have to do it yourself some time," Niamh said crossly. "I need every moment I can get, to work my own business. I don't have enough hours in the day as it is, what with the kids and Gav to look after as well."

Val was annoyed with her. "Well, the least you can do is to help me put up the stuff on the computer. I haven't a clue," she nagged.

Niamh sighed but agreed to help her.

Things were much better since she'd set up her office at

her mother's. She had managed to persuade her mother to accept payment for her baby-sitting and the arrangement suited everybody concerned. Without Bridget standing over her, and knowing that the kids were happy, Niamh could get through the paperwork in no time at all. She was very much more organised.

Sharon had turned out to be a gem. She was doing all the deliveries now, by herself, thus giving Niamh more time to recruit. She now had fifty-two reps and her bank balance was growing daily. She couldn't resist going online to open her account every night, enjoying the thrill as she saw the figure going higher and higher.

The only fly in the ointment was Gav. She was very disappointed with the lack of support from him. He thought it was enough that he was allowing her to do it without actually having to help out. She'd hoped that when he saw the money coming in, he might become more supportive and of course there was always the possibility of the car. She'd tried to get him to agree to baby-sit once a week so that she could hold parties. He baby-sat the night she'd held a party for Andy's wife, Bree, but she knew he'd done it to please Andy and not her. He still steadfastly maintained that he couldn't commit himself to any baby-sitting.

They'd started rowing over money again. Not the lack of it, this time, but the fact that she wouldn't spend it. Very early on, Gavin had asked her to buy him a leather jacket. When she'd refused, telling him she wouldn't touch the money, not even to buy a pair of tights, let alone a leather jacket, he'd stormed out. It was for their future home, she'd explained. Next, he'd pleaded with her to give him the money to go with the guys to Manchester to see his favourite team play.

"No, Gav, we're not touching this money until we have the deposit for our house," she'd told him.

He'd sulked for days after this exchange. She'd been very tempted to tell him that if he'd get a job, he could afford to go, but she bit her tongue. He didn't get it – he didn't understand how badly she wanted them to have a home of their own. She worried that he was showing no sign of growing up. She couldn't understand it. Then she came up with a great idea. She'd had requests from Sharon and Bree's friends for parties but she needed a baby-sitter to allow her to do this. Bridget wouldn't hear of a stranger coming into her house to baby-sit so Niamh decided on a strategy. She knew how much Gav wanted to go to see Man. United play so she sat him down and put her proposal to him.

"If you will agree to baby-sit two evenings a week," she told him, "I'll give you the money to go to Manchester. How does that sound?" She had her fingers crossed, hoping he'd agree, but not letting him see how much she wanted him to.

He considered it, but only for a moment.

"Okay, babe. Deal," he said, beaming at her.

She let her breath out slowly – unaware that she'd been holding it. She'd make the money for his trip in one party but she wouldn't let him know that. Anything else she earned from these parties would go into "House Account". They were both happy!

Rosie regretted that she hadn't learned about computers years ago. It was fantastic. It had opened up a whole new world to her. David had sent her the money to buy herself a new laptop for Christmas. It was extremely generous of him but, as he put it, it would benefit him too as it meant she could email him in Australia – every day if she so wished. He mentioned something about Skyping – but that was a little beyond her at the moment. She had just got the hang of emailing. First thing every morning, she rushed to the computer and it was also the last thing she did every night before she retired. It was miraculous.

Hugo, the nice man in her computer class, emailed her regularly, as practice for them both. It was amazing how a relationship could flourish through emailing. Somehow, it was easier than talking to someone and she found herself telling him things she'd never told another soul. She shared her feelings of grief and depression with him and he told her that she was helping him with his own grief. They sat together at the coffee break every night at the course. It was all very pleasant and easy.

She'd also discovered the internet and couldn't believe how much information she could get by Googling. It was exhilarating. Hugo had explained how they could play bridge via the internet. She'd thought he was joking. Could you believe it!

"Maybe you'd be interested in taking it up again. I need a partner and so do you, so how about it?" he'd asked her.

"Let me practise online first and then we'll give it a go."

"Fine," he'd replied, smiling.

He'd also mentioned something called eBay that he found great.

"Let me tackle the bridge first!" she'd laughed.

Gail was delighted with her mother's new interest and received regular "please help" phone calls during the first days of the computer but they were coming less and less frequently.

Eileen's phone rang. It was Val.

"Hi, Mam. I need a favour. I want to come back home

and move into Niamh's old room. Keith and I are finished."

Eileen couldn't believe it. Val knew that Niamh was now using it as an office. Did she expect her to turf Niamh out?

"Not possible, Val. You know Niamh is using it."

"Mam, this is an emergency," she cried. "Keith has moved another girl in. I can't stay there."

"Well, you can't stay here either, Val. I just don't have the room. Have you no friend you can go to?"

"No," Val sniffled.

Eileen was adamant. She was enjoying the children so much and it was lovely having Niamh around every day too. She was not going to renege on her agreement with Niamh. The poor kid needed all the support that she could give her.

"No, Val," Eileen insisted. "You'll just have to find somewhere else. That's final."

Val couldn't believe her ears. She'd been sure that her mother would welcome her back with open arms, but no – Niamh again! Everything revolves around *her*, she thought viciously.

She had to leave Keith's. No question about it! She'd arrived home yesterday to find him in bed with a young chick, both of them stoned out of their minds. He hadn't batted an eye when she'd walked in on him.

"Babe, either pack your bags and go, or join me and Chelsea here in bed," he'd said, moving over to make room for her.

Chelsea had thought this was hilarious and had laughed so much that she fell out of the bed. Keith had rolled out after her.

"Nah, she's not my type. Too old," Chelsea had sniggered, rolling about on the floor. She didn't look any older than sixteen.

Val grabbed the wine bottle that they'd been drinking from and poured it over them both, to shrieks of laughter from Chelsea who tried to catch it in her mouth.

"I take it you're leaving then. Leave your key before you go," Keith had said, turning his back on her as he started to snog Chelsea who was still writhing on the floor. Val flung the key at him, hitting him on the head with it. It gave her some satisfaction. And now here she was, homeless, and her own mother wouldn't take her in. She had no one else she could ask – Val had never been big into girl-friends.

In desperation, she rang Phoebe and asked if she could stay with her, explaining the situation.

"Okay darling, but only for a few nights till you get somewhere permanent," Phoebe said, somewhat reluctantly.

That would have to do.

She took a taxi to the address Phoebe had given her as it was way out in the sticks. From the way Phoebe talked, Val expected a beautiful big house set in its own grounds. What she found was quite different – a small terraced house in a council estate, surrounded by hundreds of similar small houses. Typical, Phoebe with her big talk and her big ideas – I should have guessed, Val thought disconsolately.

"Welcome, darling," Phoebe gushed, air-kissing Val on both cheeks. "Let me introduce you to my beautiful daughter, Talika."

Talika – what kind of a name is that? Val wondered, shaking hands with a shy sixteen-year-old girl who could not, by any stretch of the imagination, be called beautiful.

The poor kid was blushing like mad, obviously mortified by her mother's description of her. Val felt sorry for her. Imagine having a mother like Phoebe!

She was shown to her room which was so small that you couldn't have swung a mouse in it, let alone a cat. Well, she should be grateful, she supposed, but it was obvious that she couldn't stay here for long. She'd have to think of something.

Pete had hoped that Amber would ring him after their night out but she didn't. He couldn't get her out of his mind. There was something about her. He wondered if it was because she'd spurned him, which had come as quite a shock to him. It was not something he experienced often with women. God, maybe Tim was right. He'd rung Tim and told him how he was feeling about Amber.

"I knew someone would finally reel you in," Tim had laughed. "It's called love," he'd added, still laughing.

"Whatever it's called," Pete said forlornly, "I just can't stop thinking about her."

"What about the other girl – Lesley, wasn't it?" Tim asked. "What's happening with her?"

"Oh, we're not involved," Pete said dismissively. "It's just a sexual relationship."

"Does she know that?" Tim wanted to know. Pete could be so blind sometimes, not seeing when women were falling in love with him.

"I'm sure she does," he replied.

When he'd come off the phone Pete thought about what Tim had said. Lesley was beginning to get on his nerves. He'd had to turn off his mobile because she was calling him so often. Then she started texting him – morning, noon and night. She had this fixation about seeing his apartment but the last thing he wanted to do was take her there. He'd done that once before with a married woman and her husband had arrived on his doorstep a week later, threatening to cut off his goolies. Luckily, he'd managed to calm him down and they'd ended up getting drunk together but he'd learnt his lesson. No more women – especially attached women – in his pad. Now Amber was something else. He'd have *her* there anytime.

He called her and asked her out to dinner. He was as nervous as a teenager dialling her number. She sounded warm and friendly on the phone but she refused to see him.

"Thanks, Pete, but honestly, I'm up to my eyes at the moment," she said. "Business is just fantastic. I'm having parties almost every night now."

"I hope you're not mad at me about the coming-up-for-coffee mix-up," he stammered.

"Of course not!" Her voice tinkled with laughter.

God, she sounded delicious! He really wanted to see her again. He sent her a bouquet of white roses and freesia the next day. He missed her call, thanking him, but listened a dozen times at least to the message she'd left. Bloody Lesley! If it wasn't for her, he'd have had his phone on. He would see Amber at the sales meeting the following week and he couldn't wait. He hoped Lesley wouldn't cause any problem. He'd have to cool it there but at the same time he didn't want to antagonise her. Maybe he should take her out again before the meeting – as an insurance against trouble.

Chapter 27

Carlo and Amber had their first date the following Tuesday. He took her to the famed King Sitric restaurant in Howth where they ate delicious fresh fish, beautifully cooked. Amber was a little nervous at first, not least because she found Carlo so attractive, but he put her at her ease straight away. She sipped the delicious Chablis wine slowly, terrified of getting drunk. She fancied him so much that she was afraid of how she might behave if she did get drunk.

He was a charming, interesting companion and she had a great time. When he drove her home, he took her hand and kissed it, thanking her for a lovely evening. She was disappointed that it wasn't more than that. She was afraid that he didn't find her attractive after all, while she fancied him more than ever.

He'd been a perfect gentleman all evening and she had to admit that Tessa was right about him. He was a lovely guy. Unfortunately, she thought that he probably wouldn't ask her out again. Maybe that was just as well. That meant no complications, no heartbreak.

They all gathered in the Portmarnock Country Club Hotel the following day, for their first sales meeting together. They had been operating for just one month. Grace and Carlo hugged them all and looked very pleased indeed. Pete couldn't take his eyes off Amber. She looked stunning. Her eyes were glowing and she seemed happy and vibrant as she laughed and chatted with the girls. Carlo was aware of this too.

Pete had his work cut out for him, trying to avoid Lesley's gaze. They'd spent Monday night together and though the sex was as good as ever, somehow his heart wasn't in it. Lesley had felt his despondency and kept asking him what the problem was.

"Just leave it, for Christ's sake," he'd snapped at her, leaving her sulking for over an hour. He would definitely have to cool it after this.

The meeting started and Grace rose to address them. Smiling broadly, she welcomed them all.

"It's hard to believe that it's only a month since we last met and even harder to believe that you have made such a success of the business in such a short time," she told them. "Your sales are truly amazing and have exceeded our wildest dreams."

Carlo and Pete nodded their agreement, beaming broadly as they applauded the girls.

Grace then gave a PowerPoint presentation on the sales to date and they all agreed that they were quite staggering. The girls gasped at the figures and looked at each other, grinning happily. There was a buzz and excitement in the air that was almost tangible.

"Some of you have done better than others, of course," Grace paused.

She then broke the figures down and went through each woman's sales, individually. It was obvious that although Amber and Lesley had done extremely well and Tessa and Rosie to a lesser extent, Niamh was way ahead of them all. When her sales were exhibited on the screen, there was a collective gasp and as Amber, Tessa and Rosie hugged her she blushed to the roots of her pretty auburn hair.

Val was fuming. There she goes again! Everyone's pet. The fact that Niamh had done it all through sheer effort was lost on her. Phoebe shrugged, as if to say "It doesn't bother me", although her sales were pathetic and the lowest of all. Lesley clapped politely but was furious. She really had thought she would be top, as she had poached many of her previous reps from the cosmetic company she'd worked for, which had given her a head start. What was absolutely galling was the fact that Amber had beaten her too and Pete was now smiling and kissing them both on the cheeks. Ooohhh! She could barely contain her jealousy. Tessa noticed her narrowed eyes and taut lips. If looks could kill, poor Niamh and Amber would both be dead.

After the congratulations were over Grace turned to Niamh.

"Well, that's certainly a very impressive start, Niamh," she said, smiling at the young girl. "I wonder if you wouldn't mind saying a few words, telling us how you managed it? I'm sure we'd all like to learn the secret of your success. Will you share it with us?"

Niamh blushed again and shyly stood up in front of them. She started hesitantly but seeing how interested the others were, she soon relaxed. Her green eyes were sparkling as she spoke and Pete thought that she had never looked prettier.

Lesley was green with envy but she wanted to know how Niamh had achieved such sales so she listened politely, hoping to pick up some tips. Hesitantly at first, Niamh told them how she was operating. However, she gained in confidence as she went on and was amazed to discover when she'd finished that she'd spoken for almost half an hour. She stressed the importance of recruiting good representatives and told them of the little incentives she had devised for hers.

The others listened, fascinated, except for Val who sat in barely controlled fury. Phoebe looked interested but in fact her mind was miles away. Lesley was taking notes. Amber, Tessa and Rosie were taking it all on board, delighted for their young friend.

"I offer any rep who throws a party for me, one pair of shoes at 50% discount. All it means is that I am foregoing my commission on that pair of shoes, as the rep would have 25% commission anyway. Somehow, it appeals to them and they are all keen to hold parties as often as they can. It certainly pays off."

"What a great idea!" Grace said.

The others murmured their agreement.

Niamh showed them her list of reps and they couldn't believe that she'd recruited so many, so quickly.

"And you with three small children to look after, not like the rest of us who are free!" Rosie said.

"Well, Mam is a wonderful help," Niamh smiled.

Bloody wonderful to you, not to me, Val thought savagely. She was very surprised to hear Niamh say that she'd taken on Sharon Murphy to help her. Val remembered her

233

from school, a chubby, shy girl, whom she had teased unmercifully because of her weight. She'd been very surprised when she'd heard that Sharon had married Dean, who was a bit of all right. She'd been pregnant of course, how else could she have landed him! Val had slept with him a few times. Maybe I should have got pregnant by him. Missed the boat there, she thought. She decided that she'd ask Sharon to deliver her shoes as well. Why not? If she was doing it anyway for Niamh, what difference would a few more pairs make?

When Niamh had finished, they all applauded her loudly, Val barely bringing her hands together.

They broke for coffee. Lesley hoped for an opportunity to have a quiet word with Pete but he was busy talking to Carlo so she abandoned it and went outside for a cigarette with Val and Phoebe.

"Can I have a quick word, Pete?" Carlo asked, as they took their coffee.

"Sure, man," Pete smiled.

Carlo spoke in a low voice, not wanting to be overheard. "I don't wish to intrude on your personal life but I feel I must say something." He felt very uncomfortable speaking about the situation but felt it had to be done. "It has come to my attention that you are – how can I put it? – having an affair with one of our managers."

Pete's smile faded. "It is, in fact, none of your business. May I enquire from whom you heard this?" he asked, his fists clenching with annoyance at this intrusion.

"From the lady in question," Carlo replied.

Pete's face gave nothing away but inside he was seething. How dare Lesley discuss him with someone else –

and Carlo of all people! He was furious with her. The stupid cow! I'll kill her when I get my hands on her!

"It's just that, as the lady is married," Carlo continued apologetically, "Grace and I both feel it could lead to complications."

Pete's smile was back in place. "No need to worry, old boy," he replied. "That was just a little dalliance, if you know what I mean." He winked at Carlo. "Between you and me," he continued, lowering his voice confidentially, "I am wooing another young lady who is unattached and who I'm sure you will approve of."

"Who is that?" Carlo asked, curious.

Pete looked around to be sure he was out of earshot. "Amber," he grinned.

"Amber?" Carlo repeated, not sure if he'd heard correctly.

"Yes," Pete smiled. "We went out together last Saturday night and to tell you the truth, I'm quite smitten."

Carlo tried to pull himself together. He couldn't believe that Amber would be interested in Pete. He had felt that there was a chance he could develop a relationship with her himself. He dearly wanted to meet a lovely woman and settle down. He'd hoped that perhaps Amber was that woman, but now . . .!

Pete had no idea of the bombshell he'd just delivered. He chatted on about how sweet and intelligent Amber was but Carlo didn't hear him. He felt shell-shocked. Luckily, at that moment, Grace called the meeting back to order again.

"I'd like to try something now," Grace said when they had regrouped. "A little exercise, if you will." She smiled at their expectant faces. "I'd like each of you to tell us what, if any, incentives you can come up with to motivate your reps. A brainstorming session, if you like to call it that. Anyone like to start?"

Tessa put her hand up. "Yes, Tessa?"

"Well, I've offered a prize of a meal out for two, to the rep with the best sales in the next month."

"Good idea," Carlo smiled at her.

"I give a bottle of champagne to anyone who holds a party for me," Amber said, "but I think Niamh's idea of commission is better, so I'm going to start that from now on." She smiled her thanks to Niamh.

"Yes, I think that really is something you should all consider," Grace agreed. "It really won't cost you much more than a bottle of wine," she continued, "and I should think it would really motivate your reps. Thanks for that tip, Niamh. Phoebe? Have you any ideas?"

"So many, I don't know where to start . . ."

Grace cut her short. "Then I suggest you email them to me and I can then share them with everybody." Grace's voice brooked no argument, much to Phoebe's disappointment. She was crestfallen, her moment of glory snatched away from her.

The girls breathed a sigh of relief. Carlo and Pete tried to hide smiles. If Phoebe started on her no doubt crazy ideas they would be there for a week.

"How about you, Lesley?" Grace asked.

"I give my representatives the opportunity to earn commission on every pair of shoes they sell," Lesley stated arrogantly, staring the others down. "That, I think, is motivation enough." She tossed her head, making her curls bounce madly.

"Well, I suppose that's one way of looking at it," Grace commented drily, raising her eyebrows.

Pete sniggered, much to Lesley's annoyance. The other girls, with the exception of Val, tried to hide their amusement.

"And Val. Have you anything to add?" Grace asked her.

Val had no ideas whatsoever, so she replied, "I agree with Lesley," and was awarded with a bright smile from her friend. Grace frowned and Niamh wanted to shake Val. Surely she could have come up with something rather than just parrot Lesley?

"And lastly, Rosie . . ." Grace smiled at her.

"I hold a draw once a month for all those who have had a party for me and the winner gets the pair of shoes of their choice."

"Another terrific idea," Grace smiled at her. "Thanks, Rosie."

She then asked them to take ten minutes to try and come up with some more ideas for incentives. They amazed themselves with the amount of ideas they came up with. Phoebe's contribution was, as expected, completely off the wall. The others had to restrain themselves from laughing out loud at her ridiculous proposals. Lesley scoffed openly at her ideas while Val was torn between impressing Lesley or supporting Phoebe. She was, after all, indebted to Phoebe for taking her in but she didn't want to alienate Lesley, so she said nothing.

"That was very illuminating," Grace remarked when they'd finished. "Well, ladies, it may be hard to believe, but we are now into the peak Christmas shopping period, which means you have a fantastic opportunity to reach more customers this month and thereby greatly increase your sales. Amber has already made great progress in this regard – she has a great idea on how to target husbands and boyfriends, particularly at this time of year, and I've asked her to share this with you all. Amber?" She beckoned, inviting her up to address the meeting.

Pete thought Amber looked radiant. She had her blonde waves tied up on top of her head but tendrils had escaped and were framing her face and falling on her neck. She looked adorable, like a heroine from one of Jane Austen's novels. Lesley was watching him watching her, and she saw the admiration in his eyes. She has them all drooling over her, she thought, furiously. She noticed that Carlo seemed to be mesmerised by her too. Lesley just couldn't understand what they saw in her. Stuck-up bitch!

Amber told them about Luke's party and all the parties and sales that had resulted from it and when she'd finished they all agreed that this was a terrific way to increase sales over the next few weeks.

Tessa saw that Carlo seemed uneasy and kept raking his hand through his hair as he listened to Amber talk. She wondered had something happened between them. Amber had seemed quite keen after their date on Monday night. Don't tell me she's changed her mind. The poor guy, he really didn't deserve it.

After lunch, they filed back into the room to find a display of stunning bags set out. The two men laughed at the reaction of these grown women to the bags. They were squealing with delight like eight-year-old girls. Even Rosie, a very mature lady, was behaving like a kid in a sweetshop. They went from bag to bag stroking the soft supple leather and suede and inhaling the delicious smell of them. The men marvelled at the effect shoes and bags seemed to have on the whole female race. Men would never understand it.

The girls realised that the six bags matched the shoes they had been selling.

"Oh, look at this purple one!" Niamh squealed.

"What about this red clutch?" Amber asked. "Isn't it divine?"

They were in seventh heaven. Amber and Tessa recognised that the bags were very similar indeed to the latest designer bags. Chanel, Prada, Gucci, Dior, Marc Jacobs and Balenciaga – they were all there.

"Okay, girls, calm down," Grace laughed, clapping her hands. "Now these bags are obviously matching the shoes that you have been selling and are available from today for you to sell. They retail at between €60 and €80 and hopefully your customers who bought shoes will want the bag to match. I have brochures here for you to take with you and, as a bonus, to thank you for all your good work, you can choose whichever bag you'd like!" She smiled at their delight. "Let Carlo know your choice and we'll deliver it to you with your order next week."

Amber decided on the red, Tessa on the pale gold, Rosie on the grey patent and Niamh was in a tizzy trying to make up her mind. "I adore the purple suede bag just as much as I love the purple suede shoes but, honestly, the large black one would be more practical," she said, pursing her lips and looking from one to another.

"Decisions, decisions," Amber laughed.

"The black is classic Dior, it will last forever," Tessa advised her.

"The black one, so," Niamh decided.

"Well, actually, Niamh, you can have both," Grace told her, "as we've decided to give you a second bag in recognition of your terrific sales."

Niamh was afraid she might cry. "Thank you so much, Grace, that's fantastic," she said, her voice wobbly with emotion. "I'll have the purple one too then." The others applauded her, except for Val who was seething at Niamh's bloody luck once again.

"We have another few things to say before we wrap up for the day," Grace announced. "As the business has taken off so well, thanks to you, we have decided to expand outside Dublin and recruit seven more managers who will start in January. Carlo will explain."

She sat down as Carlo took the floor.

"As Grace has said, ladies, it's thanks to you that we are in a position to expand so soon. You have shown us what can be done." He smiled at them. "I will be spending the next week here in Ireland, setting it up. If any of you know of anybody suitable, we would be delighted to consider them – especially in counties Meath, Kildare and Wicklow. Also, if I can be of any help to any of you with your own business, please let me know. This is my new Irish mobile number." He began to hand out his business cards to them. "I know some of you are interested in talking to Pete about your tax situation and he will be happy to meet up with you, if needs be." He looked at Pete who nodded, smiling broadly.

As the meeting adjourned, Grace took Val and Phoebe aside and told them, in no uncertain terms, that they would have to pull their socks up or they would not have their contract renewed. Phoebe gave the excuse that she was buying an apartment in Spain and was having untold problems with it. Val looked at her in amazement. Was she for real? Buying an apartment in Spain indeed, I'll believe that when I see it, she thought. Val gave the excuse that her personal life was a problem at the moment.

"I'm sorry, ladies, but your personal lives are not my problem," Grace told them firmly. "I have a business to run and you have to deliver."

They were surprised at this. They'd thought that Grace was a pushover but they now realised that they had misjudged her. She could be a woman of steel when she needed to be.

As they were leaving, Carlo took Tessa aside and asked her if she would mind staying behind for a few moments as he wanted to have a word with her in private. Intrigued, she agreed and told the girls that she would follow them into the bar shortly.

"I hope you don't mind my asking you this, Tessa," he said, running his hand through his hair again, as she'd seen him do earlier. "I know you're a good friend of Amber's and I'm really concerned about her. Pete tells me that they're starting a relationship. Is this true?" His large brown eyes were solemn as he looked at her.

Tessa now understood why he had looked so agitated earlier. "Well, she has been out with him," she began but seeing how dejected he looked, she couldn't help adding, "I wouldn't worry about it. I don't think she's that interested in him."

She saw the relief wash over Carlo's face as he straightened his shoulders and she wished it was her and not Amber who was the cause of this.

"That's good to know. I'm very concerned for her," he replied. "Pete is a nice guy but a bit of a heartbreaker, I'm afraid!" He gave her a dazzling smile that sent her pulses racing.

How can Amber be so stupid as to let this gorgeous man get away, she wondered.

"As you know, we had dinner together on Monday

night," Carlo said. "Of course, if I thought she was serious about Pete then I wouldn't pursue her."

"No, really, I don't think she is," Tessa assured him. "I'll put in a good word for you, if you like?"

"Thank you, Tessa," he smiled, his brown eyes lighting up. "I'm sure she'll listen to you."

He insisted on accompanying her into the bar where he ordered a round of drinks for the girls but he refused to join them.

"I'm sure you have lots to talk about without me interrupting," he told them laughingly. Then taking Tessa's hand and bringing it to his lips, he whispered, "*Grazie, mi amica.*"

She blushed.

As she sat down, Amber whispered, "What was all that about?"

"Tell you later," Tessa replied in a low voice.

Amber was dying with curiosity and no sooner were they in the car than she said, "Well, what's going on? Has Carlo asked you out?"

"I wish," Tessa sighed as she fastened her seatbelt. "It was about you, actually."

"About me?" Amber asked, making the car lurch forward in her surprise.

"Hey, watch out!" Tessa shrieked as she pitched forward. "Yes, Carlo is concerned about you. He's heard you're going out with Pete and he's worried."

"Where did he hear that?" Amber asked, as she eased the car into the evening traffic.

"From the man himself, seemingly. 'Discreet', as we know, is not Pete's middle name. Carlo asked me if you were serious about Pete."

"What did you tell him?"

"I told him I didn't think you were."

"I'm not. Seriously!" Amber said, concentrating on the road again. "He asked me to go out with him again this week but I explained that I'm just too busy."

Tessa wouldn't let go. "Amber, Carlo would like to take you out again and you'd be crazy to turn him down. He is gorgeous. Honestly, I don't know why you don't give him a chance."

"I'm scared of him," Amber admitted. "He's too damn good looking."

"That's not his fault." Tessa couldn't see the logic here.

"No, true," Amber agreed. "I suppose it's my Catholic upbringing. After thirteen years of indoctrination by the nuns and then Dermot's behaviour, is it any wonder that I don't trust men? I'm afraid of Carlo, or maybe . . ." she added with a resigned, "maybe I'm afraid of my own feelings."

"You have to get over that, Amber, or you'll be alone all your life."

"You seem quite smitten by Carlo yourself," Amber teased her. "Why don't you go out with him?"

"Yeah, I think he's divinely attractive and I also think he's a lovely sensitive man," Tessa sighed. "Sadly, he's not interested in me. It's you he fancies. He wants to ask you out to dinner again. Will you not go?"

"I don't know . . ." Amber hemmed and hawed.

"Please, Amber, do it for me?"

"Oh, God," Amber laughed. "You're so bloody persuasive. Okay, okay, I'll go out with him – *if* he rings."

"Great!" Tessa grinned happily as Amber parked the car in the garage.

"God, men are like buses," Amber said seriously, turning off the engine. "You wait forever for one and then three come along together – not that we know much about waiting for buses!" She looked at Tessa and they both burst out laughing.

"Yeah, Pete, Carlo and Luke – all together!" Tessa said, still grinning.

"Go way with you!" Amber cried, punching her friend in the arm, and they pealed with laughter once more.

Chapter 28

Val rang Sharon just as soon as she left the hotel.

"Hi, Sharon. Val here, Niamh's sister."

Sharon was instantly wary. Val never spoke to her and had been her prime tormentor at school. She'd even come on to Dean when she'd been pregnant with Willow. Sharon was not even sure that Dean hadn't taken her up on it. You just never knew with Dean and she wouldn't trust Val as far as she could throw her.

"Niamh tells me that you do her deliveries for her and I was wondering if you could maybe fit mine in at the same time?" Val went on, her voice wheedling.

"I don't think so, Val," Sharon replied. "It's all I can do to fit Niamh's deliveries in my car and at the rate her sales are growing . . ." It gave Sharon great satisfaction to say this. She knew how jealous Val was of Niamh. Let her put that in her pipe and smoke it, she thought, uncharitably. She heard Val's intake of breath.

"Are you saying you won't help me?" she asked sharply, in the voice that Sharon was more familiar with.

"That's exactly what I'm saying," Sharon replied.

"God, you were always a stupid cow!" Val couldn't resist saying, before hanging up.

Sharon was shaking as she put the phone down. She'd never stood up to Val before and was exhilarated that she had the courage to do so now. Before she'd started to work with Niamh she'd never have been able to say no to Val, but seeing how gutsy Niamh was had increased her own confidence.

She rang Niamh immediately and told her of Val's request.

"The nerve of her!" Niamh was furious. She was even more furious when she heard what Val's parting shot to Sharon was.

"Don't pay any attention to her, Sharon. She's the stupid one. What has she ever achieved in life?"

Niamh couldn't wait to get home to tell her mother what Val was up to now.

"Why are you surprised?" Eileen asked her. "You know the latest? She wants to move back in here, into your old room."

"She what?" Niamh couldn't believe her ears. "But she knows that I'm using it as an office now."

"She expects me to throw you out, I suppose, but I refused."

"That's it! I'm finished with her," Niamh said, furiously. "I've tried to help her as much as I could but she tries to do me down, every chance she gets."

"She's a bad egg. I don't know where I got her from," Eileen said sadly.

Val bumped into Gavin on Henry Street.

"Hi, handsome, what are you doing here?"

"Oh, hi, Val," he said, accepting the kiss she planted on his lips. "I was just looking at leather jackets."

"As if you're not sexy enough already," she said coyly.

"Well, I'm only looking," he said grumpily. "Doesn't look like I'll be able to buy one." He made a face. "Your sister is very tight with her money, you know that?"

This was music to Val's ears. "What's she done now?" she asked him, acting all innocent.

"She's turning into a right miser. I told her I needed a leather jacket, but no dice. She's giving me the money to go to the Man. United match in January but only after I promised to baby-sit two nights a week. You'd swear I wanted to go to the moon! I don't know. This job has gone to her head. And to think of all the help I've given her!" He looked to Val for confirmation.

This was too good to be true, she thought.

"Poor baby!" she said, rubbing his arm. "You'd think she'd appreciate that and show her gratitude, especially with all the money she's earning."

She saw the surprise on his face and decided to stick the knife in.

"Did she tell you that she had the best sales of any of us?" she asked him, pretending to be upset. "She's raking it in, and how!"

It was obvious that Niamh hadn't shared this bit of news with her husband.

"You're joking," Gavin said, looking at her with those gorgeous big blue eyes.

"Dead serious! I should think the very least you deserve is a leather jacket." She took his arm. "Come on, show me which one you like," she cooed persuasively.

Delighted that somebody understood him, he took her

arm and they went to see the jacket that he had set his heart on.

Her heart lurched as she saw him posing and turning this way and that in the gorgeous tan jacket. He was soooo sexy! God, she wanted him so much!

"You have to have it," she urged him. "It was made for you."

He agreed. His dole money was burning a hole in his pocket.

"You deserve it," she cooed, smiling up at him admiringly.

She was right, he thought. "I'll take it," he told the salesman. Niamh could lump it. It was time he asserted himself in his own house. He missed the irony in this – it wasn't his own house. He took Val for a drink, it was the least he could do, to celebrate his new jacket. They had more than a drink – they had five – and he thought how understanding Val was. Not at all like her sister!

Niamh was surprised that Gavin was so drunk when he arrived home that evening. She also knew that he was hiding something. She could read him like a book and knew shifty when she saw it. She found out what it was when she asked him that evening for the housekeeping money for the week.

"I don't have it," he replied, avoiding eye contact with her.

"What do you mean, you don't have it?" she asked, wondering why not.

"I bought that leather jacket I told you about," he told her sullenly.

Niamh tried to keep calm but it was all she could do not

to scream at him. She was aware that Bridget was in the kitchen and could hear them.

"What do you mean you bought a leather jacket?" she cried. "You know we can't afford to spend a penny. How could you? You know your dole money is for the groceries and to pay your mother!" She paced up and down the tiny room in agitation.

"Val says that you're raking it in," he answered her. "You didn't tell me that you had the highest sales of all of them." He was accusing her now, aware that attack was the best method of defence, crossing his arms angrily in front of him. "I don't even know how much you've earned. You can use that money for food."

"I told you that every penny of it is going towards a house for us! I will not use it for anything else," she hissed at him, her green eyes fiery.

"Well, Val says –"

"What the hell has Val got to do with anything?" she screamed at him. She was past caring now whether Bridget heard them or not.

"I met her in town and she came with me to buy the jacket," he mumbled, starting to feel guilty. "She said I deserved it."

"I bet she did! Well, maybe you'd like to ask her to buy some food for your children this week!" She was so angry she wanted to hit him. Instead she grabbed her coat and stormed out. The look she gave Bridget as she passed froze the words on her mother-in-law's lips.

Chapter 29

The following Sunday was Susie's lunch and as Amber had known they would, Tessa and Susie got on like a house on fire. Tessa had also hit it off really well with her sister, Deirdre, who was heavily pregnant, and Susie's kids, Rachel and Joshua. While Susie and Amber were preparing lunch, Tessa sat barefoot on the floor playing with them, her long legs curled under her. Rachel, who was five, loved Tessa's hair and kept stroking it.

"Can I play with your hair?" she asked Tessa, her big blue eyes imploring.

"Rachel, leave Tessa's hair alone," Susie admonished her little daughter.

"Oh, no, it's okay," Tessa told her. "I love having my hair played with. So did my dad and when I was little he used to pay me to play with his hair." She smiled at the memory.

"Will you pay me to do it?" Rachel asked, not believing what she was hearing.

"Yeah, sure, how much do you charge?" Tessa asked, all business-like.

"What used your dad pay you?" the little one enquired.

"Threepence – about five cents in today's money!" she laughed.

"Oh, but that was a long time ago," Joshua butted in. His ears had pricked up at this talk of money. "That's at least a euro today," he added, to the amusement of the adults. "Will you pay me, if I do your hair too, Tessa?"

"You mercenary little monkey!" she laughed. "I'll pay you not to do it!"

"Cool!" he replied. "I'll go and watch a DVD." He turned to his dad. "Imagine, getting paid to watch *Power Rangers*! That's really cool!" He scampered off and they all laughed at his precociousness.

Tessa luxuriated as Rachel brushed, plaited and tried all kinds of styles on her hair.

"I think this little lady has a great future as a hair stylist," she told Susie as she coughed up €5 to each of the kids and they sat down to lunch.

Luke felt right at home and had a great store of jokes which kept them all entertained.

Susie asked Tessa to help with the dessert and alone in the kitchen they discussed Luke and Amber in a whisper.

"He's really sweet, isn't he?" Tessa murmured.

"A dote. They are so suited to each other. But don't even suggest romance or she'll run a mile," Susie whispered.

"I wish she could put her marriage behind her. What was Dermot like?"

"An out-and-out shit!" Susie replied vehemently, taking the profiteroles from the tin. "I really didn't like him at all. He sapped all her confidence and made her feel useless. I was really worried about her after the divorce. This job saved her life."

"So she's told me." Tessa nodded. "Do you think she and Luke could get together? He seems awfully keen."

"I hope so," Susie replied as she set about melting the chocolate. "They'd be perfect together. What's this Pete like?"

"Yeuch!" Tessa said, making a vomiting motion with her fingers. "He's a total Casanova. I can't understand that she doesn't see it."

"Believe it or not, Amber's a bit naïve when it comes to men."

"You've heard her talk of Carlo," Tessa said, as she licked a piece of cream that had missed its mark. "He's a lovely guy and cracked about her. I know she likes him but she's resisting him all the time." She shook her head and made a face. "He wants to take her out again and I practically had to beg her to go."

"I'd really like her to meet someone," Susie said earnestly.

Amber didn't suspect for a minute that her friends were talking about her while she and Luke were having a lovely time chatting. It was nice to have an uncomplicated male friendship without anything being expected of her. She was really extremely fond of him. He fitted in so well with her life and she could tell that her friends really liked him too, as he did them.

They stayed well into the evening, drinking wine and talking together and Amber was sorry when it had to end.

Val knew very quickly that living with Phoebe was not going to work out. The woman was mental! She spent all day on the phone and Val had never heard anyone tell as many lies as Phoebe.

She'd spend the morning in bed and then watch TV all afternoon, letting her voicemail take all the calls. Then she'd ring people back, telling them that she was exhausted as she'd been out working all day, without even a break for lunch. Val would look at her disbelievingly but Phoebe didn't so much as bat an eyelid. What was really awful was that she expected everyone else to lie for her too. Poor Talika was a nervous wreck but didn't seem able to disobey her mother.

"Tell them I'm not here," was Phoebe's mantra and poor Talika told the lie, time after time. She tried the same thing on Val, but Val was having none of it. She refused to lie for Phoebe so as a result was told not to answer the phone at all. A lot of Phoebe's time was taken up harassing the two previous men in her life, her ex-husband and Talika's father, for more money. Val was sure they'd have paid her any amount just to get her off their backs. They must be so relieved to be shut of her and not living with her any more.

How right Mam was, thought Val. *"If you want to know me – come and live with me."* One week of Phoebe and she'd had enough. But where could she go? Her sales were much improved but she wasn't earning enough to rent a place of her own. There was only one thing for it, she'd have to contact Boxer again and see if he'd take her back.

Boxer owned a lap-dancing club in the city centre, called Hot Bods, and Val had been one of his top dancers. She'd lived with him for a while but had left when she'd met

Keith. Boxer had been very annoyed with her so she was a bit apprehensive about how he would receive her now. "Desperate is as desperate does," she thought, as she rang him. She was relieved when he sounded pleased to hear from her and told her to come and see him. She went straight away before he changed his mind.

She got the feeling that he'd actually missed her and he appeared to be very impressed with her new boobs. After kneading them for five minutes, which hurt like hell because of her nipple ring, she was actually relieved when he finally entered her, knowing it would be over in less than two minutes. She tried to blank her mind, perusing his shaved head and the tattoos on his shoulders, because she knew there was no such thing as a free lunch. She would have to do as he wanted, and what he wanted was that she would service him, whenever he felt the need. Okay, give and take – that was fair enough. Then he said he also wanted her back in the club, working, but she was adamant.

"No! No way! I've got a regular job now and I don't want to go back there," she told him.

"A regular job! Val, don't make me laugh," he said, doing exactly that.

"I don't see what's so funny," she said huffily.

"You'll never stick it," he said, still laughing. "There's nothing regular about you, babe." He hugged her to him roughly. "Anyway, within a month you'll see just how much money you could be making here and I've no doubt you'll change your mind," he sniggered.

She looked at him imperiously. "That's what you think," she told him, but deep in her heart she acknowledged that he was probably right. Thank God he'd taken her back. Bad as it would be, it would be better than Phoebe's. She moved back in with him that night.

Niamh had headed to her mother's after the showdown with Gavin. She told her mother what had happened.

"Oh, love, he's never going to change," Eileen said, shaking her head. "Don't even think of touching that money. You and the kids can eat here with me this week and let Bridget feed him. They're well matched. I can always lend you some money if you're stuck. I haven't touched the money you put into my post office account for looking after the children. Use it if you need it."

For the hundredth time, Niamh said, "Mam, what would I do without you?"

She couldn't bring herself to forgive Gavin so things were very strained in the house during the following week. He was furious that she was taking her meals with her mother and refusing to touch her savings. Bridget was naturally taking her son's side, so Niamh spent more time than ever at her mother's in the following days. Thank God for Mam.

When she arrived home from the school the following Friday, her mother was dancing with excitement.

"Niamh, I've got some fantastic news. You know my friend, Mrs Flanagan, from Number 26? Well, she's gone into a home but the family don't want to sell the house in case she doesn't like it there. I spoke to her daughter, Carmel, today, and she said that she'd be delighted to let you have it for six months, by which time she'll know whether her mother will be happy to stay in the home or not."

"Oh my God, Mam, that is fantastic! Are you sure they won't mind having the kids there?"

"No, she knows you have three children. She'll put away anything valuable. You can see the place this evening."

Niamh could hardly believe her luck and counted the minutes till Mrs Flanagan's daughter arrived. She wondered how Gav would take the news. She worried that he wouldn't want to move from his mother's. Well, whether he did or not, she was going. She'd had her fill of Bridget.

The house was fantastic. It was bigger than her mother's, and had four bedrooms. They weren't big but it meant that Ian could have his own room, which he would love. He hated having to accommodate the girls' Baby Annabelles, Polly Pockets and Sylvan Families in his bedroom. She could also have an office of her own. And there was a TV in the bedroom. Bliss! She wouldn't have to miss *Strictly Come Dancing* while Gav watched his football. The kids could also watch their programmes in peace. There was an Aga in the kitchen and a leather suite in the living-room. It was heaven.

Mrs Flanagan's daughter, Carmel, assured her that she was delighted to have someone in the house, keeping it aired, and refused any rent for it.

"No, honestly, I'm just pleased that it won't lie empty and I know you'll look after it and cut the grass and that," Carmel told her. "I wouldn't let a stranger in here," she confided, handing Niamh the key. "You'll have to change the electricity and phone to your name, of course, and then you can move in anytime you want."

Niamh sat down and cried. She couldn't believe her luck. Everything seemed to be coming up roses lately. Hopefully, by the time the six months was up, she would be buying a house of her own.

As expected, she didn't get a great response from Gavin about the house.

"What about Ma?" he asked.

"What about her? She's constantly complaining about us and it was never meant to be long-term. Either you come with us or you stay with your mother. Either way, we're going. Let me know."

Gavin looked at her in surprise. She was turning into a woman to be reckoned with. She had matured so much since she took on this job. He couldn't help but feel a new respect for her. Her star was on the rise, no doubt about it. And let's face it, could he live with his mother on his own? It didn't take him long to make up his mind.

"Okay, I'll come too." Smiling at her, he put his arms around her. "Let's go out and celebrate tonight, babe."

She didn't want to spoil the mood by asking where they'd get the money from but he had obviously kept enough drinking money. She was relieved that they were talking again but she made him promise that he would never again spend money like he had on the leather jacket, without her agreeing to it first. He wore the jacket out that night and she had to admit that he looked damn sexy in it. They made fantastic love later and everything was back on track.

Niamh rang Rosie, Amber and Tessa the next day, to tell them her good news. They were all thrilled for her and wished her good luck in the new house. She still couldn't believe her luck. Life was really looking up!

Chapter 30

Rosie was in a bit of a tizzy. She checked again that everything was in place on the table and then put the roast beef in the oven. It was the first time that she had entertained since Jack's death. He'd always been such a good host, taking care of drinks and keeping people entertained while she did her thing in the kitchen. Now she had to do it all.

Okay, it wasn't a state reception. It was only Gail and Hugo and his daughter for Sunday lunch, but still she was apprehensive – worried that they wouldn't get along. Gail had been delighted that her mum had found a new friend and it seemed that he was lonely too. When he'd mentioned to Rosie that he missed his wife's roast beef dinners, without thinking she had invited him over for lunch the following Sunday and now here she was, cooking roast beef with all the trimmings.

Not wanting it to be just Hugo and herself, she had also invited Gail, as Mike was away on a golfing trip, and

Ursula, Hugo's daughter, whose husband was in the army and was currently serving overseas.

Gail arrived first, with Holly, and was amused to see her mother fussing so much. How things had changed since she'd started that job! She was like a new woman and her computer had opened up a whole new world for her.

Hugo and Ursula arrived a few minutes later with Ursula's baby daughter, Megan. Holly was delighted to have a playmate and the two toddlers played happily on the carpet while Gail and Ursula talked about babies and everything else under the sun. Rosie smiled at how easily the young people gelled and remembered how easy it had been to make friends when she was a young mum herself. It was so much more difficult now, at this stage of her life.

Hugo had brought a big bunch of flowers and a bottle of wine and Ursula had given her a box of Belgian chocolates.

"How lovely, you really shouldn't have, but thank you very much all the same," she said, smiling at them. She asked Gail to pour the wine for her guests as she took the flowers into the kitchen, to put them in water. A few minutes later, Hugo knocked on the kitchen door.

"May I come in?" he asked.

"Of course," Rosie said.

"Glass of wine for the cook," he smiled. "My, that smells delicious. I was just thinking how easy it is for young people to make friends," he echoed Rosie's thoughts. "It's not so easy when you get older, is it?"

Not for the first time, Rosie marvelled at how in tune their thoughts seemed to be. They often said exactly the same thing together.

"We're not doing too badly," she laughed. "We made friends fairly quickly."

"Yes, well, we seem to think alike," he replied, and she laughed out loud. There he goes again, she thought, thinking the same thoughts as me. Strange!

The lunch was delicious and Hugo could not stop saying how good it was. She was secretly pleased and happy that Gail liked him so much. He was very easy company and the two girls looked like they were going to be good friends. They were planning to meet up the following week. Hugo smiled at Rosie over his Irish Coffee.

"My turn next," he said. "Although I have to tell you, the meal won't be a patch on this."

"Don't be so modest, Dad," Ursula scolded him. "You're not a bad cook." She turned to Rosie and Gail. "He's just a bit limited in his repertoire. You'll have either lasagne, or lasagne," she laughed.

"I love lasagne," Rosie said, winking at him.

When they'd left, she and Gail chatted together.

"Mum, he's so nice. He reminds me of Dad, gentle and sweet, and did you see him with the kids? He's a sweetheart."

For some reason Rosie was inordinately pleased that Gail liked him.

"Yes, he's a good friend. I'm glad I met him."

She felt at peace that night as she spoke to Jack and she knew that he was up there, looking down on her, glad that she was moving on with her life.

Amber knew that Carlo was back in Dublin recruiting but she guessed that she was not going to hear from him any more, so was caught unawares when he rang on Tuesday asking her to dinner on Wednesday night. As luck would have it, she was free that night so she accepted and by Wednesday night she was a bundle of nerves. It amused

Tessa to see her behaving like a teenager on a first date. So much for not being interested in him, Tessa thought. Amber was obviously in deep. Lucky thing, Tessa thought, wishing it was she getting ready for a date with the divine Carlo.

"I'm so nervous," Amber announced, as she tried on one dress after another. "I need a drink." She poured a vodka and orange for herself.

"Do you think that's wise?" Tessa asked her, a frown on her lovely face. "You'll be drinking wine later."

"I'll be fine," Amber said. "I need something to calm me down. I've a feeling tonight could be an important night in my life."

"Lucky you!" Tessa grinned. "I wouldn't mind being in your shoes."

Just then the doorbell chimed and Amber threw back the last of the vodka before she went to greet Carlo.

He took her to Bon Appétit, the best restaurant in Malahide, where she had a glass of Sancerre as they perused the menu.

After the maitre d' had taken their order, they talked a little shop as she told him about her parties and how great sales were and he kept her amused with tales of the applications he'd received for the new manager positions. Amber was thoroughly enjoying herself.

After they'd finished the delicious starters and the waiters had whisked their plates away, Carlo looked at her, his eyes serious.

"Can I ask you something? I know you're good friends with Tessa. Is everything okay between her and her husband? I got the feeling, last week, that something was wrong there."

"Oh, George is not her husband," Amber explained. "He did ask her to marry him but she didn't feel she loved him enough. Anyway," she continued, as she sipped her wine, "she's left him. The crunch came when he gave her grief about taking this job. He wouldn't accept it and gave her an ultimatum – the job, or him. She chose the job. I think she did the right thing. He was a control freak. She's staying with me for the moment, till she gets a place of her own."

"Oh, I'm so sorry for her," he said. "I had no idea. She's such a lovely person."

"The best," Amber said, as their main course arrived.

The food was delicious and the wines superb. He'd decided on Italian wines tonight and Amber was pleasantly surprised at just how good they actually were. She had never tasted any wine as good as the Sassicaia that he ordered to go with the duck. Mmmmm . . . the taste lingered forever on her palate.

He was pleased that she liked it so much and shared his passion and knowledge of Italian wines with her. She discovered that he knew a lot about French wines also. In fact, he was the most interesting, knowledgeable man that she had ever met. He was also funny, charming and very entertaining, not to mention gorgeous to look at. She could see the other women in the restaurant eyeing him up. It felt good to be the woman with him.

As the evening wore on and the wine took effect, Amber found herself relaxing and, when Carlo asked her about herself, she found herself spilling out all the details of her life; her marriage, her downward spiral, and how this job had made such a difference to her.

As she spoke, he reached over and took her hand. He listened in silence, seeing the hurt in her eyes and hearing the bitterness in her voice. He could tell that she was still suffering and he was surprised at how insecure she actually was and how lacking in self-confidence. He had thought that she was exactly the opposite – confident and self-assured. When Amber saw the sympathy and kindness in his eyes, it touched her, and to her mortification she started to cry.

"I'm so sorry," she whispered. "This is so embarrassing."

He handed her a pristine white handkerchief.

Dabbing her eyes, she smiled through her tears. "Thank you," she said. "I'll just go to the Ladies', if you don't mind."

Looking at her mascara-streaked face in the mirror, Amber chastised herself. How could I have been so stupid! Spilling my guts – and then crying – I'll never get over this embarrassment. After cleaning her face and reapplying her make-up, she returned to the table.

"Sorry about that," she mumbled.

He reached for her hand but she pulled away slightly. She was very quiet for the rest of the meal.

As he drove her home he reached for her hand again but removed it when he felt her stiffen. He couldn't understand why she had changed. They'd been having such a lovely evening but then she had started to withdraw from him. He gave a little sigh.

Amber was furious with herself for revealing so much to him. He'd lulled her into a sense of security and she'd let down her guard. Now she regretted it. Damn! Then she decided that maybe it was for the best. She'd been getting far too fond of him. He was far too charming. She really didn't need this in her life right now.

When they reached the apartment she felt she had to invite him up for a nightcap, or coffee if he preferred.

"Actually, a coffee might be a good idea," he smiled.

Tessa was curled up on the sofa watching *CSI Miami* when they came in.

"Oh, hi, Carlo," she greeted him, embarrassed to be seen in her scanty nightie.

"Sorry, we're interrupting you," he started to apologise.

"No, not at all," she insisted, turning off the TV and attempting to cover herself up. "I'll just make myself scarce."

"Don't be daft," Amber said. "Join us for a coffee."

Tessa realised that to get up would reveal more than she wished. Staying put seemed the best option.

"If you could just bring me my robe, from the bedroom," she appealed to Amber.

Amber grinned as she went to get it while Carlo tried to hide a smile. He thought that Tessa looked quite beautiful, sitting there in that wisp of a negligée, no make-up on and her long hair falling like a silk curtain. She looked about eighteen.

Amber returned with her robe, still grinning at Tessa's obvious discomfiture. When Carlo wasn't looking, Tessa shook her fist at Amber, which made her grin even more.

"May I use your bathroom?" Carlo asked Amber.

She showed him where it was and when he had left the room, Tessa jumped up, preparing to make her escape.

"Where are you going?" Amber asked.

"Where do you think?" Tessa whispered. "I'm not staying around playing gooseberry. You'll want to be alone with him. I'm off to bed."

Amber grabbed her arm. "Please don't go!" she said, panic in her voice. "Please stay! I don't want to be alone with him!"

Tessa thought she was crazy. *She* wouldn't mind being alone with Carlo! Honestly, Amber didn't realise how lucky she was!

"Okay," she replied, as Amber's fingers dug into her arm. "I'll stay."

Amber served the coffee and Tessa was aware of a tension in the room that she couldn't understand.

When Carlo had left, kissing both girls on the hand, Tessa turned to Amber, eyebrows raised.

"What on earth was that all about? Didn't you have a good night?"

"It was fantastic," Amber told her, plonking down on the couch and hugging her arms around her. "But it scares me," she continued. "He's too damn nice and too damned charming."

"Oh, so you want another shit like your ex-husband, is that it?" Tessa demanded.

"Of course not," Amber cried, "but I just can't bring myself to let go. I just am not ready to get involved again."

"Oh, Amber," Tessa said sadly, putting her arms around her friend, "I'm worried you'll never be ready." She held Amber as she cried softly, fearing that this was truly the case.

Carlo dove back to his hotel, wondering where the evening had gone wrong. He really liked Amber – more than liked her – but just when he had thought they were getting somewhere, after she'd opened up to him, she'd pulled back from him. He couldn't understand it. Women! Why were they so complicated? He wished he knew the answer to that one.

Chapter 31

Lesley was still seeing Pete, although she felt that he'd changed towards her. Something was bugging him. She had a suspicion that it was Amber. There was one way to find out. She rang Val.

"Val, I need a favour. Could you find out for me if Pete and Amber are dating? I'm sure Niamh will know. But don't mention that I want to know," she added quickly.

Val would have done anything Lesley asked her. "No problem, Les," she replied.

Lesley winced at this shortening of her name but refrained from chastising her. She needed this information.

Val rang back that afternoon. "Yes, Pete and Amber have been out together, but from what I can gather, she's not that interested. She's seeing Carlo at the moment!" Val knew that Lesley would be happy to hear that.

"Thanks, Val," Lesley said, hanging up.

Well, I like that, Val grumbled. She'd thought that

Lesley would be so grateful that she might invite her out for a drink. No such luck!

Lesley mulled over the information that Val had given her. What to do about it? "Stuck-up cow!" she said savagely, wondering where Pete had taken Amber and whether they'd made love or not. Highly unlikely, Lesley thought. These posh bitches were hardly going to put it out on a first or even second date. And Pete liked his sex. Not just liked – he needed it – as others needed air. Well, maybe she'd play Amber's game. She knew she was too available for him. He was calling all the shots. Whenever he called, she went running. Well, that was going to change. She wasn't going to do the chasing any more.

She didn't call him for two days. Finally, he rang.

"Hi, sweetheart, where've you been? Haven't heard from you in a while."

"No, Pete," she replied, coolly. "It *is* the busy Christmas period. I'm up to my eyes with work."

"Not too busy to meet me tonight, I hope," he said.

"Afraid so."

"Tomorrow night, then?" he asked hopefully.

"Sorry, no can do," she told him.

He couldn't believe it. What was she playing at? She was always so keen to see him. She seemed to need sex as much as he did, yet here she was, turning him down. What was happening?

"Sorry, have to dash, Pete," she said.

"Well, give me a call when you're free," he told her.

"Sure," she replied, hanging up.

Put that in your pipe and smoke it, she thought smugly, knowing that he was smarting from her refusal to meet him. She realised that she'd been too pushy with him. He was like all men. They needed to do the chasing. How quaint! Don't they realise we we're in the twenty-first century? Well, he'd be waiting for her, although she was so horny for him that it would take all of her willpower not to call him.

Pete was feeling deflated. He'd always been able to rely on her when he needed her. Maybe she was genuinely too busy. He felt sure that she'd be calling him soon.

He had given up calling Amber. She really was too busy to meet up with him as she had parties every night, or so she said. He hoped that, after Christmas, she'd be able to make some time for him. In the meantime there was always Lesley.

Chapter 32

Niamh woke at 6 a.m. the morning they were due to move house. She lay in bed listening to Gavin's light breathing and willing the clock hands to hurry forward. Not able to stand it any longer, she got out of bed at seven and decided to do some work on her laptop. Things were manic with the business. There weren't enough hours in the day for her. She now had sixty-seven reps and it took her all her time to manage them. The sales were phenomenal and she reckoned that she had to be in the lead amongst all the managers. She knew she had higher sales than Amber, Tessa, Rosie and Val. Phoebe didn't count and the only one she wasn't sure about was Lesley. She hoped Lesley hadn't overtaken her. She wanted that car more than anything. It would make her life so much easier getting around, not having to rely on Bus Éireann or bothering Sharon.

She did a last check that everything was in order for the move before waking the children and getting them out to school. She met Sharon at the school and returning to the house they started loading Sharon's car with the boxes and cases. To her exasperation, Gavin was still in bed and she had to practically throw a bucket of water over him to get him to wake up. Eventually, he did, and arrived sleepily into the kitchen just as the last of the boxes were being loaded. Niamh went upstairs to take the linen off the bed and finish clearing their things from the bathroom and then they were all set.

Bridget sat watching all this packing, a scowl on her face.

"Well, Bridget, we're all set," Niamh said to her. "I hope you'll come over for lunch on Sunday."

"Huh," Bridget replied, sulkily. "You'll have no time for me now that you're in a grand house," she sniffed.

"Don't be daft, Ma," Gavin said, giving her a hug. "You'll always be welcome."

"I'll be so lonely here on my own." Bridget started to cry. "Can't you stay with me for a while, Gavin," she asked him, her eyes pleading.

Gavin looked at Niamh helplessly.

"No, he can't," Niamh said sharply. "I need him to unpack and get us settled in our new home." Silly old bag, Niamh thought. You never stopped complaining when we were here. She felt not a scrap of sympathy for Bridget.

Gavin heard the steel in Niamh's voice and so he didn't argue.

"Ah, Ma," Gavin tried to calm Bridget down, "sure I'll be calling in every day and you can call over any time you want."

I hope not, Niamh thought with alarm, giving Bridget a quick goodbye kiss.

As the car pulled away, she whooped with joy. "Yipee! Freedom at last!" She was in high spirits.

Sharon laughed at her and even Gavin smiled at her exuberance.

It took them only an hour and a half to put everything away and when it was done Niamh said, "We have to celebrate." She took the bottle of champagne she'd won on the course out of the fridge. Taking down the champagne glasses that she'd bought for this special occasion, she opened the bottle and poured the three of them a glass, spilling some of it in her excitement.

"Just a small glass for me," Sharon squealed. "I have to drive."

"Oh, one glass won't kill you," Niamh said, laughing.

"Did you buy these glasses, Niamh?" Gav asked her.

"Yes," she smiled at her handsome husband. "I reckoned that we'll have many more occasions to use them in the next year. To our new home and our new life!" She raised her glass.

They clinked glasses, all three smiling. Niamh's excitement was catching.

When Sharon had left, Gavin took Niamh's hand and grabbed the bottle of champagne.

"Come on, babe. Let's really celebrate," he said huskily, leading her up to the bedroom.

There they christened the new bed, sipping the champagne in between their bouts of lovemaking. Then they christened the shower and it was the most exciting sex they'd ever had. He poured the champagne over her and then licked it off. Then she did the same to him. Niamh felt uninhibited and cried out as she pleased, not having to worry about Bridget overhearing her. Oh, yes! Things were going to be just perfect.

They got up just in time to go and collect the kids from

school. Niamh insisted that Gavin come with her although he would have preferred to stay in bed. Opening her own front door, when they got back home with the kids, gave Niamh such joy that she thought she might cry. The kids' antics as they ran from room to room and out into the garden quickly turned her tears to laughter. They loved the house and the freedom it gave them. As they finally sat down to their first meal in their own home, Niamh felt a sense of contentment she'd never known. She just knew that they were going to be a happy family from now on.

Boxer had been right. It wasn't even a month before Val went back to work at the club. She just wasn't earning enough selling shoes. She couldn't understand how Niamh managed it. She was now meeting the other dancers at the club, amazed at the money they had to spend on clothes and having a good time. She was tired of being skint. Why not? She told Boxer that she was ready to come back to work.

Same old perverts, Val thought on her first night back as she gyrated in front of them, casting off her mini-skirt.

"Come on, baby, show us those knockers!" one asshole in the front row leered at her.

Her return to the club had caused a stir with all the regular customers who remembered her and were thrilled and excited by her new, bigger boobs. This of course caused jealousy with the other girls.

"Who does she think she is?" Kitten asked. "She pissed off for a year and now she swans back, straight into Boxer's bed, thinking she can have star billing again."

Kitten was furious, her nose seriously out of joint. She'd been the big attraction in the club after Val had left but

now she had to take a backseat again. She'd also been Boxer's favourite lay, although he spread his favours around all the girls whenever he chose. They knew this was part of the job description. She'd enjoyed being his favourite – it gave her a certain cachet with the other girls. Now, here was Val, behaving like she was the Queen Bee again and Kitten could do nothing about it. Grudgingly she had to admit that Val was good, as she watched her play to the audience. The men loved her and were going crazy over her new tits. I'll have to get mine done again, she decided, although any more enlargement and she'd rival Pamela Anderson.

In fact, it wasn't Val's body that drove the men wild – it was the way she used it – and her attitude. She was good and she knew it. The first night back she made €120 in tips alone. Beats dragging around flogging shoes, she thought. What she really wanted was enough money so that she could rent an apartment of her own. She was getting tired of living off men and having to do their bidding all the time. Once she'd established herself in the club, she'd start looking. Boxer wasn't stupid, he knew a good thing when he saw it and Val was good for business – very good for business. Already, word was spreading and customers were leaving other clubs to come and watch her. She knew he'd kick up a fuss if she wanted to move into her own place but she'd promise to give him regular blow-jobs and that would keep him happy.

Ironically, things had improved dramatically for her with her shoe business. She had signed up all the dancers in the club as reps and they were selling shoes like hot cakes. Things were looking up, she thought, smugly. If only she could hook Gavin, then everything would be perfect.

Chapter 33

Niamh was happier than she'd ever been. The kids were delighted with the new house and even Gavin agreed it was great. Niamh was so looking forward to their first Christmas in it. True, they'd probably have to have Bridget for Christmas Day, as well as Eileen and Val, but Niamh was so happy now that she felt she could be magnanimous. Her sales had almost doubled in the last two weeks and there were still two more orders to go before Christmas. There was no way that Sharon could cope with all the deliveries so Niamh had hired a van and Gavin had driven it, delivering the orders to her reps. He loved being involved.

Niamh's reps had worked so hard that she wanted to reward them in some way. She thought that taking them out for a night might be a good way to say thank you. She rang Carlo to run it by him.

"That's a lovely thought, Niamh," he said. "Better still, maybe we could get all the other managers to join in and

274

I'm sure the company will help out with the cost. Leave it with me. I'll suss out Grace and the others."

Gosh, that would be great, she thought. Amber, Tessa and Rosie all rang her that afternoon to say they thought it was a wonderful idea. Val thought it was a bit over the top and grumbled about the cost but agreed to join in if it wouldn't cost too much. Niamh sighed. Val was always on the make. However the Christmas spirit was taking hold and in a weak moment, Niamh said she'd help her out if she couldn't afford it. In the end it wasn't necessary as Grace agreed to foot the bill in total and even offered some spot prizes.

Carlo rang Niamh back with this news.

"Unfortunately, Lesley feels she doesn't owe her girls anything, so count her out," he told her, his voice full of disapproval. "And Phoebe is considering taking her girls to either Paris or Barcelona, for a weekend in the spring," he added.

Niamh couldn't help it: she burst out laughing and Carlo joined in.

"Yes, I know. I'll believe it when I see it too," he said, still chuckling. "Anyway, you can rule her out too. I've been in touch with the Red Cow and they say they can take us for the twentieth of December, as luckily they've had a cancellation. How does that suit?"

"Oh, Carlo, that's fantastic. I'll let the others know and then invite my reps."

"Actually, Grace has decided to hold a meeting that day too, in the same venue. She's coming over for it and we could finish early and get the room ready for the party. We'll bring posters and balloons with us, to make it festive."

Gosh, he was a gem. She hoped that he and Amber would get together.

"One other thing," he continued, "Grace wondered if you could all get together and hire a group or a DJ for dancing. She said this was absolutely essential for any party of Irish women."

Niamh heard the doubt in his voice. "She's absolutely right. We couldn't possibly have a party without dancing," she laughed. "Leave it to me."

She rang the other girls, who were delighted with all of this. They agreed to pool resources to hire the music. Val grumbled about this but reluctantly agreed, if it wouldn't cost too much. Niamh sighed resignedly.

Pete looked in the mirror, not believing what he was seeing. He looked closer. No doubt about it – it was a grey hair. "Oh, God no!" he cried. "I'm too young for grey hairs." It was really depressing. It was bad enough that he seemed to be losing his touch with women – and now this!

Lesley hadn't contacted him and it was bugging him. What had happened there? She'd been so keen. He'd rung Tim and explained the position to him.

"Maybe she got tired of sex in the back of your BMW," Tim told him. "Women like to be spoiled. Can't you think of something she'd really like, that would get her interested?"

"Yeah, well, she's always going on about my taking her to my pad," Pete admitted.

"There you are then," Tim said smugly. "Offer to cook dinner for her in your place."

"I can't cook," Pete wailed.

"Oh, for God's sake, Pete, you don't have to be able to cook. All you have to do is stick things in the microwave."

Tim sounded exasperated. "You can buy ready-made meals everywhere. M & S is always good. Trust me, she'll be impressed."

"You think so?" Pete asked hopefully.

"Definitely," Tim assured him.

Pete rang Lesley that afternoon. She was secretly thrilled but tried to play it cool. However, when he said he'd like to invite her for a meal in his apartment, she warmed to him considerably.

"Oh, that would be lovely," she said.

"Tomorrow night?" he asked hopefully. (He hadn't had sex for two weeks and was quite desperate!)

"Great," she replied.

Yeessss! He punched the air. They made arrangements and he was surprised by how much he was looking forward to it. Next he had to think about what he would cook – or re-heat – which is what he would be doing. This had to be good. He wanted her back to the hot babe he remembered. He got horny just thinking about it.

It was Gavin's night to baby-sit. Niamh kissed him goodbye as she headed off to a party organised for her by the local Curves fitness club. They were expecting a large turnout and Niamh was looking forward to great sales.

"Please don't let the kids stay up longer than seven o'clock," she told Gavin. "Otherwise, I'll never get them up in the morning."

"Don't worry, babe," he replied, kissing her and squeezing her bum, "I'll have them snug in bed by then."

He certainly would. There was a match he wanted to see on the telly at seven fifteen and he didn't want his three terrors interfering with that.

He was engrossed in the match when the doorbell rang.

"Damn!" he said, thinking he wouldn't answer it. On second thoughts, maybe it was Eileen, and Niamh wouldn't be too happy to hear that he had refused to answer the door to her mother. Groaning, he went to the door.

"Hi, handsome," Val greeted him, kissing him on the lips and pushing past him into the hall.

"Hey, Val. Niamh's not here. She's got a party on tonight."

"I know that, stupid," she grinned wickedly at him. "I'm here to see you and the new house of course," she said, going into the living-room.

"Give over, Val. Niamh will be annoyed that you're here," he said, following her in. "Anyway, I'm watching a match," he added grumpily.

"No problem. I'll keep you company," she said, taking a bottle of wine out of her bag.

"Christ," he said.

"You watch the match and I'll open this," she said, prancing into what she saw was the kitchen. "Nice house," she called out to him.

He was sweating. Jesus Christ, Niamh would have a fit. How could he get rid of her?

She arrived back in to the living-room carrying two glasses of wine. She had taken off her coat and his eyes were out on sticks when he saw the skimpy top and micro-skirt she was wearing. She handed him his wine and then sat down on the couch beside him, too close for his comfort.

"Gosh, you were lucky to find this house," she said, chattily, "but then Niamh always falls on her feet, doesn't she?"

Gavin tried to concentrate on the match but he was

distracted by her body which was pressing against him. He could see straight down her top and again she was wearing no bra. Despite himself, he found himself getting aroused and he took a big gulp of the wine.

"God, Val, that skirt is so short I can practically see your knickers," he complained.

"Maybe I'm not wearing any," she replied, her voice husky. "Do you want to find out?" She took his hand and placed it on her crotch.

She wasn't!

This was too much for him. He ached to take her right there and then, on the couch. He put down his glass of wine and was about to slip her top off when he heard Ian calling out, "Daddy, I have a sore head. I want a glass of water!"

Like a scalded cat, he pulled back and jumping up went to see to his son.

"Oh, leave him!" Val cried, trying to pull him back.

He shook her off and went to minister to Ian.

Bloody kids! Val thought viciously. She'd almost had him. She was sure of it! She hoped that he'd return to take up where he'd left off, but as soon as he walked in again she knew that wasn't going to happen.

"Val, I'd like you to drink up and leave," he told her coldly. "And if you call around here again when Niamh isn't here, I won't let you in."

Furiously, she drained her glass. "I'll just pop into the loo, if I'm allowed to stay that long," she snarled at him.

"Of course – but then I want you gone," he said firmly.

Sitting on the loo she thought how close she'd come to having her heart's desire. Bloody Niamh! She probably had the kids programmed to interfere. Niamh's life was charmed. And she had so nearly come close to wrecking it until that bloody child had cried out. Val felt like screaming. She felt the envy eating her up. And then she spotted the laundry basket and Gavin's shirt sitting on top. With a vicious glint in her eye, she took up his shirt. Refreshing her lipstick, she plonked a kiss right on the collar. She then took out her perfume – Chanel's Allure – and sprayed it on the shirt. Hah! Let Niamh cope with that!

Grabbing her coat, she called out goodnight to Gavin as she let herself out.

"Phew," he said, as he heard the door close after her. "That was close." He then had to decide whether to tell Niamh, or not, about Val's visit.

He still hadn't decided when Niamh arrived home, flushed with excitement.

"Oh, Gav! It was fantastic," she exclaimed, throwing her arms around him. Stepping back, but still with her arms around his neck, she looked up at him, her eyes aglow. "They loved the shoes and I sold forty-four pairs! Can you believe it?" She threw back her head, laughing excitedly.

God, she's beautiful, Gavin thought, feeling himself getting aroused. He loved her when she was like this. She was so vibrant and alive. Am I crazy? he asked himself. Risking all of this for a slut like Val? I must be out of my mind. Niamh is twice as lovely and sexy as her sister. Never again! I swear I will not go within a mile of Val after this. Phew! Thank God, nothing happened with her.

He kissed Niamh on the neck and within minutes they were pulling their clothes off and making love on the rug in front of the fire.

"I love you so much," he whispered tenderly to her when they were done.

"I love you too," she replied. "I'm the happiest woman in the world."

He took her up to bed where they made love again.

"Forty-four pairs," was the last thing he heard her murmur before she fell asleep.

Chapter 34

Pete was rushing around his penthouse apartment in Ballsbridge doing a last-minute check on everything. He checked off the list that he had stuck on the fridge. Smoked salmon rolls in the fridge: check. White wine and champagne, ditto: check. Pasta ready to go in the microwave: check. Tiramisu out of the box: check. Table set: check. He just had to put on some music and light the candles and he was ready. Lesley was due in – whew – two minutes! He just had time to whip off his apron when he heard the doorbell ring. He buzzed her up to the apartment and was surprised at how pleased he was to see her.

"Hey, sweetie, you look sensational," he said, taking her in his arms. "It's been too long."

"Hi, Pete," she replied, as coolly as she could. But it was difficult. She wanted him so badly but she couldn't let him know. She had to play this smart. Extricating herself from his grasp, she took off her coat and handed it to him along with the bottle of wine she'd brought. Looking around the room she drew in her breath. It was gorgeous – bigger and more luxurious than she'd expected. The address itself had greatly impressed her. It was in the most upmarket area of Dublin.

"Nice pad," she said, walking around and taking in the wonderful views from the large corner, balcony window. "Wow!" she exclaimed as she looked across Dublin Bay and saw the lights of the north side twinkling merrily.

He came up behind her and putting his arms around her waist, rested his chin on her shoulder. "Glad you like it, Princess," he mumbled, nuzzling her neck.

"Hey, I thought I was invited here for dinner," she laughed, pushing him away although she wanted more than anything to respond to him. She tried to cool it.

"Of course," he told her. "All ready, but first an aperitif for my lady." He brought out the champagne and made a big production of opening it. Hmm . . . she thought, champagne! He *is* pleased to see me. She enjoyed toying with him, flirting and teasing him, knowing that she was driving him crazy and that soon they would be in bed having great sex together. If anything, making him – and herself – wait, was heightening the excitement.

The meal was lovely and he was the perfect host. After they'd finished the pasta, Eric Clapton's "Wonderful Tonight" started playing on the music centre and taking her hand, he bowed and said, "May I have the pleasure, Madam?"

"My pleasure," she curtsied, moving into his arms. They danced close for a few moments, rocking to the music. She could feel his hardness through her dress and when he started caressing her body, she couldn't restrain herself any more. Letting go, she moved sensuously with him and when he pulled her down on the rug in front of the fire, they made delicious love with the flickering light of the fire and candles playing across their bodies.

"Oh, it's been far, far too long," he sighed, burying his face in her hair.

She threw back her head and laughed huskily. "I agree," she replied as he kissed her throat. God! He was a fantastic lover.

They finally got to eat the tiramisu about two hours later and after they finished the wine he carried her into bed where he took her once more. They fell asleep, wrapped around each other, both satiated and happy. She smiled smugly as she dropped off. She had him now. She knew how to please him. She'd make sure from now on that he'd need her by his side, forever.

Niamh was putting out the bin on Wednesday night when she spotted the empty bottle of wine.

"Where did this come from, Gav?" she asked him, coming into the living-room with it in her hand.

He dragged his eyes away from the match on the telly and blushed when he saw what she was holding. "Oh, that . . ."

"Yes, that," she said grimly, knowing from the shifty way he couldn't meet her eye that he was hiding something.

"Oh, Val brought it over with her the other night," he mumbled.

"What other night?" she wanted to know although she knew exactly when it was.

"The night you were at your party," he muttered, still unable to look her in the eye.

"My sister was here, drinking wine with you while I was

out working, and you didn't bother to mention it?" she said, her voice rising with every word.

"Well, I meant to . . . but you know . . . ahem," he coughed, quaking under her ferocious gaze. "Well, eh . . . when you got home we started smooching," he stammered, picking at his nail, still avoiding her gaze, "and it went clean out of my head," he ended lamely.

"You wouldn't have told me at all if I hadn't found this bottle, would you?" she demanded, her eyes and cheeks blazing.

He didn't answer and she turned her back, flinging the bottle so hard into the bin that it broke. She went up to the bedroom and sat on the bed, shaking. Why had Val called around on a night when she knew Niamh, was out at a party and why had she brought a bottle of wine? Nothing Val did surprised Niamh, but why, oh why, had Gav not mentioned it? What was he hiding?

Niamh was very upset and didn't know what to think. She was so angry with him but more than that, she was scared. He'd always been truthful with her, or so she'd thought. Now she didn't know what to think.

He came up a little later and tried to make up to her but she didn't want to know.

"I'm sorry, babe, truly I am," he said, stroking her hair. "I should have told you and I'm really sorry now that I didn't." He took her in his arms. "I love you, hon – you know that. Look at the great sex we had that night." He moved his hand down to her breast. "It put Val's visit right out of my head and then yesterday I'd forgotten about it." He reached over and slid his tongue over her bottom lip, at the same time slipping his hand inside her bra, rubbing her nipple gently with his fingers.

She couldn't help it. She found herself melting and before she knew what was happening he was pulling her clothes off and they were both panting as he rolled on top of her. It was wild and passionate and she climaxed almost immediately. Afterwards, relieved that she wasn't angry with him any more, he lay cradling her in his arms until she fell asleep.

Chapter 35

Niamh couldn't believe how much she had saved and went online every night to check her bank balance. It was incredible. She already almost had the money for the deposit for their house. She hoped the bank manager would keep his word. She needn't have worried. As she was waiting in line at the bank the following morning, he spotted her and smiling broadly came over to her. "Niamh, lovely to see you again. If you have a moment, perhaps you'd drop into my office before you leave."

She felt a sinking in her stomach and hoped that nothing was wrong. He had been smiling but that didn't mean anything. Nervously, she knocked on his door.

"Niamh, thank you for stopping by. Please take a seat." He pulled out a chair for her. She perched nervously on the edge of her seat, wondering what was coming. He peered at the computer, tapping at the keys with one finger.

"Hmmm . . . as I thought. I saw this last week and couldn't believe it. How have you managed to save so much in such a short time?"

For a brief moment Niamh wondered if he thought she was laundering money but then he continued. "This shoe business seems to be very successful. Congratulations!" He gave her a big smile. "You must be working very hard."

"Yes, it is great, especially at the moment," she smiled shyly back at him. "I have over seventy representatives at the moment which is the secret of my success."

"Well, I never!" he exclaimed. "Maybe you could drop me in a brochure of your shoes. Perhaps my wife would like a pair for Christmas."

"I have one right here," Niamh grinned, handing him a brochure of the shoes and the bags.

"Well, you're on the ball, no doubt about that," he laughed. "No wonder you're so successful. I'll give you a call if my wife decides she'd like a pair. She's a devil for shoes and bags," he sighed.

"She's not alone," Niamh laughed. "That's why I'm doing so well."

"It goes without saying that any time you want this mortgage, you let me know. There won't be any problem if you can keep going like this."

Niamh flushed with pleasure. "Thank you so much, Mr Shannon," she said. "I'll hold you to that and don't forget to call me about your wife's shoes."

"I won't," he laughed, as he showed her out.

The following day, Niamh had a call from Mr Shannon asking her if she could drop in more brochures as some of his colleagues were interested and could she also please call his wife as she was crazy about the shoes and so were all her friends. Niamh could see her bank balance growing by the minute.

Chapter 36

Carlo couldn't get Amber out of his mind all week. He wanted to know what had caused her withdrawal from him. They had been getting on so well. She'd opened up to him and he'd begun to think that he was really getting to know her and then *wham* – she'd shut down on him. It disturbed him and he wanted to get to the bottom of it. On the spur of the moment, he called her on Saturday evening.

Amber was surprised to hear from him. She was feeling quite low as Tessa had gone down to Ballyfern to stay with her friend Kate and the apartment was very lonely without her.

"I know it is short notice," he said, his voice sounding more Italian than ever over the phone, "but I would really like to talk to you, Amber. Would you meet me for a drink tonight?"

Something in his voice touched her and before she knew it, she was saying yes.

He arrived at her door less than an hour later and

Amber let him in, feeling once again the strong attraction he held for her. He was proffering a bottle of Masi Amarone.

"One of my favourite wines – I hope you'll like it," he smiled.

She took it from him, her hand shaking. "Thank you, that's lovely. I've heard Tessa raving about this wine."

"Better drink it before she gets her hands on it then," he laughed.

"Don't worry, she's gone away for the weekend," Amber said. She hesitated for a moment before saying, "Would you prefer me to open this now and we could stay in? The pubs are pretty packed around here on a Saturday night."

"That would be perfect," Carlo replied, his smile melting her heart.

She took down the glasses while he opened the wine. She had some cheese in the fridge – Italian, as it turned out – so she put this on a cheese board with some water biscuits.

"Fantastic!" he whistled, as she set it down. "Pecorino and Gorgonzola – I'm in heaven. You are obviously a fan of all things Italian."

"Oh, yes," she said earnestly. "I love Italian cuisine."

"Italian men, I meant," he grinned, making her blush.

"Not until now," she grinned back at him.

"That'll do," he laughed, throwing his head back as he did so.

They sipped the wine as they left the cheese to warm up. They chatted easily and Carlo was amazed, yet again, at how well they got on. Amber was relaxed and enjoying herself when he reached across to take her hand. She tried to pull away but Carlo held fast. Then he reached over and kissed her on the lips. For a moment she responded but then he felt her freeze and pull away from him.

"Amber, what is it? Why do you shy away from me? You know I'm very fond of you but whenever I try to get close, you push me away."

"I'm sorry, Carlo," she whispered, her lower lip trembling. "I'm very fond of you too but somehow I can't let go. I don't know why. I'm too scared of getting hurt. I suppose I'm just not ready. I'm still not over my marriage."

He wanted to take her in his arms and quell her fears but he knew she wouldn't allow it. Defeated, he let her go.

"Do you think you could still be in love with your ex-husband?" he asked.

"I don't know," she murmured. "I just don't know. But I do know that I'm not ready to love again."

Carlo gathered up his coat. "I can't tell you how much this saddens me, Amber," he said quietly. "I think we really could have made it and I wish we had, but obviously it's not meant to be." As he left, he looked at her sadly, "I truly hope you find yourself, my darling. You're a wonderful woman."

After he'd left, she sat crying softly. Was it true, what he'd said? Was she still in love with Dermot? If so, then her life was well and truly fucked. All she knew was that she was afraid of where her feelings with Carlo would take her. She was scared of surrendering herself to him and losing herself, as she had done with Dermot. She recognised that Carlo had that same power and this was what frightened her. She wished Susie was not in New York on a weekend break or Tessa in Ballyfern. She badly needed to talk to one of them. Breaking her promise never to drink alone, she opened another bottle of wine and polished it off, wallowing in her misery.

Tessa was having a lovely time in Ballyfern. Napoleon was overjoyed to see her and never left her side all weekend. Kate had pulled out all the stops. She'd invited her friends, Lauren, Jenny and Tara around for supper and over a bottle of champagne, they laughingly welcomed Tessa into the Because We're Worth It club.

"Now, you must tell me – you promised you would. What club is that?" Tessa asked.

Kate explained that when they'd first got together, in Tara's slimming club, they'd given each other such support and friendship that it had raised their self-esteem and made them feel worthwhile.

"Hence the name 'Because We're Worth It'." On cue, all four girls flicked back their hair, just like in the L'Oréal ad.

"Oh, I get it," Tessa laughed, turning her head so that her long silky hair swirled out behind her. "I am very honoured to be admitted into this illustrious club," she announced, swirling her hair once more.

They all roared with laughter.

Tessa had a wonderful evening and Kate was delighted to see how relaxed and happy she had become.

"Life in Dublin obviously suits you," she remarked.

"Well, I'm very happy at the moment although I miss Napoleon and Kilkenny, of course, but once I get my own place and can have them back with me, everything will be fine. I'm actually thinking of looking for a place between here and the city – I guess I'm a country girl at heart." She smiled around the table at the girls.

"How's the love life?" Lauren asked her, grinning. "Anyone special?"

"Sadly, no," Tessa said wistfully.

Kate sensed there was something she wasn't telling them and hoped to find out when the two of them were alone.

She got her chance as she and Tessa sat finishing their wine later.

"Have you met somebody?" she asked Tessa.

"Well, I fancy somebody but unfortunately he only has eyes for Amber," she replied, her eyes downcast.

"Is Amber keen on him?" Kate wanted to know.

"That's the problem," Tessa told her, coiling her hair up in a knot. "She fancies him okay but doesn't want to get involved. She's still hurting from her divorce."

"That's crazy," Kate said. "It's been a while now, hasn't it?"

"Yeah, over a year," Tessa replied, "but she just can't seem to put it behind her."

"Love is so complicated," Kate sighed. "Changing the subject, have you any plans for Christmas?"

"I'm going to Galway to visit my parents," Tessa said. "I haven't seen them since the summer."

"Well, you're very welcome to spend Christmas with us if your plans should change, although it's like a madhouse here when all the boys are home."

"Thanks, but I think you'll have enough to cope with," Tessa said, laughing. "You're so kind, Kate," she added, hugging her friend.

On Sunday, she took Kilkenny for a long trek and felt sad having to leave both him and Napoleon and head back to the big smoke.

Chapter 37

Rosie was delighted with the way her business was growing and, as she told Gail, laughingly, there weren't enough hours in the day for her. Gail was so happy to see the change in her mother. It was like a miracle. Rosie was also getting great mileage out of her computer and was delighted to be in such close contact with David in Australia. It was lovely to hear what he and his family were doing on a day-to-day basis and to receive photographs of her grandchildren regularly. She missed David dreadfully, especially since Jack's death, but she would never let him know how much. She would be eternally grateful to him for giving her the computer, as she told him often.

Hugo was emailing her more than ever and at times the frequency of it irritated her so much she didn't reply. He didn't understand that her business was now taking up so much of her time and she really didn't feel the need to justify herself to him. When she'd mentioned to him that she was dreading Christmas without Jack, he asked her if she would spend it with him. She politely turned him down. She was beginning to realise that he was becoming dependant on her and it scared her. She was just beginning to find her own feet and the last thing she wanted now was a needy man. She was happy to have him as a friend but she feared that he wanted more. She most definitely wasn't ready for a romantic relationship with anyone. How to cool it without hurting his feelings? It was a dilemma. However, she was too busy right now to give it much thought.

Niamh had really fallen behind with the housework. Although Gavin was free every day and the kids at school, he did the bare minimum around the house, such as loading the dishwasher. Anything else, in Gavin's book, was woman's work. Bridget had certainly nurtured this thinking. She decided to tackle the washing the following Saturday night when she realised that there were no clean clothes left in the hot press.

She emptied out the wash basket, sorting the clothes as she did so. She thought she smelt something unusual and sniffing around realised that it was coming from Gavin's shirt. She sniffed again. No mistake – it was perfume – and not her Body Shop White Musk either. She recognised the scent but couldn't quite place it. What was it doing on Gav's shirt? It was then that she saw the lipstick on the collar.

She sank to the floor, feeling as if someone had punched her in the stomach. What could this mean? How did this lipstick get on Gav's shirt – and the perfume? She felt sick as she realised that there could be only one explanation. Would he really do this to her? Had he been with another woman? He had every opportunity. She was out working every day and he was out most nights. She never questioned where he went. She trusted him. Maybe that was a mistake. He was still very attractive to women and could have had anyone he wanted. Oh, God! What should she do? Everything was going so well for them right now. She loved him so much. She couldn't bear to think of her life without him. She was sure that he loved her too. Would he really have gone with someone else? The thought made her feel ill.

In a trance, she put the washing in the machine and then curled up in bed to think what she could do. If she tackled him he would surely deny it – wasn't that what all men did? Was it a one-night-stand? That she could probably forgive. Or was it a full-blown affair? Suddenly, she was very afraid. Her whole world, everything she'd worked for, would be worthless if Gav wasn't by her side. She couldn't bear to think about it? Was it her fault? Was she too involved in the business and neglecting him? Her mind went round and round until she fell into a fitful sleep.

She woke to feel Gav's arm around her as he lay spooned into her in the bed. She hadn't heard him coming in. She lay in the warmth of his body, wide awake now and thinking things over in her head. Before she finally fell back asleep again, around dawn, she'd made up her mind to say nothing to him but to keep a close eye on him in the coming days. This she did, hating herself for going through his pockets and checking his mobile phone for text messages and incoming calls. She found nothing suspicious and it was all she could do to keep her mind on her work as she worried herself sick about the problem.

December was the busiest month of the year in the Hot Bods club and so Val found herself working every single night. She should have been having parties for If the Shoes Fit but she was making so much money in the club that she couldn't see the point. She enjoyed the attention from the hordes of men who flocked to the club to round off their annual Christmas parties. Being well tanked up with alcohol, they were absurdly generous with their tips, vying with each other to be the most generous, often flashing fifty and one-hundred-euro notes at the girls. Val got more than her fair share of these as she gyrated and flirted with the clientele.

Boxer smiled as he watched her perform. He was delighted that she was back in his stable. She was a great asset and he knew he'd have to look after her well to prevent any other club from poaching her.

Val was never happier than when she was performing and suspected that her shoe sales would not be enough for Grace to renew her contract. She didn't care. Niamh would always do better than her and she hated having to be second-best to her sister. She had been half expecting a call from Niamh with a tirade about her visiting the house when she knew she wasn't there. But she hadn't heard a dickey-bird. She wondered if Gav had told Niamh at all. Probably not.

Amber had been in very bad form since her last date with Carlo. His suggestion that she was still in love with Dermot had jolted her considerably. Could it be true? Whether she was or not, one thing was for sure, she was not capable of getting involved again. Would she ever be, she wondered. Meanwhile, she kept herself from thinking about it by throwing herself into her work. It was so satisfying and she loved it. She was also very scared at the way she had lapsed and polished off the bottle of wine on her own. She was terrified of going down that road again.

She was glad now that Tessa and Susie had not been available the night she and Carlo broke up. It was better if they didn't know about it, so she said nothing. The only person she confided in was Luke. They'd got into the habit of having supper together every Sunday night. Sometimes he cooked, other times she cooked or, if they were both tired, they'd order in a pizza or Chinese. Occasionally, they went out for an Indian meal, which they both loved.

Luke was very understanding and it was so easy to talk to him. He was a very dear friend.

They'd all been so busy that they hadn't had a chance to get together socially, so they were looking forward to seeing each other again on the twentieth. The last orders had been delivered and all the girls were tired but happy as they convened for the last meeting of the year. They hugged and kissed and caught up with each other's news. Although they had been phoning each other regularly, it wasn't quite the same as actually being together.

Grace welcomed them all and Carlo did his usual hand-kissing. Amber found it hard to meet his eyes but relaxed when she saw that he was treating her exactly like the others. No lingering kiss or meaningful glances. He seemed to be over her.

Grace greeted them all warmly and introduced the seven new managers who would be starting after Christmas.

Amber thought that Niamh was very subdued and asked her if everything was okay. She wasn't totally convinced by Niamh's answer that it was. Something was bothering the girl.

"My God, Lesley looks a wreck," Tessa whispered to Amber.

"Probably shagging herself to death," Amber whispered back, taking in the dark circles under Lesley's eyes.

Tessa giggled. "That's meant to give you a bloom," she informed her friend.

"She's sticking like glue to Pete – I take it he's the shagger," Amber remarked, watching him chatting up the new managers.

"She'll have a job keeping him to herself," Tessa said, as she too spotted Pete in action.

Lesley caught their glances and gave them each a dagger's look back.

The new managers were all very impressed when they heard how well the women had done in just three months and Niamh, Amber, Tessa and Rosie remembered how excited and enthusiastic they'd been at *their* first meeting. And If the Shoes Fit hadn't let them down. It had fulfilled their wildest dreams. All of them were in a better place now than when they'd joined.

When Grace posted the sales on the screen there was an audible gasp from everyone present.

Niamh's sales were way ahead of everyone else's. The girls cheered and hollered as she went up to collect her prize. She took the envelope from Grace, blushing as she did so. Opening it as she sat back down, she gasped as she saw the contents.

"What is it?" Rosie asked, leaning in to see, as did Amber and Tessa.

"I don't believe it!" she exclaimed. "It's a weekend for two in Paris, all expenses paid, and €300 spending money!" she cried, her green eyes open wide with delight.

"Fantastic!" Amber said, clapping her on the back.

"Paris is wonderful. You'll love it," Tessa said smiling.

"I'm so happy for you," Rosie said, hugging her.

Val and Lesley glowered.

Amber had the next best sales. She was presented with a beautiful leather purse.

Tessa was surprised to be third. Grace gave her a lovely wide leather belt. "Oh, it's lovely, thank you," she said, surprised and delighted. She'd been sure Lesley would be third. Lesley thought so too. She couldn't believe that the Giraffe had beaten her. This was the nickname that, in her jealousy, she'd given Tessa. She could see the car she hoped to win receding into the distance. It was all Pete's fault. She spent far too much time with him but she couldn't help herself. She was addicted to him.

Since he had brought her into his pad, things had changed between them. She knew how to keep him happy. Sex, sex and more sex, in every possible position and permutation! He was hooked, no doubt about it!

She now spent three or four nights a week there, sleeping over. No more sex in the back of his Beamer. Her husband, Paul, never questioned where she was spending her nights. It was none of his business. She wouldn't be with him for much longer anyway.

She knew she had neglected the business. She would be sorry to lose the car to Niamh but what the hell! Pete would surely buy her a car to replace her old banger as soon as they became a permanent couple, which wouldn't be long now.

They broke for lunch which was a fun affair as the Christmas spirit took hold. Carlo sent two bottles of wine to their table and they tucked in with gusto. They were all looking forward to the evening and to giving their representatives a good time. Niamh had organised a DJ so it had the makings of a good night.

After lunch, they returned to the room to find the new collection of shoes on display. They were as beautiful as the first collection and all fourteen managers were thrilled with them. They would be selling them from the fourth of January. The new women were particularly excited by the fabulous shoes. After they'd *oohed* and *aahed* over them, Grace called the meeting to order and opened up the floor to the new people who had many questions to ask of the established managers. Niamh was very much in demand and answered as helpfully as she could.

Val was seething as she watched her holding forth. Thinks she's the bee's knees, Val thought viciously. Winning a trip to Paris, indeed!

As the meeting ended, Grace advised them to enjoy the Christmas break and forget about If The Shoes Fit while they recharged their batteries. They had two full weeks off before they started back again, when they would have the new collection of shoes to introduce. The atmosphere in the room was electric as they broke up and Grace and Carlo wished those who were leaving a Happy Christmas.

The four girls adjourned for coffee while Val went off home to get ready for the evening.

"Typical," Amber said to Tessa and Rosie when Niamh was out of earshot. "Not only is Val not coughing up for the DJ but she's not helping to get the room ready either." She liked Val less and less every time she met her.

The girls were thrilled to see what Grace and Carlo had planned for the evening. The big ballroom was very festive with a big Christmas tree and decorations and Carlo and

Grace had brought balloons and posters which the girls happily put up. They also arranged a display, of both the old and new collections of the shoes, on a table in the centre of the room. The shoes were to be the stars of the evening. Finally, they set out the spot prizes on the stage, where the DJ was setting up his equipment. When they were finished the girls stood back to admire the result and they all agreed that it was very splendid indeed.

Amber and Tessa had booked a room in the hotel for the night and Rosie and Niamh joined them there, to dress for the evening. Amber was still fretting about Niamh. Finding herself alone with Rosie, she mentioned it to her.

"I'm worried about Niamh," she said quietly. "Something's bothering her. She's not her usual self at all."

Rosie looked at her thoughtfully. "You know, Amber, I was thinking the same thing," she said. "She's much quieter than usual. Have you asked her if anything's wrong?"

"Yes," Amber replied, a worried frown on her face. "She said no, but I'm not so sure. Maybe she'll talk to you. You two get on great."

"I'll try," Rosie said, worried now about her young friend.

She got her chance as she and Niamh left together to go down to the party.

"Is everything okay, Niamh?" Rosie asked her gently. "You seem very quiet. Is anything the matter?"

Seeing Rosie's concern and hearing the kindness in her voice brought tears to Niamh's eyes.

"Rosie, promise you won't tell anyone, but I think Gav is having an affair and I'm worried sick about it."

Rosie sat her down on a sofa in the corridor. "Surely not, Niamh! What makes you think that?" she asked, her heart going out to the young woman.

Niamh told her about the shirt with the lipstick stain and perfume.

"There could be a simple explanation for that," Rosie said, taking Niamh's hands in hers. "Have you asked him about it?"

"No," Niamh replied, miserably. "I'm checking his phone for evidence but I've found nothing. It's killing me. It's on my mind all the time."

She started to cry softly and Rosie gathered her in her arms. She couldn't imagine what Niamh was going through. She only knew that if she'd ever suspected Jack of having an affair, it would have broken her heart.

"There, there," she crooned to Niamh. "You must ask him straight out, tonight. It could be nothing and here you are, worrying yourself sick." Handing Niamh a handkerchief, she said, "Now, dry your eyes and put on a smile and let's go and meet these reps of ours."

Like a small child, Niamh did as she was told.

"Thanks, Rosie. It's a relief to talk about it. You're right," she said. "I'll talk to Gav tonight." Blowing her nose and checking that her mascara hadn't run all over her face, she smiled brightly.

Linking arms they made their way downstairs.

The managers formed a reception line and greeted the representatives as they came in the door. The women handed out name badges to their own reps and introduced them to Grace and Carlo. Val was late and Niamh, furious with her, had to greet Val's ten reps. Even without these, it was obvious that Niamh's reps far outnumbered everyone else's. Grace was impressed with the way she treated them and everyone she spoke to sang Niamh's praises. The girl was a gem, no doubt about it.

"Where have you been?" Niamh hissed at Val when she finally turned up.

"You'd be surprised," she smirked back at Niamh. Now what does she mean by that? Niamh wondered.

The evening went with a bang and Niamh forgot about her troubles as she danced the night away.

The reps had a wonderful time and adored the new shoes. Carlo marvelled at the way the women were all up on the floor like a shot, every time the DJ changed the music.

"Where do you all get your energy from?" Carlo asked Tessa, who dragged him up to dance with her. "I feel ridiculous. I'm the only man here," he cried, laughing, throwing back his head in that way that he had.

"*Blessed art thou amongst women,*" Tessa laughed back, twirling around him as she danced.

Carlo thought she looked fantastic in her bright red mini-dress and was surprised to see that she was such a great mover. For someone so tall, she was extraordinarily graceful. They looked spectacular together, both so tall and attractive, and the others cleared a circle on the floor around them, clapping as they danced.

"What a gorgeous couple," one of Amber's reps remarked to her.

With a pang Amber had to agree with her. Tessa was glowing as she smiled and swayed to the music. After two dances, Carlo begged for mercy and taking her hand led her off the floor. They sat down together and he gulped down a glass of water, still panting.

Amber couldn't help but feel a little envious as she saw the easy way Tessa and Carlo were chatting. She remembered what great company he had been and how sympathetic. What a pity it hadn't worked out. Well, *c'est la vie*, she thought.

Lesley was sorry now that she had opted out of the party. If she'd known that the company was going to pay for it, she'd have opted in but she'd thought that she'd have to pay for it herself and no way was she spending her own money on her reps.

Pete had intended going to the party but she'd kicked up such a song and dance about it over the phone that he'd agreed to stay home.

He was expecting her for the night but when he opened the door he saw that she had two suitcases with her and it looked like she was planning on staying longer.

"I've left Paul," she announced as she marched past him.

"You've what?" he cried, blanching as he realised that she wasn't joking.

"Kaput! My marriage is over," she said matter-of-factly, throwing off her coat and plonking down on the couch. "I told Paul about us and he agreed that the best thing was for me to leave and move in with you. Pour me a drink, sweetheart, I need it badly." She smiled at him, unaware of the turmoil she had created in Pete.

He felt he needed a drink far more than she did. As he poured himself a large whisky and a glass of wine for her, he thought feverishly. How could he get rid of her? He handed her the glass, then sat down opposite her, sipping his whisky, and tried not to panic.

"Don't you think that was a bit premature?" he asked her. "Don't you think that you should have discussed it with me first?"

"Why? I'm practically living here anyway," she replied glibly.

"There's a big difference between sleeping here a couple of times a week and actually living together! I'm not sure I'm ready for that." He raked his hands through his hair. God, this had got out of control. He should have stuck to his guns and never had her over to his place.

"It's that bitch Amber, isn't it?" she blazed at him.

"What's Amber got to do with it?" he asked, mystified.

"I've seen you looking at her. You still have the hots for her, don't you?" she hissed, her eyes accusing.

"Oh, for God's sake," he shouted at her, slamming out of the room. God, he needed to talk to Tim.

Tim was out at the office Christmas party and was a little the worse for drink.

"Hey, man, I warned you," he slurred his words.

"What can I do?" Pete asked him.

"What can you do?" Tim hiccupped. "You can't very well throw her out on her ear."

Pete could hear that someone was trying to take Tim's phone from him.

"Get lost," he heard Tim say, then laugh at whoever it was. "Sorry, man, have to go. Knew this would happen one day, Pete, ol' boy. 'Fraid you've made your bed and now you must lie on it." And he hung up.

That was a great help. Pete threw back his whisky in one gulp and went into the living-room to refill his glass. Lesley was opening the buttons on her dress and then let it slip to the floor. He saw that she was wearing his favourite red bra, thong and black fishnet stockings. She sauntered over to him, taking the glass from his hand.

"Come here, baby," she whispered in her husky voice.

Slipping her bra off, she pulled his head down to her big beautiful breasts. He couldn't help himself. All of a sudden he wanted her desperately and he pushed her down on the sofa, snapping her thong as he entered her forcefully. They both climaxed simultaneously and over his shoulder Lesley gave a smug little smile. She knew how to handle him. Everything would be okay.

Chapter 38

The party was over and the post mortem was taking place in the bar. The reps had all gone home, thanking everyone effusively. They'd had a wonderful time. Grace and Carlo had joined the girls for a last drink. They all agreed that it had been a terrific success and that they would have to repeat it next year.

Val sat quietly drinking and, when she did speak, Niamh realised that she was quite drunk.

"How are you getting home?" Niamh asked her.

"Dunno," she slurred, "taxi, I suppose."

"For God's sake, Val, it's the twentieth of December," Niamh said, shaking her head in exasperation. "There isn't a taxi to be had anywhere in Dublin. I booked mine a week ago."

"You can give me a lift so," Val mumbled.

"I suppose I don't have any choice, do I?" Niamh sighed, fed up to the teeth of her sister. She was impossible but what could Niamh do? Amber shook her head in disgust. Niamh was far too soft.

Rosie was the first to go when Gail's husband, Mike, arrived to collect her. Carlo and Grace were next and left for the City West Hotel, where they were staying.

"I'm bunched," Tessa said, yawning. "It's been a long day. I'm off to bed."

"Me too," Amber said, also yawning. "Will you be okay?" she asked Niamh as she stood up. "I'll stay with you if you like."

"No, go ahead," Niamh replied, grateful for her friend's concern. "My taxi is due in ten minutes. Thanks, anyway," she said, hugging them both goodnight and wishing them a Merry Christmas. They ignored Val, whose eyes were glazed over by now.

"No goodnight for me, I notice," she drawled. "Only for Little Miss Sunshine."

Niamh had had enough. "For fuck's sake, Val, drink up," she snapped, gathering up her things. "I'm going."

Drunk as she was, Val was shocked to hear Niamh curse. Niamh *never* cursed.

"Uh, oh, naughty, naughty," Val needled her. "Miss Perfect isn't so perfect after all!"

"For your information, I'm Mrs, not Miss," Niamh shot back at her.

"Sure," Val hiccupped. "Pity your husband can't remember that," she added, smirking.

Niamh froze. "What's that supposed to mean?" she asked, her voice quivering.

"What do you think delayed me this evening?" Val slurred. "I was paying your husband a little visit. Some lover boy you have there. Boy, is he ever good in bed!" She laughed, enjoying the look on Niamh's shocked face.

Niamh was frozen to the spot. Standing close to Val,

about to strike her, it hit her like a ton of bricks. That perfume . . . of course . . . it was Val's favourite, Allure. She could smell it now. It made her feel sick. And that lipstick . . . she was staring at it now. Val wasn't lying. Gavin had been screwing her own sister. Niamh thought she was going to throw up. She felt as if all the air had been sucked out of her lungs. She ran from the room and out the door, her tears blinding her.

That was why she never saw the car coming. She was tossed like a rag doll high in the air. The screech of brakes was the last thing she remembered.

Val was finishing her drink when someone came running into the bar.

"Is there a doctor here?" he yelled. "There's been a terrible accident outside."

"I'm a doctor," said one man, running out.

Everyone followed him and Val joined them, weaving from side to side. Niamh should have the taxi by now, she thought, looking around, realising that she was very drunk. The sight that met her eyes sobered her up pretty quickly. Niamh was lying motionless on the ground, a pool of blood around her head and her body twisted in a strange way. There was bedlam everywhere.

"Keep back, keep back!" someone was yelling.

"I can feel a pulse, she's still alive!" called the doctor who was ministering to her. "Give her some air, for God's sake!"

"She ran straight out in front of me, honestly," cried the driver of the car. "I just didn't see her, she ran straight out without looking. I swerved to avoid her. Will she be okay?" He was shaking and in shock.

"Here's her handbag," someone else called out.

Val was rooted to the spot. She thought she was going

to faint. Oh my God! It's all my fault. I've killed her. She let out a scream.

Running forward, kneeling down by the inert body, she cried out, "Niamh! Niamh! Open your eyes! Please talk to me! I'm sorry, none of it's true! Niamh, please forgive me!" she sobbed.

"You know this girl?" the doctor asked.

"She's my sister," Val replied, her face streaked with tears and mascara.

The ambulance arrived just then, blue light flashing and siren wailing, followed by two police cars, sirens and lights also going.

Tessa and Amber, getting ready for bed on the fourth floor of the hotel, heard the din. Tessa peeked out the window, checking that it wasn't a fire engine.

"No, it's an ambulance. Must be an accident," she told Amber.

"Poor soul," Amber replied. "I hope they're okay. Lousy timing – Christmas week."

"Probably someone drunk," Tessa replied, turning out the light.

"Goodnight."

"Sweet dreams."

Eileen was watching Tubridy on the telly when she got the phone call. At first she couldn't make out who it was or what they were saying. Then all her worst nightmares came to life.

"Mam, Mam, it's Niamh!" Val was sobbing. "She's had an accident."

Eileen felt her heart stop. "What kind of accident? Is she badly injured?"

"I don't know. She's not moving," Val gulped. "A car knocked her down."

"Oh, dear sweet Jesus," Eileen cried. "Where is she now?" She had grabbed her coat and was already on her way out the door.

"I'm in the ambulance with her, on our way to St James's Hospital. Hold on . . . oh . . . the doctor says that she's breathing okay."

Eileen heaved a sigh of relief. "Thank God she's alive." She was running now towards Niamh's house.

"It's all my fault, Mam," she heard Val say. "I'm so sorry."

How could it be her fault? Eileen wondered, hammering on Niamh's door.

Gavin opened it, wondering what the rumpus was.

"Niamh's been knocked down by a car but she's alive," Eileen managed to get out, her breath coming fast. "She's on her way to St James's. I'll get Johnny from next door to drive us and Sissy will stay with the children. Come on, hurry!" She ran next door.

Gavin was in shock. What had Eileen said? This couldn't be happening. Not to his Niamh. His heart was hammering as he checked on the kids and thanked Sissy for taking over.

Gav remembered nothing of the drive to the hospital. He sat, head bowed, clutching Eileen's hand.

"What will I do if anything happens to her?" he said, anguish in his eyes. "I couldn't live without her."

"Shush," she reassured him. "She's still alive and you know what a fighter she is. She'll pull through." She prayed that this would be the case. She was praying like she'd never prayed before.

"Oh, Niamh, Niamh, my poor baby!" Gavin cried over and over again.

They dashed into the A & E department of the hospital, barely noticing the bedlam that reigned there. They saw Val coming towards them, her face streaked with mascara and eye-shadow.

She burst out crying when she saw them.

"I'm so sorry, I'm so sorry!" she bawled.

"Where is she?" he asked, shaking Val to stop her gabbling. "Is she okay?" His eyes were wild.

"They're examining her now," Val told him, in between her sobs.

"I have to see her," he said. He ran to the reception desk. "My wife, where is she? She's been in an accident. I have to see her."

"Her name?" the nurse asked kindly.

"Niamh. Niamh Byrne," he replied, wringing his hands.

Eileen put her arms around him as the nurse made a phone call. "They've finished examining her and she's going into theatre shortly but you can have a moment with her. Come this way." She felt sorry for the handsome young man who was obviously distraught. His wife had not been a pretty sight when she'd been admitted. The nurse hoped he would be up to the shock.

Eileen followed her too. She had to see her baby and comfort her. The nurse led them to a waiting room and a doctor came out to greet them.

"Mr Byrne?"

Gavin nodded numbly.

"Your wife has had a very lucky escape. She took quite a knock and she's unconscious but she's alive and holding her own. We'll do a CT scan to be sure there's no brain injury. Our main concern is to ensure that she is not bleeding internally."

Gavin nodded numbly, trying to grasp all of this.

"But don't worry," the doctor assured them. "She's in good hands and she seems like a fighter."

"Oh she is, doctor," Eileen said, tears in her eyes.

"I take it you're her mother," the doctor smiled. "I can see the resemblance."

He brought them into a room where a nurse gave them gowns and masks and plastic shoes and made them wash their hands with antiseptic. She then brought them into a very bright room with green-clad figures milling around. There were machines and instruments everywhere but Gavin had eyes only for the tiny still figure lying on the stretcher. She had an oxygen mask over her face and numerous tubes going into her body. She looked so pale and fragile that Gavin started to sob.

"Niamh, babe, it's going to be okay. I'm here now," he said, taking her tiny lifeless hand. He could hear the bleep-bleep of the heart monitor. Only for that, he would have thought she was dead. Her hair was all matted with blood but he thought she still looked beautiful. Like a physical blow it hit him just how much he loved her.

Eileen took her daughter's hand and whispered "St Jude will take care of you, sweetheart. I love you."

"Time now, I'm afraid," the doctor said.

Gavin touched her hair. "I'll love you forever, my darling," he whispered, kissing her forehead.

Then they wheeled Niamh away from him.

"Come back to me, babe, please!" he cried.

Both Eileen and he were crying as they left the room, their arms around each other.

Val was sitting white-faced, waiting for them. Eileen told her what the doctor said. She started wailing again.

"It's my fault, it's all my fault!" she cried.

"How is it your fault?" Gavin asked.

Val was gabbling incoherently. They caught the words "running away" and "I didn't mean it" before she started bawling again.

"Oh, shut up, Val!" her mother snapped. She turned to Johnny, who had waited for them.

"Johnny, would you mind dropping Val home? She's not doing anyone any good here. Gavin and I are staying."

"Of course, Eileen," Johnny said. "Let us know if there's any news, won't you? And don't worry, Gavin," he nodded at him, "Sissy will stay with the kids as long as you want. You stay here with Niamh."

"Thanks, Johnny," Gavin replied.

Eileen smiled at him gratefully.

"Come on, Val," Johnny said, taking Val by the arm. She went with him meekly, still snivelling.

It was over three hours later when the doctor came for them. He looked weary as he took his cap and mask off but he was smiling.

"Please, St Jude," Eileen whispered, one last time.

"Well, good news," he told them and Gavin practically collapsed with relief. "She has no brain damage. We've stitched up the head wound but it will be pretty sore for a couple of days. Luckily, we were able to stop the internal bleeding." He smiled at them. "She has a broken wrist and some broken ribs but quite honestly it's amazing her injuries were not more severe. She's pretty stable now but we're keeping her under observation. Don't worry, she's in good hands."

315

Eileen made the sign of the cross and said a prayer of thanks.

Gavin found himself crying with the relief. "Can I see her now?" he asked.

"Yes," the doctor replied. "She's in intensive care so I'm afraid it's only one visitor at a time."

"Is she still unconscious?" Eileen asked nervously.

"She came round, just before surgery, but of course she's sedated now, so I don't expect she'll even know you're there."

He directed them to Intensive Care. They rang the bell and a nurse came and let Gavin in. Again, all the hygiene precautions, but he would have agreed to anything just to be by Niamh's side. She looked peaceful and had a little more colour in her cheeks but she still looked like a porcelain doll. His heart contracted with love for her. Rubbing her forehead, he whispered to her as he held her hand in his other one. He thought he felt her pressing his hand as he told her how much he loved her but she never opened her eyes. Kissing her gently, he left.

"She won't come around for a long time yet," a nurse told them after Eileen had visited too. "Sleep is the best thing for her now and we're keeping her heavily sedated. Why don't you go home and get some rest and come back after midday, when she should be waking up? If there's any change, we'll ring you of course."

They returned home, speaking little. Eileen had never had much time for Gavin but she had to admit that he'd gone up in her estimation during the past couple of hours. Whatever she thought of him, she was sure of one thing: he loved Niamh deeply.

Gavin grabbed a couple of hours' sleep and then got the

children up for school. It was their last day before the Christmas holidays and they were all excited about it. Santa Claus was coming to visit the school so Gavin decided not to tell them about Niamh's accident just yet.

"Where's Mammy?" Lily wanted to know.

"Yes, I want Mammy to dwess me!" Rose stamped her little foot.

"Mammy stayed in the hotel last night, after the party," Gavin lied, bouncing Rose on the bed and then tickling her, "so Daddy is going to dwess you today!"

"Me too, me too," Lily squealed, jumping on top of him.

He tickled her too and then hugged them both tightly. God, he was so lucky.

He arrived back from school to find Val waiting on his doorstep.

"What do you want, Val?" he asked her wearily. He sighed, brushing her aside. "You're not coming in."

"Please, Gav, I have to talk to you," she muttered, looking at the ground. "It's important. I have something to tell you."

He didn't know whether to believe her or not. Last night – God, it seemed so long ago now – while Niamh had been at the party – Val had arrived, all dolled up and obviously intending to hit on him again. He had turned her away unceremoniously. "Get lost, Val," he'd told her.

Now here she was again. "You're not coming in," he told her. "Say what you have to say right here."

Slowly, haltingly, she told him what she'd said to Niamh the night before – told him what had caused her to rush out into the oncoming car.

He couldn't believe what he was hearing. He grabbed

her by the shoulders. "You told her what?" he shouted at her, shaking her as hard as he could.

"I'm sorry," she whimpered.

He let go of her. "Jesus Christ!" he shouted, even louder, his fists clenching and unclenching by his side. "Get out of my sight! You're despicable! You make me want to vomit!" It took all of his self-control not to put his hands around her neck and choke the life out of her. "You'd better be at the hospital when your sister wakes up, to tell her what a liar you are and that none of it is true or, so help me God, I'll come and drag you in by the hair of your head!" He turned on his heel, slamming the door in her face.

He was shaking. How could she? Had Niamh believed her? Oh, God! He sank to the couch, his head in his hands. He'd meant what he said. He'd drag her in – physically, if necessary – to make sure Niamh learnt the truth. Val had been right about one thing. It *was* her fault that Niamh had met with the accident.

Eileen organised for her older daughter, Brenda, to come and stay with the kids while she and Gavin went to the hospital. Niamh was still sleeping but the staff nurse assured them that she was doing fine.

"I'll call you in when she wakes," she told them as they took their seats in the waiting room.

Eileen was surprised to see Val waiting there for them.

"What are you doing here?" she asked her.

Val looked at Gavin who glared back.

"Tell your mother," he said grimly.

"I can't," she wailed.

"Tell me what?" Eileen asked, mystified, looking from one to the other.

"Tell her," Gavin repeated, menacingly.

Val had no choice. She told her mother the horrible thing she'd done.

Eileen was shocked to the core.

"I knew you were bad, Val, but I never thought you'd stoop to this. You're to blame for Niamh lying here, injured. She could have been killed, for God's sake," she said, her voice shaking. "She could still die."

At that moment, the nurse appeared. "Niamh is waking up," she announced. "Would you like to come in, Mr Byrne?"

They donned gowns and Gavin went in first. When he entered the room, he saw that Niamh's colour had returned and her eyes were flickering.

"Darling," Gavin whispered, "how are you feeling?" Her eyes opened and he saw the pain in them. Not just the pain of her injuries but something else.

"Darling, I love you. There's never been anyone else. Only you," he whispered as he stroked her face. She turned away from him and he saw a tear roll down her cheek. "Please believe me, sweetheart. Val is here to tell you that she lied to you. I've never been with her. I've never been unfaithful to you." He desperately wanted her to believe in him. He saw a flicker of hope in her eyes before she closed them again.

"Okay, Mr Byrne," the nurse said, "time to go."

Niamh motioned to the nurse, who pulled the oxygen mask aside. "Val," she whispered, making a come-hither sign with her hand.

"I think she wants to see her sister," Gavin said, praying that this would make everything all right.

Gavin left and Val went in, her feet dragging on the

floor. She was terribly shocked at how frail Niamh looked and started crying softly.

"I'm so sorry, Niamh. I'm so sorry," she sobbed. "I lied to you."

Niamh's eyes flickered open and focused on Val who was shocked at the pain she saw there.

"None of it was true. None of it! I've never been with Gavin. I wanted to but he would have nothing to do with me." She continued to cry softly. "I even put lipstick and perfume on his shirt in the linen basket so that you'd think we were having an affair. Please forgive me."

Niamh listened, shocked at what Val had tried to do to her. Then she closed her eyes but not before Val had seen the relief that flooded them.

The nurse came in then and asked Val to leave. She shuffled out, still crying.

Unable to look her mother or Gavin in the face she whispered, "I told her that I lied and that I'm dreadfully sorry. I am, really I am."

"Get out of here," her mother said, spitting the words out. "And don't come near Niamh or me, ever again." And she turned her back on her spiteful daughter.

"Mam, I'm truly sorry!" Val cried, grabbing her mother's arm but Eileen pulled away out of her grasp and went in to see her injured daughter.

Gavin looked at Val in disgust and turned his back on her too.

The next time Gavin was allowed in, Niamh was much more alert. She reached for his hand.

Pulling the mask to one side, she whispered. "I'm sorry for doubting you, Gav."

"It's okay, babe. Don't try to talk. You're going to be okay now," he told her gently rubbing her cheek. "You're the only woman in the world for me, surely you know that." She smiled and nodded her head, wincing at the pain.

Eileen went in after that and sat holding her daughter's hand as Niamh closed her eyes and drifted off to sleep.

Chapter 39

Like wildfire, the news of Niamh's accident spread. Gavin was inundated with calls from the If the Shoes Fit girls, both managers and representatives. He assured them all that Niamh was on the mend but would not be ready for visitors until after Christmas. Amber and Tessa felt particularly bad when they realised that it was their friend who'd been in the accident that they'd seen from their hotel window.

"How could we have known?" Tessa said to Amber, who was very upset.

They managed to speak to Niamh two days later, on the hospital phone, and she assured them that she was fine, if a little sore.

"We'd really love to come and see you before we go away for Christmas. Do you think we might?" Amber asked.

"I'd love to see you both but I better warn you, I get tired very quickly."

"We'll only stay five minutes, promise," Tessa told her.

"We couldn't bear to go away without seeing you," Amber explained. She was heading to Spain and Tessa to Galway.

They hit Brown Thomas and bought a luxurious emerald velvet dressing-gown and matching slippers, pretty nighties and a host of Molton Brown toiletries which they wrapped up beautifully and took with them to the hospital.

Niamh smiled as she opened up the gifts. "Trust you pair to know exactly what I'd need and not send flowers, like everyone else," she said, throwing her eyes to heaven, which hurt her like hell. Indeed, her hospital room resembled a florist's shop – so many flowers had arrived for her. "One old dear, who's a patient in another ward, popped her head in this morning and seeing all the flowers, exclaimed, 'Oh, you've had a baby, how lovely, my dear!' before noticing the bandage around my head and this cast." Niamh, laughed, waving her arm.

The girls pealed with laughter.

"Okay, we promised we wouldn't tire you," Amber said, "so we'll go now."

"We just couldn't bear to go away without making sure you were okay," Tessa said gently.

"I'm so glad you called in," Niamh told them. "It's been lovely to see you and I hope you both have a great Christmas."

"We'll visit you the minute we get back," they promised, blowing kisses as they left.

Niamh was exhausted when they'd gone and was sleeping when Gavin called in some time later. He sat quietly, looking at her, thinking how beautiful she was and how goddamn lucky *he* was.

When she woke she showed him what the girls had brought in.

"Beautiful!" he let out a whistle. "Exactly the colour of your eyes."

She told him that Carlo, bless him, had sent a case of champagne and Grace a voucher for €200 for Marks & Spencer, which would come in very handy for the sales. They had sent their love and best wishes for her speedy recovery.

Niamh was fretting that she wouldn't be home for Christmas Day. It was the first year that the girls understood all about Santa Claus and they were hyper with excitement, looking forward to the presents they'd asked for. Niamh thanked her lucky stars that she'd done all her Christmas shopping early in December. The only thing that was bothering her was how they'd cope without her on Christmas Day.

Rosie was desperately upset when she heard of Niamh's accident. She was thinking of their conversation and hoped that her advice to confront Gavin had been the right one. She feared that maybe Niamh had been in a rush to get home which might have caused the accident. If that was the case, then Rosie would feel responsible. She couldn't rest easy until she got to talk to Niamh. On Christmas Eve morning she went to the hospital and, when Niamh heard it was Rosie, she asked the nurse to allow her in.

Rosie got a shock when she saw how fragile Niamh looked but felt relief when Niamh held out her arms to her, smiling.

"Oh, Niamh, I've been so worried about you," Rosie said, dabbing the tears from her eyes.

"I'm fine, don't worry. It looks much worse than it is," Niamh grinned.

Pulling up a chair, Rosie took her friend's hand. It felt so tiny.

"I was really worried that the advice I gave you might have contributed in some way to your accident," she admitted.

"You needn't have," Niamh reassured her, then told her about Val and what had happened.

"But what about the lipstick and perfume on Gavin's shirt?" Rosie wanted to know.

Grimacing, Niamh explained that Val had confessed to placing them there, to cause trouble.

"What a bitch!" Rosie said, not used to using such language. She reckoned there wasn't language bad enough to describe Val.

"Everything's fine between Gav and me now. In fact, better than fine," Niamh said, blushing.

"I'm so happy for you," Rosie said, giving her a hug.

"Ouch!" Niamh winced as her ribs hurt.

"Oh, I'm so sorry," Rosie apologised.

"I've never had so many hugs in my life," Niamh laughed, "each one more painful than the last!"

"Thank God you're okay," Rosie told her, handing her a box tied up with ribbons. "A little present for you."

Niamh opened it up to find a bottle of Allure perfume. "Oh, no," she moaned.

"What's wrong?" Rosie asked, alarmed.

"Sorry, Rosie. It's just that this is the perfume that Val used to try and sabotage my marriage. I'm not sure I could wear it. It would forever remind me of her. I'm sorry!"

"My mistake, sorry," Rosie said, dismayed. "Of course

you couldn't wear it! I can change it for Mademoiselle Coco, if you'd like. I actually almost chose that."

"That would be great," Niamh said, smiling.

The nurse bustled in. "Sorry, Niamh, you need to rest now," she said, giving Rosie the bum's rush.

"I'm so pleased you're okay," Rosie said as she got up to leave. She took great care not to hurt Niamh as she hugged her goodbye.

Greatly relieved, Rosie drove home. *Thank God for that, Jack,* she thought, looking to the sky as she always did when talking to her late husband. *I really wish you were here. Christmas is so difficult without you.*

She was dreading the next couple of days and always felt his loss more than ever at this time. She was going to Gail's for Christmas Day but the season was always so dragged out in Ireland. She'd always hated that. The country practically closed down for two weeks. Why couldn't we be like other countries? Two, three days at most! She sighed as she turned the car into her driveway.

She was preparing her lunch when there was a knock at the door. Who is it now, she wondered grumpily, as she went to answer the door.

"Happy Christmas!" was the sound that greeted her.

"Oh my God!" she cried, placing her hand on her heart.

Standing on her doorstep was her son David, all the way from Australia. Behind him was Gail with Holly and Mike, all grinning broadly. Amid the flurry of hugs and kisses, she chastised David.

"Why didn't you tell me you were coming?" she cried.

"I wanted to surprise you," David beamed.

"You did that all right," she said. "You practically gave me a heart attack."

"Ah, Mum, you're a tougher old bird than that," he replied amid much laughter.

She was delighted to see him. She ushered them in.

What a lovely surprise, indeed!

"What about Clara and the children?" she asked him, her face full of concern. "Didn't they mind you coming away for Christmas?"

"No, not at all. In fact, it was Clara's idea and she's taking the kids to her parents in Perth for the holiday, so everyone's happy." He beamed at his mother.

Chatting to Jack that night as she got ready for bed, she told him that it wasn't going to be such a bad Christmas after all. Firstly, Niamh was okay and then David had arrived. She had the strangest feeling that Jack had had a hand in this.

Chapter 40

Tessa left for Galway on Christmas Eve. She called in to Kate to deliver their Christmas presents and collect Napoleon, who was going to Galway with her. As always, he was delighted to see his mistress and even more delighted to discover that he was going in the car with her. She had to very firmly order him to "Sit", as he was trying to lick her face as she was driving and she was worried she'd have an accident.

She was looking forward to seeing her father again but less keen to see her stepmother, Claudia. Although she was now thirty-six years old, her stepmother still treated her like a child and constantly criticised and disapproved of her. Tessa guessed that she would always be like that.

Tessa was shocked at the change in her father. In the six months since she'd seen him, he'd lost a lot of weight and seemed to have shrunk. He had always been a larger than life figure but now seemed frail. Very worried about him, she asked Claudia if he was ill.

"No, just getting old, I suppose," was her stepmother's vague reply. "If you came to visit more often, you wouldn't see such a change in him."

Here we go again, Tessa thought irritably.

Niamh was feeling very down on Christmas morning. The hospital was like a morgue as most people had gone home for the festival. She was missing the thrill of the children and Santa Claus and feeling very sorry for herself when Gavin arrived, the three kids in tow.

"Happy Chwismas, Mammy!" the twins chorused, climbing up on her bed. She winced as they hugged her, pressing against her painful ribs.

"Down girls, down!" Gavin grabbed them and plonked them on the floor.

"Is it sore, Mammy?" Ian asked her, his little face full of concern as he kissed her, taking great care not to hurt her.

She ruffled his hair affectionately, tears in her eyes.

"Now for the best Christmas present of all," Gavin said, smiling at her, and after kissing her deeply on the lips he placed a bag on the bed.

"What's this?" she asked, opening the bag to find some of her clothes inside.

"You're coming home with us," he grinned. "You didn't think we'd spend Christmas Day without you?"

She saw the nurse behind him, smiling and nodding. "You'll have to take it easy, of course, Niamh," she said. "You must lie on the couch for the day, that's the very most you can do."

Niamh was overwhelmed. "I'm coming home!"

"Mammy's coming ho-ome, Mammy's coming ho-ome!" sang Rose, clapping her hands and dancing up and down.

"Mammy's coming ho-ome!" Lily parroted her twin, clapping her hands and dancing around Rose.

"And Santa Claus left a message to say that we couldn't open our presents till you're home," Ian explained to her, earnestly.

"Well, I'd better hurry up then," she replied, tears in her eyes as she smiled gratefully at her husband.

"Thank you," she mouthed to him, silently.

"I love you," he mouthed back.

She arrived home in a wheelchair but that didn't bother Niamh. She was home for Christmas! To her surprise, she found she was exhausted after the excitement of the kids opening their presents, so she went for a lie-down.

She got up in time for the delicious dinner that Eileen had prepared. Even her mother-in-law, Bridget, who joined them for it, was unusually kind and when she did once venture a criticism, Gavin silenced her with a look. He was wonderful and when he caught Niamh yawning at around seven o'clock that evening, insisted on taking her to bed. After he had undressed her tenderly and administered her medication, he lay down beside her, gently stroking her until she fell asleep. It had been a wonderful Christmas.

Chapter 41

Amber had flown out to Spain the evening after she'd visited Niamh, relieved to know that her friend was on the mend. Susie and Tony were spending Christmas in their villa in Marbella and had persuaded her to join them. The fact that Tessa would be away and that Luke was also going to be in Marbella at the same time made it a much more attractive proposition than spending it with her mother and her three old aunts, who did nothing but watch dreadful TV programmes all day. It was no contest.

She was tired after the busy selling period and she was glad to have the break. It was wonderful to be lying by the pool on Christmas Day and Amber found herself relaxing as the hot sun warmed her skin. They ate their Christmas dinner outdoors and Amber felt truly happy.

She met Luke the following day and they went for lunch at the famous Trader Vic's restaurant. She had a lovely time and was quite a bit tiddly as she toasted him for about the tenth time with the champagne they were knocking back as if there was no tomorrow.

Suddenly she had an eerie feeling that someone was staring at her and turning around to check, found herself looking into Dermot's eyes.

"Oh my God," she whispered, growing pale.

"What's the matter?" Luke asked, worried.

"It's my ex-husband, Dermot," she said, her voice shaking.

"Do you want to leave?" Luke asked her.

"No, why should I?" she demanded.

"You're right," he agreed.

She stayed, trying to make normal conversation with Luke, while desperately aware that Dermot was just yards from her. Eventually, a shadow fell over their table.

"Hello, Amber," Dermot said quietly.

"Hello, Dermot," she replied, her mouth going dry.

"How are you?" he asked.

"I'm fine, thank you," she said, feeling ludicrous to be having this stilted conversation with a man she'd been married to for fifteen years. Dermot was looking towards Luke.

"This is my friend, Luke," she said, surprised at how calmly she spoke.

"How do you do?" Dermot said formally. "Could I have a word with Amber, please, in private?"

"Certainly," Luke replied, looking at Amber to make sure that this was what she wanted.

She nodded at him. "It's okay, Luke," she assured him.

He left them alone. She gestured to Dermot to take a seat.

She looked at her ex-husband, noticing how tired he looked and how grey he'd become. He, who had always been so particular about his appearance, looked quite haggard. She felt a quiet satisfaction that she was looking great and hoped he noticed.

"You look great, Amber," was the first thing he said.

So he had noticed. Good!

"How have you been?" he enquired.

"Wonderful," she replied. "Life is good now. I've started a new business, which I love, and it's very successful."

"And . . ." he hesitated, "who is this . . . em . . . Luke? Anyone special?" He was looking at her intently.

She couldn't resist it! "Not that it's any of your business – but we're good friends. We worked together for a long time. He's a pilot."

"Oh, I see," he said, looking suitably downcast.

"What about you?" she enquired politely. "What are you doing here?"

"I'm here with Jeff. You remember him? Well, he's going through a pretty awful divorce from Maeve and he wanted to get out of her firing range over the Christmas period. She's being a bitch," he added, by way of explanation.

"She always was," Amber remarked, delighted to hear that Maeve was finally getting her come-uppance.

"Yes, I remember that she was always very nasty to you," said Dermot.

Amber was dying to ask him if his new young wife was with him but the word "wife" stuck in her throat, so she curbed her curiosity.

"Amber, I need to talk to you. Will you meet me for dinner tonight or whenever suits you?"

She couldn't help it. She just had to ask. "What about your wife?"

"Actually, we divorced. We only lasted six months. She met someone else."

Hah! Amber thought jubilantly. So you got a taste of your own medicine!

He reached across and took her hand.

She pulled away and he looked hurt.

"Amber, please can we meet and talk? There is so much I need to say . . ."

"I don't think so, Dermot. I think you said it all at our last meeting, in Brussels."

He looked devastated at her refusal. "Please, Amber," he begged. "Just let's talk."

She thought about it, remembering Carlo's remark about how she might still be in love with Dermot. What better time to find out! What harm could it do?

"Okay," she said. "I'll meet you, but not tonight – tomorrow night."

"Thank you, Amber," he said, gratefully. "Can I pick you up at your place?'

"No," she replied, quickly. "I'll meet you here. Eight o'clock?"

"I look forward to it," he said, smiling for the first time. "I'll book Cipriano's."

He looked confident again, more like his old self. Typical of him, she thought, taking her to the top restaurant around. Trying to impress – as always! They were doubtless completely booked out but Dermot would grease palms.

At that moment she saw Luke coming back. "I think you'd better go now," she said.

"Everything okay?" Luke asked, as he arrived back.

"Fine, I'm just leaving," Dermot said. "Amber, Luke," he said, bowing slightly from the waist.

Christ, he hasn't changed, Amber thought.

"My God, how did you stay married to such a stiff prick for so long?" Luke asked her.

Amber roared with laughter. "You do have a way with words, Luke."

Luke grinned sheepishly. "Well, honestly, look at how he was dressed. A pin-striped suit and tie! He looked completely out of place here."

Amber looked around the bar. She had to admit he was right. All the men were casually dressed in open-necked shirts and white suits or chinos. Luke himself was dressed like that and looked very relaxed. He had a point.

"And the way he talks," Luke was in full flow now. "All clipped vowels and so formal. Brrrrr . . ." he shivered dramatically, "What a cold fish, your ex-husband!"

Amber pealed with laughter again. Luke was a tonic. She patted his hand affectionately. He really was great company and good fun and his assessment of Dermot was spot-on. He had nailed him perfectly!

"You're what?" Susie roared at Amber. "Tell me I didn't hear that."

Tony, hearing the commotion, came running into the kitchen to investigate the cause of his wife's roars.

"What's wrong?" he asked, looking from Susie to Amber.

"You won't believe what she's doing," Susie wailed at him, pointing an accusing finger at Amber.

"What?" Tony couldn't imagine what Amber had done to so infuriate his normally calm wife.

"She met Dermot at Trader Vic's and meekly agreed to have dinner with him, tomorrow night," Susie cried.

"It wasn't meek . . ." Amber started to say.

"Can you believe it?" Susie ranted on, hands stretched towards him, asking him to agree with her.

"Calm down, Suz," he said. "What's so wrong with that?"

"What's wrong with it?" Susie looked at him incredulously. "Have you both forgotten what a total shite he was and how despicably he behaved? He almost ruined you, Amber, and I don't want you to give him the chance to do it again!"

"Don't worry," Amber reassured her, putting her hands on Susie's shoulders to stop her pacing. "I'm not the fool I was when he left me. I think it will be good for me to hear him out and have closure," she said calmly.

"Closure – *hrrump*!" Susie snorted, shaking her head in disbelief.

"I think that's a good idea," Tony remarked, immediately aware that he'd said the wrong thing when he saw the withering look his wife threw him.

Amber hadn't told Susie that Carlo had suggested she was still carrying a torch for Dermot. Luckily, she thought now, as she saw Susie's reaction to the news that she was meeting Dermot tomorrow.

"I hope he's not calling here to pick you up," Susie remarked angrily.

"No," Amber smiled. "I have more sense than that. The poor man might never make it to dinner if he crossed your path." She winked at Tony, who sniggered.

"Tony, don't you have anything better to do than stand there like an idiot?" Susie asked her husband.

Wow! She really is riled up about this, he thought, as he slunk out of the kitchen.

"All I can say is, I hope you know what you're doing," Susie said to Amber, calming down a little.

"Trust me," Amber told her, giving her a hug. "Now let's have a drink."

"I need it, after that bombshell," Susie said, heading to the drinks cabinet.

Amber noticed that she was smiling.

Chapter 42

Tessa became concerned when her father refused to go hunting on Boxing Day. It was unlike him to miss a hunt. She was happy to spend the day with her father, alone, although Claudia had insisted that they go along for the after-hunt party.

Her stepmother had, as she always had done, arranged an endless round of parties for every day over the Christmas period. Tessa could see that her father found it tiring but still Claudia insisted that they not miss a single drinks party, or brunch or dinner. Even Tessa was exhausted by the constant partying and drinking.

"Are you okay, Dad?" she asked him as they walked around the estate.

"Just slowing down," he said, sighing.

"Claudia's not giving you much chance to slow down," Tessa said irritably.

"Don't blame you stepmother, Tess," he said, gently. "She doesn't know any other way to live."

"She could at least slow down a little," Tessa said critically. "She always has to be socialising."

"She is the way she is," he replied, as always supportive of his wife.

Tessa was angry with her stepmother and it came to a head between them the next day.

"Why are you driving Dad so hard?" Tessa demanded.

"Oh, stop babying him!" Claudia shot back angrily. "He's still a virile man."

"For God's sake, look at him! He's not well," Tessa cried. "Can you not make him go to a doctor?"

"Nonsense, he's fine," was her stepmother's reply.

Tessa sighed, realising she was beating her head against a brick wall.

Next she tackled her father. "Dad, I'm worried about you. You don't look well. Would you come to Dublin and I'll arrange a medical check-up for you?"

"Oh, no," he replied. "That would worry Claudia too much."

Tessa wasn't too sure about that!

Tessa kept trying to change his mind but he was a stubborn old git. She left for Ballyfern the following day, still worried about him, but with nothing resolved. She was relieved to be getting away from her stepmother and looking forward to spending the New Year with Kate and her family and also to taking Kilkenny out for some long rides. She hoped the weather would allow it.

Rosie had had a very nice Christmas and it was lovely having David around. The only thing missing was Jack. Somehow, now that Christmas was over, she was beginning to come to terms with his death. Life was good and she now accepted that she had to live every day to the full.

She had rung Hugo on Christmas morning to wish him a Merry Christmas and give him the news of Niamh's accident and David's surprise visit.

"I was wondering why you weren't answering my emails," he said, petulantly.

"Well, I've just been too busy, Hugo, to be honest," she told him. "The internet is great but it's no substitute for real life." She knew that he was sulking but he would just have to get over it. Men could be such children! He was somewhat mollified when she asked him around for a drink on Stephen's Night.

"That would be lovely, Rosie. Have a nice day! I look forward to tomorrow night."

Val was miserable. In other years, the family had all got together at Christmas and it had always been great fun. This year she was an outcast. None of her brothers and sisters wanted anything to do with her when they heard what she'd done. She was feeling desperately low and couldn't face into work. Boxer was furious with her.

"This is a business, ducky," he'd said, "and the show must go on, regardless of how you're feeling."

She hadn't had the nerve to tell him what she'd done. She spent Christmas Day alone and drank herself into oblivion. Her mood wasn't helped three days later when she received a letter from Grace telling her that they were sorry, but that they would not be renewing her contract in January. Great, she thought. Niamh wins again! She'd accepted that Gavin was now forever beyond her reach.

She rang Phoebe to discover that she too had received a similar letter.

"Oh, I'm not bothered! I've got a fantastic new venture in the pipeline. This will make me millions," she gushed.

"I'm sure," Val said flippantly. God, Phoebe was such a pain.

She then rang Lesley, who was in the middle of yet another blazing row with Pete.

"I really can't talk now, Val," she said snottily. "Could you call me back tomorrow?"

Val felt very alone. She had hoped that Lesley would have given her some sympathy and support. But as always, Lesley was only thinking of Lesley.

Pete realised very quickly that he'd made a dreadful mistake. Lesley was a selfish bitch and as hard as nails. The only good thing that he could say about her was that she was a hottie in bed. Unfortunately, they couldn't stay in bed 24/7 and when out of it they fought constantly.

She threw a major tantrum whenever he wanted to go out with mates so that in the end he stayed in, for the sake of peace. They did have a lovely Christmas Day, when they stayed in bed all day, making love and drinking champagne. Tim and Lucy invited them over for Stephen's Day and it was hate at first sight. Lesley was happily occupied, telling some dirty jokes to a group of men who surrounded her, ignoring the dagger's looks being thrown her way by their wives. Pete wasn't too happy about the very low, tight, sequinned dress she had insisted on wearing, although he had to admit it showed off her voluptuous body to perfection. They weren't twenty minutes in the house when Tim motioned Pete into the kitchen.

"For God's sake, Pete," he hissed. "What are you doing with her? She's a nightmare."

"She has her moments," Pete replied sheepishly.

"I can imagine what *they* are," Tim grimaced. "Pete, you've been out with some pretty dreadful women in the past – as even you'll agree – but this one takes the biscuit." He put his hands on his friend's shoulders. "Seriously, Pete, you have to get rid of her. She's not for you." Tim looked at him earnestly.

"Well, I've got a problem there," Pete said, not looking too happy. "She's moved in with me."

"She's what?"

Just then Lucy came into the kitchen to refill a tray of canapés. "Who's what?" she asked.

"Lesley has moved in with Pete," Tim explained grimly to his wife.

"She's *what*?" Lucy's reaction mirrored that of her husband's.

"Yeah, she left her husband," Pete told them. "What could I do?" he asked, refilling his whisky glass.

Lucy said nothing but her grim expression said it all.

Matters didn't improve when Lesley proceeded to get disgustingly drunk and he had to practically carry her out to the taxi.

From the looks he got he knew that they'd never be invited again. He was furious with Lesley and they'd pretty much been fighting ever since.

Chapter 43

Tessa had just returned from a three-hour trek with Kilkenny and was rubbing him down when Amber rang her.

"Hi there, how's everything in sunny Spain? Fallen in love with any Señor?" Tessa laughed.

"No, but I have a date with my ex-husband tonight," Amber announced, knowing that this would completely floor Tessa, which it did.

Tessa almost dropped the phone on hearing this. "Oh my God! How did this come about?"

"Well, I met him in a bar and he said he wanted to talk. In the beginning I wasn't too keen but then I thought of what Carlo had said and decided that maybe it would be a good idea. I needn't tell you that Susie is going ballistic."

"Yeah, well, I see where she's coming from," Tessa said, thinking about it. "But I think you're right. Maybe you'll see him for the asshole that he really is and then you'll be over him, once and for all, and able to move on with your life."

"Thank God you understand," Amber told her friend. "That's exactly what I'm hoping will happen." She let out a sigh of relief. "How was Galway?"

"Same old, same old, where my stepmother is concerned, anyway," Tessa confided, rubbing Kilkenny's nose. "I'm very concerned about Dad, though. I'm really worried that he's not well but Claudia doesn't want to see it. He's definitely not himself."

"Oh, I'm sorry, Tessa. I hope he'll be okay," Amber sympathised, knowing how difficult Tessa's stepmother could be. "How's Kate? And everyone in Ballyfern?"

"They're all great. I'm really looking forward to New Year here. There's so much love in this house. I really wish you could be here."

"I'll be back on the second so we can celebrate New Year again together, and catch up," Amber said, missing her friend, suddenly.

"Good luck tonight, hon," Tessa said softly.

"Thanks, Tessa. It's good that you understand. Miss you."

"Miss you too."

Amber was amazed at how calm she felt as she prepared to go out to meet her ex-husband. Despite Susie's warnings and misgivings, she knew she was doing the right thing. He was waiting for her at Trader Vic's and as she walked towards him, she basked in the admiring glances she was getting from the men she passed. She wanted Dermot to see what he'd thrown away.

"Amber, you look stunning," he said, admiration in his voice.

Round one to me, she thought.

He reached over to kiss her and just in time she turned her head so that his lips missed their mark and landed in the region of her ear.

"I took the liberty of ordering a bottle of champagne. I hope that's okay?" he asked.

He hasn't changed, Amber thought wryly. Taking control again!

"Actually, I'd prefer a Martini," she smiled sweetly, amused at how surprised Dermot was at this show of independence.

"A Martini it is then," he smiled back at her, but Amber could see the annoyance behind it.

"You've changed," he said, surprise in his voice. "I like it." Reaching over to take her hand he said, "I've missed you dreadfully."

Snatching her hand back, she replied, "Yes, well, we all make mistakes."

"I made the biggest mistake of all, leaving you." He leaned across the table towards her. "Could you ever find it in your heart to forgive me, my dear?"

Amber wondered what in the world he wanted from her. She soon found out.

"Amber, darling, could we start over? I never stopped loving you, you know."

His eyes had that look she remembered when he wanted something and was sure that he was going to get it.

"Dermot, I –"

"Darling, let me say one thing." He gave her that patronising smile which he'd always used when he was about to bestow some gift on her. "I'm even willing for us to have a baby, if that's what you really want." He sat, like a small boy waiting for a pat on the head.

She looked at him incredulously. Was he serious? She realised that he was, and in that moment she also realised that she was well and truly over him. In fact, looking at his smug face, she wondered, as Luke had yesterday when he'd met him, how she'd ever stayed married to such a pompous ass for so long.

She started to laugh and seeing the shock on his face, laughed even harder.

"I don't see what's so funny," he said, obviously deeply offended.

"No, you wouldn't," she replied, still laughing. "Did you really seriously think that you could crook your little finger and that I'd come running? You know, Dermot," she said, rising to leave, "you're an even bigger prick than I remember."

His face was suffused with anger.

"The fact is," she continued, "I don't love you any more and the thought of suffering your pompous arrogance for even one whole evening is too much for me. Goodbye!" And with a flounce worthy of an Oscar winner, she made her exit.

She was still laughing at his sheer neck when she rang Luke three minutes later.

"Hey, if you're free I'd love to take you to dinner tonight, to celebrate," she told him.

"Will I like this celebration?" he asked warily, wondering why she wasn't having dinner with her ex in Cipriano's.

"Very much," she laughed. "Meet me in La Cantina as soon as you can."

"Be there in five," he said, his hopes rising.

While she waited for him, she rang Susie who was amazed to hear from her.

"You were right," were Amber's first words to her. "He

346

is a shite and a bastard and all the other things you've ever called him, and more besides." She briefly told Susie what had happened and her friend was as flabbergasted at what Dermot had suggested as Amber had been. Amber described her parting shots to him with gusto.

"Good girl and good riddance!" was Susie's response. She was secretly thrilled when she heard that Amber had asked Luke to dinner.

"Go, girl, go!" she said, smiling, after Amber had rung off.

When Luke walked in, Amber was sipping champagne and smiling. She poured a glass for him and raised her glass. "Cheers," she clinked it against his, smiling broadly.

"Can I ask what we're celebrating?" Luke asked her.

"Freedom – mine! I'm free at last!" she announced. "I'm finally free of him!" The grin was still plastered all over her face.

"To you!" he toasted her, smiling.

"To us!" she responded, setting his pulses racing.

Luke had realised quite some time ago that he was falling in love with Amber but had thought that it was a lost cause. He'd lost count of the times she'd told him that she wasn't ready for another relationship. Now it looked like maybe she was.

The evening was magical and Amber was more animated and alive than he'd ever seen her. He also thought that she had never looked more beautiful. They laughed and joked all through the meal and by the time they'd demolished the bottle of champagne and a bottle of wine, they were both a little tipsy. Leaving the restaurant, they walked along by the harbour, holding hands. It seemed the most natural thing in the world to be kissing and, when Luke asked her to come home with him, she didn't think twice about it.

She rang Susie to tell her that she would be spending the night with Luke and laughed at Susie's reaction. "Yes, yes, yes!" she'd cried.

He was very gentle with her, taking it very slowly and when he finally entered her, she was ready for him. It was so different from anything she'd ever experienced with Dermot that when Luke cradled her in his arms afterwards the tears flowed down her face.

"That was the most wonderful love I've ever experienced," she told him, smiling through her tears.

"Me too," he said, holding her face in his hands and kissing away her tears.

She fell asleep, wrapped in his arms thinking how perfect it was.

Chapter 44

Niamh was getting a little stronger every day but was still depending on painkillers every four hours. The strapping on her ribs was driving her crazy with itch but she knew it was necessary.

"I feel like a mummy in all this strapping," she'd remarked to her mother.

"You are a mummy, Mammy," said Ian, who had overheard.

Eileen and Niamh pealed with laughter at this.

"Ouch!" Niamh cried out. Laughing was painful but she'd laughed more in the past few days than ever before.

Something had subtly changed between Niamh and Gavin since her accident. It was as if he felt he was getting a second chance. He'd almost lost her and it had brought it home to him just how much he loved her. He couldn't do enough for her and watched over her as tenderly as if she were a china doll. He hadn't been out with his mates since she'd come home from the hospital.

"Gav, why don't you take a break and go out with the guys?" she'd suggested.

"I don't want to go out," he'd replied, kissing her in between each of the words, "I-prefer-to-be-with-you. I-love-you."

He had also cancelled the trip to Manchester to see Man. United play. Niamh urged him to go, saying that Eileen would look after things while he was away but he was adamant.

"I'm not leaving you, and that's that," he said, placing his hands on her shoulders. "I can go see them another time, when you're better." This, to Niamh was the biggest declaration of love he could ever have made.

The accident had changed Niamh's perspective also. When it finally hit her just how lucky she was to have survived, she realised what really mattered most to her – Gav and the kids – that was it! She kept them close to her and suffered their hugs and kisses, despite the pain it caused. She was so lucky. Somebody up there loved her. She'd even started praying to St Jude, thanking him!

"Cooeee, I'm home!" Amber cried as she turned her key in the lock. Tessa jumped up off the couch and ran excitedly to meet her, hair flying behind her. Amber had one foot against the door as she tried to pull her case in, a huge bouquet of flowers in her other hand. Tessa grabbed the flowers before they met an untimely death, as pealing with laughter Amber finally got herself inside the door.

"How I missed you!" Tessa said, hugging her, then standing back to look at her friend. "Good God, girl, you look fantastic. I'd like some of whatever it is you're on," she exclaimed. She had never seen Amber look so radiant.

Her glowing tanned skin couldn't match the glow in her eyes. She was vibrant and exhilarated and for a moment Tessa wondered if she was high on something.

"Whatever it is, I want the secret," she said, leading the way into the living-room.

"Love," Amber replied, almost causing Tessa to drop the beautiful bouquet of roses.

"Oh no!" Tessa cried, fearing that Amber had reunited with her ex-husband. "Not Dermot again!"

"That pompous asshole?" Amber snorted, making a puke-like sound. "No, it's Luke," she announced, beaming broadly.

This time Tessa did drop the bouquet. Nothing could have surprised her more.

"Luke?" she asked, stupidly. "What happened to Dermot?"

"Go open a bottle of wine – no, make that champagne – and I'll tell you the whole story," Amber told her dumb-founded friend.

Tessa's eyes opened wide as Amber told her everything and they toasted each other at every new revelation. When Amber told her how she'd walked out on Dermot, Tessa convulsed with laughter.

"I'd love to have seen his face, at that moment," she squeaked through her laughs. "It must have been priceless."

"Believe me, it was," Amber told her. "I've never had so much satisfaction in my life."

"And Luke," Tessa exclaimed. "I'm shocked."

"Not as shocked as I am, believe me," Amber smiled, remembering the last few wonderful days that she'd spent with him. "It's wonderful. Being with him is so easy and relaxing – just what I need!"

"What about *va-va-voom*?" Tessa asked. "Is that there? Does he make your heart pound when you see him?"

"Oh yes," Amber replied. "He maybe hasn't as much *va-va-voom* as Carlo, but he has more than enough of it for me."

She smiled again and Tessa thought how wonderful love was, to have this effect on someone. Amber looked radiant – lit up from within.

"I take it that's curtains for Carlo, then?" Tessa asked.

"'Fraid so," Amber grinned wickedly, "which leaves the coast clear for you to do a seduction number on him." She poked her friend in the arm.

"I'm afraid I'm not the seducing type," Tessa sighed.

She then told Amber all about her Christmas and New Year and it was after midnight when they finally crept into bed, Amber to dream of Luke and Tessa to wish she had someone special too.

Chapter 45

Rosie felt that her life was getting back on track also. It had been wonderful to have David home for Christmas. For the New Year he had suggested they go down to Clare to visit her family. She hadn't been back there since Jack's death but, with David by her side, it wasn't too difficult and she'd had a lovely time. She'd almost forgotten how beautiful it was there and enjoyed walking the empty beaches and the Burren. And of course the Irish music, which one heard everywhere, took her back to her wonderful youth. More than anything it was the warmth of the people she met that made her feel whole again. It was quite invigorating and she left with regret, thinking that it was a much nicer place to live than Dublin. Her two sisters and two brothers were sad to see her leave but she promised she'd come back soon.

The following day, with tears in her eyes, she saw David off at Dublin Airport but not before he'd extracted a promise from her to visit him in Australia, the following

Christmas. *I'll go, Jack, I promise*, she said, looking heavenward as she drove home alone.

Val was furious with Lesley, who hadn't returned any of her calls. When she did finally get her on the phone, Lesley was very brusque with her. Some friend she was turning out to be! She knew Lesley was living with Pete now and Val wanted to retrieve the DVDs that she'd lent her.

Furious with Lesley, she decided to ring Lesley's old home to see if she could get them back. Paul, Lesley's husband, answered the phone to her.

"Yeah sure," he'd replied to her request. "Come and get them and you can take her whole bloody collection for all I care." He gave her the address and directions.

Val went out there the next evening and was pleasantly surprised by how nice Paul was. Having listened to Lesley's description of him, she'd expected a moron. She picked out her DVDs and took a few others that she quite fancied as well.

"Hey, do you want her CDs as well? They're in my way and she sure as hell ain't comin' back for them."

"Gee, thanks," Val said, greedily rummaging through the vast collection.

He poured them both a beer and they chatted happily as she looked through the CDs. She admired his tattoos – he had quite an imposing collection of them on his body – and by the time they got around to showing all of their intimate tattoos to one another . . . well . . . one thing led to another and they ended up naked, having sex. Val thought he was really cool and it gave her an added thrill to be with Lesley's ex. Lesley didn't want him but she sure as hell wouldn't have wanted Val to have him either. She chuckled at the thought of Lesley's face when she would break the news to her.

She stayed with him for three days and they hit it off wonderfully. Boxer had been giving her a hard time lately, pushing her back to work. She'd go back when she was good and ready. In the meantime, he was probably doing his nut, wondering where the hell she was. Serve him right!

Val did not want to go back to work in Hot Bods. Somehow, since Niamh's accident, she'd lost her confidence. She felt very alone so Paul's attention was making her feel better about herself. He was very nice which surprised Val. Listening to Lesley anyone would have thought he was a complete nerd. When Val confided her predicament to him and how she dreaded going back to Boxer and Hot Bods, he'd said, "Why don't you move in here? I could do with someone to look after me. I can't iron a shirt or cook to save my life!"

Val didn't need a second invitation. She moved her stuff in the very next day. The fact that she couldn't cook or iron a shirt either didn't bother her. Paul would find out soon enough but in the meantime she had somewhere to stay again and someone who liked her, for herself.

Amber was surprised to get a phone call from Carlo.

"I'm sorry for calling during the holidays but it's quite urgent that I meet with you as soon as possible," he told her.

"Fine," she replied, wondering what on earth could be so urgent.

"Is tomorrow morning too soon?" he asked.

"No, that's okay. What time?"

"Ten, in the Merrion?"

"Okay."

"Thanks, Amber. See you then."

Carlo rang Tessa two minutes later and asked the same question. She was as intrigued as Amber.

"I'm sorry for the short notice," he said, "but it is important. Twelve noon tomorrow okay for you?"

"Sure. Great," Tessa replied loving the sound of his deep Italian voice but mystified as to why he wanted to see her so urgently.

Amber met up with Carlo the next morning and he greeted her warmly.

"You look wonderful, my dear," he said, kissing her hand. "Radiant, in fact," he added, causing her to blush bright red. She felt a little guilty at the way she'd treated him. But it was all water under the bridge, she told herself. She was happy now and Luke was right for her. She just knew it in her heart.

"Well, Amber," he said, "Grace and I have done a lot of thinking over the Christmas break, and we've come to the conclusion that, as the business has grown far faster than we'd anticipated, I can't possibly run it alone."

She wondered why he was telling her this.

"And . . ." he hesitated, smiling at her, "we've decided that you would be the best person to take over as Regional Manager, with responsibility for the Dublin area." He laughed at the incredulous look on her face.

"Oh, my! I don't know what to say," she stammered. "I'm very honoured that you chose me . . . but what would it entail?"

"Well, you'd be running the business here in Dublin and

perhaps further afield in Leinster, as we get more established. You would be in charge of all the managers, recruiting, training, orders, and of course, liasing with us in Rome." He drummed his fingers on the table. "We want to expand into the rest of Ireland as soon as possible. There is incredible potential here and we want to tap into it before someone else does. I'll be very involved with that and will have no time to be here in Dublin."

"This sounds so exciting," she said breathlessly, "but very challenging."

"Yes, indeed," he replied, "but both Grace and I feel you'll be more than up to that challenge."

He outlined the job specification for her and the hefty salary and expenses that went with it. She could hardly believe it.

"This is quite a promotion for you," he smiled. "Will you think about it and get back to me? As soon as possible."

"Wow! What can I say? Yes, of course I will." She beamed at him. "Thank you for considering me, Carlo."

"It was no contest," he smiled back at her. "I'll be looking forward to your call."

Dazed, she left the room. She thought about it all the way home and by the time she got there, she had made up her mind. She rang Carlo immediately and accepted the position. She also rang Tessa who had just arrived at the Merrion for her meeting with him. Amber was so excited that the words came out in a jumble and she wasn't making sense.

"Hang on, hang on," Tessa cried. "What's all this about?"

Amber told her what Carlo had offered her.

"Congratulations! That's fantastic," Tessa said, delighted for her friend. "Does that mean I can have your area?"

"God, you don't let the grass grow under your feet," Amber laughed. "I'll have to think about that. It depends on how nice to me you are."

"Then I'll have to ask him for it," Tessa shot back. "Lord, but you're going to be a much harder boss than Carlo," she sighed. "I'd better run. It's almost noon. I wonder what he wants with me?" Then she added thoughtfully, "Maybe it *is* to offer me your area."

Nothing could have prepared her for what he did offer her.

"Contessa!" he greeted her, making her smile as he kissed her hand.

Her heart beat a little faster as it always did when he was around. He'd obviously been somewhere sunny for Christmas as his skin was more tanned than ever and she noticed that his hair was longer too, brushing the collar of his jacket. It made him even sexier.

"I feel like Santa Claus this week," he smiled, and she relaxed a little.

This couldn't be anything bad, if he felt like Santa.

"I want to talk to you about our advertising campaign," he informed her. "We are growing at such a rate, not just here in Ireland, but our shoe empire worldwide and we need to step up our brochures and make them as glamorous and classy as our products." He was looking at her intently.

As always, she was mesmerised by his eyes and voice but she was wondering why he was telling her all this.

"That's where you come in," he continued. "Grace and I think that you would be the perfect model for our shoes and bags and would like to offer you a contract for three years to model them exclusively for us."

Tessa was as stunned as Amber had been earlier in the day.

"It would only mean three or four photo-shoots a year in Rome, of course, so you could keep on your business here. What do you think?"

He looked at her with his large velvet brown eyes and there was no way she could refuse. His smile when she agreed was worth it.

"If Amber is not going to be working her area any more, can I have some of it?" she asked.

"You're not wasting any time," Carlo said, throwing back his head – in that manner that sent Tessa weak at the knees – and laughing with gusto. "How about joining me for lunch and we can discuss it? If you don't have other plans, that is."

"No, no other plans," she smiled at him.

They had good fun over lunch, he teasing her unmercifully and she falling for it every time.

"Actually, it will be up to Amber now to designate the areas," he told her, as they finished their lunch. "But I imagine you'll have no problem persuading her to give you another area."

"So you got me to have lunch with you under false pretences!" she cried, in mock horror.

"Guilty," he replied, holding his hands up in front of him. "I didn't know how else I could have persuaded you to join me," he said sheepishly.

Tessa looked at his twinkling eyes, thinking – if only he knew! He only had to ask and she'd have lunch, dinner and breakfast the following morning with him, if he so wished. She cast her eyes down, knowing that she was blushing and not wanting him to know how she felt, when her phone rang.

"Excuse me," Tessa said, standing up to leave and take the call. "Hello?" she said into the phone. Then her eyes widened in horror as she listened. "Oh my God! Oh no!" She groped for the chair and sank down onto it and Carlo saw that she had gone deathly pale.

"When? How bad is it?" she spoke in a whisper into the phone. "Oh God no!" she wailed. "I'm on my way."

She stood up but her legs wouldn't hold her and she sank down again.

"What is it?" Carlo asked, aware that something awful had happened.

"It's my father," she whispered hoarsely. "That was the hospital. He collapsed and he's unconscious. I have to go to him."

"I'll take you," he said. "You're in no condition to drive."

"It's in Galway," Tessa said. "It's too far for you to come."

"Nonsense," Carlo said. "You're shaking like a leaf, you couldn't possibly drive." He had his arm around her now. "Please let me help."

She realised that he was right. She couldn't possibly drive in this state and she had to get to her father as quickly as possible.

"If you're sure you don't mind," she said weakly, grateful for his strong presence.

For the first part of the journey, Tessa hardly said a word. She sat wringing her hands and twisting a handkerchief till it was almost a rag. From time to time she sat crying silently and Carlo wanted to reach out and comfort her but he was driving so fast that he dare not take his hands from the wheel.

Eventually, after they had passed Athlone, she slowly started to talk, quietly, as if to herself, blaming herself for not insisting that her father seek medical advice.

Carlo tried to comfort her. "You couldn't make him go if he didn't want to," he assured her. "You did try. If anyone is to blame it's your stepmother."

"She only cares about herself," Tessa said bitterly. She then told him about how demanding and selfish Claudia had always been, in contrast to the loving, caring person that was her father. He let her talk on, thinking that it would do her good to get it all out and take her mind off the fact that the father she obviously adored was now lying unconscious in a hospital bed.

As they came to the outskirts of Galway city, he noticed the flashing blue light in his mirror and within minutes he was being pulled over by a police squad car.

"Have you any idea what speed you're doing, sir?" the burly young Garda asked him.

Tessa leaned across Carlo, her beautiful eyes brimming with tears. "My father is unconscious in Calvary Hospital, Garda. I have to get to him as quickly as possible but we don't know the way. Everything has changed so much since last I was here. Can you help us, please?"

Carlo thought that there was not a man alive who would not be moved by her plea and this policeman was no exception.

"Just follow me," he ordered. "Stay right on my tail and I'll take you there." He was rewarded by a dazzling smile from Tessa.

"Thank you so much," she said. "I'll never forget your kindness."

The young Garda blushed.

Siren wailing, he pulled out and Carlo followed him closely, through red lights and traffic queues and in no time at all they were pulling up outside the hospital. Tessa jumped out and, waving goodbye to the Garda, ran to the main entrance, Carlo hot on her heels.

They were directed to Intensive Care where Jeffrey and Bart, two of Edward's close friends were waiting. They both kissed her, hugging her tight.

"How is he?" Tessa asked tersely, afraid of what they might say.

"He's still the same, Tessa, no change," said Jeffrey.

"Thank God." She gave him a grim smile.

"You can see him, Tessa, if you ring the bell there," Bart informed her.

"Where's Claudia?" Tessa asked as she rang the bell.

"She's at home. She said she couldn't cope with it all," Jeffrey replied, disapproval written all over his face.

Tessa said nothing but pursed her lips in anger.

Just then a nurse came to the door and, when Tessa explained who she was, opened the door to let her in. "And this gentleman?" the nurse asked politely, nodding at Carlo.

"I'm her husband," Carlo answered quickly, ignoring Tessa's look of surprise.

They were admitted and Tessa started crying gently as she saw how emaciated her father was. She kissed him and held his hand, shocked at how ill he looked. He'd failed so much, even in the week since she'd last seen him. Now he lay pale and lifeless, a shadow of his former self. The only sound in the room was the bleep-bleep of the heart monitor.

"Daddikins, it's Tessa," she said, lapsing back into her childhood name for him. She kept talking to him, non-stop, although it appeared that he couldn't hear her. She'd read somewhere that even though people were unconscious and didn't respond to you, it didn't mean that they couldn't hear you. She was determined to get through to her father.

Carlo looked at her with pity, wishing he could do something positive to help.

"Would you like me to leave?" he asked her.

"Please stay," she beseeched him, reaching out to him.

He stroked her hair, wanting to comfort her. He hoped that his presence was helping her a little.

They sat by her father's bedside as Tessa talked and stroked his hand and head. It was three hours later when he finally responded.

She felt him squeeze her hand.

"Daddikins, it's me, Tessa. I love you so much!" she cried. "Please don't leave me."

His eyelids flickered momentarily and he seemed to be making a monumental effort to open his eyes, but he managed it.

"Love you, Princess," he whispered hoarsely. "It's time."

His eyes moved to Carlo and he gave a little smile. "Good," he said, looking back at Tessa, "die happy."

The heart monitor suddenly stopped its bleeping.

"No, Daddikins, no!" she cried, but with a huge sigh he was gone.

Carlo rang for the nurse.

When she came in she looked sadly at Tessa. "I'm sorry my dear, but there is nothing we can do for him now. He's at peace."

Carlo folded her in his arms, stroking her hair as she sobbed. Her grief brought tears to his eyes but he was happy to be the shoulder that she cried on.

He finally persuaded her to leave and Jeffrey and Bart hugged her when they realised that Edward was gone.

"Would you like us to call Claudia?" Bart asked.

"I'd appreciate that. I'd better call out to see her," she said, unable to keep the contempt from her voice.

Carlo saw the sympathy for Tessa in the two men's faces and also the underlying disapproval of Edward's wife. They both went in to say a last goodbye to their dear friend and Tessa asked Carlo if he wouldn't mind driving her to her childhood home.

"Of course not," he replied gently, keeping his arm around her waist as they walked to the car. She was such a tall, confident woman but right now she was like a little girl lost.

Carlo was unprepared for Gloucester House, the beautiful Georgian house which Tessa called home. As they drove up the long driveway he admired the wonderful horses grazing in the fields.

"Dad loved it here," she sighed. "It was his life's work and his passion. I don't know what will happen to it now. Claudia has no interest in it aside from entertaining her cronies here."

They entered the magnificent house, Carlo taking in the beautiful furniture and paintings. This was the house of someone with exquisite taste.

"Dad had great taste," Tessa broke into his thoughts as if she'd read them. "This is all his doing."

"It's beautiful," he exclaimed, awe in his voice as he looked around.

She led the way into the grand drawing-room where a number of people had gathered and were talking quietly.

Carlo saw a small dark woman, impeccably made-up, hair upswept in a chignon and dressed in a black dress which fitted her petite figure perfectly. She looked like the hostess at an elegant soirée.

"Tessa, darling," she said, detaching herself from a group and coming towards Tessa with outstretched arms. She embraced her stepdaughter awkwardly and Tessa had to stop herself from recoiling at her touch. Claudia was so tiny and Tessa so tall that they looked incongruous together.

"How can I cope with this?" Claudia cried, dabbing at her eyes. "What will I do without your father?"

"It's always about you, isn't it?" Tessa said through gritted teeth, bitterness oozing from every syllable.

"Not here, darling," Claudia said quietly, drawing her out of the room into the large hall.

"My stepmother can't stand scenes," Tessa remarked to Carlo, "sure you can't, Claudia? Which is probably why you missed a very sad scene a short while ago when Dad passed away." She looked at her stepmother accusingly. "You couldn't even be with him at the end."

"There was no point, dear," Claudia excused herself. "He was unconscious."

"He came round at the end," Tessa hissed. "And before you ask – no, he didn't mention you."

Her stepmother recoiled a little at the vehemence in Tessa's voice.

"Go back to your friends, Claudia. The party must go on, as always."

She saw her stepmother go pale as she put her hand up to her throat.

"I will never forgive you for this," Tessa continued, her

voice breaking, "never, as long as I live. You're truly on your own now." She turned on her heel and swept out, Carlo following.

Looking back Carlo saw Tessa's stepmother re-enter the salon, a smile on her face, as if the devastating scene had never taken place.

Chapter 46

Pete was at his wits' end. Lesley had become a total nightmare and was ruining his life. Gone was the fun, sexy girl who'd moved in with him. In her place was an argumentative, demanding, jealous witch. He had even tired of the sexual games she demanded night after night and longed for a straightforward, caring relationship with normal loving sex. More and more he was thinking of Amber and how it would have been with her. What a mistake he'd made! Why hadn't he waited for Amber? Now his problem was how to get rid of Lesley. He didn't know how he could stick her for another day and yet what choice did he have?

He was staying out more and more but then he eventually had to face home and the tantrums and screaming match that would ensue. And that was when she was sober! If she'd been drinking, then it became like hell on earth.

His beautiful pad, which had been his haven of peace,

had now been turned into a battle zone. In desperation he enlisted Tim's help but for once his friend was not willing to help him.

"I warned you," was all Tim said. "Maybe this will teach you a lesson."

Great! With friends like that, who needed enemies?

Finally, last weekend, things had come to a head. He'd come home late that night, having downed more pints than usual, to find Lesley practically foaming at the mouth. They'd had an unmerciful row and he'd finally told her to pack her bags and get out. She'd looked at him disbelievingly.

"You're not serious?" she'd asked, her big blue eyes wide with hurt.

"Deadly serious," he'd replied. "Out!"

He went into his office. Some time later he'd heard the door slam and then . . . peace! He couldn't believe his luck. Coming into the living-room he quickly locked the door, just in case she changed her mind. Plonking down on the sofa he let out a long sigh. Never, never again, he swore. Never would he bring another woman into this place. What a close shave!

Lesley was livid. How dare he throw her out like a piece of shit – and after she'd been so good to him! She'd even ironed some of his poncy shirts! Maybe she'd been too hasty. Maybe he hadn't really meant it. She decided that she'd go and stay with her sister for the night, although they couldn't stand one another, and then tomorrow she'd go back and make up with him. Yes, that's what she'd do. Let him miss her and the great sex, for one night, and tomorrow he'd be waiting with open arms for her. Yes, let him suffer and he'd be crawling all over her when she went back.

Amber was beginning to worry. She'd heard nothing from Tessa since she'd had her meeting with Carlo. She'd tried Tessa's mobile at least ten times and left messages for her but so far had received no reply.

"Don't worry," Luke assured her. "Maybe she and Carlo got it together."

"You think so?" Amber said, twirling a curl around her finger. "I hope so. She really fancies him, you know."

Luke pulled her close and was just nibbling her ear when her phone rang. Checking the number, she jumped up when she saw it was Tessa.

"Hi, where've you been? I've been worried about – what? Oh, Tessa, I'm so, so sorry. Why didn't you ring me? Oh my God! Where are you now?"

As Tessa explained, Amber covered the mouthpiece with her hand and whispered to Luke, "Tessa's father died in Galway today. She's on her way back from there." The shock on his face mirrored her feelings.

After the call, Amber sank down on the sofa and Luke put his arms around her.

"How awful for poor Tessa," he said. "Was she with her father when he died?"

"Yes, thank God. Carlo drove her to Galway and she spoke to her father before he died." She kissed Luke and added, "Sorry I can't stay but Tessa will need someone to be with her tonight."

"Of course you must go," he said, kissing her gently.

"Thank you. I love you," she told him, slipping into her coat.

"Love you too," he replied. "Call me if you need me."

It had been a shattering day and an emotional one too, thought Carlo. On the drive home from Galway, Tessa had opened up to him about her childhood and he understood now just why she'd been so angry with her stepmother. The more he heard of Tessa's life story, the more he admired her. He was happy when she finally fell asleep and he tried to drive as smoothly as possible so as not to wake her. She woke with a start as he pulled up in front of the apartment.

"Oh, I'm sorry, I didn't mean to drop off," she apologised, flustered. "God, I must look a mess," she added, smoothing her hair.

"You look beautiful," he smiled at her.

"Carlo, I can't ever thank you enough and –"

"Don't say another word," he said gently, reaching forward to stroke her hair. "I'm glad I was able to be with you today. I have to fly to Rome in the morning but if you need me I can be on the next flight back here."

His kindness touched her and she felt the tears starting again. He reached over and kissed her cheek, tasting the salt of her tears. "Have a good sleep and I'll call you tomorrow," he said, getting out of the car to open her door for her.

"Goodnight, *carissima*."

She went up in the lift touching her cheek where he'd kissed her. She was so confused with everything that had happened that she was afraid to read anything into it. He was probably just being kind.

Amber hugged her and sat her down to eat the supper she'd prepared for her. To Tessa's surprise she was ravenous and wolfed it down. Then after soaking in the bath that

Amber ran for her, she fell into bed exhausted to dream of her father and Carlo, the two men she loved most in the world.

Lesley arrived back at Pete's apartment the following evening. She'd had a dreadful row with her sister, Yvonne – what's new, she thought – and was looking forward to seeing Pete again. She was feeling really hot for him now after a night without him and was wearing her black leather underwear as a special treat for him. It would be one of those nights! She tried her key in the door and was surprised when it wouldn't open. She rang the bell. No reply. She began to have a scary feeling in her stomach. She rang his mobile and was relieved when he answered. Time to eat humble pie, she decided.

"Pete, honey, I'm so sorry –" she began, but that's as far as she got.

"It's no good, Lesley," he said. "Sorry won't cut it, I'm afraid."

"I can't get into the apartment!" she wailed.

"That's because I've had the locks changed."

"Oh babe, I've missed you," she said, in her best little girl voice.

"Well, I'm afraid you'll have to go on missing me, Lesley. It's over. Finished," he said in his coldest voice.

She resorted to the only ploy she had left. "I'm so hot for you, babe. I'm wearing my –"

"I don't give a damn what you're wearing. Just give me an address where I can send your things. I don't ever want to have anything to do with you again."

And with that, he hung up.

He realised what an ass he'd made of himself. Now he'd

probably have to change his mobile number. Lesley wasn't the type to let go easily. He'd also probably have to cut his ties with If the Shoes Fit. He couldn't very well stay on if it meant bumping into Lesley all the time. He'd really miss all that. Well, that was the price he'd have to pay for his stupidity. Tim was right. It was time to settle down. He must give Amber a ring when this was all settled. Hopefully she wouldn't be too busy now to see him.

Lesley was distraught. He was really a louse. After all she'd given him! Where could she go now? Not back to Yvonne's, that's for sure. Yvonne had told her never to darken her door again. Maybe she shouldn't have called her all those names . . . Well, there was only one thing for it – she'd have to go back to Paul. She was sure he'd be delighted to have her back and in a way it suited her better. She'd have the garage again to store her orders now that Yvonne's was no longer available. Yes. That's what she'd do.

She pulled up outside her old house, checking her make-up in the mirror and fixing her hair. Not that she ever gave a damn how she looked for Paul – but better to make an effort, just in case.

She opened the door gingerly, calling out, "Hey, babe, I'm home," as if she'd just been gone for a couple of hours, not three weeks. At least *he* hadn't changed the locks! There was no reply.

She crept into the living-room, thinking that he was probably engrossed in some sport on television. He was engrossed all right – but the sport was sex. Lesley took in the sight of female legs wrapped around her husband's naked butt.

"What the hell!" she cried, as she belted him on his very vulnerable rear.

"Ouch!" he yelled, jumping up in pain. "Give over!"

It was then that she saw the owner of the legs. "Val! What the fuck are you doing here screwing my husband?" she yelled.

"Don't talk to her like that," Paul yelled back at her. "We're a couple now."

She didn't know what surprised her more, the fact that he'd said he was with Val or the fact that he'd shouted at her. She felt that her whole world had turned upside down. Nothing was working out the way that she'd planned it.

She sank down on the armchair, finally finding her voice.

"What do you mean you're 'a couple'?" she asked him, her voice coming out in a squeak.

Val finally spoke, grinning wickedly. "He means that I've moved in here now."

Lesley wanted to punch her and wipe that smirk off her face.

"What about me?' she asked her husband.

"What about you?" Paul replied.

"Where am I supposed to live?" Lesley looked at him appealingly.

"With your lover boy – or has he turfed you out already?" He saw from the look in her eyes that this was exactly what had happened. "He saw through you pretty quickly, then. Now if you don't mind, you interrupted us at a very bad moment."

Val smirked at her again.

"You little tramp!" Lesley hissed at her. "You'll never last here." Turning to Paul she tried to cajole him. "Paul, babe, I have nowhere to stay tonight and after all this is my home."

"Well, if Val doesn't mind you can sleep in the spare room." He turned to Val. "Is that okay with you, honey?"

"Sure, why not?" Val replied, enjoying every moment of this crazy scenario. "As long as she leaves us alone now," she added.

"You heard the lady," Paul said, returning his attentions to Val.

With gritted teeth Lesley turned on her heel, not able to watch any more. "Lady, my arse," she muttered as she slammed the door and marched up to the spare room.

Chapter 47

Niamh was feeling stronger every day but Gavin was still clucking over her like a mother hen, insisting that she put her feet up and keeping the kids away when she was resting. Her mother was, as always, a great help and between the two of them she felt cared for and cosseted.

A nurse, Moira, came every day to change her dressings and was surprised by how quickly Niamh was recovering.

"My, but you're a strong wee lassie," she'd said in her Scottish brogue. She agreed that it was good for Niamh to walk about a little and told Gavin this.

"Yes, but she wants to start back to work next week," he complained.

"Well, that might be no harm," Moira said, "as long as she takes it easy. Niamh tells me that she can work from home and it would keep her occupied. No driving of course," she added, "until that wrist is better."

Gavin looked dubious but he presumed Moira knew

what she was talking about. He reluctantly agreed on condition that Niamh would allow him to help.

"What a lucky wee lassie you were," Moira said, at least ten times a day.

Niamh was idyllically happy with the house and looking forward to being back to full strength. In the meantime, she had to be patient and was taking it one day at a time. Even though she was aching still, she was beginning to think that maybe her accident had been for a reason. The change in Gav was unbelievable. He seemed to have grown up overnight and was more loving towards her than ever before. He had assumed responsibility for his family, at last, and seemed to be taking it in his stride. He was discovering how much fun his children actually were and every afternoon took them out to give Niamh a chance to rest. They went to the park, to a film or McDonald's and he even took them to a pantomime once and to the zoo. What's more, he seemed to be enjoying these outings as much as the kids. They would be back to school in a couple of days, of course, and then things would be back to normal.

Niamh and Gavin were sitting quietly on the sofa one evening, chatting, as the children played on the floor. Their favourite game nowadays was doctors and nurses.

"I want to be the doctor," came Ian's plaintive little cry. "I'm always the sick one."

"No! I'm the doctor," Lily stamped her little foot, "and Wose is the nurth."

She stood with both hands on her hips and Ian, recognising when he was beaten and outnumbered, obediently lay down on the floor.

Gavin winked at Niamh, smiling, as they watched their children play.

"I'm Nurth Wose. Come in to the hostipul," Rose said to Ian, dragging him into her doll's buggy which was posing as a wheelchair. She wheeled him, wobbling dangerously, to where Lily was waiting for him.

"My, but you're a stwong wee lathie," Lily said, mimicking Moira as she stuck a pen, which was standing in for a syringe, in Ian's little arm.

"Ouch!" he squealed.

"Quiet now. I'm going to dwess your head with this bandage," Rose said, practically strangling the poor little fellow. "What a lucky wee lathie you are," she added, standing arms akimbo, just like Moira did every day.

Niamh and Gavin convulsed with laughter, she holding her sides where her ribs hurt.

"I guess we'll have to be careful what we say around here in future," Gavin laughed.

"Yes, they don't miss much," Niamh agreed with him. "They really are growing up fast."

"Maybe it's time we had another one," he said, stroking her hair.

"Are you serious?" she said, looking at him incredulously. "You never wanted another baby."

"Well, I've changed my mind," he smiled at her. "What do you say we start to try tonight for one? I'll be gentle, I promise."

Niamh sighed blissfully. Life didn't get any better than this.

Amber rang Niamh and arranged for Tessa and her to visit the following day.

"I'm dying to see you both and hear all your news," Niamh said, delighted that they were coming over. "I'll ask

Rosie if she can make it too. It will be nice for the four of us to get together, after all that's happened."

"Are you sure you're up to it?" Rosie asked Niamh on the phone, worried that it might be too much for her.

"Absolutely!" Niamh assured her. "It will be good for me."

"Well, I'll bake a cake and an apple tart. Don't you lift a little finger," Rosie ordered.

As soon as the girls arrived, bringing gifts of flowers, chocolates and wine, Gavin let them in and brought them into the living-room to Niamh.

"Don't hug her too tightly, she's still sore," he said, giving them his charming lopsided smile.

Amber and Tessa exchanged looks behind his back which said, "handsome devil", as they followed him in.

Niamh was in great form and looked so much better than the last time they'd seen her in the hospital when they'd been so concerned about her. Rosie arrived just then, giving Niamh the cake and tart and the Mademoiselle Coco perfume that she'd replaced, as asked.

"Thank you, I appreciate that," said Niamh, giving her a secret smile.

Gavin came in with the kids to say hello before he took them off to the park.

The girls *oohed* and *aahed* over them and gave them the sweets they'd brought for them.

"They're adorable!" Tessa exclaimed.

"You're so lucky," Amber said wistfully to Niamh.

"I know that," Niamh replied, smiling over their heads at Gavin.

"I've left all the tea things out ready on the dining-room table," he told her. "You just have to make the tea."

"We'll do that," Rosie assured him.

Amid kisses and hugs, he left with the children. The girls could feel the love in the house and were happy for Niamh. She deserved it.

Then Rosie and Niamh sympathised with Tessa on her father's death.

"When is the funeral?" Rosie asked.

"Next Friday," Tessa replied.

"I'd really like to go," Rosie said.

"You can come with me, if you like," Amber offered.

"Could I come too?" Niamh asked quietly.

"Would you be up to it, darling?" Tessa asked her. "I really wouldn't expect you to come."

"No, I'd really like to be there. I've got to get back to normal now and I'm feeling much stronger. Anyway, work starts next Monday, so the quicker I get on my feet again the better."

"Speaking of work," Amber said, twirling a curl with her finger, "I have some news for you." She looked at Rosie and Niamh's expectant faces.

Tessa, knowing what was coming, was grinning broadly.

"Miss Gileece has an announcement to make," Tessa said formally, causing the others to titter.

"Give over," Amber swatted her. "Actually, I'm taking over as Area Manager for Dublin, as from next Monday."

"Congratulations!" Rosie and Niamh hugged her.

"She's our boss now, can you imagine it?" Tessa threw her eyes to heaven.

"What about your area, Amber?" Niamh wanted to know.

"Well, I'd like to talk to you all about that. My first job is to redistribute that, and Val and Phoebe's areas. They're gone, as you've probably heard. As you know, we have seven new managers but of course you three, as the most senior," she grinned at them, "will have first call – that is, if you wish to expand."

"Great," Niamh said, her cheeks flushed. "Gav is talking about coming in with me in the business, so once I'm on my feet I'll definitely be interested in expanding."

"Hard to believe he was against your taking the job in the beginning!" said Tessa.

"That's all changed," Niamh told them, blushing. "In fact, he's changed so much since I've had my accident. He's been wonderful." She looked down at her hands, embarrassed at how emotional she felt.

Rosie had tears in her eyes and Amber and Tessa weren't far off tears either.

As they were having tea, Rosie told them about her trip to Clare and how much she'd loved it there.

"I was just thinking how much I'd like to live there again," she said wistfully. "All my family are there still."

"Maybe you can," Amber said excitedly. "Carlo is about to start recruiting all over Ireland. Limerick, Galway and Clare will be his starting points. It would be fantastic to have someone with experience based there. I'm sure he would be delighted to let you move." She looked at Rosie earnestly. "Would you consider it, Rosie?"

"Gosh, I'll have to think about it," she said. What she really meant was, I'll have to talk to Jack about it. And then there was Gail to consider, of course.

On the way home in the car Tessa and Amber discussed the afternoon.

"Niamh and Gavin are still really in love, even after three kids. Isn't it wonderful?" Tessa remarked.

"Kind of restores one's faith in marriage, doesn't it?" Amber said gently.

"Are you trying to tell me something?" Tessa asked her. She could see that Amber was twirling her curl again. Always a bad sign! "Uh-oh, spit it out!" she cried.

"Well, Luke has asked me to move in with him," Amber said, blushing. "I told him I would."

"Fantastic! If you're sure you love him," Tessa stressed.

"Yes, I'm sure," Amber smiled broadly.

"Well, what are you waiting for, girl? Go to him! In the meantime, I'll rent your apartment from you till I'm sure where I want to live. Only if that's okay with you, of course," she added.

"You just want my shoe-room!"

"Well, yes – but what are you going to do without it?" Tessa was intrigued to hear what she'd say.

"Well, Luke has promised to build me an even bigger one," Amber grinned.

"Some women have all the luck!" Tessa cried.

"Enough about me," said Amber. "I notice Carlo is ringing you every day. Is there anything *you* want to tell me?"

"Sadly, no, he's just being kind," Tessa said wistfully.

Amber wasn't so sure. "You're really fond of him, aren't you?"

"Actually, I think I'm in love with him," Tessa admitted. "But unfortunately, it's all on my side." She was glad that they had arrived back at the apartment as she didn't want to discuss it further.

As they walked in the door her phone rang and it was Carlo. After talking to him, she came into the kitchen to Amber, her eyes shining.

"Carlo is flying over for Dad's funeral. He says he'll drive me down, if that's okay with you."

"Of course, sweetie," Amber hugged her. It was as obvious as the nose on your face that Carlo was interested in Tessa but she was afraid to believe it. Amber hoped with all her heart that it would work out for them. She wanted everyone to be as happy as she was.

Rosie was really excited on the drive home from Niamh's. She was beginning to understand that she needed a new start and Amber had handed her that possibility this afternoon. She talked to Jack all the way home and felt that he was behind her one hundred per cent. The only problem was Gail. She had been such a wonderful support over the past year that Rosie felt she couldn't just up sticks and move back to Clare. That would have seemed so ungrateful and of course she'd miss seeing Holly every day. *No, Jack,* she said that night. *I really couldn't move away from them. That's final!*

The following morning when Gail called in for coffee, Rosie sensed that something was bothering her.

"Is something wrong, pet?" she asked her daughter, seeing how agitated she was.

"Mum, I don't know how to tell you this but Mike has been offered a job in Limerick University and he desperately wants to take it. I told him I can't possibly go as I couldn't leave you but he says he has to take it as it's such a wonderful opportunity." Gail looked at her mother, her lower lip quivering.

She looked aghast as her mother started laughing crazily.

"Mum!" Gail cried, wondering if her mother had gone mad.

"Oh sweetheart," Rosie cried, "I can't believe this! I've been thinking of going back to Clare but I wouldn't go because of you and Holly." She pealed with laughter once more. "Now you're telling me you won't go to Limerick because of me. Oh, girl, your dad has outdone himself this time!"

Gail didn't know what her mother was on about, although she knew that she spoke to Jack every day.

"Well, it looks like we can both go," Rosie said, her eyes shining. "I'll go back to Clare and you to Limerick."

"Mike will be so pleased," Gail said, hugging her mother, "and we'll be practically next-door neighbours!"

Oh Jack, you're something else, Rosie chuckled to her late husband after Gail had gone. "You're my guardian angel now, aren't you?" she whispered, looking heavenward.

Chapter 48

Luke wanted to attend Tessa's father's funeral and after numerous phone calls managed to get someone to fill in for him on the New York route the following Friday.

On the Thursday, Niamh rang Tessa to tell her that she would not be able to travel to the funeral after all.

"My wrist is giving me grief," she explained, "and Gav has arranged to take me into the hospital tomorrow to let them have a look at. Anyway he's dead set against me going. He thinks it's too soon."

"Sweetheart, I understand completely," Tessa replied. "Actually, Gavin's right. I was worried it might be too much for you too."

"Thanks, Tessa. I'll be thinking of you," Niamh said sweetly. "Is Amber there? I'd better tell her I'm not travelling with her."

Tessa called Amber and gave her the phone, quickly explaining that Niamh would not be travelling after all.

"Don't worry about it," Amber told Niamh. "You take

care of yourself, honey, and of that beautiful family you have. I'll call you when we get back."

Niamh was relieved that they understood and blushed with pride at Amber's comment.

Tessa had arranged to pick Carlo up at the airport and head straight to Galway from there.

Coming off the plane, he kissed her cheek, shocked at the circles he saw under her eyes. He reckoned that she'd had a bad week and hadn't slept much.

"All set?" he asked.

"More or less," Tessa answered, not very convincingly.

As they went to retrieve the car he put his arm around her shoulder and felt that she was trembling. "Would you like me to drive?" he asked, as they reached her car. "I can never resist driving a Porsche. It's my Italian blood."

"Would you?" She smiled at him, relieved. "I'd appreciate that. And Carlo," she continued shyly, "I really appreciate you coming over for Dad's funeral. Thanks."

"It's the least I could do," he replied gently.

Tessa relaxed and smiled back at him as they set off for Galway.

As they neared the church, Tessa felt the butterflies start to dance around in her stomach. Carlo felt her tension and reached over to hold her hand.

They arrived at the church to find a large crowd milling around outside. Her stepmother was in the centre of these people, shaking hands and smiling as if, for all the world, she was Queen Elizabeth greeting people at the annual garden party at Buckingham Palace. Tessa turned away in disgust.

Jeffrey and Bart broke away from the crowd to come and greet Tessa but Claudia never left her coterie of admirers.

"Be brave, sweetheart, for your father's sake," Jeffrey whispered in her ear.

Bart squeezed her hand. "Ignore her," he whispered. "Think of Edward."

She was very grateful to them both – her father's two best friends. They stayed with her, arms protectively about her as they greeted Carlo.

"I think Edward would be very happy to think that Tessa has you with her," Bart said to him.

"Oh, Carlo is . . ." Tessa started to say but Carlo put his finger over her lips. "Sshh," he said, looking into her eyes intimately.

She saw from the smiles of her father's two friends that they obviously thought Carlo and she were a couple.

Just then Luke and Amber arrived, together with Rosie, followed closely by Kate and Kevin from Ballyfern.

"Oh, thank you all so much for coming," she said as she hugged them. "It's so good of you all to travel so far." She was moved at their kindness.

"Of course we'd be here for you," Kate said, squeezing her. "And this must be Carlo," she added, giving him a big hug.

He instantly loved this warm, motherly woman and understood why Tessa was so fond of her.

Then it was time to enter the church and Tessa watched her stepmother walk regally up the church to the front pew. All her hangers-on piled into the seat beside her and when Tessa reached it she found that there was no space left for her. Jeffrey led her into the pew opposite and as one, Carlo, Bart and all her friends moved in beside her.

For a brief moment, Tessa felt sorry for her stepmother. Now that her father was dead it meant Claudia's biggest supporter was gone. Tessa recognised the people surrounding her stepmother as sycophants – she had no real friends – whereas Tessa herself was surrounded by the greatest bunch of friends anyone could ask for. Having Jeffrey and Bart, her father's true friends, on her side was like the icing on the cake. She realised how lucky she was.

The funeral passed her by in a daze. She couldn't even remember the eulogy that she gave her father from the altar, but afterwards they told her that there wasn't a dry eye in the house. Carlo thought that she'd never looked more beautiful. She was wearing a short black coat-dress with gilt buttons down the front and black suede boots over black opaque tights. Her hair hung like silk under a simple wide-brimmed hat but it was her face, suffused with sadness as she spoke about her father that captivated him most. Her stepmother finished proceedings by inviting everyone back to the house for a party to celebrate Edward's life.

"Any excuse for a party," Bart said bitterly, watching the masses rush out and away from the church, not even bothering to go to the graveside.

Tessa stood on one side of the grave, pale and silent, while Claudia stood on the other side, weeping copious tears.

"Crocodile tears," Jeffrey muttered under his breath.

Tessa had had enough and, when her father's coffin was lowered into the ground and the prayers finished, she turned and left without a backward glance at her stepmother.

Carlo kept his arm around her all the time, a fact that didn't escape Amber, Rosie or Kate, much to their delight. Tessa and her little group went to the local hotel where Bart and Jeffrey had organised a lunch for them.

"We guessed you'd want to be with real friends, not that other circus," Bart nodded.

"Thank you both so much," Tessa said, shedding her first tears of the day. "You're wonderful. No wonder Dad loved you so dearly."

"He was a great man," Bart said.

"Aye, and a great friend," Jeffrey added.

Tessa felt loved and cared for as never before as the two men told hilarious tales of her dad's fantastic life. They had all her friends in stitches and she felt that they came to know a little of the wonderful man that was her father. After many, many, drinks – she lost count – it was time for everyone to leave.

Tessa was staying on in Galway as the reading of her father's will was taking place the next day.

"I suppose my stepmother will be there," she remarked to Bart.

"Without a doubt," he replied. "But don't you worry, little lady, Jeffrey and I will be there to look after you, as your father asked us."

This started her crying again.

"Now, Carlo, I think it's time you took the lady home," Jeffrey said. "She's had a tough day."

"I thought you'd never ask," Carlo sighed dramatically and they all laughed.

Hugging everyone goodbye she felt the tears flow again. "Oh, God, I'm becoming a real blubberer," she said. What she didn't realise was that all her friends had tears in their eyes also as they hugged her goodbye.

On the way out Kate caught up with Amber. "Does she really not believe that guy is in love with her?" she asked.

"She just doesn't know it yet," Amber replied, smiling

with satisfaction, as she linked arms with Luke and headed towards the car.

Rosie left the funeral and travelled on to Clare. She was very excited about the news she was going to spring on her family there. She'd had a quiet word with Carlo in the aftermath of the funeral and he'd said that he'd be delighted to have her start again in Clare. "And would you consider covering Limerick City?" he'd asked her. "It's very close to Clare and I'd dearly like to have someone in there as soon as possible." Would she ever!

"We didn't expect to see you so soon again," her brother joked, as they all gathered in her sister's house that evening. She was so excited telling them her news that she could hardly get the words out. The news that Gail and her family were also moving to Limerick was also a cause for celebration and they certainly knew how to do that in Clare, Rosie told Jack as she lay in bed that night, her feet aching from all the Clare sets that she'd danced.

"Thank you for looking after me, love," she whispered to the sky, as she turned the light out.

Carlo had booked a luxury two-bedroom suite for them, in a hotel overlooking Galway Bay. When they got there, he sat her down on the luxurious sofa and poured her a brandy while he went and ran a bath for her in the sumptuous marble bathroom.

"You look exhausted," he said gently. "Go and have a long soak and I'll order some food from room service for when you're finished."

She gratefully accepted his suggestion. In the bath she lay back, letting the warm water soothe her as she reflected on the day. One hour later she emerged, wrapped in the cosy towelling bathrobe. Her hair was piled on top of her head and her face scrubbed clean and Carlo thought she looked more like sixteen than her thirty-six years.

"Oh, that felt good," she said, stretching.

"You needed it," he replied, happy at how easy and relaxed she felt with him.

"Dinner," he announced, as there was a knock on the door.

When the waiter had left, Carlo lifted the silver domes from the plates to reveal a delicious meal of scallops, prawns and lobster.

"Perfect," she smiled at him as he poured her a glass of Chablis. The meal was delicious and when she was finished she sat back, feeling very sleepy. Within seconds, she was sound asleep. He smiled at her as she slumped on his shoulder. For all her sophistication, she was really just like a little girl. Gently lifting her, he carried her into her bed, surprised that she weighed so little for such a tall girl. He left her sleeping and went back into the living-room and poured himself a brandy.

He was finally accepting that he loved this woman. She was beautiful both inside and out. He had been so proud of her today and how she had carried herself. It hurt him to think how devastated she was by her father's death and her stepmother's behaviour. He wanted to protect her and care for her, if she would have him.

Going into bed, he fell into a restless sleep. He woke some time later aware of a noise in the living-room. Getting up to investigate, he found Tessa at the fridge, pouring a glass of milk.

"I had a terrible nightmare," she told him. "I had to get up to get over it."

Putting his arms around her, he said, gently, "Come to bed with me."

She took his hand and followed him meekly into his room. He slipped her robe from her shoulders and started kissing her face and then her neck. Within seconds they were on the bed, caressing and kissing each other, escaping from the world into each other. He was gentle and passionate with her and, just before she climaxed, he took her face in his hands and, looking into her eyes, said, "I love you, Tessa."

"I love you too," she replied as she lost herself in the joy and pleasure that erupted in her being.

Afterwards they lay spooned together, his arms around her as he buried his face in her silken hair. He loved the scents of her body, from the coconut of her hair to the musky smell of her skin. He felt that he would never get enough of her as he inhaled deeply.

Tessa loved his strong body and felt safe and secure as she fell into a warm, dreamless sleep.

They made love again the next morning, slowly and sensuously this time and she was amazed at how easy they were with each other. It felt like they'd been together forever. She was amazed to hear him say he loved her once more. It hadn't been a dream after all, she told herself, smiling.

They arrived at the solicitor's office at the appointed time, to find Bart and Jeffrey waiting for her. They were joint executors of her father's estate. There was no sign of her stepmother. They were ushered into the room and she asked that Carlo be allowed in also. He was holding tightly to her hand throughout, a fact not lost on Bart and Jeffrey, who winked at each other.

They couldn't start without Claudia who arrived, fashionably late, to the annoyance of everyone present. She was dressed in a bright red suit and accompanied by a very dapper younger man. She ignored Tessa.

"Her mourning didn't last long," Bart muttered to Jeffrey.

Carlo overheard and had to agree that the red was a touch tasteless. Tessa was wearing a black trouser suit over a white shirt and looked very businesslike.

The elderly solicitor began and after outlining a few bequests by her father to some of the staff and both Bart and Jeffrey, he continued: "I leave the bulk of my estate, the land, the horses and the house to my beloved daughter, Tessa. I know she'll take good care of them for me."

There was an audible gasp from everyone present, not least Tessa and Claudia.

"He can't do that!" her stepmother cried.

"I'm afraid he can, and he just has," the solicitor remarked coldly. "Pray, let me continue."

"To my wife, Claudia, I leave €1,000,000, our house in Barbados, where I know she would prefer to live, and an annuity of €25,000 a year, until such time as she may remarry."

"That won't be long, I'm sure," Jeffrey muttered to Bart. Luckily no one else heard.

"That concludes proceedings," the solicitor said, smiling at Tessa who sat looking dazed.

"I'll appeal," Claudia cried shrilly, sweeping out of the room, her lackey chasing after her.

"Can she do that?" Carlo asked.

"She can try but she doesn't have a leg to stand on. The land and house have been in Edward's family for generations and he very wisely got her to sign a prenuptial agreement before their marriage. No, she won't get far with an appeal."

"Well, I think this calls for a celebratory lunch," Bart said.

"This one's on me," Carlo said as he took Tessa's hand. It was finally beginning to sink into her brain that she was now the owner of Gloucester.

Chapter 49

It was back to business for the girls.

"God, so much has happened to us all since the Christmas party," Amber remarked to Tessa as they headed down to La Spa Therapie in Malahide the following Saturday. They had decided to treat themselves once a week to the fantastic treatments on offer and both of them were really enjoying it.

They were having a girls-only weekend as Carlo had gone back to Rome and Luke was working the Los Angeles route.

"Niamh had that dreadful accident, Rosie decided to decamp to Clare, you've found Carlo and I've found Luke," she laughed.

"We don't hang around, do we?" Tessa grinned. "Not to mention Phoebe and Val getting the boot," she added, making a face.

"They bloody deserved it," Amber said vehemently. She would never forgive Val for her part in Niamh's accident.

"And what about Lesley's little fling with Pete and then finding Val having it off with her husband," they both pealed with laughter at the vision. This little snippet had come to them via Grace's brother Tim. They both found it hilarious.

"Well, we've a lot more changes to come," Tessa said, thoughtfully. "I really have to decide soon what I'm going to do with Gloucester."

"What do you want to do?" Amber asked her.

"Well, seeing as how Dad has entrusted it to me, I really would like to keep it up and running," she confided to Amber. "I love it there. I'm a country girl at heart."

"Have you discussed it with Carlo?" Amber wanted to know.

"We've talked about nothing else for the past week." Tessa blushed as she spoke. "He's very keen for me to move there and, as he's going to be working in Ireland for the foreseeable future, he could make it his base."

"Wow!" Amber cried. "That would be fantastic. I take it this is the real thing?" she teased.

"Definitely." Tessa blushed again. "Actually, he's asked me to marry him," she said, grinning from ear to ear.

"I hope you said yes," Amber said threateningly.

"Of course," Tessa laughed.

"Oh my God!" Amber whirled her round in the middle of Malahide. "I bags to be chief bridesmaid!"

"I'll think about it," Tessa said with a deadpan face.

"Go on, you!" Amber punched her in the arm. "Just try and stop me!"

Gosh, Amber thought – life was wonderful!

Niamh agreed with Gavin that Sharon couldn't possibly handle all the deliveries on her own. Now with half of

Amber's area and also half of Val's, the business had really grown and it would take two people to run it. Gavin had turned out to have a very good business head, much to Niamh's surprise. He was also great at doing the deliveries and all the girls were charmed by him. He loved it. As he said to his mates, "Meeting gorgeous women all day and delivering designer shoes to them – which makes them blissfully happy – what more could a guy ask for?" In fact, none of the women he met could hold a candle to his Niamh.

They decided that hiring a van every week was proving too costly so when Andy said that he was trading in his Hyundai van for a larger one, Niamh jumped in and offered him €2,500 for it, which he accepted. He liked Niamh and thought she was very good for Gavin. And what a plucky little bird she was! The van was taxed up till the end of the year so they only had to pay the insurance – which she could claim off expenses, as well as the cost of the van.

Gavin was in his element. It was only a van – but it had wheels! The first evening he went for a drive with the kids who were giddy with excitement at being so high up and sitting beside Dad.

"Maybe you can come out and help me with deliveries someday," he whispered to Ian, who puffed up with pride at the very idea.

"Cool – but no girls," he whispered back conspiratorially. "They couldn't do deliveries."

"Definitely not, son," Gavin replied with a wink. "It's men's work."

Ian beamed back at him and gave him a thumbs-up sign. Niamh had never been happier. They had taken the cast off her wrist which was a great relief, although she still had to keep it in a sling. It was her left wrist, thank God, so she could still use the computer with her right hand. The bandages were gone from her head and a little plaster covered the scar where her hair was now growing back, spiky-looking. She realised how lucky she'd been and thanked God every day.

Rosie had put her house in Dun Laoghaire up for sale and was thrilled that a buyer materialised so quickly. She'd found an adorable little cottage in Clare, overlooking the Atlantic, and she put an offer in on it straight away. Within a month she was on her way to her new home. Mike and Gail were renting out their house and would be down in Limerick by Easter. Hugo wasn't at all happy about this state of affairs but she didn't care. She didn't owe him anything. "We can get great practice now, emailing," she'd told him but she figured that wasn't quite what he had wanted.

Tessa had moved back to Galway where she hoped to continue with her shoe business. Carlo reckoned that with the terrific staff her father had bequeathed to her she could run the stud farm and still keep her hand in with If the Shoes Fit, albeit in a small way. He wanted her on his team and needed her experience. She loved being back in the country taking up the reins where her father had left off and was also excited about the prospect of introducing the designer shoe business to Galway.

On her way back there with Carlo she called in to Kate to collect Napoleon and Kilkenny. She was overjoyed to have them back with her again. She hadn't realised just how much she'd missed them. Nap took to Carlo like a duck to water and she eventually had to order him to sit or he would have licked him to death.

They planned to get married in April in Rome and Tessa went into overdrive planning it all. She'd been over there to do the photo-shoot for the advertising campaign and he'd introduced her to all his family that weekend. She'd had a wonderful time and they made her feel very welcome. They all loved her, not that it would have made any difference to Carlo. He loved her enough for them all.

Amber had intended moving in with Luke but with Tessa gone they finally decided to move into Amber's apartment and rent out Luke's house.

"It makes sense," Amber told Tessa. "Malahide is closer to the airport for Luke and we won't need to build another shoe-room," she joked.

"First thing I'm going to install in Gloucester," Tessa informed her. "You've certainly set the bar for the rest of us where shoe-rooms are concerned!"

Niamh really felt life couldn't get any better when her mother arrived on the doorstep one morning with Carmel, the daughter of Mrs Flanagan, the owner of the house.

"Hi, come in," Niamh greeted her, putting on the kettle for tea.

Eileen was practically jumping out of her skin with excitement and Niamh wondered what it was that had her so high. She soon found out.

"Carmel has something exciting to tell you!" She couldn't get the words out quick enough.

Niamh looked at Carmel expectantly.

"Well, you know Mam is in a retirement home," Carmel started. "Well, the fact is, she loves it and wants to stay there ... which means that the house will have to be sold."

Niamh drew in her breath.

"However, Mam is adamant that she wants the house to go to someone who will love it and be as happy here as she was for fifty years. So, if you're interested in buying it, we'll be happy to sell it at a very good price."

Niamh thought she might faint. Was this really happening? Was her dream about to come true?

"Wow!" she said, sitting down. "This is so sudden. Gosh, we would love nothing more than to be able to buy this house. We're so happy here!"

Eileen stood by, beaming and nodding her head.

Carmel then told her the price her mother would be willing to sell for which seemed very fair to Niamh. She couldn't wait to tell Gav and also to get to the bank and talk to Mr Shannon.

Niamh had great hopes that the bank manager would keep his promise to her. He'd sent a bouquet of flowers to her when she was in hospital which all her friends told her was unheard of. The fact that she'd expanded her area and that Gav was now in the business with her should surely count for something. She needn't have worried. Mr Shannon knew a good thing when he saw it and Niamh's accomplishments had impressed him greatly. He was delighted to be able to help her out and surprisingly that husband of hers had turned out to be not a bad sort after all. He had no compunction about giving her the small mortgage she asked for in the sure knowledge that she would pay it back in jig time.

So it was that one month later, Niamh and Gavin held

the keys to the first home of their own. They held a big party and invited all their friends and family, with the exception of Val. Niamh felt a bit bad about that but it was Val's own doing. As Gav kept saying, "You could have been killed, babe, and then how would the kids and I have kept going?" She had to agree with him there. The girls were all there and Niamh was delighted to see Carlo and Luke, both obviously in love as they never left Tessa and Amber's sides all night. Rosie had travelled all the way from Clare and was glowing from the fresh Atlantic air. She already had twice the representatives that she'd had in Dublin. As she told them, "The women of Limerick just can't get enough of our shoes and bags!"

"I'm bloody delighted she moved," said Carlo, making them all laugh.

"Spoken like a true Irishman," Amber cried. "God, Tessa, it didn't take you long to educate him in our language!"

They all parted company looking forward to their next meeting, which was for Tessa's hen party and after that the trip to Rome, for which they'd all qualified, followed by Tessa's wedding there. Amber, Niamh and Rosie were all going to be bridesmaids as well as Kate from Ballyfern.

"Please don't call us matrons of honour?" Amber begged. "I can't bear that word 'matron'."

"Absolutely not," Tessa said. "You'll be my handmaidens, which means you have to wait on me every second and give me my heart's desire."

"Forget it," Rosie said with a deadpan face. "We'll settle for matrons," which cracked everybody up.

Chapter 50

It was an unusually warm sunny Monday in April that saw the four women meet up at Dublin Airport for their trip to Rome. They had thought that Lesley would be joining them but she had seemingly gone totally off the rails and packed the job in. The latest word was that she had run off to England with a married man, thirty years her senior. Nobody expected that that would last very long. Obviously, living with her husband and Val had driven her quite crazy so she'd had no other choice. Pete was still working with the company and deeply involved with one of the new managers whose husband had walked out on finding out about the affair. *Plus ça change*!

The girls were flying out to Rome on the company jet which meant being whisked past all the queues of ordinary passengers and into the VIP lounge where Carlo greeted them with champagne. Tessa had her wedding dress over her arm and the girls their bridesmaids'/matrons' dresses too.

"Before we board, may I just say congratulations to you all on winning this trip and I promise it will be a trip you'll never forget," he smiled at them. "It will be first class all the way."

They all cheered.

Taking Tessa's hand he added, "Can I also say that I'm the happiest man alive that this wonderful woman will be my wife in one week's time and how honoured we both are that you will be with us to celebrate our love." He reached over and kissed Tessa, making her blush as her friends roared and cheered again.

Kate, her husband Kevin, Luke and Gavin would all be joining them the following Friday, for Tessa's wedding. The company jet was going to transport them, along with Jeffrey and Bart whom Tessa had asked to give her away.

"Two men to give you away?" Amber had teased her.

"Well, I couldn't ask one without the other," Tessa had explained. "Either way, one of them would never have forgiven me."

The two men were tickled pink at the idea of a limousine coming to whisk them to a private jet.

"Did we ever think we'd see the day when Edward's little lass would be taking us to Rome on a private jet?" Bart said, thrilled at the idea.

"What a shame he isn't here to give her away himself," Jeffrey sighed.

"Well, we'll do a damn good job in his place," Bart said, "for his sake."

"Her mother, God rest her, would be very happy to see her daughter getting married in Rome," Jeffrey said.

"Yes, Tessa told me that it's always been a special place for her."

In the VIP lounge, as the girls sipped their champagne and nibbled on Beluga caviar, Carlo continued.

"Before I forget, I did promise a car to the manager with the highest sales and it will come as no surprise to any of you to learn that the winner is Niamh."

Niamh could hardly believe it. "Oh my God, Gav is going to love this!" she cried, to the cheers and clapping of her friends.

"The choice is yours, Niamh," he said handing her a brochure. "You can choose between the sports car, the family saloon, or the larger people-carrier."

"Thank you so much," she said, kissing Carlo on the cheek. She looked at the brochure. "Gav would love the sports car and the family car is lovely but I'm afraid it will be too small for my family soon," she blushed. "Gav and I are expecting another baby in late September."

The others fell on her, whooping and cheering. "Congratulations!" they cried, hugging her.

"I guess that means the people carrier," Carlo smiled at her.

"I guess so," she replied, laughing. "I'd like to propose a big thank you to If the Shoes Fit. I am so grateful for it. It has changed my life completely." There were tears in her eyes.

"Hear, hear!" echoed, Amber, Tessa and Rosie whose lives had also been greatly changed for the better.

"The shoes certainly fit!" Amber said, raising her glass to her friends.

"And she has them in every colour!" Tessa cried, as they all dissolved into laughter.

If you enjoyed *If the Shoes Fit*
by Pauline Lawless why not try
Because We're Worth It also published by Poolbeg?
Here's a sneak preview of Chapter One.

Because We're Worth it

PAULINE LAWLESS

POOLBEG

Chapter 1

"Perfect!" said Kate O'Mara as she bit into the crisp, but gooey on the inside, meringue that she had just taken out of the Aga. "Mmm . . . delicious!" Too late, she remembered her diet. "Oh damn! That's at least another hundred calories. There goes my diet again! Suppose I may as well be hung for a sheep as a lamb!" . . . and another meringue bit the dust. She then turned her attention to the chocolate mousse – couldn't resist tasting it and then licked the spoon clean when she had finished. The brandy snaps and Bailey's ice cream suffered the same fate. After all, she reasoned, if I don't taste it how will I know if it's okay? She was busy preparing a very special dinner and everything had to be absolutely perfect.

Her husband, Danny, had stressed the importance of this evening so she had pulled out all the stops. He ran a highly successful building company and often entertained his business clients at home. He maintained it was better than any restaurant as Kate was a superb cook but she suspected that he also wanted to show off their lovely home, of which he was very proud. Kate was painfully shy with strangers and found it an ordeal having to make conversation with them at the dinner table. She would much rather stay in the kitchen all night. However, she knew how important these dinners were to Danny and so she tried her best to overcome her shyness. It had got a little easier since he had convinced her to have a glass or two of wine which helped her to relax, but that was her limit. She could not risk having any more than that or she would be drunk and the meal would become a disaster.

Tonight there was a very influential Dublin property developer, Michael Traynor, coming with his two directors and their wives. They had plans to build a big development in Canary Wharf in London – luxury apartments, hotel, shopping centre to start with – and Danny was the front-runner to win this contract. Secretly he hoped to clinch the deal tonight. She knew how badly he wanted it so she had done everything she possibly could to make it a success.

Kate stood surveying herself critically in the dressing-room mirror. She didn't like what she saw. Looking back at her was a very attractive woman who could have passed for much less than her thirty-nine years – thanks to her dewy youthful complexion and a look of innocence in her big blue eyes. She had shoulder-length honey-blonde hair that was a mass of waves and curls that always had that "just-got-out-of-bed" look. Although she often tied it up in an attempt to look neat, curls and tendrils kept escaping around her face which drove her crazy but only added to her charm. It was, however, the sweetness of her expression and the warmth and kindness in her eyes that drew people to her like a magnet. Men wanted to protect her – women confided in her.

Looking in the mirror, she saw none of this. She had so little self-esteem that all she could see was fat and bulges everywhere not to mention boobs that she felt were far too big. Piled on the bed were the entire contents of her wardrobe which she had tried on and discarded.

"Oh dear God, I look so frumpy and nothing fits me!" she sighed. "I really will have to do something about it. I suppose it'll have to be my black silk tunic and pants again! At least they hide my stomach and hips and they're comfortable."

Less than a mile away Diana Rafferty had none of these problems as she prepared for the dinner. She sat in front of the mirror in her dressing-room admiring her new hairstyle. Gary had excelled himself – the plum highlights, which he'd insisted on, looked terrific in her her sleek, black shiny hair.

Yep, I like it, she thought as she preened, turning her head this way and that. Very edgy and now – just what I wanted.

Appearance was everything to Diana and she devoured all the latest "crap magazines" – as Kevin called them – to see what all her favourite celebrities were wearing. How she envied these women and their lifestyles: jetting around the world in private jets, partying in all the best places, paparazzi following their every step, glamorous men lusting after them! She sighed . . . that was the life she wanted!

Diana had a typical hour-glass figure: tall, with long slim legs, a surprisingly small waist, curvaceous hips and big full breasts. "Voluptuous" was the word that sprang to mind when people first set eyes on her. She was "sex-on-legs" and she knew it. She flaunted her body at every opportunity and men fell for it every time. Consumed with lust, they never noticed her cold grey calculating eyes. Women disliked her intensely and none of them trusted her.

She'd spent the morning in Dublin getting her weekly manicure, pedicure, waxing, massage and spray-tan. Then, after lunch in the Shelbourne with some girlfriends, she'd spent the afternoon in the top hair salon in the city having her hair cut, highlighted and treated.

She was busy applying a bevy of make-up products to her face when her husband Kevin emerged from the bathroom, a towel around his waist and his dark curly hair sprinkling little droplets of water everywhere. Once upon a time, the sight of his toned muscled body and smooth tawny skin would have excited her and she'd have dragged him to bed. His resemblance to Antonio Banderas had been a huge turn-on for her but that was like . . . in another life! Now he was just annoying her as he bent to kiss the top of her head.

"Don't touch me!" she shrieked. "You'll mess up my hair!"

He pulled back.

"Do you like it?" she asked, turning to face him.

"It's different. It will take some getting used to."

"God, you haven't a clue! This is the very latest trend."

He saw the new coral silk dress lying on the bed. "Very nice," he whistled as he read the label on the dress. "How much did this cost me?"

"Don't be such a tightwad. You know you like me to look well!"

"You look great in anything. You don't need Gucci for that."

"Well, these women at Danny's tonight will certainly be in

designer gear and I don't want to feel like the poor relation. By the way, I bought a pair of Jimmy Choos to go with it."

"I won't even ask. I suppose I'll need to take out a bank loan for those. You can bet Kate won't be wearing Gucci and Jimmy Choos tonight."

"Kate is such a frump," she added viciously. "She could well afford them if she wanted them. Danny is always on at her to go shopping but she has no interest. He even opened an account for her in Brown Thomas and she has never used it. Can you believe it? How I wish I were in her place. Money no object there!"

"Darling, you can't complain. When do you ever want for anything? Anyway, let's get a move on. I promised Danny I would be there early to lend some moral support. Tonight is very important for him."

"Oh sure, he needs you to hold his hand!" she replied sarcastically.

Kevin held his tongue. The last thing he wanted now was an argument with her. Why is she so resentful all the time, he asked himself as he dressed. She's never happy – always envious. Women! I'll never understand them!

Meanwhile Kate was laying out the titbits to have with the pre-dinner drinks – or the '*amuse-gueule*' to have with the '*apéritifs*' – as Diana insisted on calling them. God, thought Kate, Diana could be so pretentious sometimes. I hope she doesn't flirt too much with the men tonight. One of these nights some wife will clock her! She giggled as she imagined the scene. How on earth Kevin put up with her she'd never understand. He had the patience of Job.

She helped herself to another Parmesan crisp. Stop it, she chided herself. There'll be none left if I keep this up.

Just then the doorbell rang. Danny was delighted to see that their first guests were Kevin and Diana. He brought them through the foyer and enormous reception room and out on to the terrace which overlooked the romantically floodlit pool.

"It's such a lovely balmy evening that I thought we would have drinks out here."

"Perfect. I just love these sofas," Diana said as she sank into the butter-soft white leather while hoisting her skirt up as high as she dared so that Danny could get a good look at her long shapely legs. She was also aware that the contours of her nipples were highly visible through the light silk of her dress. Danny could hardly take his eyes off them. She loved the effect she had on men. It gave her a sense of power. He wanted her and she knew it and he knew that she knew it. Of course, out of loyalty to Kevin he would never make a move on her, much as he wanted to.

"And what can I get you both? I've made a jug of Wallbangers but perhaps you'd prefer champagne or something else?"

"Champoo for me, please, sweetie," she replied coquettishly.

Kevin opted for a Harvey Wallbanger.

Danny brought them their drinks and filled them in on the other guests who were coming and just how much the night meant to him.

"Michael is the main man. It will be his decision to give me this contract or not – so try and charm him for me, Diana, will you?"

"No probs, darling," she purred, crossing and uncrossing her legs. "Anything for you!"

As Kate came in from the kitchen the doorbell pealed again. Danny nervously straightened his tie and went to the door. It was Michael and his wife Marcia, with one of his directors and his wife. As Danny ushered them in the other couple arrived. They were all beautifully dressed and groomed and reeked of money – lots of it!

Danny led them out to the terrace and made the introductions all round. He was so good at this sort of thing, Kate thought, whereas she was useless. People gravitated to him and he could keep a whole room entertained for the night with his stories and jokes. He wasn't tall but his personality was larger than life. He used to be devilishly handsome but now his dark-blond hair was thinning on top and he had the start of a double chin. Even so, he could still charm the birds off the trees, Kate thought fondly.

Danny got drinks for everyone and after they were all seated, with the men on one side and the women on the other – things never change in Ireland, Kate smiled to herself – Marcia turned to her.

"What a beautiful home you have! It's so big and bright and the view across to the mountains is fantastic. And what a glorious pool! I would love one but we get so little good weather here that it hardly seems worth it. And I must say I love the white leather sunbeds too."

"Thank you." said Kate.

I'm afraid I'm responsible for the pool. It's been my biggest extravagance," replied Danny suavely. "It's always been a dream of mine. Kate and I only use it in the really fine weather but the boys use it all summer long when they're home from boarding school, regardless of the weather. We do enjoy sitting out here in the evenings and in

415

winter we can enclose the terrace with double-glazed doors and a sliding roof, so we can have the view while still being snug and warm." He smiled around the room.

"That sounds wonderful. How many children do you have?" Marcia asked Kate.

"Four boys," Kate replied shyly.

"We have two daughters," said Marcia, adding sadly, "Michael would have loved a son also but it wasn't to be."

Kate wondered what had happened but, of course, couldn't ask.

"Diana, I love your shoes!" remarked Amanda, the youngest of the wives. "I almost bought an exact pair of those Jimmy Choos last week but in the end I opted for these Christian Louboutin." She lifted a perfectly pedicured foot, clad in a very high beige-suede stiletto. Diana and Louise, the other wife, made a big deal of admiring the shoes. Kate wondered how on earth she could walk in them.

"I prefer Manolo Blahnik," Marcia said. "I find them more comfortable."

Kate felt like a complete outsider as they rattled on about shoes. Looking around at the other women's feet she realised that they were all wearing the same vertiginously high heels. She prayed nobody would notice her feet, clad in their €12.99 flat ballet pumps from New Look. They were the most comfortable shoes she had ever put on. Before they could draw her into the conversation she quickly made her escape to the sanctuary of her kitchen. She remembered Diana once telling her that she had spent €590 on a pair of Louboutin shoes. Is this for real, she'd wondered. How could anyone justify spending that amount on a pair of shoes?

Overhearing the ladies' conversation, Michael remarked,

"I just don't get it with you women. What is it about shoes that sends the whole female race gaga?"

"Well, for one thing they always fit. Whether you gain weight or lose it - your shoes always fit," Marcia answered him, to the cries of "Absolutely!" and "Hear, hear!" from Amanda and Louise. "Likewise bags," she continued, getting really into it. "My bags always fit me!"

The women all pealed with laughter. They were really enjoying this!

"Tell me, Diana. How many pairs of shoes do you own?" Michael asked.

"Mmm . . . probably about sixty – not counting boots."

"See!" He asked Amanda and Louise the same question and got much the same reply. Then he turned to his wife. "Okay, Marcia. Honestly now. How many pairs? A hundred? More?"

"Gosh, this is embarrassing but eh . . . okay . . . I'll come clean. A hundred and five pairs, last count."

"See what I mean? I rest my case."

"Hey, I've had some of them for over thirty years!"

"It doesn't matter, still counts."

"Oh, get lost! You can afford it!"

This brought more guffaws.

Kate, who had come back in from the kitchen, felt completely out of her depth. Was there something wrong with her? She had four, maybe five pairs of shoes – and that included her gardening ones. Why would I need more, she wondered? Am I a total misfit in the female race? She made a quick getaway to the kitchen once again before Michael could ask her about her shoes. She would have been mortified to let them know the truth. She put this out of her mind as she prepared the asparagus hollandaise for the first course of the meal.

Meanwhile, back on the terrace, Marcia watched Diana in action, flirting with all the men and Michael in particular. Oh, she knew her type so well! How many Dianas had she met over the years? This one had very striking looks but there was a hard edge to her. She was the ultimate high-maintenance woman – the kind that made other women feel they needed a makeover – with not a hair out of place and groomed to within an inch of her life. She was a Jezebel who would take any man she wanted, married or not. With dismay, she saw the way Michael was responding to Diana. No doubt about it – she was just his type! Marcia felt helpless.

Danny led his guests into the dining-room and he was pleased with their *oohs* and *aahs* as they took in the beautiful elegant room with its red silk wallpaper and crystal chandelier. The snow-white place mats and napkins and the large centrepiece of white roses made a lovely contrast to the rich mahogany table and the red walls. The many candles reflected the lights of the Waterford crystal and the Old Irish Silver cutlery.

"It's really beautiful," remarked Marcia and the others all agreed.

Diana meanwhile was turning herself inside out trying to impress Michael, batting her eyelashes at him and laughing heartily at his jokes. She was talking in that little-girl voice which she reserved specifically for men. When they took their places at the table she plonked herself down beside him although Kate's name was on the place card. Not wanting to make a scene, Kate silently sat down in Diana's place. Danny saw what had happened and shrugged his shoulders helplessly at Kate.

As they ate the starter, Diana leaned in to Michael at

every possible chance and kept laying her hand on his arm as she whispered to him. She ignored the other guests and Kate felt embarrassed for Kevin. Marcia appeared not to notice but she had to be aware of it.

After the asparagus, Kate served a fish course of coquilles St Jacques. "These scallops are heavenly, Kate!" said Michael. "They just melt in the mouth!"

Danny gave her a wink. The dinner was going very well and the conversation was flowing easily. There was much laughter which was getting louder with every glass of the superb Burgundy wines that Danny was so generously pouring. The main course of mustard crusted rack of lamb was very well received and Kate heaved a great sigh of relief.

Then, as she was clearing away the plates from the main course she almost dropped them all in shock when she saw that beneath the table, unseen by the others, Michael had his hand up under Diana's skirt. She was doing nothing to stop him and, from the look on her face, appeared to be enjoying it. Kate blushed with embarrassment and looked over at Kevin and Marcia to make sure they hadn't seen it. Apparently not, thank God, as they were deep in conversation with one another.

When she came in with the dessert trolley all the ladies groaned . . . "I couldn't eat another bite . . ." until they saw what was on offer: white and dark chocolate mousse terrine, meringue nests filled with raspberries, cream and toasted almonds, brandy-snap baskets filled with Baileys ice cream topped with spun sugar and finally oranges in Cointreau.

"I really shouldn't indulge," declared Amanda," but how can we resist this?"

"I think I've died and gone to heaven!" Louise remarked.

"Forget the diets, girls! We'll start again tomorrow," advised Marcia.

They tried everything, much to Kate's delight. Desserts were her speciality and tonight she had outdone herself. It always amused her that even when people claimed to be completely stuffed they still found a space for dessert. Over the Irish coffees and liqueurs the compliments were coming so fast that Kate could feel herself blushing.

"That is the best meal I've eaten in years," announced Michael.

"Wonderful!" said Kevin and Amanda in unison.

"Superb!" said Marcia. "You just have to give me the name of your caterer, dear. I will absolutely have to get them to cater for my next party."

"There's no caterer – Kate did all this herself," Danny said proudly. "She's a terrific cook. Everything you ate tonight is home-made."

"You lucky man!" remarked Michael as the women looked at Kate in disbelief.

"You did all of this yourself?" asked Marcia, admiringly.

"Incredible!" said Amanda.

"Don't you even have help in the kitchen?" Louise asked her.

"No way! I tried that – they were more of a hindrance than a help, getting in my way. I prefer to do it myself, though Danny doesn't agree with me."

"Well, you seem to be able to cope admirably, my dear," Marcia smiled kindly at her. "It was wonderful."

Diana was noticeably silent.

"Thank you," said a blushing Kate. "I'm glad you all enjoyed it."

420

"I'd like to propose a toast. To Kate! The best housewife in Ireland!" said Danny.

"Housewife?" asked Marcia archly, raising her eyebrows. "You mean 'wife', surely."

"Yes, of course," replied Danny with an embarrassed laugh. "To Kate!" They all raised their glasses to her.

Diana was seething at all the attention Kate was getting, especially from Michael. She grudgingly admitted that the meal was good and Kate was an okay cook. That's all she's good for, she thought. Look at the state of her in that old black tunic that she wears all the time! Danny must be sick of looking at it. He deserves better. To think she could have a full wardrobe of designer gear if she wanted it! Some women are downright stupid. And she really is piling on the weight . . . I'll take that smile off her face . . .

"Kate, I've something important to tell you."

Everyone turned to look at Diana expectantly.

"There's a new Slimming Club opening in Naas on Monday night," she said, smiling sweetly. "It's called Slimforever and seemingly the girl running it can work absolute miracles. I thought you might be interested."

Kate almost died with embarrassment and wished the ground would open up and swallow her. She felt self-conscious enough about her weight without Diana calling everyone's attention to it. How cruel of her!

She felt the colour spreading up her face as she muttered, "I must check it out."

"I've heard about that girl," Marcia chimed in. "I believe she's fantastic. Some of my friends are travelling all the way from Foxrock to Maynooth to her classes. They say she can talk the weight off you!"

"I wish," sighed Louise, to everyone's amusement.

After the guests had left, thanking her profusely yet again, Danny took her in his arms.

"What a great success! You did me proud with the meal. I think the job is mine. Michael hinted as much to me before he left. Let's go to bed and celebrate!"

Kate tingled with anticipation. Their lovemaking was as good as ever, even after nineteen years of marriage and four children, and she loved the intimacy and pleasure she derived from it.

But tonight she had a niggling thought at the back of her mind. For the first time ever she felt self-conscious about her body while making love. She couldn't quite relax and as they were drifting off to sleep she murmured,

"I was very hurt by Diana's remark about that Slimming Club."

"Darling, you're much too sensitive. Pay no attention to her. You know Diana well enough by now. Her nose was out of joint because of all the praise you were getting. She was jealous. Don't let it bother you . . ." Then, after a pause, he added, "But perhaps it might be a good idea to check it out and see if they can help you lose some weight."

Was he serious? She couldn't see his face in the dark, but she knew he wasn't smiling. It wasn't a joke. She felt dejected and hurt. Danny – who frequently told her he loved her curves and who discouraged her from all those diets she was constantly on – was he now saying she was too fat?

That decided her. I'll join that club on Monday, she vowed.

If you enjoyed this chapter from
Because We're Worth it by Pauline Lawless
why not order the full book online
@ www.poolbeg.com
and enjoy a 10% discount on all
Poolbeg books

See next page for details.

POOLBEG WISHES TO

THANK YOU

for buying a Poolbeg book.
As a loyal customer we will give you
10% OFF (and free postage*)
on any book bought on our website
www.poolbeg.com

Select the book(s) you wish to buy
and click to checkout.

Then click on the 'Add a Coupon' button
(located under 'Checkout') and enter
this coupon code

 **USMWR15173**

(Not valid with any other offer!)

WHY NOT JOIN OUR MAILING LIST
@ www.poolbeg.com and get some
fantastic offers on Poolbeg books

*See website for details